KU-222-291

Black & Blue

An Inspector Rebus Novel

IAN RANKIN

ORION

Copyright © 1997 Ian Rankin

All rights reserved.

The right of Ian Rankin to be identified as the author
of this work has been asserted by him in accordance
with the Copyright, Designs and Patents Act 1988.

This edition first published
in 1997 by Orion
An imprint of Orion Books Ltd
Orion House, 5 Upper St Martin's Lane
London WC2H 9EA

Second impression 1997
Third impression 1997
Fourth impression 1997

A CIP catalogue record for this book
is available from the British Library

Typeset by Deltatype Ltd, Birkenhead, Merseyside

Printed and bound in Great Britain by
Clays Ltd, St Ives plc

O would, ere I had seen the day
That treason thus could sell us,
My auld grey head had lien in clay,
Wi' Bruce and loyal Wallace!
But pith and power, till my last hour,
I'll mak' this declaration;
We're bought and sold for English gold –
Such a parcel of rogues in a nation.

Robert Burns,
'Fareweel to a' Our Scottish Fame'

If you have the Stones ... to say I can rewrite history to my own specifications, you can get away with it.

James Ellroy
(Capitalisation the author's own)

Empty Capital

Weary with centuries
This empty capital snorts like a great beast
Caged in its sleep, dreaming of freedom
But with nae belief . . .

Sydney Goodsir Smith,
'Kynd Kittock's Land'

1

'Tell me again why you killed them.'

'I've told you, it's just this *urge*.'

Rebus looked back at his notes. 'The word you used was "compulsion".'

The slumped figure in the chair nodded. Bad smells came off him. 'Urge, compulsion, same thing.'

'Is it?' Rebus stubbed out his cigarette. There were so many butts in the tin ashtray, a couple spilled over on to the metal table. 'Let's talk about the first victim.'

The man opposite him groaned. His name was William Crawford Shand, known as 'Craw'. He was forty years old, single, and lived alone in a council block in Craigmillar. He had been unemployed six years. He ran twitching fingers through dark greasy hair, seeking out and covering a large bald spot at the crown of his head.

'The first victim,' Rebus said. 'Tell us.'

'Us' because there was another CID man in the biscuit-tin. His name was Maclay, and Rebus didn't know him very well. He didn't know anyone at Craigmillar very well, not yet. Maclay was leaning against the wall, arms folded, eyes reduced to slits. He looked like a piece of machinery at rest.

'I strangled her.'

'What with?'

'A length of rope.'

'Where did you get the rope?'

'Bought it at some shop, I can't remember where.'

Three-beat pause. 'Then what did you do?'

'After she was dead?' Shand moved a little in the chair. 'I took her clothes off and was intimate with her.'

'With a dead body?'

'She was still warm.'

3

Rebus got to his feet. The grating of his chair on the floor seemed to unnerve Shand. Not difficult.

'Where did you kill her?'

'A park.'

'And where was this park?'

'Near where she lived.'

'Where's that?'

'Polmuir Road, Aberdeen.'

'And what were you doing in Aberdeen, Mr Shand?'

He shrugged, running his fingers now along the rim of the table, leaving traces of sweat and grease.

'I wouldn't do that,' Rebus said. 'The edges are sharp, you might get cut.'

Maclay snorted. Rebus walked over towards the wall and stared at him. Maclay nodded briefly. Rebus turned back to the table.

'Describe the park.' He rested against the edge of the table, got himself another cigarette and lit it.

'It was just a park. You know, trees and grass, a play park for the kids.'

'Were the gates locked?'

'What?'

'It was late at night, were the gates locked?'

'I don't remember.'

'You don't remember.' Pause: two beats. 'Where did you meet her?'

Quickly: 'At a disco.'

'You don't seem the disco type, Mr Shand.' Another snort from the machine. 'Describe the place to me.'

Shand shrugged again. 'Like any other disco: dark, flashing lights, a bar.'

'What about victim number two?'

'Same procedure.' Shand's eyes were dark, face gaunt. But for all that he was beginning to enjoy himself, easing into his story again. 'Met her at a disco, offered to take her home, killed her and fucked her.'

'No intimacy then. Did you take a souvenir?'

'Eh?'

Rebus flicked ash on to the floor, flakes landed on his shoes. 'Did you remove anything from the scene?'

Shand thought it over, shook his head.

'And this was where exactly?'

'Warriston Cemetery.'

'Close to her home?'

4

'She lived on Inverleith Row.'

'What did you strangle her with?'

'The bit of rope.'

'The same piece?' Shand nodded. 'What did you do, keep it in your pocket?'

'That's right.'

'Do you have it with you now?'

'I chucked it.'

'You're not making it easy for us, are you?' Shand squirmed with pleasure. Four beats. 'And the third victim?'

'Glasgow,' Shand recited. 'Kelvingrove Park. Her name was Judith Cairns. She told me to call her Ju-Ju. I did her same as the others.' He sat back in the chair, drawing himself up and folding his arms. Rebus reached out a hand until it touched the man's forehead, faith-healer style. Then he pushed, not very hard. But there was no resistance. Shand and the chair toppled backwards on to the floor. Rebus was kneeling in front of him, hauling him up by the front of his shirt.

'You're a liar!' he hissed. 'Everything you know you got straight from the papers, and what you had to make up was pure dross!' He let go and got to his feet. His hands were damp where he'd been holding the shirt.

'I'm not lying,' Shand pleaded, still prone. 'That's gospel I'm telling you!'

Rebus stubbed out the half-smoked cigarette. The ashtray tipped more butts on to the table. Rebus picked one up and flicked it at Shand.

'Are you not going to charge me?'

'You'll be charged all right: wasting police time. A spell in Saughton with an arse-bandit for a roomie.'

'We usually just let him go,' Maclay said.

'Stick him in a cell,' Rebus ordered, leaving the room.

'But I'm him!' Shand persisted, even as Maclay was picking him off the floor. 'I'm Johnny Bible! I'm Johnny Bible!'

'Not even close, Craw,' Maclay said, quietening him with a punch.

Rebus needed to wash his hands, splash some water on his face. Two woolly suits were in the toilets, enjoying a story and a cigarette. They stopped laughing when Rebus came in.

'Sir,' one asked, 'who did you have in the biscuit-tin?'

'Another comedian,' Rebus said.

'This place is full of them,' the second constable commented. Rebus didn't know if he meant the station, Craigmillar itself, or the city as a whole. Not that there was much comedy in Craigmillar police station. It

5

was Edinburgh's hardest posting; a stint of duty lasted two years max, no one could function longer than that. Craigmillar was about as tough an area as you could find in Scotland's capital city, and the station fully merited its nickname – Fort Apache, the Bronx. It lay up a cul-de-sac behind a row of shops, a low-built dour-faced building with even dourer-faced tenements behind. Being up an alley meant a mob could cut it off from civilisation with ease, and the place had been under siege numerous times. Yes, Craigmillar was a choice posting.

Rebus knew why he was there. He'd upset some people, people who mattered. They hadn't been able to deal him a death blow, so had instead consigned him to purgatory. It couldn't be hell because he knew it wasn't for ever. Call it a penance. The letter telling him of his move had explained that he would be covering for a hospitalised colleague. It had also stated that he would help oversee the shutting down of the old Craigmillar station. Everything was being wound down, transferred to a brand new station nearby. The place was already a shambles of packing cases and pillaged cupboards. Staff weren't exactly expending great energy solving ongoing cases. Nor had they put any energy into welcoming Detective Inspector John Rebus. The place felt more like a hospital ward than a cop-shop, and the patients were tranquillised to the hilt.

He wandered back to the CID room – the 'Shed'. On the way, he passed Maclay and Shand, the latter still protesting his guilt as he was dragged to the cells.

'I'm Johnny Bible! I fucking am and all!'

Not even close.

It was nine p.m. on a Tuesday in June and the only other person in the Shed was Detective Sergeant 'Dod' Bain. He glanced up from his magazine – *Offbeat*, the L&B newsletter – and Rebus shook his head.

'Thought not,' Bain said, turning a page. 'Craw's notorious for grassing himself up, that's why I left him to you.'

'You've as much heart as a carpet tack.'

'But I'm as sharp as one, too. Don't forget that.'

Rebus sat at his desk and considered writing his report of the interview. Another comedian, another waste of time. And still Johnny Bible was out there.

First there had been Bible John, terrorising Glasgow in the late 1960s. A well-dressed young man with reddish hair, who knew his Bible and frequented the Barrowland Ballroom. He picked up three women there, beat them, raped them, strangled them. Then he disappeared, right in the middle of Glasgow's biggest manhunt, and never resurfaced, the case open to this day. Police had a cast-iron description of Bible John from the sister of his last victim. She'd spent close on two hours in his company, shared a taxi with him even. They'd dropped her off; her sister had waved goodbye through the back window ... Her description hadn't helped.

And now there was Johnny Bible. The media had been quick with the name. Three women: beaten, raped, strangled. That was all they'd needed to make the comparison. Two of the women had been picked up at nightclubs, discos. There were vague descriptions of a man who'd been seen dancing with the victims. Well-dressed, shy. It clicked with the original Bible John. Only Bible John, supposing he were still alive, would be in his fifties, while this new killer was described as mid-to-late twenties. Therefore: Johnny Bible, spiritual son of Bible John.

There were differences, of course, but the media didn't dwell on those. For one thing, Bible John's victims had all been dancing at the same dancehall; Johnny Bible ranged far and wide through Scotland in his hunt for victims. This had led to the usual theories: he was a long-distance lorry driver; a company rep. Police were ruling nothing out. It might even be Bible John himself, back after a quarter century away, the mid-to-late twenties description flawed – it had happened before with apparently watertight eyewitness testimony. They were also keeping a few things quiet about Johnny Bible – just as they had with Bible John. It helped rule out the dozens of fake confessions.

Rebus had barely started his report when Maclay swayed into the room. That was the way he walked, from side to side, not because he was drunk or drugged but because he was seriously overweight, a metabolism thing. There was something wrong with his sinuses too; his breathing often came in laboured wheezes, his voice a blunt plane against the grain of the wood. His station nickname was 'Heavy'.

'Escorted Craw from the premises?' Bain asked.

Maclay nodded towards Rebus's desk. 'Wants him charged for wasting our time.'

'Now that's what I call a waste of time.'

Maclay swayed in Rebus's direction. His hair was jet black, ringed with slick kiss-curls. He'd probably won Bonniest Bairn prizes, but not for a while.

'Come on,' he said.

Rebus shook his head and kept typing.

'Fuck's sake.'

'Fuck him,' Bain said, getting to his feet. He unhooked his jacket from the back of the chair. To Maclay: 'Drinkie?'

7

Maclay wheezed out a long sigh. 'Just the job.'

Rebus held his breath until they'd gone. Not that he'd been expecting to be asked along. That was their whole point. He stopped typing and reached into his bottom drawer for the Lucozade bottle, unscrewed the cap, sniffed forty-three per cent malt and poured in a mouthful. With the bottle back in its drawer, he popped a mint into his mouth.

Better. 'I can see clearly now': Marvin Gaye.

He yanked the report from the typewriter and crumpled it into a ball, then called the desk, told them to hold Craw Shand an hour, then release him. He'd just put down the phone when it started ringing.

'DI Rebus.'

'It's Brian.'

Brian Holmes, Detective Sergeant, still based at St Leonard's. They kept in touch. His voice tonight was toneless.

'Problem?'

Holmes laughed, no humour. 'I've got the world's supply.'

'So tell me the latest.' Rebus opened the packet one-handed, in mouth and lit.

'I don't know that I can, with you being in shit.'

'Craigmillar's not so bad.' Rebus looked around the stale office.

'I meant the other thing.'

'Oh.'

'See, I'm ... I might have gotten myself into something ...'

'What's happened?'

'A suspect, we had him in custody. He was giving me a shit load of grief.'

'You smacked him.'

'That's what he's saying.'

'Filed a complaint?'

'In the process. His solicitor wants to take it all the way.'

'Your word against his?'

'Right.'

'The rubber-heels will kick it out.'

'I suppose so.'

'Or get Siobhan to cover your arse.'

'She's on holiday. My partner for the interview was Glamis.'

'No good then, he's as yellow as a New York cab.'

A pause. 'Aren't you going to ask me if I did it?'

'I don't *ever* want to know, understood? Who was the suspect?'

'Mental Minto.'

'Christ, that brewhead knows more law than the procurator-fiscal. OK, let's go talkies.'

It was good to be out of the station. He had the car windows rolled down. The breeze was almost warm. The station-issue Escort hadn't been cleaned in a while. There were chocolate wrappers, empty crisp bags, crushed bricks of orange juice and Ribena. The heart of the Scottish diet: sugar and salt. Add alcohol and you had heart *and* soul.

Minto lived in one of the tenement flats on South Clerk Street, first floor. Rebus had been there on occasions past, none of them savoury to the memory. Kerbside was solid with cars, so he double-parked. In the sky, fading roseate was fighting a losing battle with encroaching dark. And below it all, halogen orange. The street was noisy. The cinema up the road was probably emptying, and the first casualties were tearing themselves away from still-serving pubs. Night-cooking in the air: hot batter, pizza topping, Indian spice. Brian Holmes was standing outside a charity shop, hands in pockets. No car: he'd probably walked from St Leonard's. The two men nodded a greeting.

Holmes looked tired. Just a few years ago he'd been young, fresh, keen. Rebus knew home life had taken its toll: he'd been there in his own marriage, annulled years back. Holmes's partner wanted him out of the force. She wanted someone who spent more time with her. Rebus knew all too well what she wanted. She wanted someone whose mind was on her when he was at home, who wasn't immersed in casework and speculation, mind games and promotion strategies. Often as a police officer you were closer to your working partner than your partner for life. When you joined CID they gave you a handshake and a piece of paper.

The piece of paper was your decree *nisi*.

'Do you know if he's up there?' Rebus asked.

'I phoned him. He picked up. Sounded halfway to sober.'

'Did you say anything?'

'Think I'm stupid?'

Rebus was looking up at the tenement windows. Ground level was shops; Minto lived above a locksmith's. There was irony there for those who wanted it.

'OK, you come up with me, but stay on the landing. Only come in if you hear trouble.'

'You sure?'

'I'm only going to speak to the man.' Rebus touched Holmes's shoulder. 'Relax.'

The main door was unlocked. They climbed the winding stairs without speaking. Rebus pushed at the bell and took a deep breath. Minto started to pull the door open, and Rebus shouldered it, propelling Minto and himself into the dimly lit hallway. He slammed the door shut behind him.

Minto was ready for violence until he saw who it was. Then he just snarled and strode back to the living room. It was a tiny room, half kitchenette, with a narrow floor-to-ceiling cupboard Rebus knew held a shower. There was one bedroom, and a toilet with a doll-house sink. They made igloos bigger.

'Fuck do you want?' Minto was reaching for a can of lager, high-alcohol. He drained it, standing.

'A word.' Rebus looked around the room, casually as it were. But his hands were by his sides, ready.

'This is unlawful entry.'

'Keep yapping, I'll show you unlawful entry.'

Minto's face creased: not impressed. He was mid-thirties but looked fifteen years older. He'd done most of the major drugs in his time: Billy Whizz, skag, Morningside speed. He was on a meth programme now. On dope, he was a small problem, an irritation; off dope, he was pure radge. He was Mental.

'Way I hear, you're fucked anyway,' he said now.

Rebus took a step closer. 'That's right, Mental. So ask yourself: what have I got to lose? If I'm fucked, might as well make it good and.'

Minto held up his hands. 'Easy, easy. What's your problem?'

Rebus let his face relax. 'You're my problem, Mental. Making a charge against a colleague of mine.'

'He laid into me.'

Rebus shook his head. 'I was there, didn't see a thing. I'd called in with a message for DS Holmes. I stuck around. So if he'd assaulted you, I'd've known, wouldn't I?'

They stood facing one another silently. Then Minto turned and slumped into the room's only armchair. He looked like he was going to sulk. Rebus bent down and picked something off the floor. It was the city's tourist accommodation brochure.

'Going somewhere nice?' He flicked through the lists of hotels, B&Bs, self-catering. Then he waved the magazine at Minto. 'If one single place in here gets turned, you'll be our first stop.'

'Harassment,' Minto said, but quietly.

Rebus dropped the brochure. Minto didn't look so mental now; he looked done in and done down, like life was sporting a horseshoe in one

10

of its boxing gloves. Rebus turned to go. He walked down the hall and was reaching for the door when he heard Minto call his name. The small man was standing at the other end of the hall, only twelve feet away. He had pulled his baggy black T-shirt up to his shoulders. Having shown the front, he turned to give Rebus a view of the back. The lighting was poor – forty-watt bulb in a flyblown shade – but even so Rebus could see. Tattoos, he thought at first. But they were bruises: ribs, sides, kidneys. Self-inflicted? It was possible. It was always possible. Minto dropped the shirt and stared hard at Rebus, not blinking. Rebus let himself out of the flat.

'Everything all right?' Brian Holmes said nervously.

'The story is, I came by with a message. I sat in on the interview.'

Holmes exhaled noisily. 'That's it then?'

'That's it.'

Perhaps it was the tone of voice that alerted Holmes. He met John Rebus's stare, and was the first to break contact. Outside, he put out a hand and said, 'Thanks.'

But Rebus had turned and walked away.

He drove through the streets of the empty capital, six-figure housing huddled either side of the road. It cost a fortune to live in Edinburgh these days. It could cost you everything you had. He tried not to think about what he'd done, what Brian Holmes had done. The Pet Shop Boys inside his head: 'It's a Sin'. Segue to Miles Davis: 'So What?'

He headed in the vague direction of Craigmillar, then thought better of it. He'd go home instead, and pray there were no reporters camped outside. When he went home, he took the night home with him, and had to soak and scrub it away, feeling like an old paving slab, walked on daily. Sometimes it was easier to stay on the street, or sleep at the station. Sometimes he drove all night, not just through Edinburgh: down to Leith and past the working girls and hustlers, along the waterfront, South Queensferry sometimes, and then up on to the Forth Bridge, up the M90 through Fife, past Perth, all the way to Dundee, where he'd turn and head back, usually tired by then, pulling off the road if necessary and sleeping in his car. It all took time.

He remembered he was in a station car, not his own. If they needed it, they could come fetch it. When he reached Marchmont, he couldn't find a parking space on Arden Street, ended up on a double yellow. There were no reporters; they had to sleep some time, too. He walked along Warrender Park Road to his favourite chip shop – huge portions, and they sold toothpaste and toilet-rolls too, if you needed them. He walked back slowly, nice night for it, and was halfway up the tenement stairs when his pager went off.

2

His name was Allan Mitchison and he was drinking in a hometown bar, not ostentatiously, but with a look on his face that said he wasn't worried about money. He got talking to these two guys. One of them told a joke. It was a good joke. They bought the next round, and he bought one back. They wiped tears from their eyes when he told his only gag. They ordered three more. He was enjoying the company.

He didn't have many pals left in Edinburgh. Some of his one-time friends resented him, the money he still made. He didn't have any family, hadn't had for as long as he could remember. The two men were company. He didn't quite know why he came home, or even why he called Edinburgh 'home'. He had a flat with a mortgage on it, but hadn't decorated it yet or put in any furniture. It was just a shell, nothing worth coming back for. But everyone went home, that was the thing. The sixteen days straight that you worked, you were supposed to think about home. You talked about it, spoke of all the things you'd do when you got there – the booze, the minge, clubbing. Some of the men lived in or near Aberdeen, but a lot still had homes further away. They couldn't wait for the sixteen days to end, the fourteen-day break to begin.

This was the first night of his fourteen days.

They passed slowly at first, then more quickly towards the end, until you were left wondering why you hadn't done more with your time. This, the first night, this was the longest. This was the one you had to get through.

They moved on to another bar. One of his new friends was carrying an old-style Adidas bag, red plastic with a side pocket and a broken strap. He'd had one just like it at school, back when he was fourteen, fifteen.

'What have you got in there,' he joked, 'your games kit?'

They laughed and slapped him on the back.

At the new place, they moved to shorts. The pub was heaving, wall-to-wall minge.

'You must think about it all the time,' one of his friends said, 'on the rigs. Me, I'd go off my head.'

'Or blind,' said the other.

He grinned. 'I get my share.' Downed another Black Heart. He didn't used to drink dark rum. A fisherman in Stonehaven had introduced him to the stuff. OVD or Black Heart, but he liked Black Heart best. He liked the name.

They needed a carry-out, keep the party going. He was tired. The train from Aberdeen had taken three hours, and there'd been the paraffin budgie before that. His friends were ordering over the bar: a bottle of Bell's and one of Black Heart, a dozen cans, crisps and smokes. It cost a fortune, buying that way. They split it three ways even, so they weren't after his cash.

Outside, there was trouble finding a taxi. Plenty about, but already taken. They had to pull him out of the road when he tried to flag one down. He stumbled a bit and went down on one knee. They helped him back up.

'So what do you do exactly on the rigs?' one of them asked.

'Try to stop them falling down.'

A taxi had stopped to let a couple out.

'Is that your mother or are you just desperate?' he asked the male passenger. His friends told him to shut up, and pushed him into the back. 'Did you see her?' he asked them. 'Face like a bag of marbles.' They weren't going to his flat, there was nothing there.

'We'll go back to our place,' his friends had said. So there was nothing to do but sit back and watch all the lights. Edinburgh was like Aberdeen – small cities, not like Glasgow or London. Aberdeen had more money than style, and it was scary, too. Scarier than Edinburgh. The trip seemed to take for ever.

'Where are we?'

'Niddrie,' someone said. He couldn't remember their names, and was too embarrassed to ask. Eventually the taxi stopped. Outside, the street was dark, looked like the whole fucking estate had welshed on the lecky bill. He said as much.

More laughter, tears, hands on his back.

Three-storey tenements, pebble-dashed. Most of the windows were blocked with steel plates or had been infilled with breeze blocks.

'You live here?' he said.

'We can't all afford mortgages.'

14

True enough, true enough. He was lucky in so many ways. They pushed hard at the main door and it gave. They went in, one friend either side of him with a hand on his back. Inside, the place was damp and rotten, the stairs half-blocked with torn mattresses and lavatory seats, runs of piping and lengths of broken skirting-board.

'Very salubrious.'

'It's all right once you get up.'

They climbed two storeys. There were a couple of doors off the landing, both open.

'In here, Allan.'

So he walked in.

There was no electricity, but one of his friends had a torch. The place was a midden.

'I wouldn't have taken youse for down and outs, lads.'

'The kitchen's OK.'

So they took him through there. He saw a wooden chair which had once been padded. It sat on what was left of the linoleum floor. He was sobering up fast, but not fast enough.

They hauled him down on to the chair. He heard tape being ripped from a roll, binding him to the chair, around and around. Then around his head, covering his mouth. His legs next, all the way down to the ankles. He was trying to cry out, gagging on the tape. A blow landed on the side of his head. His eyes and ears went fuzzy for a moment. The side of his head hurt, like it had just connected with a girder. Wild shadows flew across the walls.

'Looks like a mummy, doesn't he?'

'Aye, and he'll be crying for his daddy in a minute.'

The Adidas bag was on the floor in front of him, unzipped.

'Now,' one of them said, 'I'll just get out my games kit.'

Pliers, claw-hammer, staple-gun, electric screwdriver, and a saw.

Night sweat, salt stinging his eyes, trickling in, trickling out again. He knew what was happening, but still didn't believe it. The two men weren't saying anything. They were laying a sheet of heavy-duty polythene out on the floor. Then they carried him and the chair on to the sheet. He was wriggling, trying to scream, eyes screwed shut, straining against his bonds. When he opened his eyes, he saw a clear polythene bag. They pulled it down over his head and sealed it with tape around his neck. He breathed in through his nostrils and the bag contracted. One of them picked up the saw, then put it down and picked up the hammer instead.

Somehow, fuelled by sheer terror, Allan Mitchison got to his feet, still tied to the chair. The kitchen window was in front of him. It had been boarded up, but the boards had been torn away. The frame was still there, but only fragments of the actual window panes remained. The two men were busy with their tools. He stumbled between them and out of the window.

They didn't wait to watch him fall. They just gathered up the tools, folded the plastic sheet into an untidy bundle, put everything back in the Adidas bag, and zipped it shut.

'Why me?' Rebus had asked when he'd called in.

'Because,' his boss had said, 'you're new. You haven't been around long enough to make enemies on the estate.'

And besides, Rebus could have added, you can't find Maclay or Bain.

A resident walking his greyhound had called it in. 'A lot of stuff gets chucked on to the street, but not like this.'

When Rebus arrived, there were a couple of patrol cars on the scene, creating a sort of cordon, which hadn't stopped the locals gathering. Someone was making grunting noises in imitation of a pig. They didn't go much for originality around here; tradition stuck hard. The tenements were mostly abandoned, awaiting demolition. The families had been relocated. In some of the buildings, there were still a few occupied flats. Rebus wouldn't have wanted to stick around.

The body had been pronounced dead, the circumstances suspicious to say the least, and now the forensic and photography crews were gathering. A Fiscal Depute was in conversation with the pathologist, Dr Curt. Curt saw Rebus and nodded a greeting. But Rebus had eyes only for the body. An old-fashioned spike-tipped set of railings ran the length of the tenement, and the body was impaled on the fence, still dripping blood. At first, he thought the body grossly deformed, but as he stepped closer he saw what it was. A chair, half of it smashed in the fall. It was attached to the body by runs of silver tape. There was a plastic bag over the corpse's head. The bag, once translucent, was now half-filled with blood.

Dr Curt walked over. 'I wonder if we'll find an orange in his mouth.'

'Is that supposed to be funny?'

'I've been meaning to phone. I was sorry to hear about your ... well ...'

'Craigmillar's not so bad.'

'I didn't mean that.'

'I know you didn't.' Rebus looked up. 'How many storeys did he fall?'

'Looks like a couple. That window there.'

There was a noise behind them. One of the woolly suits was vomiting on to the road. A colleague had an arm around his shoulders, encouraging the flow.

'Let's get him down,' Rebus said. 'Get the poor bastard into a body bag.'

'No electricity,' someone said, handing Rebus a torch.

'Are the floors safe to walk on?'

'Nobody's fallen through yet.'

Rebus moved through the flat. He'd been in dens like it a dozen times. Gangs had been in and sprayed their names and their urine around the place. Others had stripped out anything with even a whiff of monetary value: floor coverings, interior doors, wiring, ceiling roses. A table, missing one leg, had been turned upside down in the living room. There was a crumpled blanket lying on it, and some sheets of newspaper. A real home from home. There was nothing in the bathroom, just holes where the fittings had been. There was a large hole, too, in the bedroom wall. You could look right through into the adjoining flat, and see an identical scene.

The SOCOs were concentrating on the kitchen.

'What have we got?' Rebus asked. Someone shone their torch into a corner.

'Bag full of booze, sir. Whisky, rum, some tinnies and nibbles.'

'Party time.'

Rebus walked to the window. A woolly suit was standing there, looking down on to the street, where a team of four were trying to manoeuvre the body from the railings.

'That's just about as potted heid as you can get.' The young constable turned to Rebus. 'What's the odds, sir? Alky commits suicide?'

'Get used to that uniform, son.' Rebus turned back into the room. 'I want prints from the bag and its contents. If it's from an off-licence, you'll probably find price stickers. If not, could be from a pub. We're looking for one, more likely two people. Whoever sold them the hooch might give a description. How did they get here? Their own transport? Bus? Taxi? We need to know. How did they know about this place? Local knowledge? We need to ask the neighbours.' He was walking through the room now. He recognised a couple of junior CID from St Leonard's, plus Craigmillar uniforms. 'We'll split the tasks later. It could all be some hideous accident or joke gone wrong, but whatever it was the victim wasn't here on his tod. I want to know who was here with him. Thank you and good night.'

Outside, they were taking final photographs of the chair and the bonds around it, before separating chair from body. The chair would be bagged, too, along with any splinters they found. Funny how orderly it all became; order out of chaos. Dr Curt said he'd do the post mortem in the morning. That was fine by Rebus. He got back into the patrol car, wishing it were his own: the Saab had a half bottle of whisky tucked under the driver's seat. Many of the pubs would still be open: midnight licences. Instead, he drove back to the station. It was less than a mile away. Maclay and Bain looked like they'd just got in, but they'd already heard the news.

'Murder?'

'Something like it,' Rebus said. 'He was tied to a chair with a plastic bag over his head, mouth taped shut. Maybe he was pushed, maybe he jumped or fell. Whoever was with him left in a rush – forgot to take their carry-out.'

'Junkies? Dossers?'

Rebus shook his head. 'New jeans by the look of them, and new Nikes on his feet. Wallet with plenty of cash, bank card and credit card.'

'So we've got a name?'

Rebus nodded. 'Allan Mitchison, address off Morrison Street.' He shook a set of keys. 'Anybody want to tag along?'

Bain went with Rebus, leaving Maclay to 'hold the fort' – a phrase overused at Fort Apache. Bain said he didn't make a good passenger, so Rebus let him drive. DS 'Dod' Bain had a rep; it had followed him from Dundee to Falkirk and from there to Edinburgh. Dundee and Falkirk weren't exactly spa towns either. He sported a nick in the skin beneath his right eye, souvenir of a knife attack. Every so often, his finger strayed to the spot; it wasn't something he was conscious of. At five-eleven he was a couple of inches shorter than Rebus, maybe ten pounds lighter. He used to box middleweight amateur, southpaw, leaving him one ear which hung lower than the other and a nose which covered half his face. His shorn hair was salt-and-pepper. Married, three sons. Rebus hadn't seen much at Craigmillar to justify Bain's hardman rep; he was a regular soldier, a form-filler and by-the-book investigator. Rebus had just dispatched one nemesis – DI Alister Flower, promoted to some Borders outpost, chasing sheep-shaggers and tractor racers – and wasn't looking to fill the vacancy.

Allan Mitchison's flat was in a designer block in what wanted to be called 'the Financial District'. Scrapland off Lothian Road had been transformed into a conference centre and 'apartments'. A new hotel was in the offing, and an insurance company had grafted its new headquarters on to the Caledonian Hotel. There was room for more expansion, more road-building.

'Desperate,' Bain said, parking the car.

Rebus tried to remember the way the area had looked before. He only had to think back a year or two, but found the process difficult nonetheless. Was it just a big hole in the ground, or had they knocked things down? They were half a mile, maybe less, from Torphichen cop-shop; Rebus thought he knew this whole hunting-ground. But now he found that he didn't know it at all.

There were half a dozen keys on the chain. One of them opened the main door. In the well-lit lobby there was a whole wall of letter-boxes. They found the name Mitchison – flat 312. Rebus used another key to open the box and remove the mail. There was some junk – 'Open Now! You Could Have Scooped Life's Jackpot!' – and a credit-card statement. He opened the statement. Aberdeen HMV, an Edinburgh sports shop – £56.50, the Nikes – and a curry house, also in Aberdeen. A gap of just under two weeks, then the curry house again.

They took the narrow lift to the third floor, Bain shadow-boxing the full-length mirror, and found flat 12. Rebus unlocked the door, saw that an alarm panel was flashing on the wall in the small hallway, and used another key to disable it. Bain found the light-switch and closed the door. The flat smelled of paint and plaster, carpets and varnish – new, uninhabited. There wasn't a stick of furniture in the place, just a telephone on the floor beside an unrolled sleeping-bag.

'The simple life,' Bain said.

The kitchen was fully equipped – washing machine, cooker, dishwasher, fridge – but the seal was still across the door of the washer-drier and the fridge contained only its instruction manual, a spare lightbulb, and a set of risers. There was a swing-bin in the cupboard beneath the sink. When you opened the door, the lid of the bin opened automatically. Inside, Rebus saw two crushed beer cans and the red-stained wrappings from what smelled like a kebab. The flat's solitary bedroom was bare, no clothes in the built-in wardrobe, not even a coat-hanger. But Bain was dragging something out of the tiny bathroom. It was a blue rucksack, a Karrimor.

'Looks like he came in, had a wash, changed clothes and buggered off out again pronto.'

They started emptying the rucksack. Apart from clothing, they found

19

a personal stereo and some tapes – Soundgarden, Crash Test Dummies, Dancing Pigs – and a copy of Iain Banks's *Whit*.

'I meant to buy that,' Rebus said.

'Take it now. Who's watching?'

Rebus looked at Bain. The eyes seemed innocent, but he shook his head anyway. He couldn't go handing anyone any more ammunition. He pulled a carrier bag out of one of the side pockets: new tapes – Neil Young, Pearl Jam, Dancing Pigs again. The receipt was from HMV in Aberdeen.

'My guess,' Rebus said: 'he worked in Furry Boot town.'

From the other side pocket, Bain produced a pamphlet, folded in four. He unfolded it, opened it, and let Rebus see what it was. There was a colour photograph of an oil platform on the front, beneath a headline: 'T-BIRD OIL – STRIKING THE BALANCE', and a sub-head: 'Decommissioning Offshore Installations – A Modest Proposal'. Inside, besides a few paragraphs of writing, there were colour charts, diagrams and statistics. Rebus read the opening sentence:

'"In the beginning there were microscopic organisms, living and dying in the rivers and seas many millions of years ago."' He looked up at Bain. 'And they gave their lives so that millions of years on we can tank around in cars.'

'I get the feeling Spike maybe worked for an oil company.'

'His name was Allan Mitchison,' Rebus said quietly.

It was getting light when Rebus finally arrived home. He turned the hi-fi on so that it was just audible, then rinsed a glass in the kitchen and poured an inch of Laphroaig, adding a dribble of water from the tap. Some malts demanded water. He sat down at the kitchen table and looked at the newspapers laid out there, cuttings from the Johnny Bible case, photocopies of old Bible John stuff. He'd spent a day in the National Library, fast-tracking the years 1968–70, winding a blur of microfilm through the machine. Stories had leapt out at him. Rosyth was to lose its Royal Navy Commander; plans were announced for a £50 million petrochemical complex at Invergordon; *Camelot* was showing at the ABC.

A booklet was advertised for sale – 'How Scotland Should be Governed' – and there were letters to the editor concerning Home Rule. A Sales and Marketing Manager was wanted, salary of £2,500 p.a. A new house in Strathalmond cost £7,995. Frogmen were searching for clues in Glasgow, while Jim Clark was winning the Australian Grand Prix. Meantime, members of the Steve Miller Band were being arrested in London on drug charges, and car parking in Edinburgh had reached saturation point ...

1968.

Rebus had copies of the actual newspapers – purchased from a dealer for considerably more than their sixpenny cover price. They continued into '69. August. The weekend that Bible John claimed his second victim, the shit was hitting the fan in Ulster and 300,000 pop fans were turning up (and on) at Woodstock. A nice irony. The second victim was found by her own sister in an abandoned tenement ... Rebus tried not to think of Allan Mitchison, concentrated on old news instead, smiled over an August 20 headline: 'Downing Street Declaration'. Trawler strikes in Aberdeen ... an American film company seeking sixteen sets of bagpipes ... dealings in Robert Maxwell's Pergamon suspended. Another headline: 'Big drop in Glasgow crimes of violence'. Tell that to the victims. By November, it was reported that the murder rate in Scotland was twice that of England and Wales – a record fifty-two indictments in the year. A debate on capital punishment was taking place. There were anti-war demos in Edinburgh, while Bob Hope entertained the troops in Vietnam. The Stones did two shows in Los Angeles – at £71,000 the most lucrative one-night stand in pop.

It was November 22 before an artist's impression of Bible John appeared in the press. By then he *was* Bible John: the media had come up with the name. Three weeks between the third murder and the artist's impression: the trail grown good and cold. There'd been an artist's drawing after the second victim too, but only after a delay of almost a month. Big, big delays. Rebus wondered about them ...

He couldn't quite explain why Bible John was getting to him. Perhaps he was using one old case as a way of warding off another – the Spaven case. But he thought it went deeper than that. Bible John meant the end of the sixties for Scotland; he'd soured the end of one decade and the beginning of another. For a lot of people, he'd all but killed whatever dribble of peace and love had reached this far north. Rebus didn't want the twentieth century to end the same way. He wanted Johnny Bible caught. But somewhere along the road, his interest in the present case had taken a turning. He'd started to concentrate on Bible John, to the point where he was dusting off old theories and spending a small fortune on period newspapers. In 1968 and '69, Rebus had been in the army. They'd trained him how to disable and kill, then sent him on tours – including, eventually, Northern Ireland. He felt he'd missed an important part of the times.

But at least he was still alive.

He took glass and bottle through to the living room and sank into his chair. He didn't know how many bodies he'd seen; he just knew it didn't get any easier. He'd heard gossip about Bain's first post mortem, how the pathologist had been Naismith up in Dundee, a cruel bastard at the best of times. He'd probably known it was Bain's first, and had really done a job on the corpse, like a scrap merchant stripping a car, lifting out organs, sawing the skull open, hands cradling a glistening brain – you didn't do that so lightly these days, fear of hepatitis C. When Naismith had started unpeeling the genitals, Bain had dropped deadweight to the floor. But credit where due, he'd stuck around, hadn't bolted or hughied. Maybe Rebus and Bain could work together, once friction had smoothed their edges. Maybe.

He looked out of the bay window, down on to the street. He was still parked on a double yellow. There was a light on in one of the flats across the way. There was always a light on somewhere. He sipped his drink, not wanting to rush it, and listened to the Stones: *Black and Blue*. Black influences, blues influences; not great Stones, but maybe their mellowest album.

Allan Mitchison was in a fridge in the Cowgate. He'd died strapped to a chair. Rebus didn't know why. Pet Shop Boys: 'It's a Sin'. Segue to the Glimmer Twins: 'Fool to Cry'. Mitchison's flat hadn't been so different from Rebus's own in some respects: under-used, more a base than a home. He downed the rest of his drink, poured another, downed that too, and pulled the duvet off the floor and up to his chin.

Another day down.

He awoke a few hours later, blinked, got up and went to the bathroom. A shower and shave, change of clothes. He'd been dreaming of Johnny Bible, getting it all mixed up with Bible John. Cops on the scene wearing tight suits and thin black ties, white bri-nylon shirts, pork-pie hats. 1968, Bible John's first victim. To Rebus it meant Van Morrison, *Astral Weeks*. 1969, victims two and three; the Stones, *Let It Bleed*. The hunt went on into 1970, John Rebus wanting to go to the Isle of Wight Festival, not managing it. But of course Bible John had disappeared by then ... He hoped Johnny Bible would just sod off and die.

There was nothing in the kitchen to eat, nothing but newspapers. The nearest corner shop had closed down; it wasn't much more of a walk to the next grocer's along. No, he'd stop somewhere on route. He looked out of the window and saw a light-blue estate double parked outside, blocking three resident cars. Equipment in the back of the estate, two men and a woman standing on the pavement, supping coffee from take-away beakers.

'Shit,' Rebus said, knotting his tie.

Jacketed, he walked outside and into questions. One of the men was hoisting a video camera up to his shoulder. The other man was speaking.

'Inspector, could we have a word? Redgauntlet Television, *The Justice Programme.*' Rebus knew him: Eamonn Breen. The woman was Kayleigh Burgess, the show's producer. Breen was writer/presenter, loved himself, RPIA: Royal Pain in Arse.

'The Spaven case, Inspector. A few minutes of your time, that's all we need really, help everybody get to the bottom—'

'I'm already there.' Rebus saw the camera wasn't ready yet. He turned quickly, his nose almost touching the reporter's. He thought of Mental Minto breathing the word 'harassment', not knowing what harassment was, not the way Rebus had grown to know.

'You'll think you're in childbirth,' he said.

Breen blinked. 'Sorry?'

'When the surgeons are taking that camera out of your arse.' Rebus tore a parking ticket from his windscreen, unlocked the car, and got in. The video camera was finally up and running, but all it got was a shot of a battered Saab 900 reversing at speed from the scene.

Rebus had a morning meeting with his boss, Chief Inspector Jim MacAskill. The boss's office looked as chaotic as any other part of the station: packing cases still waiting to be filled and labelled, half-empty shelves, ancient green filing cabinets with their drawers open, displaying acre upon acre of paperwork, all of which would have to be shipped out in some semblance of order.

'The world's hardest jigsaw puzzle,' MacAskill said. 'If everything gets to the other end unscathed, it'll be a miracle on a par with Raith Rovers winning the UEFA Cup.'

The boss was a Fifer like Rebus, born and raised in Methil, back when the shipyard had been making boats rather than rigs for the oil industry. He was tall and well-built and younger than Rebus. His handshake was not masonic, and he'd not yet married, which had caused the usual gossip that maybe the boss was a like-your-loafers. It didn't worry Rebus – he never wore loafers himself – but he hoped that if his boss was gay there was no guilt involved. It was when you wanted a secret kept that you fell prey to blackmailers and shame merchants, destructive forces both interior and exterior. Jesus, and didn't Rebus know about that.

Whatever, MacAskill was handsome, with plenty of thick black hair – no grey, no sign of dyeing – and a chiselled face, all angles, the geometry of eyes, nose and chin making it look like he was smiling even when he wasn't.

'So,' the boss said, 'how does it read to you?'

'I'm not sure yet. A party gone wrong, a falling out – literally in this case? They hadn't started on the booze.'

'Question one in my mind: did they come together? The victim could have come alone, surprised some people doing something they shouldn't—'

Rebus was shaking his head. 'Taxi driver confirms dropping off a party of three. Gave descriptions, one of which matches the deceased pretty well. The driver paid him most attention, he was behaving the worst. The other two were quiet, sober even. Physical descriptions aren't going to get us far. He picked up the fare outside Mal's Bar. We've had a word with the staff. They sold them the carry-out.'

The boss ran a hand down his tie. 'Do we know anything more about the deceased?'

'Only that he had Aberdeen connections, maybe worked in the oil business. He didn't use his Edinburgh flat much, makes me think he used to work heavy shifts, two weeks on, two off. Maybe he didn't always come home between times. He was earning enough to pay off a mortgage in the Financial District, and there's a two-week gap between his latest credit-card transactions.'

'You think he could have been offshore during that time?'

Rebus shrugged. 'I don't know if that's the way it still works, but in the early days I had friends who went to seek their fortune on the rigs. The stints lasted two weeks, seven days a week.'

'Well, it's worth following up. We need to check family, too, next of kin. Priority for the paperwork and formal ID. Question one in my mind: motive. Are we sticking with an argument?'

Rebus shook his head. 'There was too much premeditation, way too much. Did they just happen to find sealing-tape and a polythene bag in that tip? I think they brought them. Do you remember how the Krays got to Jack "the Hat" McVitie? No, you're too young. They invited him to a party. He'd been paid to do a contract, but bottled it and couldn't pay them back. It was in a basement, so down he comes crying out for birds and booze. No birds, no booze, just Ronnie grabbing him and Reggie stabbing him to death.'

'So these two men lured Mitchison to the derelict flat?'

'Maybe.'

'To what end?'

'Well, first thing they did was tie him up and wrap a bag around his head, so they didn't have any questions to ask. They just wanted him crapping himself and then dead. I'd say it was straight assassination, with a bit of malicious cruelty thrown in.'

'So was he thrown or did he jump?'

'Does it matter?'

'Very much, John.' MacAskill stood up, leaned against the filing cabinet with his arms folded. 'If he jumped, that's tantamount to suicide, even if they *had* been planning to kill him. With the bag over his head and the way he was trussed up, we've got maybe culpable homicide. Their defence would be that they were trying to scare him, he got *too* scared and did something they hadn't been expecting – jumped through a window.'

'To do which he must have been scared out of his wits.'

MacAskill shrugged. 'Still not murder. The crux is, were they trying to scare him, or kill him?'

'I'll be sure to ask them.'

'It's got a gang feel to it: drugs maybe, or a loan he'd stopped repaying, somebody he'd ripped off.' MacAskill returned to his chair. He opened a drawer and took out a can of Irn-Bru, opened it and started to drink. He never went to the pub after work, didn't share the whisky when the team got a result. Soft drinks only: more ammo for the like-your-loafers brigade. He asked Rebus if he wanted a can.

'Not while I'm on duty, sir.'

MacAskill stifled a burp. 'Get a bit more background on the victim, John, let's see if it leads anywhere. Remember to chase forensics for fingerprint ID on the carry-out, and pathology for the PM results. Did he do drugs, that's question one in my mind. Make things easier for us if he did. Unsolved, and we don't even know how to frame it – not the sort of case I want to drag to the new station. Understood, John?'

'Unquestionably, sir.'

He turned to go, but the boss hadn't quite finished. 'That trouble over … what was the name again?'

'Spaven?' Rebus guessed.

'Spaven, yes. Quietened down yet, has it?'

'Quiet as the grave,' Rebus lied, making his exit.

3

That evening – a long-standing engagement – Rebus was at a rock concert at Ingliston Showground, an American headliner with a couple of biggish-name British acts supporting. Rebus was part of a team of eight, four different city stations represented, providing back-up (meaning protection) for Trading Standards sniffers. They were looking for bootleg gear – T-shirts and programmes, tapes and CDs – and had the full support of the bands' management. This meant backstage passes, liberal use of the hospitality marquee, a lucky-bag of official merchandising. The lackey passing out the bags smiled at Rebus.

'Maybe your kids or grandkids ...' Thrusting the bag at him. He'd bitten back a remark, passed straight to the booze tent, where he couldn't decide between the dozens of hooch bottles, so settled for a beer, then wished he'd taken a nip of Black Bush, so eased the unopened bottle into his lucky-bag.

They had two vans parked outside the arena, way back behind the stage, filling with counterfeiters and their merchandise. Maclay weaved back to the vans nursing a set of knuckles.

'Who did you pop, Heavy?'

Maclay shook his head, wiping sweat from his brow, a Michelangelo cherub turned bad.

'Some choob was resisting,' he said. 'Had a suitcase with him. I punched a hole right through it. He didn't resist after that.'

Rebus looked into the back of a van, the one holding bodies. A couple of kids, hardening already to the system, and two regulars, old enough to know the score. They'd be fined a day's wages, the loss of their stock just another debit. The summer was young, plenty festivals to come.

'Fucking awful racket.'

Maclay meant the music. Rebus shrugged; he'd been getting into it, thought maybe he'd take home a couple of the bootleg CDs. He offered Maclay the bottle of Black Bush. Maclay drank from it like it was lemonade. Rebus offered him a mint afterwards, and he threw it into his mouth with a nod of thanks.

'Post mortem results came in this afternoon,' the big man said.

Rebus had meant to phone, hadn't got round to it. 'And?'

Maclay crushed the mint to powder. 'The fall killed him. Apart from that, not much.'

The fall killed him: little chance of a straight murder conviction. 'Toxicology?'

'Still testing. Professor Gates said when they cut into the stomach, there was a strong whiff of dark rum.'

'There was a bottle in the bag.'

Maclay nodded. 'The decedent's tipple. Gates said no initial signs of drug use, but we'll have to wait for the tests. I went through the phone book for Mitchisons.'

Rebus smiled. 'So did I.'

'I know, one of the numbers I called, you'd already been on to them. No joy?'

Rebus shook his head. 'I got a number for T-Bird Oil in Aberdeen. Their personnel manager's going to call me back.'

A Trading Standards officer was coming towards them, arms laden with T-shirts and programmes. His face was red from exertion, his thin tie hanging loose at the neck. Behind him, an officer from 'F Troop' – Livingston Division – was escorting another prisoner.

'Nearly done, Mr Baxter?'

The Trading Standards officer dumped the T-shirts, lifted one and wiped his face with it.

'That should about do it,' he said. 'I'll round up my soldiers.'

Rebus turned to Maclay. 'I'm starving. Let's see what they've laid on for the superstars.'

There were fans trying to breach security, teenagers mostly, split half and half, boys and girls. A few had managed to inveigle their way in. They wandered around behind the barriers looking for faces they would recognise from the posters on their bedroom walls. Then when they did spot one, they'd be too awed or shy to talk.

'Any kids?' Rebus asked Maclay. They were in hospitality, nursing bottles of Beck's taken from a coolbox Rebus hadn't noticed first time round.

Maclay shook his head. 'Divorced before it became an issue, if you'll pardon the pun. You?'

'One daughter.'

'Grown up?'

'Sometimes I think she's older than me.'

'Kids grow up faster than in our day.' Rebus smiled at that, Maclay a good ten years his junior.

A girl, squealing resistance, was being hauled back to the perimeter by two burly security men.

'Jimmy Cousins,' Maclay said, pointing out one of the security bears. 'Do you know him?'

'He was stationed at Leith for a while.'

'Retired last year, only forty-seven. Thirty years in. Now he's got his pension *and* a job. Makes you think.'

'Makes me think he misses the force.'

Maclay smiled. 'It can turn into a habit.'

'That why you divorced?'

'I dare say it played a part.'

Rebus thought of Brian Holmes, feared for him. Stress getting to the younger man, affecting work and personal life both. Rebus had been there.

'You know Ted Michie?'

Rebus nodded: the man he'd replaced at Fort Apache.

'Doctors think it's terminal. He won't let them cut, says knives are against his religion.'

'I hear he was handy with a truncheon in his day.'

One of the support bands entered the marquee to scattered applause. Five males, mid-twenties, stripped to the waist with towels around their shoulders, high on something – maybe just from performing. Hugs and kisses from a group of girls at a table, whoops and roars.

'We fucking killed them out there!'

Rebus and Maclay drank their drinks in silence, tried not to look like promoters, succeeded.

When they walked back outside, it was dark enough for the light-show to be worth watching. There were fireworks, too, reminding Rebus that it was the tourist season. Not long till the nightly Tattoo, fireworks you could hear from Marchmont, even with the windows closed. A camera crew, stalked by photographers, was itself stalking the main support band who were ready to go on. Maclay watched the procession.

'You're probably surprised they're not after you,' he said, mischief in his voice.

'Fuck off,' Rebus replied, making for the side of the stage. The passes were colour-coded. His was yellow, and it got him as far as the stage-wings, where he watched the entertainment. The sound system was a travesty, but there were monitors nearby and he concentrated on those. The crowd seemed to be having fun, bobbing up and down, a sea of disembodied heads. He thought of the Isle of Wight, of other festivals he'd missed, headliners who weren't around any more.

He thought of Lawson Geddes, his one-time mentor, boss, protector, his memory rippling back through two decades.

John Rebus, mid-twenties, a detective constable, looking to put army years behind him, ghosts and nightmares. A wife and infant daughter trying to be his life. And Rebus maybe seeking out a surrogate father, finding one in Lawson Geddes, Detective Inspector, City of Edinburgh Police. Geddes was forty-five, ex-army, served in the Borneo conflict, told stories of jungle war versus The Beatles, no one back in Britain very interested in a last spasm of colonial muscle. The two men found they shared common values, common night sweats and dreams of failure. Rebus was new to CID, Geddes knew everything there was to know. It was easy to recall the first year of growing friendship, easy now to forgive the few hiccups: Geddes making a pass at Rebus's young wife, almost succeeding; Rebus passing out at a Geddes party, waking in the dark and pissing into a dresser-drawer, thinking he'd found the toilet; a couple of fist-fights after last orders, the fists not connecting, turning into wrestling matches instead.

Easy to forgive so much. But then they landed a murder inquiry, Leonard Spaven Geddes' chief suspect. Geddes and Lenny Spaven had been playing cat-and-mouse for a couple of years – aggravated assault, pimping, the hijacking of a couple of cigarette lorries. Even whispers of a murder or two, gangster stuff, trimming the competition. Spaven had been in the Scots Guards same time as Geddes, maybe the bad blood started there, neither man ever said.

Christmas 1976, a gruesome find on farmland near Swanston: a woman's body, decapitated. The head turned up almost a week later, New Year's Day, in another field near Currie. The weather was sub-zero. From the rate of decay, the pathologist was able to say that the head had been kept indoors for some time after being severed from the body, while the body itself had been dumped fresh. Glasgow police semi-interested, the file on Bible John still open six years on. Identification from clothing initially, a member of the public coming forward to say the description sounded like a neighbour who hadn't been seen for a couple of weeks. The milkman had kept on delivering until he decided no one was home, that she had gone away for Christmas without telling him.

Police forced the front door. Unopened Christmas cards on the hall carpet; a pot of soup on the stove, speckled with mould; a radio playing quietly. Relatives were found, identified the body – Elizabeth Rhind, Elsie to her friends. Thirty-five years old, divorced from a sailor in the merchant navy. She'd worked for a brewery, shorthand and typing. She'd been well liked, the outgoing type. The ex-husband, suspect one, had a steel-toecapped alibi: his ship was in Gib at the time. Lists of the victim's friends, especially boyfriends, and a name came up: Lenny. No surname, someone Elsie had gone out with for a few weeks. Drinking companions provided a description, and Lawson Geddes recognised it: Lenny Spaven. Geddes formed his theory quickly: Lenny had zeroed in on Elsie when he learned she worked at the brewery. He was probably looking for inside gen, maybe thinking of a truck hijack or a simple break-in. Elsie refused to help, he got angry, and he killed her.

It sounded good to Geddes, but he found it hard to convince anyone else. There was no evidence either. They couldn't determine a time of death, leaving a twenty-four-hour margin of error, so Spaven didn't need to provide an alibi. A search of his home and those of his friends showed no bloodstains, nothing. There were other strands they should have been following, but Geddes couldn't stop thinking about Spaven. It nearly drove John Rebus demented. They argued loudly, more than once, stopped going for drinks together. The brass had a word with Geddes, told him he was becoming obsessed to the detriment of the inquiry. He was told to take a holiday. They even had a collection for him in the Murder Room.

Then one night he'd come to Rebus's door, begging a favour. He looked like he hadn't slept in a week, or changed his clothes over that time. He said he'd been following Spaven, and had tracked him to a lock-up in Stockbridge. He was probably still there if they hurried. Rebus knew it was wrong; there were procedures. But Geddes was shivering, wild-eyed. All idea of search warrants and the like evaporated. Rebus insisted on driving, Geddes giving directions.

Spaven was still in the garage. So were brown cardboard boxes, piled high: the proceeds from a South Queensferry warehouse break-in back in November. Digital clock-radios: Spaven was fitting plugs to them, preparing to hawk them around the pubs and clubs. Behind one pile of boxes, Geddes discovered a plastic carrier bag. Inside were a woman's hat and a cream shoulder-bag, both later identified as having belonged to Elsie Rhind.

Spaven protested his innocence from the moment Geddes lifted up the carrier bag and asked what was inside. He protested all the way through the rest of the investigation, the trial, and as he was being hauled back to the cells after being handed down a life sentence. Geddes and Rebus were in court, Geddes back to normal, beaming satisfaction, Rebus just a little uneasy. They'd had to concoct a story: an anonymous tip-off on a consignment of stolen goods, a chance find ... It felt right and wrong at the same time. Lawson Geddes hadn't wanted to talk about it afterwards, which was strange: usually they dissected their cases – successful or not – over a drink. Then, to everyone's surprise, Geddes had resigned from the force, with promotion only a year or two away. Instead, he'd gone to work in his father's off-sales business – there was always a discount waiting for serving officers – made some money, and retired at a youthful fifty-five. For the past ten years, he'd been living with his wife Etta in Lanzarote.

Ten years ago Rebus had received a postcard. Lanzarote had 'not much fresh water, but enough to temper a glass of whisky, and the Torres wines need no adulteration'. The landscape was almost lunar, 'black volcanic ash, so an excuse not to garden!', and that was about it. He hadn't heard anything since, and Geddes hadn't furnished his address on the island. That was OK, friendships came and went. Geddes had been a useful man to know at the time, he'd taught Rebus a lot.

Dylan: *Don't Look Back*.

The here and now: light-show stinging Rebus's eyes. He blinked back tears, stepped away from the stage, retreated to hospitality. Pop stars and entourage, loving the media interest. Flash-bulbs and questions. A spume of champagne. Rebus brushed flecks from his shoulder, decided it was time to find his car.

The Spaven case should have remained closed, no matter how loudly the prisoner himself protested. But in jail, Spaven had started writing, his writings smuggled out by friends or bribed jailers. Pieces had started to see publication – fiction at first, an early story picking up first prize in some newspaper competition. When the winner's true identity and whereabouts were revealed, the newspaper got itself a bigger news story. More writing, more publication. Then a TV drama, penned by Spaven. It won an award somewhere in Germany, another in France, it was shown in the USA, an estimated audience of twenty million worldwide. There was a follow-up. Then a novel, and then the non-fiction pieces started appearing – Spaven's early life at first, but Rebus knew where the story would lead.

By this time there was loud support in the media for an early release, nullified when Spaven assaulted another prisoner severely enough to cause brain damage. Spaven's pieces from jail became more eloquent than ever – the man had been jealous of all the attention, had attempted to murder Spaven in the corridor outside his cell. Self-defence. And the crunch: Spaven would not have been placed in this invidious position were it not for a gross miscarriage of justice. The second instalment of Spaven's autobiography ended with the Elsie Rhind case, and with mention of the two police officers who'd framed him – Lawson Geddes and John Rebus. Spaven reserved his real loathing for Geddes, Rebus just a bit-player, Geddes' lackey. More media interest. Rebus saw it as a revenge fantasy, planned over long incarcerated years, Spaven unhinged. But whenever he read Spaven's work, he saw powerful manipulation of the reader, and he thought back to Lawson Geddes on his doorstep that night, to the lies they told afterwards ...

And then Lenny Spaven died, committed suicide. Took a scalpel to his throat and opened it up, a gash you could fit your hand inside. More rumour: he'd been murdered by jailers before he could complete volume three of his autobiography, detailing his years and depredations in several Scottish prisons. Or jealous prisoners had been allowed access to his cell.

Or it was suicide. He left a note, three drafts crumpled on the floor, maintaining to the end his innocence in the Elsie Rhind killing. The media started sniffing their story, Spaven's life and death big news. And now ... three things.

One: the incomplete third volume of autobiography had been published – 'heart-breaking' according to one critic, 'a massive achievement' for another. It was still on the best-seller list, Spaven's face staring out from bookshop windows all along Princes Street. Rebus tried to avoid the route.

Two: a prisoner was released, and told reporters he was the last person to see or speak to Spaven alive. According to him, Spaven's last words were: 'God knows I'm innocent, but I'm so tired of saying it over and over.' The story earned the ex-offender £750 from a newspaper; easy to see it as flannel waved at a gullible press.

Three: a new TV series was launched, *The Justice Programme*, a hard-hitting look at crime, the system, and miscarriages of justice. High ratings for its first series – attractive presenter Eamonn Breen scooping women viewers – so now a second series was on the blocks, and the Spaven case – severed head, accusations, and suicide of a media darling – was to be the showcase opener.

With Lawson Geddes out of the country, address unknown, leaving John Rebus to carry the film-can.

Alex Harvey: 'Framed'. Segue to Jethro Tull: 'Living in the Past'.

He went home by way of the Oxford Bar – a long detour, always worthwhile. The gantry and optics had a quietly hypnotic effect, the only possible explanation as to why the regulars could stand and stare at them for hours at a stretch. The barman waited for an order; Rebus did not have a 'usual' drink these days, variety the spice of life and all that.

'Dark rum, and a half of Best.'

He hadn't touched dark rum in years, didn't think of it as a young man's drink. Yet Allan Mitchison had drunk it. A seaman's drink, another reason to think he worked offshore. Rebus handed over money, downed the short in one sour swallow, rinsed his mouth with the beer, found himself finishing it too quickly. The barman turned with his change.

'Make it a pint this time, Jon.'

'And another rum?'

'Jesus, no.' Rebus rubbed his eyes, bummed a cigarette from his drowsy neighbour. The Spaven case ... it had dragged Rebus backwards through time, forcing him to confront memory, then to wonder if his memory was playing tricks. It remained unfinished business, twenty years on. Like Bible John. He shook his head, tried to clear it of history, and found himself thinking of Allan Mitchison, of falling headlong on to spiked rails, watching them rise towards you, arms held fast to a chair so there was only one choice left: did you confront doom open-eyed or closed? He walked around the bar to use the telephone, put money in and then couldn't think who to call.

'Forgotten the number?' a drinker asked as Rebus got his coin back.

'Aye,' he said, 'what's the Samaritans' again?'

The drinker surprised him, knew the number pat.

Four blinks from his answering machine meant four messages. He lifted the instruction manual. It was open at page six, the 'Playback' section boxed with red pen, paragraphs underlined. He followed the instructions. The machine decided to work.

'It's Brian.' Brian Holmes. Rebus opened the Black Bush and poured, listening. 'Just to say ... well, thanks. Minto's recanted, so I'm off the hook. Hope I can return the favour.' No energy in the voice, a mouth tired of words. End message. Rebus savoured the whiskey.

Blip: message two.

'I was working late and thought I'd give you a call, Inspector. We spoke earlier, Stuart Minchell, personnel manager at T-Bird Oil. I can confirm that Allan Mitchison was in our employ. I can fax through the details if you have a number. Call me at the office tomorrow. Bye.'

Goodbye and bingo. A relief to know something about the deceased other than his taste in music. Rebus's ears were roaring: the concert and the alcohol, blood pounding.

Message three: 'It's Howdenhall here, thought you were in a hurry but I can't find you. Typical CID.' Rebus knew the voice: Pete Hewitt at the police lab, Howdenhall. Pete looked fifteen, but was probably early twenties, smart-mouthed with a brain to match. Fingerprints a speciality. 'I got mostly partials, but a couple of beauties, and guess what? Their owner's on the computer. Past convictions for violence. Phone me back if you want a name.'

Rebus checked his watch. Pete doing his usual tease. It was gone eleven, he'd be home or out on the ran-dan, and Rebus didn't have a home number for him. He kicked the sofa, wished he'd stayed home: carting off bootleggers a pure waste of time. Still, he had the Black Bush and a bagful of CDs, T-shirts he'd never wear, a poster of four tykes with acne close-ups. He'd seen their faces before, couldn't think where ...

One message to go.

'John?'

A woman's voice, one he recognised.

'If you're home, pick up, please. I hate these things.' Pause, waiting. A sigh. 'OK then, look, now that we're not ... I mean, now I'm not your boss, how about some socialising? Dinner or something. Give me a call at home or office, OK? While there's time. I mean, you won't be at Fort Apache for ever. Take care.'

Rebus sat down, staring at the machine as it clicked off. Gill Templer, Chief Inspector, one-time 'significant other'. She'd become his boss only recently, frost on the surface, no sign of anything but iceberg beneath. Rebus took another drink, toasted the machine. A woman had just asked him for a date: when had *that* last happened? He got up and went to the bathroom, examined his reflection in the cabinet mirror, rubbed his chin and laughed. Twilit eyes, lank hair, hands that trembled when he lifted them level.

'Looking good, John.' Yes, and he could fib for Scotland. Gill Templer, looking as good these days as when they'd first met, *asking him out*? He shook his head, still laughing. No, there had to be something ... A hidden agenda.

Back in the living room, he emptied his lucky-bag, found that the poster of the four tykes matched the cover of one of the CDs. He recognised it: The Dancing Pigs. One of Mitchison's tapes, their latest recording. He recalled a couple of the faces from the hospitality tent: *We fucking killed them out there!* Mitchison had owned at least two of their albums.

Funny he hadn't had a ticket to the gig …

His front door bell: short, two rings. He walked back down the hall, checking the time. Eleven twenty-five. Put his eye to the spy-hole, didn't believe what he saw, opened the door wide.

'Where's the rest of the crew?'

Kayleigh Burgess stood there, heavy bag hanging from her shoulder, hair tucked up under an oversized green beret, strands curling down past both ears. Cute and cynical at the same time: Don't-Muck-Me-About-Unless-I-Want-You-To. Rebus had seen the model and year before.

'In their beds, most likely.'

'You mean Eamonn Breen *doesn't* sleep in a coffin?'

A guarded smile; she adjusted the weight of the bag on her shoulder. 'You know,' not looking at him, fussing with the bag instead, 'you're doing yourself no favours refusing to even discuss this with us. It doesn't make you look good.'

'I was no pin-up to start with.'

'We're not taking sides, that's not what *The Justice Programme*'s about.'

'Really? Well, much as I enjoy a blether on the doorstep last thing at night …'

'You haven't heard, have you?' Now she looked at him. 'No, I didn't think so. Too soon. We've had a unit out in Lanzarote, trying to interview Lawson Geddes. I got a phone call this evening …'

Rebus knew the face and tone of voice; he'd used them himself on many grim occasions, trying to break the news to family, to friends …

'What happened?'

'He committed suicide. Apparently he'd been suffering from depression since his wife died. He shot himself.'

'Aw, Christ.' Rebus swivelled from the door, legs heavy as he made for the living room, the whiskey bottle. She followed him, placed her bag on the coffee table. He motioned with the bottle and she nodded. They chinked glasses.

'When did Etta die?'

'About a year ago. Heart attack, I think. There's a daughter, lives in London.'

Rebus remembered her: a cheeky-faced pre-teen with braces. Her name was Aileen.

'Did you hound Geddes the way you've hounded me?'

'We don't "hound", Inspector. We just want everyone to have their say. It's important to the programme.'

'The programme.' Rebus shook his head. 'Well, you've not got a programme now, have you?'

The drink had brought colour to her face. 'On the contrary, Mr Geddes' suicide could be construed as an admission of guilt. It makes a hell of a punch-line.' She'd recovered well; Rebus wondered how much of her earlier timidity had been an act. He realised she was standing in his living room: records, CDs, empty bottles, books piled high on the floor. He couldn't let her see the kitchen: Johnny Bible and Bible John spread across the table, evidence of an obsession. 'That's why I'm here ... partly. I could have given you the news over the telephone, but I thought it was the sort of thing best done face to face. And now that you're alone, the only living witness so to speak ...' She reached into the bag, produced a professional-looking tape deck and microphone. Rebus put down his glass and walked over to her, hands out.

'May I?'

She hesitated, then handed over the equipment. Rebus walked down the hall with it. The front door was still open. He stepped into the stairwell, reached a hand over the guard-rail, and let go the recorder. It fell two flights, case splintering on impact with the stone floor. She was right behind him.

'You'll pay for that!'

'Send me the bill and we'll see.'

He walked back inside and closed the door after him, put the chain on as a hint, and watched through the spy-hole till she'd gone.

He sat in his chair by the window, thinking of Lawson Geddes. Typical Scot, he couldn't cry about it. Crying was for football defeats, animal bravery stories, 'Flower of Scotland' after closing time. He cried about stupid things, but tonight his eyes remained stubbornly dry.

He knew he was in shit. They only had *him* now, and they'd redouble their efforts to salvage a programme. Besides, Burgess was right: prisoner suicide, policeman suicide – it was a hell of a punch-line. But Rebus didn't want to be the man to feed them it. Like them, he wanted to know the truth – but not for the same reasons. He couldn't even say *why* he wanted to know. One course of action: start his own investigation. The only problem was, the further he dug, the more he might be creating a pit for his own reputation – what was left of it –

and, more importantly, that of his one-time mentor, partner, friend. Problem connected to the first: he wasn't objective enough; he *couldn't* investigate himself. He needed a stand-in, an understudy.

He picked up the telephone, pressed seven numbers. A sleepy response.

'Yeah, hello?'

'Brian, it's John. Sorry to phone so late, I need that favour repaid.'

They met in the car park at Newcraighall. Lights were on in the UCI cinema complex, some late showing. The Mega Bowl was closed; so was McDonald's. Holmes and Nell Stapleton had moved into a house just off Duddingston Park, looking across Portobello Golf Course and the Freightliner Terminal. Holmes said the freight traffic didn't keep him awake through the night. They could have met at the golf course, but it was too close to Nell for Rebus's liking. He hadn't seen her in a couple of years, not even at social functions – each had a gift for knowing when the other would or wouldn't be in attendance. Old scrapes; Nell picking at the scabs, obsessive.

So they met a couple of miles away, in a gully, surrounded by closed shops – DIY store, shoe emporium, Toys R Us – still cops, even off duty.

Especially off duty.

Their eyes darted, using wing mirrors and rearview, looking for shadows. Nobody in sight, they still talked in an undertone. Rebus explained exactly what he wanted.

'This TV programme, I need some ammo before I talk to them. But it's too personal with me. I need you to go back over the Spaven case – case notes, trial proceedings. Just read through them, see what you think.'

Holmes sat in the passenger seat of Rebus's Saab. He looked what he was: a man who'd got undressed and gone to bed, only to have to get up too shortly thereafter and put dayshift clothes on again. His hair was ruffled, shirt open two buttons, shoes but no socks. He stifled a yawn, shaking his head.

'I don't get it. What am I looking for?'

'Just see if anything jars. Just … I don't know.'

'You're taking this seriously then?'

'Lawson Geddes just killed himself.'

'Christ.' But Holmes didn't even blink; beyond compassion for men he didn't know, figures from history. He had too much on his own mind.

'Something else,' Rebus said. 'You might track down an ex-con who says he was the last person to talk to Spaven. I forget the name, but it was reported in all the papers at the time.'

'One question: do *you* think Geddes framed Lenny Spaven?'

Rebus made a show of thinking it over, then shrugged. 'Let me tell you the story. Not the story you'll find in my written notes on the case.'

Rebus began to talk: Geddes turning up at his door, the too-easy finding of the bag, Geddes frantic before, unnaturally calm after. The story they manufactured, anonymous tip-off. Holmes listened in silence. The cinema began to empty, young couples hugging, air-hopping towards their cars, walking like they'd rather be lying down. A gathering of engine-noise, exhaust fumes and headlights, tall shadows on the canyon walls, the car park emptying. Rebus finished his version.

'Another question.'

Rebus waited, but Holmes was having trouble forming the words. He gave up finally and shook his head. Rebus knew what he was thinking. He knew Rebus had put the squeeze on Minto, while believing Minto to have a case against Holmes. And now he knew that Rebus had lied to protect Lawson Geddes and to secure the conviction. The question in his mind a double strand – was Rebus's version the truth? How dirty was the copper sitting behind the steering wheel?

How dirty would Holmes allow *himself* to get before he left the force?

Rebus knew Nell nagged him every day, quiet persuasion. He was young enough for another career, *any* career, something clean and risk-free. There was still time for him to get out. But maybe not much time.

'OK,' Holmes said, opening the car door. 'I'll start a.s.a.p.' He paused. 'But if I find any dirt, anything concealed in the margins ...'

Rebus turned on his lights, high-beam. He started the car and drove off.

4

Rebus woke up early. There was a book open on his lap. He looked at the last paragraph he'd read before falling asleep, didn't recall any of it. Mail lying inside the door: who'd be a postman in Edinburgh, all those tenement stairs? His credit-card bill: two supermarkets, three off-licences, and Bob's Rare Vinyl. Impulse buys one Saturday afternoon, after a lunchtime sesh in the Ox – *Freak Out* on single vinyl, mint; *The Velvet Underground*, peel-off banana intact; *Sergeant Pepper* in mono with the sheet of cut-outs. He'd yet to play any of them, already had scratchy copies of the Velvets and Beatles.

He shopped on Marchmont Road, ate breakfast at the kitchen table with the Bible John/Johnny Bible material for a cloth. Johnny Bible headlines: 'Catch This Monster!'; 'Baby-Faced Killer Claims Third Victim'; 'Public Warned: Be Vigilant'. Much the same banners Bible John was earning a quarter century before.

Johnny Bible's first victim: Duthie Park, Aberdeen. Michelle Strachan came from Pittenweem in Fife, so of course all her Furry Boot pals called her Michelle Fifer. She didn't look like her near-namesake: short and skinny, mousy shoulder-length hair, front teeth prominent. She was a student at Robert Gordon University. Raped, strangled, one shoe missing.

Victim two, six weeks later: Angela Riddell, Angie to her friends. In her time she'd worked at an escort agency, been arrested in a slapper sweep near Leith docks, and fronted a blues band, husky-voiced but trying too hard. A record company had now released the band's only demo as a CD single, making money from ghouls and the curious. Edinburgh CID had spent a lot of hours – thousands of man hours – trawling through Angie Riddell's past, seeking out old clients, friends, fans of the band, looking for a prozzy punter turned killer, an obsessed blues fan, whatever. Warriston Cemetery, where the body was found, was a known haunt of Hell's Angels, amateur black magicians, perverts and loners. In the days following the discovery of the body, at dead of

39

night you were more likely to trip over a snoozing surveillance team than a crucified cat.

A month-long gap, during which the first two murders had been connected – Angie Riddell not only raped and strangled, but missing a distinctive necklace, a row of two-inch metal crosses, bought in Cockburn Street – then a third killing, this time in Glasgow. Judith Cairns, 'Ju-Ju', was on the dole, which hadn't stopped her working in a chip shop late evenings, a pub some lunchtimes, and as a hotel chambermaid weekend mornings. When she was found dead, there was no sign of her backpack, which friends swore she took everywhere, even to clubs and warehouse raves.

Three women, aged nineteen, twenty-four and twenty-one, murdered within three months. It was two weeks since Johnny Bible had struck. A six-week gap between victims one and two had been whittled to a calendar month between two and three. Everyone was waiting, waiting for the worst possible news. Rebus drank his coffee, ate his croissant, and examined photos of the three victims, culled from the newspapers, blown-up grainy, all the young women smiling, the way you only usually did for a photographer. The camera always lied.

Rebus knew so much about the victims, so little about Johnny Bible. Though no police officer would admit it in public, they were impotent, all but going through the motions. It was *his* play; they were waiting for *him* to slip up: overconfidence, or boredom, or a simple desire to be caught, the knowledge of what was right and wrong. They were waiting for a friend, a neighbour, a loved one to come forward, maybe an anonymous call – one that would prove not merely malicious. They were all waiting. Rebus ran a finger over the biggest photo of Angie Riddell. He'd known her, had been part of the team that had arrested her and a lot of other working girls that night in Leith. The atmosphere had been good, a lot of jokes, jibes at married officers. Most of the prostitutes knew the routine, those who did calming those who were new to the game. Angie Riddell had been stroking the hair of a hysterical teenager, a druggie. Rebus had liked her style, had interviewed her. She'd made him laugh. A couple of weeks later, he'd driven down Commercial Street, asked how she was doing. She'd told him time was money, and talk didn't come cheap, but offered him a discount if he wanted anything more substantial than hot air. He'd laughed again, bought her tea and a bridie at a late-opening café. A fortnight later, he found himself down in Leith again, but according to the girls she hadn't been around, so that was that.

Raped, beaten, strangled.

It all reminded him of the World's End killings, of other murders of young women, so many of them left unsolved. World's End: October '77, the year before Spaven, two teenagers drinking in the World's End pub on the High Street. Their bodies turned up next morning. Beaten, hands tied, strangled, bags and jewellery missing. Rebus hadn't worked the case, but knew men who had: they carried with them the frustration of a job left undone, and would carry it to the grave. The way a lot of them saw it, when you worked a murder investigation, your client was the deceased, mute and cold, but still screaming out for justice. It had to be true, because sometimes if you listened hard enough you could hear them screaming. Sitting in his chair by the window, Rebus had heard many a despairing cry. One night, he'd heard Angie Riddell and it had pierced his heart, because he'd known her, liked her. In that instant it became personal for him. He couldn't not be interested in Johnny Bible. He just didn't know what he could do to help. His curiosity about the original Bible John case was probably no help at all. It had sent him back in time, spending less and less time in the present. Sometimes it took all his strength to pull him back to the here and now.

Rebus had telephone calls to make. First: Pete Hewitt at Howdenhall.

'Morning, Inspector, and isn't she a beauty?'

Voice dripping irony. Rebus looked out at milky sunshine. 'Rough night, Pete?'

'Rough? You could shave a yak with it. I take it you got my message?' Rebus had pen and paper ready. 'I got a couple of decent prints off the whisky bottle: thumb and forefinger. Tried lifting from the polythene bag and the tape binding him to the chair, but only a few partials, nothing to build a case on.'

'Come on, Pete, get to the ID.'

'Well, all that money you complain we spend on computers ... I got a match within quarter of an hour. The name is Anthony Ellis Kane. He has a police record for attempted murder, assault, reset. Ring any bells?'

'Not a one.'

'Well, he used to operate out of Glasgow. No convictions these past seven years.'

'I'll look him up when I get to the station. Thanks, Pete.'

Next call: the personnel office at T-Bird Oil. A long-distance call; he'd wait and make it from Fort Apache. A glance out of the window: no sign of the Redgauntlet crew. Rebus put his jacket on and made for the door.

He stopped in at the boss's office. MacAskill was guzzling Irn-Bru.

'We have a fingerprint ID, Anthony Ellis Kane, previous convictions for violence.'

MacAskill tossed the empty can into his waste-basket. His desk was stacked with old paperwork – drawer one of the filing cabinet. There was an empty packing case on the floor.

'What about the decedent's family, friends?'

Rebus shook his head. 'Deceased worked for T-Bird Oil. I'm going to call the personnel manager for details.'

'Make that job one, John.'

'Job one, sir.'

But when he got to the Shed and sat at his desk, he thought about phoning Gill Templer first, decided against it. Bain was at his desk; Rebus didn't want an audience.

'Dod,' he said, 'run a check on Anthony Ellis Kane. Howdenhall found his prints on the carry-out.' Bain nodded and started typing. Rebus phoned Aberdeen, gave his name and asked to be put through to Stuart Minchell.

'Good morning, Inspector.'

'Thanks for leaving a message, Mr Minchell. Do you have Allan Mitchison's employment details?'

'Right in front of me. What do you want to know?'

'A next of kin.'

Minchell shuffled paper. 'There doesn't appear to be one. Let me check his CV.' A long pause, Rebus happy not to be making the call from home. 'Inspector, it seems Allan Mitchison was an orphan. I have details of his education, and there's a children's home mentioned.'

'No family?'

'No mention of a family.'

Rebus had written Mitchison's name on a sheet of paper. He underlined it now, the rest of the page a blank. 'What was Mr Mitchison's position within the company?'

'He was … let's see, he worked for Platform Maintenance, specifically as a painter. We have a base in Shetland, maybe he worked there.' More paper shuffling. 'No, Mr Mitchison worked on the platforms themselves.'

'Painting them?'

'And general maintenance. Steel corrodes, Inspector. You've no idea how fast the North Sea can strip paint from steel.'

'Which rig did he work on?'

'Not a rig, a production platform. I'd have to check that.'

'Could you do that, please? And could you fax me through his personnel file?'

'You say he's dead?'

'Last time I looked.'

'Then there should be no problem. Give me your number there.'

Rebus did so, and terminated the call. Bain was waving him over. Rebus crossed the room and stood by Bain's side, the better to see the computer screen.

'This guy's pure mental,' Bain said. His phone rang. Bain picked up, started a conversation. Rebus read down the screen. Anthony Ellis Kane, known as 'Tony El', had a record going back to his youth. He was now forty-four years old, well known to Strathclyde police. The bulk of his adult life had been spent in the employ of Joseph Toal, a.k.a. 'Uncle Joe', who practically *ran* Glasgow with muscle provided by his son and by men like Tony El. Bain put down the receiver.

'Uncle Joe,' he mused. 'If Tony El is still working for him, we could have a very different case.'

Rebus was remembering what the boss had said: *it's got a gang feel to it.* Drugs or a default on a loan. Maybe MacAskill was right.

'You know what this means?' Bain said.

Rebus nodded. 'A trip to weegie-land.' Scotland's two main cities, separated by a fifty-minute motorway trip, were wary neighbours, as though years back one had accused the other of something and the accusation, unfounded or not, still rankled. Rebus had a couple of contacts in Glasgow CID, so went to his desk and made the calls.

'If you want info on Uncle Joe,' he was told during the second call, 'best talk to Chick Ancram. Wait, I'll give you his number.'

Charles Ancram, it turned out, was a Chief Inspector based in Govan. Rebus spent a fruitless half hour trying to find him, then went for a walk. The shops in front of Fort Apache were the usual metal shutters and mesh grille affairs, Asian owners mostly, even if the shops were staffed with white faces. Men hung around on the street outside, T-shirted, sporting tattoos, smoking. Eyes as trustworthy as a weasel in a hen-house.

Eggs? Not me, pal, can't stand them.

Rebus bought cigarettes and a newspaper. Walking out of the shop, a baby buggy caught his ankles, a woman told him to mind where he was fucking going. She bustled away, hauling a toddler behind her. Twenty, maybe twenty-one, hair dyed blonde, two front teeth missing. Her bared forearms showed tattoos, too. Across the road, an advertising hoarding told him to spend £20k on a new car. Behind it, the discount supermarket was doing no business, kids using its car park as a skateboard rink.

Back in the Shed, Maclay was on the telephone. He held the receiver out to Rebus.

'Chief Inspector Ancram, returning your call.' Rebus rested against the desk.

'Hello?'

'Inspector Rebus? Ancram here, I believe you want a word.'

'Thanks for getting back to me, sir. Two words really: Joseph Toal.'

Ancram snorted. He had a west coast drawl, nasal, always managing to sound a little condescending. 'Uncle Joe Corleone? Our own dear Godfather? Has he done something I don't know about?'

'Do you know one of his men, a guy called Anthony Kane?'

'Tony El,' Ancram confirmed. 'Worked for Uncle Joe for years.'

'Past tense?'

'He hasn't been heard of in a while. Story is he crossed Uncle Joe, and Uncle Joe got Stanley to see to things. Tony El was all cut up about it.'

'Who's Stanley?'

'Uncle Joe's son. It's not his real name, but everyone calls him Stanley, on account of his hobby.'

'Which is?'

'Stanley knives, he collects them.'

'You think Stanley topped Tony El?'

'Well, the body hasn't turned up, which is usually proof enough in a perverse way.'

'Tony El's very much alive. He was through here a few days ago.'

'I see.' Ancram was quiet for a moment. In the background Rebus could hear busy voices, radio transmissions, police station sounds. 'Bag over the head?'

'How did you know?'

'Tony El's trademark. So he's back in circulation, eh? Inspector, I think you and me better have a talk. Monday morning, can you find Govan station? No, wait, make it Partick, 613 Dumbarton Road. I've a meeting there at nine. Can we say ten?'

'Ten's fine.'

'See you then.'

Rebus put down the telephone. 'Monday morning at ten,' he told Bain. 'I'm off to Partick.'

'You poor bastard,' Bain replied, sounding like he meant it.

'Want us to put out Tony El's description?' Maclay asked.

'Pronto. Let's see if we can lassoo him before Monday.'

*

Bible John flew back into Scotland on a fine Friday morning. The first thing he did at the airport was pick up some newspapers. In the kiosk, he saw that a new book had been published on World War Two, so bought that too. Sitting in the concourse, he flicked through the newspapers, finding no new stories concerning the Upstart. He left the papers on his seat and went to the carousel, where his luggage was waiting.

A taxi took him into Glasgow. He had already decided not to stay in the city. It wasn't that he had anything to fear from his old hunting-ground, but that a stay there would bring little profit. Of necessity, Glasgow brought back bittersweet memories. In the late sixties, it had been reinventing itself: knocking down old slums, building their concrete equivalents on the outskirts. New roads, bridges, motorways – the place had been an enormous building site. He got the feeling the process was still ongoing, as if the city still hadn't acquired an identity it could be comfortable with.

A problem Bible John knew something about.

From Queen Street station, he took a train to Edinburgh, and used his cellphone to reserve a room at his usual hotel, placing it on his corporate account. He called his wife to tell her where he'd be. He had his laptop with him, and did some work on the train. Work soothed him; a busy brain was best. Go therefore now, and work; for there shall no straw be given you, yet shall ye deliver the tale of bricks. The Book of Exodus. The media back then had done him a favour, and so had the police. They'd issued a description saying his first name was John and he was 'fond of quoting from the Bible'. Neither was particularly true: his middle name was John, and he had only occasionally quoted aloud from the good book. In recent years, he'd started attending church again, but now regretted it, regretted thinking he was safe.

There was no safety in this world, just as there would be none in the next.

He left the train at Haymarket – in summer it was easier to catch a taxi there – but when he stepped out into sunshine, he decided to walk to the hotel: it was only five or ten minutes away. His case had wheels, and his shoulder-bag was not particularly heavy. He breathed deeply: traffic fumes and a hint of brewery hops. Tired of squinting, he paused to put on sunglasses, and immediately liked the world better. Catching his reflection in a shop window he saw just another businessman tired of

45

travelling. There was nothing memorable about either face or figure, and the clothes were always conservative: a suit from Austin Reed, shirt by Double 2. A well-dressed and successful businessman. He checked the knot of his tie, and ran his tongue over the only two false teeth in his head – necessary surgery from a quarter-century before. Like everyone else, he crossed the road at the lights.

Check-in at his hotel took a matter of moments. He sat at the room's small circular table and opened his laptop, plugging it into the mains, changing the adaptor from 110v to 240. He used his password, then double-clicked on the file marked UPSTART. Inside were his notes on Johnny Bible so-called, his own psychological profile of the killer. It was building nicely.

Bible John reflected that he had something the authorities didn't have: inside knowledge of how a serial killer worked, thought and lived, the lies he had to tell, the guile and disguises, the secret life behind the everyday face. It put him ahead in the game. With any luck, he'd get to Johnny Bible before the police did.

He had avenues to follow. One: from his working habits, it was clear the Upstart had prior knowledge of the Bible John case. How did he gain this knowledge? The Upstart was in his twenties, too young to remember Bible John. Therefore he'd heard about it somewhere, or read about it, and then had gone on to research it in some detail. There were books – some of them recent, some not – about the Bible John killings or with chapters on them. If Johnny Bible were being meticulous, he would have consulted all the available literature, but with some of the material long out of print he must have been searching secondhand bookshops, or else must have used libraries. The search was narrowing nicely.

Another connected avenue: newspapers. Again, it was unlikely the Upstart had open access to papers from a quarter century ago. That meant libraries again, and very few libraries held newspapers for that length of time. Search narrowing nicely.

Then there was the Upstart himself. Many predators made errors early on, mistakes executed due to a lack either of proper planning or of simple nerve. Bible John himself was unusual: his real mistake had come with victim three, with sharing a taxi with her sister. Were there victims around who had escaped the Upstart? That meant looking through recent newspapers, seeking out attacks on women in Aberdeen, Glasgow, Edinburgh, tracking down the killer's false starts and early failures. It would be time-consuming work. But therapeutic, too.

He stripped and had a shower, then put on a more casual outfit: navy blazer and khaki trousers. He decided not to risk using the telephone in his room – the numbers would be logged by reception – so headed out into the sunshine. No phone boxes these days held directories, so he walked into a pub and ordered tonic water, then asked for the phone book. The barmaid – late teens, nose-stud, pink hair – handed it over with a smile. At his table, he took out notebook and pen and jotted down some numbers, then went to the back of the bar where the telephone was kept. It was next to the toilets – private enough for the purpose, especially just now with the pub all but empty. His calls were to a couple of antiquarian booksellers and three libraries. The results were, to his mind, satisfactory if by no means revelatory, but then he'd decided weeks back that this might be a drawn-out process. After all, he had self-knowledge on his side, but the police had hundreds of men and computers and a publicity machine. And they could investigate *openly*. He knew his own investigation into the Upstart had to be undertaken with more discretion. But he also knew he needed help, and that was risky. Involving others was always a risk. He'd considered the dilemma over long days and nights – on one side of the scales, his wish to track down the Upstart; on the other, the risk that in so doing, he would be putting himself – his identity – in danger.

So he'd asked himself a question: how badly did he want the Upstart? And had answered it: very badly. Very badly indeed.

He spent the afternoon on and around George IV Bridge – the National Library of Scotland and the Central Lending Library. He had a reader's card for the National Library, had done research there in the past – business; plus some reading on the Second World War, his main hobby these days. He browsed in local secondhand bookshops too, asking if they had any true-life crime. He told staff the Johnny Bible murders had kindled his interest.

'We only have half a shelf of true crime,' the assistant in the first shop said, showing him where it was. Bible John feigned interest in the books, then returned to the assistant's desk.

'No, nothing there. Do you also search for books?'

'Not as such,' the assistant said. 'But we keep requests ...' She pulled out a heavy old-style ledger and opened it. 'If you put down what you're looking for, your name and address, if we happen across the book we'll get in touch.'

'That's fine.'

Bible John took out his pen, wrote slowly, checking recent requests. He flicked back a page, eyes running down the list of titles and subjects.

'Don't people have such varied interests?' he said, smiling at the assistant.

He tried the same ploy at three further shops, but found no evidence of the Upstart. He then walked to the National Library's annexe on Causewayside, where recent newspapers were kept, and browsed through a month's worth of *Scotsman*s, *Herald*s and *Press and Journal*s, taking notes from certain stories: assaults, rapes. Of course, even if there *was* an early, failed victim, it didn't mean the attempt had gone reported. The Americans had a word for what he was doing. They called it shitwork.

Back in the National Library proper, he studied the librarians, looking for someone special. When he thought he'd found what he was looking for, he checked the library's opening hours, and decided to wait.

At closing time, he was standing outside the National Library, sunglasses on in the mid-evening light, crawling lines of traffic separating him from the Central Library. He saw some of the staff leave, singly and in groups. Then he spotted the young man he was looking for. When the man headed down Victoria Street, Bible John crossed the road and followed. There were a lot of pedestrians about, tourists, drinkers, a few people making their way home. He became just another of them, walking briskly, his eyes on his quarry. In the Grassmarket, the young man turned into the first available pub. Bible John stopped and considered: a quick drink before heading home? Or was the librarian going to meet friends, maybe make an evening of it? He decided to go inside.

The bar was dark, noisy with office workers: men with their suit jackets draped over their shoulders, women sipping from long glasses of tonic. The librarian was at the bar, alone. Bible John squeezed in beside him and ordered an orange juice. He nodded to the librarian's beer glass.

'Another?'

When the young man turned to look at him, Bible John leaned close, spoke quietly.

'Three things I want to tell you. One: I'm a journalist. Two: I want to give you £500. Three: there's absolutely nothing illegal involved.' He paused. 'Now, do you want that drink?'

The young man was still staring at him. Finally he nodded.

'Is that yes to the drink or yes to the cash?' Bible John was smiling too.

'The drink. You better tell me a little more about the other.'

'It's a boring job or I'd do it myself. Does the library keep a record of books consulted and borrowed?'

The librarian thought about it, then nodded. 'Some computerised, some still on cards.'

'Well, the computer will be quick, but the cards may take you a while. It'll still be easy money, believe me. What about if someone came in to consult old newspapers?'

'Should be on record. How long ago are we talking about?'

'It would be in the past three to six months. The papers they'd be looking at would be from 1968 to '70.'

He paid for two drinks with a twenty, opened his wallet so the librarian could see plenty more.

'It might take a while,' the young man said. 'I'll have to cross-reference between Causewayside and George IV Bridge.'

'There's another hundred if you can hurry things along.'

'I'll need details.' Bible John nodded, handed over a business card. It stated name and a phony address, but no phone number.

'Don't try to get in touch. I'll phone you. What's your name?'

'Mark Jenkins.'

'OK, Mark.' Bible John lifted out two fifties, tucked them into the young man's breast pocket. 'Here's something on account.'

'What's it all about anyway?'

Bible John shrugged. 'Johnny Bible. We're checking a possible connection with some old cases.'

The young man nodded. 'So what books are you interested in?'

Bible John handed him a printed list. 'Plus newspapers. *Scotsman*s and *Glasgow Herald*s, February '68 to December '69.'

'And what do you want to know?'

'People who've been looking at them. I'll need names and addresses. Can you do it?'

'Actual newspapers are held at Causewayside, we only stock microfilm.'

'What are you saying?'

'I may need to ask a colleague at Causewayside to help.'

Bible John smiled. 'My paper's not short of a bob or two, as long as we get results. How much would your friend want ...?'

The Whispering Rain

Mind me when mischief befalls me
from the cruel and the vain

The Bathers,
'Ave the Leopards'

5

The Scots language is especially rich in words to do with the weather: 'dreich' and 'smirr' are only two of them.

It had taken Rebus an hour to drive to Raintown, but another forty minutes to find Dumbarton Road. He hadn't been to the station before: Partick cop-shop had relocated in '93. The old station, the 'Marine', he'd been there, but not the new place. Driving in Glasgow could be a nightmare for the uninitiated, a maze of one-way streets and ill-signposted intersections. Rebus twice had to leave his car and call in for instructions, both times queuing outside phone boxes in the rain. Only it wasn't real rain, it was smirr, a fine spray-mist which drenched you before you knew it. It was blowing in from the west, moisture straight from the Atlantic Ocean. It was all Rebus needed first thing on a dreich Monday morning.

When he got to the station, he noticed a car in the car park, two figures inside, smoke billowing from an open window, radio playing. Reporters, had to be. They were the graveyard shift. At this point in a story, reporters divvied the hours into shifts, so they could go off and be somewhere else. Whoever was left on recce was on a promise to buzz any breaks in the story to the other journalists pronto.

When he finally pushed open the station door, there was scattered applause. He walked up to the desk.

'Finally made it, then?' the Duty Sergeant asked. 'Thought we were going to have to send out search parties.'

'Where's CI Ancram?'

'In a meeting. He said for you to go up and wait.'

So Rebus went upstairs, and found that the CID offices had become a sprawling Murder Room. There were photographs on the walls: Judith Cairns, Ju-Ju, in life and in death. More photos of the locus – Kelvingrove Park, a sheltered spot surrounded by bushes. A work rota had been posted – interview grind mostly, shoe-leather stuff, no big breaks expected but you had to make the effort. Officers clattered at keyboards, maybe using the SCRO computer, or even HOLMES – the major enquiry database. All murder cases – excluding those solved straight off – were put on the Home Office Large Major Enquiry System. There were dedicated teams – detectives and uniforms – who operated the system, typing in data, checking and cross-referencing. Even Rebus – no great fan of new technology – could see the advantages over the old card-index system. He stopped by a computer terminal and watched someone entering a statement. Then, looking up, he saw a face he recognised, walked up to its owner.

'Hiya, Jack, thought you were still in Falkirk?'

DI Jack Morton turned, his eyes opening wide in disbelief. He rose from his desk, took Rebus's hand and pumped it.

'I am,' he said, 'but they're short-handed here.' He looked around the room. 'Understandably.'

Rebus looked Jack Morton up and down, couldn't believe what he saw. Last time they'd met, Jack had been a couple of stone overweight, a heavy smoker with a cough that could crack patrol-car windscreens. Now he'd shed the excess weight, and the perennial ciggie was missing from his mouth. More, his hair was professionally groomed and he was dressed in an expensive-looking suit, polished black shoes, crisp shirt and tie.

'What happened to you?' Rebus asked.

Morton smiled, patted his near-flat stomach. 'Just looked at myself one day and couldn't understand why the mirror didn't break. Got off the booze and the cigs, joined a health club.'

'Just like that?'

'Life and death decisions. You can't afford to hem and haw.'

'You look great.'

'Wish I could say the same, John.'

Rebus was thinking up a comeback when CI Ancram entered the room.

'DI Rebus?' They shook hands. The Chief Inspector didn't seem keen to let go. His eyes were soaking up Rebus. 'Sorry to keep you.'

Ancram was in his early fifties, and every bit as well-dressed as Jack Morton. He was bald mostly, but with Sean Connery's style and a thick dark moustache to match.

'Has Jack been giving you the tour?'

'Not exactly, sir.'

'Well, this is the Glasgow end of the Johnny Bible operation.'

'Is this the nearest station to Kelvingrove?'

Ancram smiled. 'Proximity to the locus was just one consideration.

Judith Cairns was his third victim, by then the media had already hit on the Bible John connection. And this is where all the Bible John files are stored.'

'Any chance I can see them?'

Ancram studied him, then shrugged. 'Come on, I'll show you.'

Rebus followed Ancram along the corridor to another suite of offices. There was a musty smell in the air, more library than cop-shop. Rebus saw why: the room was full of old cardboard boxes, box-files with spring hinges, packets of curl-edged paper bound with string. Four CID officers – two male, two female – were working their way through everything and anything to do with the original Bible John case.

'We had this lot stashed in a storeroom,' Ancram said. 'You should have seen the stoor that came off when we brought them out.' He blew on a folder, fine powder rising from it.

'You do think there's a connection then?'

It was a question every police officer in Scotland had asked every other police officer, for there was always the chance that the two cases, the two killers, had nothing in common, in which event hundreds of man-hours were being wasted.

'Oh yes,' Ancram said. Yes: it was what Rebus felt, too. 'I mean, the *modus operandi* is close enough to start with, then there are the souvenirs he takes from the scene. The description of Johnny Bible may be a fluke, but I'm sure he's copying his hero.' Ancram looked at Rebus. 'Aren't you?'

Rebus nodded. He was looking at all the material, thinking how he'd like to have a few weeks with it, how he might find something no one else had spotted ... It was a dream, of course, a fantasy, but on slow nights sometimes it was motivation enough. Rebus had his newspapers, but they told only as much of the story as the police had wanted made public. He walked over to a row of shelves, read the spines of the box-files: Door to Door; Taxi Firms; Hairdressers; Tailors' Shops; Hairpiece Suppliers.

'Hairpiece suppliers?'

Ancram smiled. 'His short hair, they thought maybe it was a wig. They talked to hairdressers to see if anyone recognised the cut.'

'And to tailors because of his Italian suit.'

Again Ancram stared at him.

Rebus shrugged. 'The case interests me. What's this?' He pointed to a wall chart.

'Similarities and dissimilarities between the two cases,' Ancram said. 'Dancehalls versus the club scene. And the descriptions: tall, skinny, shy, auburn hair, well dressed … I mean, Johnny could almost be Bible John's son.'

'That's something I've been asking myself. Supposing Johnny Bible *is* basing himself on his hero, and supposing Bible John's still out there somewhere …'

'Bible John's dead.'

Rebus kept his eyes on the chart. 'But just supposing he isn't. I mean, is he flattered? Is he pissed off? What?'

'Don't ask me.'

'The Glasgow victim hadn't been to a club,' Rebus said.

'Well, she wasn't last *seen* in a club. But she'd been to one earlier that evening, he could have followed her from there to the concert.'

Victims one and two had been picked up by Johnny Bible in nightclubs, the nineties equivalent of a sixties dancehall: louder, darker, more dangerous. They'd been in parties, who were able to furnish only the vaguest descriptions of the man who had walked off into the night with their friend. But victim three, Judith Cairns, had been picked up at a rock concert in a room above a pub.

'We've had others too,' Ancram was saying. 'Three unsolveds in Glasgow in the late seventies, all three missing some personal item.'

'Like he never went away,' Rebus muttered.

'There's too much to go on, yet not nearly enough.' Ancram folded his arms. 'How well does Johnny know the three cities? Did he pick the clubs at random, or did he know them to start with? Was each locus chosen beforehand? Could he be a brewery delivery-man? A DJ? Music journalist? Maybe he writes fucking travel guides for all I know.' Ancram started a joyless laugh, and rubbed at his forehead.

'Could always be Bible John himself,' Rebus said.

'Bible John's dead and buried, Inspector.'

'You really think so?'

Ancram nodded. He wasn't alone. There were plenty of coppers who thought they knew who Bible John was, and knew him to be dead. But there were others more sceptical, and Rebus was among them. A DNA match probably wouldn't have been enough to change his mind. There was always the chance that Bible John was out there.

They had a description of a man in his late twenties, but witness evidence was notoriously uneven. As a result, the original photofits and artists' impressions of Bible John had been dusted off and put back into circulation with the media's help. The usual psychological ploys were being used too – pleas in the press for the killer to come forward: 'You obviously need help, and we'd like you to contact us.' Bluff, with silence the retort.

Ancram pointed to photos on one wall: a photofit from 1970, aged by computer, beard and glasses added, the hair receding at crown and temples. They'd been made public too.

'Could be anybody, couldn't it?' Ancram stated.

'Getting to you, sir?' Rebus was waiting for an invitation to call Ancram by his first name.

'Of course it's getting to me.' Ancram's face relaxed. 'Why the interest?'

'No real reason.'

'I mean, we're not here for Johnny Bible, are we? We're here to talk about Uncle Joe.'

'Ready when you are, sir.'

'Come on then, let's see if we can find two empty chairs in this fucking building.'

They ended up standing in the corridor, with coffee bought from a machine further along.

'Do we know what he strangles them with?' Rebus asked.

Ancram's eyes widened. 'More Johnny Bible?' He sighed. 'Whatever it is, it doesn't leave much of an impression. The latest theory is a length of washing-line; you know, the nylon stuff, plastic-coated. The forensic labs have tested about two hundred possibles, everything from rope to guitar strings.'

'What do you think about the souvenirs?'

'I think we should go public with them. I know keeping them hush-hush helps us rule out the nutters who walk in to confess, but I honestly think we'd be better off asking the public for help. That necklace, I mean, you couldn't get more distinctive. If someone out there has found it, or seen it ... housey-housey.'

'You've got a psychic working the case, haven't you?'

Ancram looked nettled. 'Not me personally, some arsehole further up the ranks. It's a newspaper stunt, but the brass went for it.'

'He hasn't helped?'

'We told him we needed a demonstration, asked him to predict the winner of the two-fifteen at Ayr.'

Rebus laughed. 'And?'

'He said he could see the letters S and P, and a jockey dressed in pink with yellow spots.'

'That's impressive.'

'Thing is though, there *was* no two-fifteen at Ayr, or anywhere else for that matter. All this voodoo and profiling, a waste of time if you ask me.'

'So you've nothing to go on?'

'Not much. No saliva at the locus, not so much as a hair. Bastard uses a johnny, then takes it with him – wrapper included. My bet is, he wears gloves too. We've a few threads from a jacket or the like, forensics are still busy with them.' Ancram raised his cup to his lips, blew on it. 'So, Inspector, do you want to hear about Uncle Joe or not?'

'That's why I'm here.'

'I'm beginning to wonder.' Rebus just shrugged, so Ancram took a deep breath. 'OK, then listen. He controls a lot of the muscle-work – and I mean that literally; he has a share in a couple of bodybuilder gyms. In fact, he has a share in just about everything that's the least bit dodgy: money-lending, protection, prozzy pitches, betting.'

'Drugs?'

'Maybe. There are a lot of maybes with Uncle Joe. You'll see that when you read the files. He's as slippery as a Thai bath – he owns massage parlours too. Then he's got a lot of the taxi cabs, the ones that don't switch their meters on when you get in; or if they do, the rate-per-mile's been hiked. The cabbies are all on the broo, claiming benefit. We've approached several of them, but they won't say a word against Uncle Joe. Thing is, if the DSS start sniffing around for scroungers, the investigators receive a letter. It details where they live, spouse's name and daily movements, kids' names, the school they go to ...'

'I get the picture.'

'So they start requesting a transfer to another department, and meantime go to their doctor because they're having trouble sleeping at night.'

'OK, Uncle Joe isn't Glasgow's Man of the Year. Where does he live?'

Ancram drained his cup. 'This is a beauty. He lives in a council house. But just remember: Robert Maxwell lived in a council house, too. You have to see this place.'

'I intend to.'

Ancram shook his head. 'He won't talk to you, you won't get past the door.'

'Want a bet?'

Ancram narrowed his eyes. 'You sound confident.'

Jack Morton walked past them, rolling his eyes: a general comment on life. He was searching his pockets for coins. As he waited for the machine to pour his drink, he turned to them.

'Chick, The Lobby?'

Ancram nodded. 'One o'clock?'

'Braw.'

'What about associates?' Rebus asked. He noticed Ancram hadn't yet said he could call him by his nickname.

'Oh, he has plenty of those. His guards are bodybuilders, hand-picked. Then he has some nutters, real headbangers. The bodybuilders might look the business, but these others *are* the business. There was Tony El, poly-bag merchant with a penchant for power tools. Uncle Joe still has one or two like him. Then there's Joe's son, Malky.'

'Mr Stanley knife?'

'Emergency rooms all over Glasgow can testify to *that* particular hobby.'

'But Tony El hasn't been around?'

Ancram shook his head. 'But I've had my grasses out sniffing on your behalf; I should hear back today.'

Three men pushed open the doors at the end of the hall.

'Aye, aye,' Ancram said in an undertone, 'it's the man with the crystal balls.'

Rebus recognised one of the men from a magazine photograph: Aldous Zane, the American psychic. He'd helped a US police force in their hunt for Merry Mac, so called because someone passing the scene of one of his murders – without realising what was happening on the other side of the wall – had heard deep gurgling laughter. Zane had given his impressions of where the killer lived. When police finally arrested Merry Mac, the media pointed out that the location bore a striking resemblance to the picture Zane had drawn.

For a few weeks, Aldous Zane was newsworthy all around the world. It was enough to tempt a Scottish tabloid to pay for him to offer his impressions in the Johnny Bible hunt. And the police brass were just desperate enough to offer their cooperation.

'Morning, Chick,' one of the other men said.

'Morning, Terry.'

'Terry' was looking at Rebus, awaiting an introduction.

'DI John Rebus,' Ancram said. 'DCS Thompson.'

The man stuck out his hand, which Rebus shook. He was a mason, like every second cop on the force. Rebus wasn't of the brotherhood, but had learned to mimic the handshake.

Thompson turned to Ancram. 'We're taking Mr Zane along to have another look at some of the physical evidence.'

'Not just a look,' Zane corrected. 'I need to touch it.'

Thompson's left eye twitched. Obviously he was as sceptical as Ancram. 'Right, well, this way, Mr Zane.'

The three men walked off.

'Who was the silent one?' Rebus asked.

Ancram shrugged. 'Zane's minder, he's from the newspaper. They want to be in on everything Zane does.'

Rebus nodded. 'I know him,' he said. 'Or I used to, years back.'

'I think his name's Stevens.'

'Jim Stevens,' Rebus said, still nodding. 'By the way, there's another difference between the two killers.'

'What?'

'Bible John's victims were all menstruating.'

Rebus was left alone at a desk with the available files on Joseph Toal. He didn't learn much more from them except that Uncle Joe seldom saw the inside of a court. Rebus wondered about that. Toal always seemed to know when police had him or his operations under surveillance, when the shit was heading fanwards. That way, they never found any evidence, or not enough to put him away. A couple of fines, that was about the sum total. Several big pushes had been made, but they'd always been abandoned for lack of hard evidence or because a surveillance was blown. As if Uncle Joe had a psychic of his own. But Rebus knew there was a more likely explanation: someone in CID was feeding gen back to the gangster. Rebus thought of the fancy suits everyone seemed to be wearing, the good watches and shoes, the general air of prosperity and superiority.

It was west coast dirt, let them sweep it up or push it into the corner. There was a hand-written notation towards the end of the file; he guessed it was Ancram's writing:

'Uncle Joe doesn't need to kill people any more. His rep is weapon enough, and the bastard's getting stronger all the time.'

He found a spare telephone, made a call to Barlinnie Prison, then, no sign of Chick Ancram, went walkabout.

As he'd known he would, he ended up back in the musty-smelling room dominated by the old monster, Bible John. People in Glasgow still talked about him, had done even before Johnny Bible had come along. Bible John was the bedtime bogeyman made flesh, a generation's scare story. He was your creepy next-door neighbour; the quiet man who lived two flights up; he was the parcel courier with the windowless van. He was whoever you wanted him to be. Back in the early seventies, parents had warned their children, 'Behave, or Bible John will get you!'

Bogeyman made flesh. Now reproducing.

The shift of detectives looked to have taken a collective break. Rebus was alone in the room. He left the door open, not sure why, and pored over the documents. Fifty thousand statements had been taken. Rebus read a couple of the newspaper headlines: 'The Dance Hall Don Juan With Murder on his Mind'; '100 Day Hunt for Ladykiller'. In the first year of the hunt, over five thousand suspects had been interviewed and eliminated. When the third victim's sister gave her detailed description, police knew so much about the killer: blue-grey eyes; straight teeth except for one on the upper-right which overlapped its neighbour; his preferred brand of cigarette was Embassy; he spoke of a strict upbringing, and he quoted passages from the Bible. But by then it was too late. Bible John was history.

Another difference between Bible John and Johnny Bible: the gaps between the killings. Johnny was killing every few weeks, while Bible John had killed to no pattern of weeks or even months. His first victim had been February '68. There followed a gap of nearly eighteen months – August '69, victim number two. And then two and a half months later, his third and final outing. Victims one and three had been killed on a Thursday night, the second victim on a Saturday. Eighteen months was a hell of a gap – Rebus knew the theories: that he'd been overseas, perhaps as a merchant seaman or navy sailor, or on some army or RAF posting; that he'd been in jail, serving time for some lesser offence. Theories, that's all they were. All three of his victims were mothers of children: so far, none of Johnny Bible's was. Was it important that Bible John's victims had been menstruating, or that they had children? He'd tucked a sanitary towel under his third victim's armpit – a ritual act. A lot had been read into that action by the various psychologists involved in the case. Their theory: the Bible told Bible John that women were harlots, and he was offered proof when married women left a dancehall with him. The fact that they were menstruating angered him somehow, fed his bloodlust, so he killed them.

Rebus knew there were those out there – always had been – who believed there to be no connection, other than pure circumstance, between the three killings. They posited three murderers, and it was true that only strong coincidences connected the murders. Rebus, no great champion of coincidence, still believed in a single, driven killer.

Some great policemen had been involved: Tom Goodall, the man who'd gone after Jimmy Boyle, who'd been there when Peter Manuel confessed; then when Goodall died, there'd been Elphinstone Dalgliesh and Joe Beattie. Beattie had spent hours staring at photos of suspects, using a magnifying glass sometimes. He'd felt that if Bible John walked into a crowded room, he would know him. The case had obsessed some officers, sent them spiralling downwards. All that work, and no result. It made a mockery of them, their methods, their system. He thought of Lawson Geddes again …

Rebus looked up, saw he was being watched from the doorway. He got up as the two men walked into the room.

Aldous Zane, Jim Stevens.

'Any luck?' Rebus asked.

Stevens shrugged. 'Early days. Aldous came up with a couple of things.' He put out his hand. Rebus took it. Stevens smiled. 'You remember me, don't you?' Rebus nodded. 'I wasn't sure, back there in the hallway.'

'I thought you were in London.'

'I moved back three years ago. I'm mainly freelance now.'

'And doing guard duty, I see.'

Rebus glanced towards Aldous Zane, but the American wasn't listening. He was moving his palms over the paperwork on the nearest desk. He was short, slender, middle-aged. He wore steel-framed glasses with blue-tint lenses, and his lips were slightly parted, showing small, narrow teeth. He reminded Rebus a little of Peter Sellers playing Dr Strangelove. He wore a cagoule over his jacket, and made swishing sounds when he moved.

'What is this?' he said.

'Bible John. Johnny Bible's ancestor. They brought in a psychic on his case, too, Gerard Croiset.'

'The *paragnost*,' Zane said quietly. 'Was there any success?'

'He described a location, two shopkeepers, an old man who could help the inquiry.'

'And?'

'And,' Jim Stevens interrupted, 'a reporter found what looked like the location.'

'But no shopkeepers,' Rebus added, 'and no old man.'

Zane looked up. 'Cynicism is not helpful.'

'Call me par-agnostic.'

Zane smiled, held out his hand. Rebus took it, felt tremendous heat in the man's palm. A tingle ran up his arm.

'Creepy, isn't it?' Jim Stevens said, as though he could read Rebus's mind.

Rebus waved a hand over the material on all four desks. 'So, Mr Zane, do you *feel* anything?'

'Only sadness and suffering, an incredible amount of both.' He picked up one of the later photofits of Bible John. 'And I thought I could see flags.'

'Flags?'

'The Stars and Stripes, a swastika. And a trunk filled with objects ...' He had his eyes shut, the lids fluttering. 'In the attic of a modern house.' The eyes opened. 'That's all. There's a lot of distance, a lot of distance.'

Stevens had his notebook out. He wrote quickly in shorthand. There was someone else in the doorway, looking surprised at the assembly.

'Inspector,' Chick Ancram said, 'time for lunch.'

They took one of the duty cars into the west end, Ancram driving. There was something different about him; he seemed at the same time more interested in Rebus and warier of him. Their conversation collapsed into point-scoring.

Eventually, Ancram pointed to a striped traffic-cone kerbside, protecting the only space left on the street.

'Get out and move that, will you?'

Rebus obliged, placing the cone on the pavement. Ancram reversed the car inch-perfect into the space.

'Looks like you've had practice.'

Ancram straightened his tie. 'Patrons' parking.'

They walked into The Lobby. It was a trendy-looking bar with too many high uncomfortable-looking bar-stools, black and white tiled walls, electric and acoustic guitars suspended from the ceiling.

There was a chalkboard menu behind the bar. Three staff were busy with the lunchtime crush; more perfume than alcohol in the air. Office girls, screeching over the slam of the music, nursing gaudy drinks; sometimes one or two men with them, smiling, saying nothing, older. They wore suits that said 'management': the banshees' bosses. There were more cellphones and pagers on the tables than there were glasses; even the staff seemed to carry them.

'What do you want?'

'Pint of eighty,' Rebus said.

'To eat?'

Rebus ran down the menu. 'Is there anything with meat?'

63

'Game pie.'

Rebus nodded. They were a row back from the bar, but Ancram had caught a barman's attention. He stood on tiptoe and yelled the order over the straw-perm heads of the teenagers in front. They turned, gave hostile looks: he'd jumped the queue.

'All right, ladies?' Ancram leered. They turned away again.

He led Rebus through the bar to a far corner, where a table groaned with green food: salads, quiche, guacamole. Rebus got himself a chair; there was one already waiting for Ancram. Three CID officers sat there, not one with a pint glass in front of him. Ancram made introductions.

'Jack you already know.' Jack Morton nodded, chewing pitta bread. 'That's DS Andy Lennox, and DI Billy Eggleston.' The two men gave curt greetings, more interested in their food. Rebus looked around.

'What about the drinks?'

'Patience, man, patience. Here they come.'

The barman was approaching with a tray: Rebus's pint and game pie; Ancram's smoked salmon salad and gin and tonic.

'Twelve pounds ten,' the barman said. Ancram handed over three fives, told him to keep the change. He raised his glass to Rebus.

'Here's tae us.'

'Wha's like us,' Rebus added.

'Gey few, and they're a' deid,' Jack Morton said, raising his own glass of what looked suspiciously like water. They all drank, got down to eating, exchanging the day's gossip. There was a table of office girls nearby; Lennox and Eggleston tried intermittently to engage them in conversation. The girls got on with their own gossip. Clothes, Rebus reflected, did not necessarily make the man. He felt stifled, uncomfortable. There wasn't enough space on the table; his chair was too close to Ancram's; the music was using him as a punchbag.

'So what do you reckon to Uncle Joe?' Ancram asked at last.

Rebus chewed on a tough crescent of pastry. The others seemed to be waiting for his answer.

'I reckon I'll be visiting him some time today.'

Ancram laughed. 'Let me know if you're serious, we'll lend you some armour.' The others laughed too, and started eating again. Rebus wondered just how much of Uncle Joe's money was floating around Glasgow CID.

'John and me,' Jack Morton was saying, 'worked the Knots and Crosses case together.'

'Is that right?' Ancram looked interested.

Rebus shook his head. 'Ancient history.'

Morton caught the tone of voice, lowered his head to his food, reached for the water.

Ancient history; and far, far too painful.

'Speaking of history,' Ancram said, 'sounds like you've got a bit of trouble with the Spaven case.' He smiled mischievously. 'I read about it in the papers.'

'It's all hype for the TV show,' was Rebus's only comment.

'We've got more problems with the DNAs, Chick,' Eggleston was saying. He was tall, skinny, starched. He reminded Rebus of an accountant; he'd bet he was good with paperwork, lousy on the street – every station needed at least one.

'They're an epidemic,' Lennox snarled.

'Society's problem, gentlemen,' Ancram said, 'which makes them our problem too.'

'DNAs?'

Ancram turned to Rebus. 'Do Not Accommodate. The council's been turfing out a lot of "problem clients", refusing to house them, even in the night shelters – druggies mostly, headers, the "psychologically disturbed" who've been returned to the community. Only the community's telling them to fuck right off again. So they're on the streets, making mischief, causing us grief. Kitting up in public, ODing on mainline Temazepam, you name it.'

'Fucking shocking,' Lennox offered. He had tight-curled ginger hair and crimson cheeks, his face heavily freckled, eyebrows and eyelashes fair. He was the only one smoking at the table. Rebus lit one up to join him: Jack Morton gave a reproachful look.

'So what can you do?' Rebus asked.

'I'll tell you,' Ancram said. 'We're going to round them up next weekend, into a fleet of buses, and we're going to drop the whole lot of them off on Princes Street.'

More laughter at the table, directed at the visitor – Ancram waving the baton. Rebus checked his watch.

'Somewhere to be?'

'Yes, and I'd better get going.'

'Well, look,' Ancram said, 'if you *do* get an invite to Uncle Joe's abode, I want to know about it. I'll be here this evening, seven until ten. OK?'

Rebus nodded, waved a general goodbye, and got out.

Once outside, he felt better. He began to walk, not very sure in which direction he was headed. The city centre was laid out American-style, a grid system of one-way streets. Edinburgh might have its monuments, but Glasgow was built to monumental scale, making the capital seem like Toytown. Rebus walked until he saw something that looked more his kind of bar. He knew he needed shoring up for the trip he was about to take. A TV was playing quietly, but no music. And what conversation there was was muffled, low-key. He couldn't make out what the two men nearest him were saying, their accents were so thick. The only woman in the place was the barmaid.

'What'll it be today?'

'Grouse, make it a double. And a half-bottle to take out.'

He trickled water into the glass, reflected that if he'd eaten a couple of pies here and had a couple of whiskies, it wouldn't have been half as expensive as The Lobby. But then Ancram had paid at The Lobby; three crisp fivers from the pocket of a sleek suit.

'Just a Coke, please.'

Rebus turned to the new customer: Jack Morton.

'You following me?'

Morton smiled. 'You look rough, John.'

'And you and your cronies look *too* good.'

'I can't be bought.'

'No? Who can?'

'Come on, John, I was making a joke.' Morton sat down next to him. 'I heard about Lawson Geddes. Does that mean the stooshie'll die down?'

'Some hope.' Rebus drained his glass. 'Look at that,' he said, pointing out a machine on the corner of the bar. 'Jelly bean dispenser, twenty pence a throw. Two things the Scots are famous for, Jack: our sweet tooth and alcohol consumption.'

'Two more things we're famous for,' Morton said.

'What?'

'Avoiding the issue and feeling guilty all the time.'

'You mean Calvinism?' Rebus chuckled. 'Christ, Jack, I thought the only Calvin you knew these days was Mr Klein.'

Jack Morton was staring at him, seeking eye-to-eye contact. 'Give me another reason why a man would let himself go.'

Rebus snorted. 'How long have you got?'

Morton to Rebus: 'As long as it takes.'

'Not nearly enough, Jack. Here, have a proper drink.'

'This is a proper drink. That stuff you're drinking, that's not really a drink.'

'What is it then?'

'An escape clause.'

Jack said he'd drive Rebus to Barlinnie, didn't ask why he wanted to go there. They took the M8 to Riddrie; Jack knew all the routes. They didn't say much during the trip, until Jack asked the question which had been hanging between them.

'How's Sammy?'

Rebus's daughter, now grown up. Jack hadn't seen her in nearly ten years.

'She's fine.' Rebus had a change of subject ready. 'I'm not sure Chick Ancram likes me. He keeps ... *studying* me.'

'He's a shrewd customer, be nice to him.'

'Any particular reason?'

Jack Morton bit back an answer, shook his head. They turned off Cumbernauld Road, approached the jail.

'Look,' Jack said, 'I can't hang around. Tell me how long you'll be and I'll send a patrol car for you.'

'An hour should do it.'

Jack Morton checked his watch. 'An hour it is.' He held out his hand. 'Good to see you again, John.'

Rebus took the hand, squeezed.

6

'Big Ger' Cafferty was waiting when he reached the Interview Room.

'Well, Strawman, this is an unexpected pleasure.'

Strawman: Cafferty's name for Rebus. The prison guard who had brought Rebus seemed disinclined to leave, and there were already two guards in the room keeping an eye on Cafferty. He'd already escaped once from Barlinnie, and now that they had him back, they were intent on keeping him.

'Hello, Cafferty.' Rebus sat down across from him. Cafferty had aged in prison, losing his tan and some musculature, putting on weight in all the wrong places. His hair was thin and greying quickly, and there was stubble on chin and cheekbones. 'I've brought you something.' He looked at the guards, eased the half-bottle out of his pocket.

'Not allowed,' one guard snapped.

'Don't worry, Strawman,' Cafferty said. 'I've plenty of hooch, this place is practically swimming in the stuff. It's the thought that counts, eh?'

Rebus dropped the bottle back into his pocket.

'I take it you've a favour to ask?'

'Yes.'

Cafferty crossed his legs, utterly at ease. 'What is it?'

'You know Joseph Toal?'

'Everyone and their dog knows Uncle Joe.'

'Yes, but you *know* him.'

'So?' There was an edge to Cafferty's smile.

'I want you to phone him, get him to speak to me.'

Cafferty considered the request. 'Why?'

'I want to ask him about Anthony Kane.'

'Tony El? I thought he was dead.'

'He left his prints at a murder scene in Niddrie.' Never mind what the boss said, Rebus was treating this as murder. And he knew the word would make more of an impression on Cafferty. It did. His lips rounded into an O, and he whistled.

'That was stupid of him. Tony El didn't used to be so stupid. And if he was still working for Uncle Joe ... There could be fallout.' Rebus knew that connections were being made in Cafferty's mind, and they all led to Joseph Toal becoming his Barlinnie neighbour. There would be reasons for Cafferty to want Toal inside: old scores, debts unpaid, territory encroached. There were always old scores to be settled. Cafferty came to his decision.

'You'll need to get me a phone.'

Rebus got up, walked over to the guard who'd barked 'Not allowed', slipped the whisky into the man's pocket.

'We need to get him a phone,' he said.

They marched Cafferty left and right through corridors until they reached a payphone. They'd had to pass through three sets of gates.

'This is as near to the outside as I've been in a while,' Cafferty joked.

The guards weren't laughing. Rebus provided the money for the call.

'Now,' said Cafferty, 'let's see if I remember ...' He winked at Rebus, pressed seven digits, waited.

'Hello?' he said. 'Who's that?' He listened to the name. 'Never heard of you. Listen, tell Uncle Joe that Big Ger wants a word. Just tell him that.' He waited, glanced at Rebus, licked his lips. 'He says what? Tell him I'm phoning from the Bar-L and money's short.'

Rebus pushed another coin home.

'Well,' Cafferty growing angry, 'tell him he's got a tattoo on his back.' He covered the mouthpiece. 'Not something Uncle Joe goes blabbing about.'

Rebus got as close as he could to the earpiece, heard a dull rasp of a voice.

'Morris Gerald Cafferty, is that you? I thought someone was winding me up.'

'Hello, Uncle Joe. How's business?'

'Loupin'. Who's listening in?'

'At the last count, three monkeys and a dick.'

'You always liked an audience, that was your problem.'

'Sound advice, Uncle Joe, but years too late.'

'So what do they want?' They: Rebus the dick and the three monkey guards.

'The dick's from Edinburgh CID, he wants to come talk to you.'

'What about?'

69

'Tony El.'

'What's to tell? Tony hasn't worked for me in a twelvemonth.'

'Then tell the nice policeman that. Seems Tony's been up to his old tricks. There's a cold one in Edinburgh, and Tony's prints on the scene.'

A low growl: human.

'You got a dog there, Uncle Joe?'

'Tell the cop I don't have anything to do with Tony.'

'I think he wants to hear it for himself.'

'Then put him on.'

Cafferty looked to Rebus, who shook his head.

'And he wants to look you in the eye while you're telling him.'

'Is he a poof or what?'

'He's old school, Uncle Joe. You'll like him.'

'Why did he come to you?'

'I'm his Last Chance Saloon.'

'And why the fuck did you agree?'

Cafferty didn't miss a beat. 'A half-bottle of *usquebaugh*.'

'Jesus, the Bar-L must be drier than I thought.' The voice not so rough.

'Send a whole bottle over and I'll tell him to go fuck himself.'

A croaky laugh. 'Christ, Cafferty, I miss you. How long to go?'

'Ask my lawyers.'

'Are you still keeping your hand in?'

'What do you think?'

'It's what I hear.'

'Nothing wrong with your hearing.'

'Send the bastard over, tell him he gets five minutes. Maybe I'll come see you one of these days.'

'Better not, Uncle Joe, when visiting time ends they might have misplaced the key.'

More laughter. The line went dead. Cafferty put down the receiver.

'You owe me, Strawman,' he growled, 'so here's my favour: put that old bastard away.'

But Rebus was already walking towards freedom.

The car was waiting for him, Morton keeping his word. Rebus gave the address he'd memorised from the Toal files. He was sitting in the back, two woolly suits in the front. The passenger turned in his seat.

'Isn't that where Uncle Joe lives?'

Rebus nodded. The woolly suits exchanged a look.

'Just get me there,' Rebus ordered.

The traffic was heavy, people heading home. Elastic Glasgow, stretching in four directions. The housing scheme, when they reached it, was much like any scheme its size in Edinburgh: grey pebbledash, barren play areas, tarmac and a smattering of fortified shops. Kids on bikes stopping to watch the car, eyes as keen as sentries'; brisk baby buggies, shapeless mothers with dyed blonde hair. Further into the estate, driving slowly: people watching from behind their windows, men at pavement corners, muttered confabs. A city within a city, uniform and enervating, energy sapped, nothing left but obstinacy: the words NO SURRENDER on a gable-end, a message from Ulster just as relevant here.

'Are you expected?' the driver asked.

'I'm expected.'

'Thank Christ for that at least.'

'Any other patrol cars around?'

The passenger laughed nervously. 'This is the frontier, sir. The frontier has a way of keeping its own law and order.'

'If you had his money,' the driver said, 'would you live here?'

'He was born here,' Rebus said. 'And I believe his house is a bit special.'

'Special?' The driver snorted. 'Well, judge for yourself.'

He brought the car to a stop at the entrance to a cul-de-sac. Rebus saw at the end of the cul-de-sac two houses which stood out from their neighbours for a single reason: they boasted stone cladding.

'One of those?' Rebus asked.

'Pick either door.'

Rebus got out of the car, leaned back in. 'Don't you dare drive away.' He slammed his door shut and walked up the cul-de-sac. He chose the left-hand of the two identical semi-detacheds. The door was opened from within, and an oversized man in a bulging T-shirt ushered him in.

'You the rozzer?' They were standing in a cramped hallway. Rebus nodded. 'Through there.'

Rebus opened the door to the living room, and did a double-take. The connecting wall between the two semis had been knocked through, providing a double-sized living space, open plan. The room also went further back than should have been feasible. Rebus was reminded of Dr Who's Tardis, and, alone in the room, walked towards the back of the house. A large extension had been added, including a sizeable conservatory. This should have minimised the space left for a garden, but the lawn outside was plentiful. There were playing-fields backing on

71

to the house, and Rebus saw that Uncle Joe had taken a chunk out of these fields for his garden.

Planning permission, of course, was out of the question.

But then who needed planning permission?

'I hope your ears don't need cleaning,' a voice said. Rebus turned and saw that a small, stooped man had entered the room. He held a cigarette in one hand, while his other was busy with a walking-stick. He shuffled in carpet slippers towards a well-used armchair and fell into it, hands gripping the greasy anti-macassars, walking-stick lying across his lap.

Rebus had seen photographs of the man, but they hadn't prepared him for the reality. Joseph Toal really *did* look like someone's uncle. He was in his seventies, stocky, with the hands and face of a one-time coalminer. His forehead was all rippled flesh, and his thin grey hair was swept back and Brylcreemed. His jaw was square, eyes watery, and his glasses hung from a string around his neck. When he raised the cigarette to his lips, Rebus saw nicotine fingers, bruised ingrown nails. He was wearing a shapeless cardigan over an equally shapeless sports shirt. The cardigan was patched, loose threads hanging from it. His trousers were brown and baggy, stained at the knees.

'Nothing wrong with my ears,' Rebus said, coming forward.

'Good, because I'll say it only once.' He sniffed, controlling his breathing. 'Anthony Kane worked for me twelve, thirteen years, not all the time – short-term contracts. But then a year ago, maybe a little over, he told me he was walking, wanted to be his own boss. We parted on amicable terms, I haven't seen him since.'

Rebus gestured to a chair. Toal nodded to let him know he could sit. Rebus took his time getting comfortable.

'Mr Toal –'

'Everybody calls me Uncle Joe.'

'As in Stalin?'

'You think that's a new joke, son? Ask your question.'

Go: 'What was Tony planning to do when he left your employ?'

'He didn't go into specifics. Our parting conversation was ... curt.'

Rebus nodded. He was thinking: I had an uncle who looked very much like you; I can't even remember his name.

'Well, if that's everything ...' Toal made a show of starting to rise.

'Do you remember Bible John, Uncle Joe?'

Toal frowned, understanding the question but not its intent. He reached down to the floor for an ashtray, stubbed his cigarette into it. 'I remember fine. Hundreds of coppers on the street, it was bad for business. We cooperated a hundred per cent, I had men out hunting the bugger for months. *Months!* And now this new bastard turns up.'

'Johnny Bible?'

Pointing to himself: 'I'm a businessman. The slaughter of innocents sickens me. I've had all my taxi drivers –' he paused – 'I have interests in a local taxi firm – and I've instructed every single driver: keep your eyes peeled and your ears open.' He was breathing heavily. 'If anything comes to me, it'll go straight to the cops.'

'Very public spirited.'

Toal shrugged. 'The public is my business.' Another pause, a frown. 'What's all this to do with Tony El?'

'Nothing.' Toal looked unconvinced. 'Call it tangential. Is it OK to smoke?'

'You're not staying long enough to enjoy it.'

Rebus lit up anyway, staying put. 'Where did Tony El go?'

'He didn't send a postcard.'

'You must have some idea.'

Toal thought about it, when he shouldn't have needed to. 'Somewhere south, I think. Maybe London. He had friends down there.'

'London?'

Toal wouldn't look at Rebus. He shook his head. 'I heard he headed south.'

Rebus stood up.

'Is it that time already?' Toal showed effort getting to his feet, steadying himself with the walking-stick. 'And here we were just getting to know one another. How's Edinburgh these days? Know what we used to say about it? Fur coat and nae knickers, that's Edinburgh.' A hacking laugh turned into a hacking cough. Toal gripped the walking-stick with both hands, knees almost buckling.

Rebus waited until he'd finished. The old man's face was puce, sweat breaking out. 'That may be true,' he said, 'but I don't see too many fur coats around here, never mind the knickers.'

Toal's face broke into a grin, showing yellow dentures. 'Cafferty said I'd like you, and you know what?'

'What?'

The grin turned to a scowl. 'He was wrong. And now I've seen you, I'm wondering more than ever why he sent you here. Not just for the price of a half-bottle, not even Cafferty's that cheap. You better get yourself back to Edinburgh, laddie. And take care of yourself, I hear it's not as safe as it used to be.'

Rebus walked to the far end of the living room, deciding to leave by the other front door. There was a staircase next to it, and someone came bounding down, nearly colliding with him. A big man in bad clothes, a face that said he wasn't too bright, arms tattooed with thistles and pipers. He'd be about twenty-five, and Rebus recognised him from the photos in the file: Mad Malky Toal, a.k.a. 'Stanley'. Joseph Toal's wife had died in childbirth, too old really to be having kids. But their first two had died, one in infancy, one in a car smash. So now there was only Stanley, heir apparent, and towards the back of the queue when the IQs were being divvied.

He gave Rebus a long look, full of grudge and threat, then loped towards his father. He was wearing the trousers from a pinstripe suit with T-shirt, white socks, trainers – Rebus had yet to meet a gangster with dress sense: they spent money, but with no style – and his face sported half a dozen good-sized warts.

'Hey, Da, I've lost my keys to the beamer, where's the spare set?'

Rebus let himself out, relieved to see that the patrol car was still there. Boys were circling it on bikes, a cherokee party with scalps on their minds. Leaving the cul-de-sac, Rebus checked the cars: a nice new Rover; BMW 3 Series; an older Merc, one of the big ones, and a couple of less serious contenders. Had it been a used car lot, he'd have kept his money and looked elsewhere.

He squeezed between two bikes, opened the back door, got in. The driver started the engine. Rebus looked back to where Stanley was making for the BMW, bouncing on his heels.

'Now,' the passenger said, 'before we leave, have you counted that you still have all your fingers and toes?'

'West end,' Rebus said, leaning back in his seat and closing his eyes. He needed another drink.

The Horseshoe Bar first, a jolt of malt, and then outside for a taxi. He told the driver he wanted Langside Place in Battlefield. From the moment he'd walked into the Bible John room, he'd known he would make this trip. He could have had the patrol car take him, but didn't want to have to explain his interest.

Langside Place was where Bible John's first victim had lived. She'd worked as a nurse, lived with her parents. Her father looked after her small son while she went out dancing. Rebus knew her original destination had been the Majestic Ballroom in Hope Street, but somewhere along the way she'd decided on the Barrowland instead. If only she'd stuck to her first choice. What force had nudged her towards the Barrowland? Could you just call it fate and be done with it?

He told the driver to wait, got out of the cab and walked up and down the street. Her body had been found nearby, outside a garage in Carmichael Lane, clothing and handbag missing. Police had spent a lot of time and effort searching for them. They'd also done their best to interview people who'd been at the Barrowland that night, only there was a problem: Thursday night there was notorious. It was Over Twenty-fives night, and a lot of married men and women went, leaving spouses and wedding rings behind. A lot of people shouldn't have been there, and made unwilling material as witnesses.

The taxi's engine was still running – and so was its meter. Rebus didn't know what he'd expected to find here, but he was still glad he'd come. It was hard to look at the street and see the year 1968, hard to get any feel for that era. Everything and everyone had changed.

He knew the second address: Mackeith Street, where the second victim had lived and died. Here was one thing about Bible John: he'd taken the victims so close to their homes, a sign either of confidence or indecision. By August 1969 police had all but given up the initial investigation, and the Barrowland was thriving again. It was a Saturday night, and the victim left her three children with her sister, who lived across the landing. In those days, Mackeith Street was tenements, but as the taxi reached its destination Rebus saw terraced housing, satellite dishes. The tenements had long gone; in 1969 they'd been awaiting demolition, many of them empty. She'd been found in one of the derelict buildings, strangled with her tights. Some of her things were missing, including her handbag. Rebus didn't get out of the taxi, didn't see the point. His driver turned to him.

'Bible John, is it?'

Surprised, Rebus nodded. The driver lit a cigarette. He'd be about fifty, thick curling grey hair, his face ruddy, a boyish gleam to the blue eyes.

'See,' he said, 'I was a cabbie back then as well. Never really seem to have got out of the rut.'

Rebus remembered the box-file with 'Taxi Firms' on its spine. 'Did the police question you?'

'Oh aye, but it was more that they wanted us to be on the lookout, you know, in case we ever got him in the back. But he looked like any other punter, there were dozens fit the description. We almost had a few lynchings. They had to give out cards to some of them: "This man is not Bible John", signed by the Chief Constable.'

'What do you think happened to him?'

'Ach, who knows? At least he stopped, that's the main thing, eh?'

'If he stopped,' Rebus said quietly. The third address was Earl Street in Scotstoun, the victim's body found on Hallowe'en. The sister, who had accompanied the victim all evening, had painted a very full picture of that night: the bus to Glasgow Cross, the walk up the Gallowgate ... shops they stopped at ... drinks in the Traders' Tavern ... then the Barrowland. They both met men called John. The two men didn't seem to hit it off. One went to catch a bus, the other stayed, sharing their taxi. Talking. It gnawed at Rebus, as it had at so many before him: why would Bible John leave such a good witness behind? Why had he gone on to kill his third victim, knowing her sister would be able to draw such a vivid portrait of him: his clothes, what he'd talked about, his overlapping front teeth? Why had he been so reckless? Had he been taunting the police, or was there some other reason? Maybe he was heading away from Glasgow, so could afford this casual exit. But heading where? Somewhere his description would mean nothing – Australia, Canada, the USA?

Halfway to Earl Street, Rebus said he'd changed his mind and directed his driver to the 'Marine' instead. The old Partick station – which had been the heart of the Bible John inquiry – was empty and near-derelict. It was still possible to gain access to the building if you unlocked the padlocks, and no doubt kids had found they could get in without undoing any locks at all. But all Rebus did was sit outside and stare. A lot of men were taken to the Marine, questioned, and put in a line-up. There were five hundred formal identity parades, and many more informal ones. Joe Beattie and the third victim's sister would stand there and concentrate on faces, physiques, speech. Then there'd be a shake of the head, and Joe would be back to square one.

'You'll want to see the Barrowland next, eh?' his driver said. Rebus shook his head. He'd had enough. The Barrowland wouldn't tell him anything he didn't already know.

'Do you know a bar called The Lobby?' he said instead. The driver nodded. 'Let's go there then.'

He paid off the cabbie, adding a fiver as a tip, and asked for a receipt.

'No receipts, sorry, pal.'

'You don't happen to work for Joe Toal, do you?'

The man glared at him. 'Never heard of him.' Then he shifted into first and sped off.

Inside The Lobby, Ancram was standing at the bar, looking relaxed, the focus of a lot of attention: two men and two women in a huddle around him. The bar was full of after-work suits, careerists plotting furtively, women on the scent.

'Inspector, what'll it be?'

'My shout.' He pointed to Ancram's glass, then to the others, but Ancram laughed.

'You don't buy them drinks, they're journos.'

'It's my round anyway,' one of the women said. 'What'll you have?'

'My mother told me never to accept drinks from strangers.'

She smiled: lip gloss, eye-shadow, tired face trying for enthusiasm. 'Jennifer Drysdale.' Rebus knew why she was tired: it was hard work acting like 'one of the boys'. Mairie Henderson had told him about it – the pattern was changing only slowly; a lot of surface gloss about equality sloshed over the same old wallpaper.

Jeff Beck on the sound system: 'Hi-Ho Silver Lining'. Stupid lyric, and a hook that had lasted two decades and more. It comforted him that a place with The Lobby's pretensions should still cling to old hooks.

'Actually,' Ancram was saying, 'we should be making tracks. Right, John?'

'Right.' The use of his first name a hint: Ancram wanted out.

The reporters didn't look so happy any more. They flung questions at Ancram: Johnny Bible. They wanted a story, any story.

'I would if I could, but there's nothing to give.' Ancram had his hands up, trying to placate the foursome. Rebus saw that someone had placed a recording Walkman on top of the bar.

'Anything,' one of the men said. He even glanced towards Rebus, but Rebus was staying out of it.

'If you want a story,' Ancram said, pushing through the bodies, 'get yourselves a psychic detective. Thanks for the drinks.'

Outside, the smile fell from Ancram's face. An act, it had been no more than that. 'Bastards are worse than leeches.'

'And like leeches, they have their uses.'

'True, but who would you rather have a drink with? I've no car, do you mind walking?'

'Where to?'

'The next bar we find.'

But in fact they had to walk past three pubs – not places a policeman could drink in safely – until they hit one Ancram liked the look of. It was still raining, but mild. Rebus could feel sweat glueing his shirt to his back. Despite the rain, *Big Issue* sellers were out in force, not that anyone was buying: good-cause fatigue.

They shook themselves dry and settled on stools at the bar. Rebus ordered – malt, gin and tonic – and lit a cigarette, offering one to Ancram, who shook his head.

'So where have you been?'

'Uncle Joe's.' Among other places.

'How did you get on?'

'I spoke to the man.' And paid my respects …

'Face to face?' Rebus nodded; Ancram appraised him. 'Where?'

'At his house.'

'The Ponderosa? He let you in without a search warrant?'

'The place was immaculate.'

'He'd probably spent half an hour before you got there sticking all the booty upstairs.'

'His son was upstairs when I got there.'

'Standing guard on the bedroom door, no doubt. Did you see Eve?'

'Who's she?'

'Uncle Joe's clippie. Don't be fooled by the wheezing old pensioner routine. Eve's around fifty, still in good nick.'

'I didn't see her.'

'You'd've remembered. So, did anything rattle loose from the shaky old bugger?'

'Not much. He swore Tony El's been off the payroll for a year, and he hasn't seen him.'

A man came into the bar, saw Ancram, and was about to do a U-turn. But Ancram had already spotted him in the bar mirror, so the man walked up to him, brushing rain off his hair.

'Hiya, Chick.'

'Dusty, how's things?'

'No' bad.'

'You're doing away then?'

'You know me, Chick.' The man kept his head low, spoke in an undertone, shuffled off to the far end of the bar.

'Just someone I know,' Ancram explained: meaning, a snitch. The man was ordering a half and a 'hauf': whisky with a half-pint of beer to chase it down. He opened a packet of Embassy, made too much of a point of not looking along the bar.

'So was that all Uncle Joe gave you?' Ancram asked. 'I'm intrigued, how did you get to him?'

'A patrol car dropped me, I walked the rest of the way.'

'You know what I mean.'

'Uncle Joe and I have a mutual friend.' Rebus finished his malt.

'Same again?' Ancram asked. Rebus nodded. 'Well, I know you

visited the Bar-L.' Jack Morton talking? 'And I can't think of *too* many people there who have Uncle Joe's ear ... Big Ger Cafferty?' Rebus gave silent applause. Ancram laughed for real this time, not a show for reporters. 'And the old sod didn't tell you anything?'

'Just that he thought Tony El had moved south, maybe to London.'

Ancram picked the lemon out of his drink, discarded it. 'Really? That's interesting.'

'Why?'

'Because I've had my friends reporting in.' Ancram made the slightest movement with his head, and the snitch from the far end of the bar slid off his stool and came towards them. 'Tell Inspector Rebus what you told me, Dusty.'

Dusty licked non-existent lips. He looked the kind who snitched to feel important, not just for money or revenge.

'Word is,' he said, face still bowed so Rebus was looking at the top of his head, 'Tony El's been working up north.'

'North?'

'Dundee ... north-east.'

'Aberdeen?'

'Up that way, aye.'

'Doing what?'

A fast shrug of the shoulders. 'Independent operator, who knows. He's just been seen around.'

'Thanks, Dusty,' Ancram said. Dusty sloped back to his end of the bar. Ancram signalled for the barmaid. 'Two more,' he said, 'and whatever Dusty's drinking.' He turned to Rebus. 'So who do you believe, Uncle Joe or Dusty?'

'You think he lied just to wind me up?'

'Or wind you down.'

Yes, down as far as London, a false trail that could have eaten into the investigation: wasted time, manpower, effort.

'The victim worked out of Aberdeen,' Rebus said.

'All roads leading to.' The drinks had arrived. Ancram handed over a twenty. 'Don't bother with change, keep it to pay for whatever else Dusty drinks, and give him what's left at the end. Plus one for yourself.'

She nodded, knew the routine. Rebus was thinking hard, routes leading north. Did he want to go to Aberdeen? It would keep him away from *The Justice Programme*, maybe keep him from thinking about Lawson Geddes. Today had been like a holiday in that respect. Edinburgh was too full of ghosts; but then so was Glasgow – Jim Stevens, Jack Morton, Bible John and his victims ...

'Did Jack tell you I'd been to the Bar-L?'

'I pulled rank on him, don't blame Jack.'

'He's changed a lot.'

'Has he been nagging you? I wondered why he chased after you at lunchtime. The zeal of the converted.'

'I don't get it.' Rebus lifted the glass to his lips, poured it in smoothly.

'Didn't he say? He's joined AA, and I don't mean breakdown insurance.' Ancram paused. 'Come to think of it though, maybe I do.' He winked, smiled. There was something annoying about his smile; it was like he was party to secrets and motives – a patronising smile. A very Glaswegian sort of smile.

'He was an alcoholic,' Ancram went on. 'I mean, he still is. Once an alky, always an alky, that's what they say. Something happened to him in Falkirk, he ended up in hospital, nearly in a coma. Sweats, spewing, slime dripping off the ceiling. Gave him a hell of a fright. First thing he did when he got out was look up the phone number for Samaritans, and they put him on to the Juice Church.' He looked at Rebus's glass. 'Christ, that was quick. Here, have another.' The barmaid already had a glass in her hand.

'Thanks, I will,' said Rebus, wishing he didn't feel so calm. 'Since you seem to be so loaded. Nice suit, too.'

The humour left Ancram's eyes. 'There's a tailor on Argyle Street, ten per cent discount for serving officers.' The eyes narrowed. 'Spit it out.'

'No, it's nothing really, just that when I was going through the files on Toal, I couldn't help noticing that he always seemed to have inside info.'

'Careful, laddie.'

The 'laddie' rankled; it was meant to.

'Well,' Rebus went on, 'everyone knows the west coast is open to bungs. Not always cash, you understand. Could be watches, ID bracelets, rings, maybe even a few suits ...'

Ancram looked around the bar, as though begging for witnesses to Rebus's remarks.

'Would you care to name any names, *Inspector*, or is hearsay good enough for Edinburgh CID? The way I hear it, there's no cupboard-space left in Fettes, they're so jam-packed with skeletons.' He picked up his drink. 'And half those skeletons seem to have *your* fingerprints all over them.'

The smile again, sparkling eyes, laughter lines. *How did he know?* Rebus turned to go. Ancram's voice followed him out of the pub.

'We can't all go running to friends in Barlinnie! I'll see you around, Inspector ...'

7

Aberdeen.

Aberdeen meant away from Edinburgh; no *Justice Programme*,
no Fort Apache, no shite for him to skite in. Aberdeen looked good.

But Rebus had things to do in Edinburgh. He wanted to see the locus
in daylight, so drove out there, not risking his own Saab; leaving it at
Fort Apache and taking the spare Escort. Jim MacAskill wanted him on
the case because he hadn't been around long enough to make enemies;
Rebus was wondering how you ever made friends in Niddrie. The place
was if anything bleaker by day: blocked-in windows, glass like shrapnel
on the tarmac, kids playing in the sunshine with no real enthusiasm,
eyes and mouths narrowing as his car cruised past.

They'd knocked a lot of the estate down; behind it was better
housing, semi-detached. Satellite dishes a status symbol: the owners'
status – unemployed. The estate boasted a derelict pub – insurance job
blaze – and one all-purpose corner shop, its window full of video
posters. The kids made this last their base. BMX bandits blowing
bubble-gum. Rebus drove past slowly, his eyes on them. The death flat
wasn't quite on the edge of the estate, not quite visible from Niddrie
Mains Road. Rebus was thinking: Tony El didn't come from round
here, and if he'd picked the spot by chance, there were other derelict
flats nearer the main road.

Two men plus the victim. Tony El and an accomplice.

The accomplice had local knowledge.

Rebus climbed the stairs to the flat. The place had been sealed, but he
had keys to both padlocks. The living room as before, upside-down
table, blanket. He wondered who'd slept there, maybe they'd seen
something. He reckoned his chances of finding them were one per cent;
of getting them to talk, slightly less. Kitchen, bathroom, bedrooms,
hallway. He kept close to the walls, so as not to fall through the floor.
There was no one living in the block, but the next block along had glass
in a couple of its windows: one on the first storey, one on the second.

Rebus knocked on the first door. A dishevelled woman answered, an infant clinging round her neck. He didn't need to introduce himself.

'I don't know anything, and I didn't see or hear anything.' She made to close the door.

'You married?'

She opened the door again. 'What's it to you?'

Rebus shrugged; good question.

'He's down the boozer, most likely,' she said.

'How many kids have you got?'

'Three.'

'Must be pushed for space.'

'That's what we keep telling them. All they'll say is our name's on the list.'

'What age is your oldest?'

Eyes narrowing. 'Eleven.'

'Any chance he saw something?'

She shook her head. 'He'd've told me.'

'What about your man?'

She smiled. 'He'd have seen everything *twice*.'

Rebus smiled too. 'Well, if you hear anything ... from the kids or your man ...'

'Aye, right.' Slowly, so as not to cause offence, she shut the door on him.

Rebus climbed the next flight. Dog shit on the landing, a used condom: he tried not to connect the two. Felt-marker graffiti on the door – Wanker, HMFC, cartoon coitus. The occupier had given up trying to wipe it off. Rebus pushed the doorbell. No answer; he tried again.

A voice from within: 'Bugger off!'

'Could I have a word?'

'Who is it?'

'CID.'

A chain rattled, and the door opened two inches. Rebus saw half a face: an old woman, or maybe an old man. He showed his warrant card.

'You're not moving me out. I'll be here when they pull the place down.'

'I don't want to move you out.'

'Eh?'

Rebus raised his voice. 'Nobody wants to move you out.'

'Aye they do, but I'm not moving, you can tell them that.' Rebus caught foul breath, a meaty smell.

83

'Look, have you heard what happened next door?'

'Eh?'

Rebus peered through the gap. The hallway was littered with sheets of newspaper, empty cat-food tins. One more try.

'Someone was killed next door.'

'Don't try your tricks with me, boyo!' Anger in the voice.

'I'm not trying any … ach, to hell with it.' Rebus turned, started back downstairs. Suddenly the outside world looked good to him in the warm sunshine. It was all relative. He walked over to the corner shop, asked the kids a few questions, handed out mints to anyone who wanted one. He didn't learn anything, but ended up with an excuse to go inside. He bought a packet of extra-strong, put it in his pocket for later, asked the Asian behind the counter a couple of questions. She was fifteen, maybe sixteen, extraordinarily pretty. A video was playing on the TV, high up on one wall. Hong Kong gangsters shooting chunks out of each other. She didn't have anything to tell him.

'Do you like Niddrie?' he asked.

'It's all right.' Her voice was pure Edinburgh, eyes on the TV.

Rebus drove back to Fort Apache. The Shed was empty. He drank a cup of coffee and smoked a cigarette. Niddrie, Craigmillar, Wester Hailes, Muirhouse, Pilton, Granton … They all seemed to him like some horrible experiment in social engineering: scientists in white coats sticking families down in this maze or that, seeing what would happen, how strong they'd have to become to cope, whether or not they'd find the exit … He lived in an area of Edinburgh where six figures bought you a three-bedroom flat. It amused him that he could sell up and be suddenly rich … except, of course, that he'd have nowhere to live, and couldn't afford to move anywhere nicer in the city. He realised he was just about as trapped as anyone in Niddrie or Craigmillar, nicer model of trap, that was all.

His phone rang. He picked it up and wished he hadn't.

'Inspector Rebus?' A woman's voice: administrative. 'Could you attend a meeting tomorrow at Fettes?'

Rebus felt a chill run the length of his spine. 'What sort of meeting?'

A cool smiling voice. 'I don't have that information. The request comes from the ACC's office.'

The Assistant Chief Constable, Colin Carswell. Rebus called him the 'CC Rider'. A Yorkshireman – as close to a Scot as the English got. He'd been with Lothian and Borders two and a half years, and so far nobody had a bad word to say about him, which should have put him in the *Guinness Book of Records*. There had been a hairy few months after the last Deputy Chief Constable resigned and before they appointed a new one, but Carswell had coped. Some were of the opinion that he was just *too* good, and therefore would never make it to Chief Constable. Lothian and Borders used to boast one DCC and two ACCs, but one of the ACC posts had now become 'Director of Corporate Services', about which no one on the force seemed to know anything at all.

'What time?'

'Two o'clock, it shouldn't take long.'

'Will there be tea and biccies? I'm not coming otherwise.'

A shocked pause, then a release of breath as she realised he was joking. 'We'll see what we can manage, Inspector.'

Rebus put down the phone. It rang again and he picked it up.

'John? It's Gill, did you get my message?'

'Yes, thanks.'

'Oh. I thought you might have tried to call me.'

'Mmm.'

'John? Is something wrong?'

He shook himself. 'I don't know. The CC Rider wants to see me.'

'Whatever for?'

'Nobody's saying.'

A sigh. 'What have you been up to this time?'

'Absolutely nothing, Gill, that's the God's honest truth.'

'Made any enemies yet at your new posting?' As she spoke, Bain and Maclay walked through the door. Rebus nodded a greeting.

'No enemies. Do you think I'm doing something wrong?' Maclay and Bain were shedding jackets, pretending not to be interested.

'Listen, about that message I left ...?'

'Yes, Chief Inspector?' Maclay and Bain dropped the pretence.

'Can we meet?'

'I don't see why not. Dinner tonight?'

'Tonight ... yes, why not?'

She lived in Morningside, Rebus in Marchmont ... make it a Tollcross rendezvous.

'Brougham Street,' Rebus said, 'that Indian place with the slat blinds. Half eight?'

'Sure.'

'See you there, Chief Inspector.'

Bain and Maclay went about their business, said nothing for a minute or two. Then Bain coughed, swallowed, spoke.

'How was Raintown?'

'I got out alive.'

'Find out anything about Uncle Joe and Tony El?' Bain's finger went to the nick below his eye.

Rebus shrugged. 'Maybe something, maybe nothing.'

'All right, don't tell us,' Maclay said. He looked funny, sitting at his desk. An inch had been sawn off each of the legs of his chair, so his thighs would fit under the lip of the desk. When Rebus had first arrived, he'd asked why Maclay hadn't just lifted the table legs up an inch. Until then, Maclay hadn't thought of it – sawing the chair legs had been Bain's idea.

'Nothing *to* tell,' Rebus argued. 'Except this – word is, Tony El's a free agent, working out of the north-east, so we need to contact Grampian CID and ask about him.'

'I'll fax them his details,' Maclay said.

'I take it there's been no sign?' Rebus asked.

Bain and Maclay shook their heads.

'I'll let you into the secret though,' Bain said.

'What?'

'There are at least *two* Indians on Brougham Street with slatted blinds.'

Rebus watched them have a good laugh about that, then asked what the background check on the decedent had produced.

'Not much,' Bain said, leaning back in his chair and waving a sheet of paper. Rebus got up, took the paper from him.

Allan Mitchison. Only child. Born in Grangemouth. His mother died in childbirth; his father went into decline, followed her two years later. Infant Allan was taken into care – no other kin found. Children's home, then a foster family. Put up for adoption, but was an unruly kid, a trouble-maker. Screaming fits, tantrums, then long sulks. He always ran away eventually, always found his way back to the children's home. Grew up into a quiet teenager, still prone to black sulks, the occasional outburst, but talented in some school subjects – English, geography, art, music – and mostly docile. Still preferred the children's home to foster life. Left school at seventeen. Having seen a documentary on life on a North Sea platform, decided he liked the look of it. Miles from anywhere, and an existence not unlike the children's home – regimented. He liked group life, dormitories, shared rooms. Painter. His work pattern was uneven – he'd spent time onshore as well as off – a spell of training at RGIT-OSC …

'What's RGIT-OSC?'

Maclay had been waiting for the question. 'Robert Gordon Institute of Technology's Offshore Survival Centre.'

'Is that the same as Robert Gordon's University?'

Maclay and Bain looked at one another, shrugged.

'Never mind,' Rebus said, thinking: Johnny Bible's first victim had attended RGU.

Mitchison had also worked at the Sullom Voe terminal on Shetland, a few other locations. Friends and workmates: plenty of the latter, precious few of the former. Edinburgh had proved a dead end: none of his neighbours had ever clapped eyes on him. And the word from Aberdeen and points north was only a little more encouraging. A couple of names: one on a production platform, one at Sullom Voe ...

'Are these two willing to be interviewed?'

Bain: 'Christ, you're not thinking of going up *there*? First Glasgow, now teuchter-land – didn't you get a holiday this year?'

Maclay's high-pitched laughter.

Rebus: 'I seem to be a sitting target down here. I had a thought today – whoever picked out that flat knew the area. I'm thinking a local. Either of you have snitches in Niddrie?'

'Of course.'

'Then get talking to them, a man answering Tony El's description, he might've been hanging around the pubs and clubs, looking for local talent. Is there anything on decedent's employer?'

Bain lifted another sheet, waved it, smiling. Rebus had to get up again, go fetch it.

T-Bird Oil got its name from Thom Bird, who had been co-founder with 'Major' Randall Weir.

'Major?'

Bain shrugged. 'That's what they call him: Major Weir.'

Weir and Bird were both Americans, but with strong Scottish roots. Bird had died in 1986, leaving Weir in charge. It was one of the smaller companies hoovering up oil and gas from below the sea bed ...

Rebus realised that he knew almost nothing about the oil industry. He had some pictures in his head, mostly disasters – Piper Alpha, the *Braer*.

T-Bird had its UK base in Aberdeen, near Dyce Airport, but the global HQ was in the US, and the company held other oil and gas interests in Alaska, Africa, and the Gulf of Mexico.

'Boring, eh?' Maclay offered.

'Is that meant to be a joke?'

'Just making conversation.'

Rebus got to his feet, put his jacket on. 'Well, much as I could listen to your dulcet tones all day ...'

'Where are you going?'
'Station to station.'

No one seemed very interested in his return to St Leonard's; a couple of woolly suits stopped to say hello – it turned out they didn't even know he'd been transferred.

'I don't know who that says more about – me or you.'

In the CID offices he saw Siobhan Clarke at her desk. She was on the phone, and waved her pen at him as he passed. She wore a white short-sleeved blouse, and her bare arms were deeply tanned, as were her neck and face.

Rebus kept looking, and acknowledged a few lukewarm greetings. Jings, but it was rare to be 'home'. He thought of Allan Mitchison and his empty flat: he'd come back to Edinburgh because it was as close to a home as he had.

Eventually he spotted Brian Holmes, chatting up a WPC, giving it plenty.

'Hello, Brian, how's the wife?'

The WPC turned red, mumbled some excuse and left.

'Ha fucking ha,' Holmes said. Now that the WPC had gone, he looked dead done in, shoulders slumped, skin grey, specks of stubble left behind by a too-casual razor.

'That favour ...' Rebus prompted.

'I'm on it.'

'And?'

'*I'm on it!*'

'Go easy, son, we're all friends here.'

Holmes seemed to deflate. He rubbed his eyes, clawed fingers through his hair.

'Sorry,' he said. 'I'm beat, that's all it is.'

'Would coffee help?'

'Only if you can buy it by the vat.'

The canteen could stretch to an 'Extra Large'. They sat down, Holmes tearing open sachets of sugar and pouring them in.

'Look,' he said, 'about the other night, Mental Minto ...'

'We don't talk about that,' Rebus said firmly. 'It's history.'

'Too much history around here.'

'What else have the Scots got?'

'You two look about as happy as nuns on a Club 18–30.' Siobhan Clarke pulled out a chair and sat down.

'Nice holiday?' Rebus asked.

'Relaxing.'

'I see the weather was lousy.'

She ran a hand up one arm. 'Took hours of work on the beach to get this.'

'You've always been conscientious.'

She sipped Diet Pepsi. 'So why's everyone so down in the dumps?'

'You don't want to know.'

She raised an eyebrow, but didn't say anything. Two tired, grey men; one young woman, tanned and brimming with life. Rebus knew he'd have to gee himself up for his evening date.

'So,' he asked Holmes casually, 'that thing I asked you to look into …?'

'It's slow going. If you want my opinion,' he looked up at Rebus, 'whoever wrote up the notes was a master of circumlocution. There's a lot of circling around the subject. I'd guess most casual readers would give up rather than plough on.'

Rebus smiled. 'Why would the writer have done that?'

'To put people off reading it. He probably thought they'd flick to the summing-up, miss out all the rubbish in the middle. Thing is, you can lose things that way, bury them in the text.'

'Excuse me,' Siobhan said, 'have I walked into a masonic meeting by mistake? Is this some code I'm not supposed to get?'

'Not at all, Brother Clarke,' Rebus said, getting to his feet. 'Maybe Brother Holmes will tell you about it.'

Holmes looked to Siobhan. 'Only if you promise not to show me any holiday snaps.'

'I wasn't intending to.' Siobhan straightened her back. 'I know naturist beaches aren't your thing.'

Rebus was purposely early for the rendezvous. Bain hadn't been lying: there *were* two restaurants with wood-slatted blinds. They were eighty yards apart, and Rebus walked relays between the two. He saw Gill rounding the corner at Tollcross and waved to her. She hadn't over-dressed for the occasion: new-looking denims, plain cream blouse, and a yellow cashmere jumper tied around her neck. Sunglasses, gold-chain necklace, and two-inch heels – she liked to make a noise when she walked.

'Hello, John.'

'Hiya, Gill.'

'Is this the place?'

He looked at the restaurant. 'There's another one just up the road if you'd prefer. Or there's French, Thai ...'

'This is fine.' She pulled open the door, walked in ahead of him. 'Did you book a table?'

'Didn't think they'd be busy,' Rebus said. The restaurant wasn't empty, but there was a spare table for two by the window, directly beneath a distorting loudspeaker. Gill removed her brown leather shoulder-bag and laid it under her chair.

'Something to drink?' their waiter asked.

'Whisky and soda for me,' Gill said.

'Whisky, no additives,' Rebus ordered. As the first waiter left, another appeared with menus, popadums and pickles. After he'd gone, Rebus looked around, saw that no one at the other tables was paying attention, and reached up to tug at the speaker-cable, disconnecting it. The music above them stopped.

'Better,' Gill said, smiling.

'So,' Rebus said, laying his napkin across his thighs, 'is this business or social?'

'Both,' Gill admitted. She broke off as the drinks arrived. The waiter knew something was wrong, eventually placed it. He looked up at the silent speaker.

'It can be easily mended,' he told them. They shook their heads, then studied the menus. Having ordered, Rebus raised his glass.

'*Slàinte.*'

'Cheers.' Gill took a gulp of her drink, exhaled afterwards.

'So,' Rebus said, 'niceties taken care of ... to business.'

'Do you know how many women make chief inspector in the Scottish force?'

'I know we're talking the fingers of a blind carpenter's hand.'

'Exactly.' She paused, realigned her cutlery. 'I don't want to screw up.'

'Who does?'

She glanced at him, smiled. Rebus: world's supply of fuck-ups, his life a warehouse filled to the rafters with them. Harder to shift than eight-track cartridges.

'OK,' he said, 'so I'm an authority.'

'And that's good.'

'No.' He shook his head. 'Because I'm *still* fucking up.'

She smiled. 'Five months, John, and I haven't made a good collar yet.'

'But that's about to change?'

'I don't know.' Another gulp of courage. 'Someone's passed me some information about a drug deal ... a biggie.'

'Which protocol dictates you should pass on to the Scottish Crime Squad.'

She gave him a look. 'And hand those lazy bastards the glory? Come on, John.'

'I've never been a great believer in protocol myself. All the same ...' All the same: he didn't want Gill fucking up. He could see this was important to her: maybe *too* important. She needed perspective, same as he needed on Spaven.

'So who passed you the info?'

'Fergus McLure.'

'Feardie Fergie?' Rebus pursed his lips. 'Wasn't he one of Flower's snitches?'

Gill nodded. 'I took over Flower's list when he moved.'

'Jesus, how much did he screw out of you?'

'Never you mind.'

'Most of Flower's grasses are worse than anyone they could possibly snitch on.'

'Nevertheless, he gave *me* his list.'

'Feardie Fergie, eh?'

Fergus McLure had been in and out of private hospitals half his life. A nervous wreck, he drank nothing stronger than Ovaltine, and couldn't watch anything more exciting than *Pets Win Prizes*. His constant supply of prescription drugs bolstered the profits of the British pharmaceutical industry. This said, he ran a nice little empire which just bordered on the legal: jeweller by trade, he also put on sales of Persian rugs, fire-damaged and water-damaged merchandise, receivership auctions. He lived in Ratho, a village on the edge of the city. Feardie Fergie was a known homosexual, but lived quietly – unlike some judges of Rebus's acquaintance.

Gill crunched on a popadum, dribbled chutney on the remaining piece.

'So what's the problem?' Rebus asked.

'How well do you know Fergus McLure?'

Rebus shrugged, lied. 'Reputation only. Why?'

'Because I want this watertight before I act on it.'

'Problem with snitches, Gill, you can't always have corroboration.'

'No, but I can have a second opinion.'

'You want me to talk to him?'

'John, for all your flaws –'

91

'For which I am famous.'

'– you're a good judge of character, and you know enough about informers.'

'My back-up subject for *Mastermind*.'

'I just want to know if you think he's on the level. I don't want to go to all the trouble and effort of opening an investigation, maybe setting up surveillance, taps, even a sting operation, only to have the carpet pulled out from under me.'

'Understood, but you know the Squaddies will be peeved if you keep them in the dark. They've got the manpower and experience for this sort of thing.'

She just stared at him. 'Since when did you start going by the book?'

'We're not talking about me. I'm the L&B bad apple – doubtless they think one's more than enough.'

Their food arrived, the table filling with platters and dishes, a nan bread big enough to be plotting world domination. They looked at one another, realising they didn't feel that hungry any more.

'A couple more of the same,' Rebus said, handing the waiter his empty glass. To Gill: 'So tell me Fergie's story.'

'It's sketchy. Some drugs are coming north in a consignment of antiques. They're going to be handed over to the dealers.'

'The dealers being ...?'

She shrugged. 'McLure thinks they're Americans.'

Rebus frowned. 'Who? The sellers?'

'No, the buyers. The sellers are German.'

Rebus went through the major Edinburgh dealers, couldn't think of a single American.

'I know,' Gill said, reading his thoughts.

'New boys trying to break in?'

'McLure thinks the stuff's headed further north.'

'Dundee?'

She nodded. 'And Aberdeen.'

Aberdeen again. Jesus. A town called malice. 'So how's Fergie involved?'

'One of his sales would be the perfect cover.'

'He's fronting?'

Another nod. She chewed on a piece of chicken, dipped nan bread into the sauce. Rebus watched her eat, remembering little things about her: the way her ears moved when she chewed, the way her eyes flicked over the different dishes, the way she rubbed her fingers together afterwards ... There were rings around her neck that hadn't been there five years ago, and maybe when she visited her hairdresser they added some colour to her roots. But she looked good. She looked great.

'So?' she asked.

'Is that all he told you?'

'He's scared of these dealers, too scared to tell them to get lost. But the last thing he wants is us catching on and putting him in jail as an accessory. That's why he's grassing.'

'Even though he's scared?'

'Mm-hm.'

'When's all this supposed to happen?'

'When they phone him.'

'I don't know, Gill. If it were a peg, you couldn't hang a fucking hankie on it, never mind your coat.'

'Colourfully put.'

She was staring at his tie as she said it. It was a loud tie, purposely so: it was supposed to distract attention from his unironed shirt with the missing button.

'OK, I'll go talkies tomorrow, see if I can wring any more out of him.'

'But gently.'

'He'll be putty in my hands.'

They ate only half the food, still felt bloated. Coffee and mints came: Gill put both mints into her bag for later. Rebus had a third whisky. He was looking ahead, seeing them standing outside the restaurant. He could offer to walk her home. He could ask her back to his flat. Only she couldn't stay the night: there might be reporters outside in the morning.

John Rebus: presumptuous bastard.

'Why are you smiling?' she asked.

'Use it or lose it, they say.'

They split the bill, the drinks coming to as much as the food. And then they were outside. The night had grown cool.

'What are my chances of finding a taxi?' Gill was looking up and down the street.

'Pubs aren't out yet, you should be OK. My car's back at the flat ...'

'Thanks, John, I'll be all right. Look, here's one.' She waved to it. The driver signalled and pulled over with a squeak of brakes. 'Tell me how you get on,' she said.

'I'll phone you straight after.'

'Thanks.' She pecked his cheek, a hand on his shoulder to steady herself. Then she got into the taxi and closed the door, giving her address to the driver. Rebus watched the cab execute a slow U-turn into the traffic heading for Tollcross.

Rebus stood there for a moment, looking at his shoes. She'd wanted a favour, that was all. Good to know he was still useful for some things. 'Feardie Fergie', Fergus McLure. A name from the past; one-time friend of a certain Lenny Spaven. Worth a morning trip to Ratho for definite.

He heard another taxi coming – unmistakable engine sound. Its yellow light was on. He waved it down, got in.

'The Oxford Bar,' he said.

*

The more Bible John thought about the Upstart … the more he learned about him … the surer he felt that Aberdeen was the key.

He sat in his study, door locked against the outside world, and stared at the UPSTART file on his laptop. The gap between victims one and two was six weeks, between victims two and three only four. Johnny Bible was a hungry little devil, but so far he hadn't killed again. Or if he had, he was still playing with the body. But that wasn't the Upstart's way. He killed them quick, then presented the bodies to the world. Bible John had worked back, and had found two newspaper stories – both in the Aberdeen *Press and Journal*. A woman attacked on her way home from a nightclub, a man attempting to drag her into an alley. She'd screamed, he'd panicked and fled. Bible John had driven out to the scene one night. He stood in the alley and thought of the Upstart standing there, biding his time till the nightclub emptied. There was a housing scheme nearby, and the route home passed the mouth of the alley. Superficially, it was the perfect spot, but the Upstart had been nervous, ill-prepared. He'd probably been waiting there for an hour or two, standing back in the shadows, afraid someone would stumble upon him. His nerve had come and gone. When he'd finally picked a victim, he hadn't disabled it quickly enough. A scream was all it had taken to send him running.

Yes, it could well be the Upstart. He'd studied his failure, come up with a better plan: go *into* the nightclub, get talking to the victim … put the victim at its ease, then strike.

Second newspaper item: a woman complaining of a peeper in her back garden. When police were called, they found marks on her kitchen door, clumsy attempts at entering. Maybe connected to the first story, maybe not. Story one: eight weeks before the first murder. Story two: a further four weeks back. A pattern of months establishing itself. And

94

another pattern on top of the first: peeper becoming attacker. Of course, there could be other stories he'd missed, ones from other cities, making for different theories, but Bible John was happy to go with Aberdeen. First victim: often the first victim was local. Once the killer's confidence was up, he would range further afield. But that first success was so very important.

A timid knock at the study door. 'I've made coffee.'

'I'll be out soon.'

Back to his computer. He knew the police would be busy compiling their own composites, their psychological profiles, remembered the one a psychiatrist had compiled of *him*. You knew he was 'an authority' because of all the letters after his name: BSc, BL, MA, MB, ChB, LLB, DPA, FRCPath. Meaningless in the wider scheme, as was his report. Bible John had read it in a book years back. The few things about him it got right, he attempted to remedy. The serial murderer was supposedly withdrawn, with few close friends, so he had forced himself to become gregarious. The type was known for a lack of drive and fear of adult contacts, so he took a job where drive and contacts were crucial. As for the rest of the thesis ... rubbish, mostly.

Serial killers not infrequently had a history of homosexual activity – not guilty.

They were usually unmarried – tell that to the Yorkshire Ripper.

They often heard two voices inside their heads, one good and the other evil. They collected weapons, and gave them pet names. Many dressed up in women's clothes. Some showed an interest in black magic or in monsters, and collected sadistic pornography. Many had a 'private place' where objects such as hoods, dolls and rubber diving-suits would be kept.

He looked around his study and shook his head.

There were only a few points where the psychiatrist got it right. Yes, he would say he was egocentric – like half the population. Yes, he was neat and tidy. Yes, he had an interest in the Second World War (but not solely Nazism or concentration camps). Yes, he was a plausible liar – or rather, people were gullible listeners. And yes, he planned his culls well in advance, as it appeared the Upstart was now doing.

The librarian had not yet finished compiling his newspaper list. A check of requests for Bible John literature had drawn a blank. That was the bad news. But there was good news too. Thanks to the recent upsurge of interest in the original Bible John case, he had newspaper details of other unsolved murders, seven of them. Five took place in 1977, one in '78, and one much more recently. These gave him a second thesis. The first had the Upstart just beginning his career; the second had him recommencing it after a long gap. He might have been out of the country, or in some institution, or even in a relationship where he did not feel it necessary to kill. If the police were being meticulous – which he doubted – they'd be looking at recent divorces of men who had married in '78 or '79. Bible John did not have the means at his disposal to do this, which was frustrating. He got up and stared at his shelves of books, not really seeing them. There was an opinion that the Upstart *was* Bible John, that the eyewitness descriptions were flawed. As a result, the police and the media had dusted off their photofits and artists' impressions.

Dangerous. He knew the only way to quash such speculation was to locate the Upstart. Imitation was *not* the sincerest form of flattery. It was potentially lethal. He had to find the Upstart. Either that or lead the police to him. One way or another, it would be done.

8

He was in a six a.m. opener, drinking off a good sleep.

He'd woken up way too early, got dressed, and decided to go for a walk. He crossed the Meadows, headed down George IV Bridge and the High Street, left on to Cockburn Street. Cockburn Street: shopping mecca to teenagers and hippies; Rebus remembered Cockburn Street market when it was a damned sight more disreputable than these days. Angie Riddell had bought her necklace in a shop on Cockburn Street. Maybe she'd worn it the day he'd taken her to the café, but he didn't think so. He switched off the thought, turned down a passageway, a steep flight of steps, and took another left on Market Street. He was opposite Waverley Station, and there was a pub open. It catered to night-shift workers, a drink or two before home and bed. But you saw businessmen in it too, bracing themselves for the day ahead.

With newspaper offices nearby, the regulars were printworkers and subs, and there were always first editions available, the ink just dry. Rebus was known here, and no one ever bothered him. Even if a reporter was having a drink, they didn't hassle him for stories or quotes – it was an unwritten rule, never breached.

This morning, three teenagers sat slumped at a table, barely touching their drinks. Their dishevelled and sleepy state told Rebus they'd just completed a 'twenty-four': round-the-clock drinking. The daytime was easy: you started at six in the morning – somewhere like this – and the pubs were licensed till midnight or one o'clock. After that, it had to be clubs, casinos, and you finished the marathon at a pizza parlour on Lothian Road, open till six a.m., at which point you returned here for the last drink of the session.

The bar was quiet, no TV or radio, the fruit machine not yet plugged in: another unwritten rule. At this time of day, what you did in this place was drink. And read the papers. Rebus poured a helping of water into his whisky, took it and a paper to a table. The sun outside the windows was skin-tone pink against a milky sky. It had been a good walk; he liked the city quiet: taxis and early risers, first dogs being exercised, clear, clean air. But the night before still clung to the place: a litter-bin upturned, a bench on the Meadows with a broken back, traffic cones hoisted on to bus shelter roofs. It was true of the bar too: last night's fug had not had time to dissipate. Rebus lit a cigarette and read his paper.

A story on the inside page caught his attention: Aberdeen was hosting an international convention on offshore pollution and the role of the oil industry. Delegates from sixteen countries were expected to attend. There was a smaller story tacked on to the article: the Bannock oil and gas field, 100 miles north-east of Shetland, was coming to the end of its 'useful economic life', and was about to undergo decommissioning. Environmentalists were making an issue of Bannock's main production platform, a steel and concrete structure weighing 200,000 tonnes. They wanted to know what the owners, T-Bird Oil, planned to do with it. As required by law, the company had submitted an Abandonment Programme to the Oil and Gas Division of the Department of Trade and Industry, but its contents had not been made public.

The environmentalists were saying that there were over 200 oil and gas installations on the UK Continental Shelf, and they all had a finite production life. The government seemed to be backing an option which would leave the majority of the deep-water platforms in place, with only minimal maintenance. There was even talk of selling them off for alternative use – plans included prisons and casino/hotel complexes. The government and the oil companies were talking cost-effectiveness, and about striking a balance between cost, safety and the environment. The protesters' line was: the environment at *any* cost. Stoked up from their victory over Shell with the Brent Spar, the pressure groups were planning to make Bannock an issue too, and would be holding marches, rallies, and an open-air concert close to the site of the Aberdeen convention.

Aberdeen: fast becoming the centre of Rebus's universe.

He finished his whisky, decided against a second, then changed his mind. Flicked through the rest of the paper: nothing new on Johnny Bible. There was a property section; he checked the Marchmont/ Sciennes prices, then laughed at some of the New Town specs: 'luxurious townhouse, elegant living on five floors ...'; 'garage for sale separately, £20,000'. There were still a few places in Scotland where £20,000 would buy you a house, maybe with the garage thrown in. He looked down the 'Country Property' list, saw more wild prices, flattering photos attached. There was a place on the coast south-east of the city, picture windows and sea views, for the price of a Marchmont flat. Dream on, sailor ...

He walked home, got in his car, and drove out to Craigmillar, one area of the city not yet represented in the property section, and not likely to be for some time to come.

The night shift was just about to come off. Rebus saw officers he hadn't seen before. He asked around: it had been a quiet night; the cells were empty, ditto the biscuit-tins. In the Shed, he sat at his desk and saw new paperwork staring up at him. He fetched himself a coffee and picked up the first sheet.

More dead ends on Allan Mitchison; the head of his children's home interviewed by local CID. A check of his bank account, nothing amiss. Nothing from Aberdeen CID on Tony El. A woolly suit came in with a package addressed to Rebus. Postmarked Aberdeen, a printed label: T-Bird Oil. Rebus opened it. Publicity material, a compliment slip from Stuart Minchell, Personnel Dept. Half a dozen A4 pamphlets, quality layout and paper, colour throughout, facts kept to a minimum. Rebus, author of five thousand reports, knew waffle when he saw it. Minchell had enclosed a copy of 'T-BIRD OIL – STRIKING THE BALAN-CE', identical to the one in the side pocket of Mitchison's rucksack. Rebus opened it, saw a map of the Bannock field, laid out across a grid showing which blocks it occupied. A note explained that the North Sea had been divided into blocks of 100 square miles apiece, and oil companies initially made bids for exploration rights to these blocks. Bannock was slap-bang up against the international boundary – a few miles east and you came to more oil fields, but this time Norwegian rather than British.

'Bannock will be the first T-Bird field to undergo rigorous decommissioning,' Rebus read. There seemed to be seven options available, from Leave In Place to Total Removal. The company's 'modest proposal' was for mothballing: leaving the structure to be dealt with at a later date.

'Surprise, surprise,' Rebus muttered, noting that mothballing 'would leave funds available for future exploration and development'.

He put the pamphlets back in their envelope and shoved it in a drawer, returning to his paperwork. A sheet of fax paper was hidden near the bottom. He pulled it out. It was from Stuart Minchell, sent the previous day at seven in the evening: further details on Allan Mitchison's two workmates. The one who worked at the Sullom Voe terminal was called Jake Harley. He was on a walking/birdwatching holiday somewhere on Shetland, and probably hadn't yet heard of his friend's demise. The one who worked offshore was called Willie Ford. He was halfway through a sixteen-day stint, and 'of course' had learned about Allan Mitchison.

Rebus picked up his telephone, reached into the drawer for Minchell's compliment slip. He got the number from it and pushed the buttons. It was early; all the same ...

'Personnel.'

'Stuart Minchell, please.'

'Speaking.' Bingo: Minchell a company man, early starter.

'Mr Minchell, it's Inspector Rebus again.'

'Inspector, you're lucky I picked up the phone. Usually I just let it ring, only way I can get some work done before the rush.'

'Your fax, Mr Minchell – why did you say "of course" Willie Ford had learned of Allan Mitchison's death?'

'Because they worked together, didn't I tell you?'

'Offshore?'

'Yes.'

'Which platform, Mr Minchell?'

'Didn't I tell you that either? Bannock.'

'The one that's being mothballed?'

'Yes. Our Public Relations team's got its work cut out there.' A pause. 'Is it important, Inspector?'

'Probably not, sir,' Rebus said. 'Thanks anyway.' Rebus put down the receiver, drummed his fingers against it.

He went out to the shops, bought a filled roll for breakfast – corned beef and onion. The roll was too floury, and stuck to the roof of his mouth. He bought himself a coffee to wash it down. When he got back to the Shed, Bain and Maclay were at their desks, feet up, tabloid reading. Bain was eating a dough-ring; Maclay burping sausage-meat.

'Snitch reports?' Rebus asked.

'Nothing so far,' Bain said, not taking his eyes from the paper.

'Tony El?'

Maclay's turn: 'Description's gone out to every Scottish force, nothing's come back.'

'I phoned Grampian CID myself,' Bain added, 'told them to check out Mitchison's Indian restaurant. Looks like he was a regular, they might know something.'

'Nice one, Dod,' Rebus said.

'Not just a pretty face, is he?' Maclay said.

The weather forecast was for sunshine and showers. It seemed to Rebus, as he drove out to Ratho, that they were coming at ten-minute intervals. Brisk black clouds, shafts of sunlight, blue skies, then clouds gathering again. At one point, it started raining when there didn't seem to be a cloud in the sky.

Ratho was surrounded by farmland, with the Union Canal bordering it to the north. It was popular in the summer: you could take a boat trip on the canal, or feed the ducks, or eat at a waterfront restaurant. Yet it was less than a mile from the M8, two miles from Turnhouse Airport. Rebus drove out along Calder Road, trusting to his sense of direction. Fergus McLure's house was on Hallcroft Park. He knew he could find it: there were only a dozen streets in the whole village. McLure was known to work from home. Rebus had decided against phoning ahead: he didn't want Fergie forewarned.

When he reached Ratho, it took him five minutes to locate Hallcroft Park. He found Fergie's address, stopped the car, and walked up to the door. There was no sign of life. He rang the bell a second time. Net curtains stopped him peering through the window.

'Should have phoned,' Rebus muttered.

A woman was walking past, terrier straining on its leash. The small dog made terrible choking sounds as it sniffed the pavement.

'Is he not in?' she asked.

'No.'

'Funny, his car's here.' She had time to nod in the direction of a parked Volvo before the dog hauled her away. It was a blue 940 estate. Rebus looked in through the windows, but all he saw was how clean the interior looked. He checked the mileage: low. A new car. The tyre-walls hadn't even had time to lose their shine.

Rebus got back into his own car – mileage to date fifty times the Volvo's – and decided to head back into town by the Glasgow Road. But as he made to drive over the canal bridge, he saw a police car at the far end of the restaurant car park, sitting on the slip-road down to the canal. There was an ambulance parked next to it. Rebus braked, reversed, and turned into the car park, crawling towards the scene. A woolly suit came to warn him off, but Rebus had his warrant card ready. He parked and got out.

'What is it?' he asked.

'Somebody went for a dip with their clothes on.'

The constable followed Rebus down to the jetty. There were cruise boats moored there, and a couple of tourist-types who looked like they'd come for a trip on one of them. The rain had started again, pockmarking the surface of the canal. The ducks were keeping their distance. A body had been hauled out of the water, clothes sodden, and laid on the wooden slats that constituted the jetty. A man who looked like a doctor was checking for signs of life, no real hope in his face. The back door to the restaurant was open, staff members standing there, faces interested but full of horror.

The doctor shook his head. One of the tourists, a woman, began to cry. Her companion, a man, cradled his video camera and put an arm around her.

'He must've slipped and fallen in,' someone said, 'banged his head.'

The doctor checked the corpse's head, found a clean gash.

Rebus looked up towards the staff. 'Anyone see anything?' Head-shakes. 'Who reported it?'

'I did.' The woman tourist, English accent.

Rebus turned to the doctor. 'How long has he been in the water?'

'I'm just a GP, not an expert. All the same, if you want a guess … not long. Certainly not overnight.' Something had rolled out of the drowned man's jacket pocket and wedged between two of the slats. A small brown bottle with white plastic top. Prescription pills. Rebus looked at the bloated face, fixed it to a much younger man, a man he'd interviewed in 1978 about his connection to Lenny Spaven.

'He's a local,' Rebus told the company. 'His name's Fergus McLure.'

He tried phoning Gill Templer, couldn't track her down, ended up leaving messages for her in half a dozen different places. Back home, he polished his shoes and changed into his best suit, picked out the shirt with the fewest creases, and found the most sober tie he had (excepting his funeral one).

He looked at himself in the mirror. He'd showered and shaved, dried his hair and combed it. The knot in his tie looked OK, and for once he'd found a matching pair of socks. He looked fine, felt anything but.

It was half past one, time to go to Fettes.

The traffic wasn't too bad, the lights with him, like they didn't want to hold up his appointment. He was early at L&B HQ, thought of driving around, but knew it would only make him more nervous. Instead, he went inside, and sought out the Murder Room. It was on the second floor, a large central office space with smaller compartments off for the senior officers. This was the Edinburgh side of the triangle Johnny Bible had created, the heart of the Angie Riddell investigation. Rebus knew some of the faces on duty, smiled, nodded. The walls were covered with maps, photographs, charts – an attempt at order. So much of police work was putting things in some kind of order: fixing chronology, getting the details right, tidying up after the mess of people's lives as well as their deaths.

Most of the people on duty this afternoon looked tired, lacking enthusiasm. They were waiting by telephones, waiting for the elusive tip-off, the missing link, a name or a sighting, waiting for the man ... They'd been waiting a long time. Someone had mocked up a photofit of Johnny Bible: horns curling from the head, wisps of smoke from the flared nostrils, fangs and a serpent's forked tongue.

The Bogeyman.

Rebus looked closer. The photofit had been done on computer. The starting-point had been an old photofit of Bible John. With the horns and fangs, he bore a vague likeness to Alister Flower ...

He examined the photographs of Angie Riddell in life, kept his eyes away from her autopsy pics. He remembered her the night he'd arrested her, remembered her sitting in his car talking, almost too full of life. Her hair seemed to be dyed a different colour in almost every picture, like she was never quite happy with herself. Maybe she'd just needed to keep changing, running from the person she'd been, laughing to stop herself crying. Circus clown, painted smile ...

Rebus checked his watch. Fuck it: it was time.

9

There was just the CC Rider himself, Colin Carswell, waiting for Rebus in the comfortable and carpeted office.

'Take a seat, won't you?' Carswell had half-risen to welcome Rebus, now sat down again. Rebus sat opposite him, studying the desktop, looking for clues. The Yorkshireman was tall, with a body that sagged towards a beer drinker's gut. His hair was brown, thinning, his nose small, almost flat like a pug's. He sniffed. 'Sorry, can't oblige with your request for biscuits, but there's tea or coffee if you want it.'

Rebus remembered the phone call: *Will there be tea and biccies? I'm not coming otherwise.* The remark had been passed along.

'I'm fine, thanks, sir.'

Carswell opened a folder, picked something up, a newspaper clipping. 'Damned shame about Lawson Geddes. I hear he was an exceptional officer in his day.'

The story concerned Geddes' suicide.

'Yes, sir,' Rebus said.

'They say it's a coward's way out, but I know *I* wouldn't have the guts.' He looked up. 'What about you?'

'I hope I never have to find out, sir.'

Carswell smiled, put the cutting back, closed the folder. 'John, we're getting flak from the media. At first it was just that TV crew, but now everyone seems to want to join the circus.' He stared at Rebus. 'Not good.'

'No sir.'

'So we've decided – the Chief Constable and myself – that *we* should make an effort.'

Rebus swallowed. 'You're reopening the Spaven case?'

Carswell brushed invisible dust off the folder. 'Not straight away. There's no new evidence, therefore no real need to.' He looked up quickly. 'Unless you know some reason why we should?'

'It was cut and dried, sir.'

'Try telling the media that.'

'I have, believe me.'

'We're going to open an internal inquiry, just to satisfy ourselves that nothing was overlooked or ... untoward ... at the time.'

'Putting *me* under suspicion.' Rebus could feel his hackles rising.

'Only if you've got something to hide.'

'Come on, sir, you reopen an investigation, *everyone* begins to look dirty. And with Spaven and Lawson Geddes dead, I'm left carrying the can.'

'Only if there's a can to carry.'

Rebus leapt to his feet.

'*Sit down, Inspector, I've not finished with you yet!*'

Rebus sat down, made his hands grip the sides of the chair. He felt if he let go, he might fly clean through the ceiling. Carswell was taking a second to regain his own composure.

'Now, to keep things objective, the inquiry will be headed by someone from outside Lothian and Borders, reporting directly to me. They'll go through the original files ...'

Warn Holmes.

'... do any follow-up interviews deemed necessary, and compile their report.'

'Is this going to be made public?'

'Not until I have the finished report. It can't look like a whitewash, that's all I'll say. If any breach of the rules has taken place anywhere down the line, it'll be dealt with. Is that clear?'

'Yes, sir.'

'Now, is there anything you'd like to tell me?'

'Just between us, or do you want to bring the strongarm in?'

Carswell allowed this as a joke. 'I'm not sure you could call him that.'

Him.

'Who's in charge, sir?'

'An officer from Strathclyde, DCI Charles Ancram.'

Oh dear Jesus fucking Christ. His goodbye to Ancram: an accusation of graft. And Ancram had *known*, all that day he'd known this was coming, the way he'd smiled, like he had secrets, the way he'd studied Rebus, like they might well become adversaries.

'Sir, there may be some bad blood between CI Ancram and myself.'

Carswell stared at him. 'Care to elucidate?'

'No, sir, with respect.'

'Well, I suppose I could get Chief Inspector Flower instead. He's the bee's knees just now, nabbing that MP's son for cannabis growing ...'

Rebus swallowed. 'I'd prefer CI Ancram, sir.'

Carswell glowered. 'It's not your bloody decision, is it, Inspector?'

'No, sir.'

Carswell sighed. 'Ancram's already been briefed. Let's stick with him ... if that's all right with you?'

'Thank you, sir.' How did I get here, Rebus thought: thanking the man for putting Ancram on my tail ... 'Can I go now, sir?'

'No.' Carswell was looking in the folder again, while Rebus tried to get his heart-rate down. Carswell read a note, spoke without looking up. 'What were you doing in Ratho this morning?'

'Sir?'

'A body was hauled out of the canal. I've had word you were there. Not exactly Craigmillar, is it?'

'I was just in the area.'

'Apparently you ID'd the body?'

'Yes, sir.'

'You're a handy man to have around.' Heavy with irony. 'How did you know him?'

Blurt it out or clam up? Neither. Dissemble. 'I recognised him as one of our snitches, sir.'

Carswell looked up. 'Whose in particular?'

'DI Flower's.'

'Were you looking to poach him?' Rebus kept his mouth shut, letting Carswell draw his own conclusions. 'On the very morning he took a tumble into the canal ... strange coincidence?'

Rebus shrugged. 'These things happen, sir.' He fixed his eyes on Carswell's. They stared one another out.

'Dismissed, Inspector,' Carswell said.

Rebus didn't blink until he was back in the corridor.

He phoned St Leonard's from Fettes, his hand shaking. But Gill wasn't there, and nobody seemed to know where she was. Rebus asked the switchboard to page her, then asked to be put through to CID. Siobhan answered.

'Is Brian there?'

'I haven't seen him for a couple of hours. Are you two cooking something up?'

'The only thing cooking around here is my fucking goose. When you see him, tell him to call. And pass the same message along to Gill Templer.'

He broke the connection before she could say anything. Probably she'd have offered to help, and the one thing Rebus didn't want right now was anyone else involved. Lying to protect himself … lying to protect Gill Templer … Gill … he had questions for her, urgent questions. He tried her home number, left a message on the answering machine, then tried Holmes's home number: another machine, same message. Call me.

Wait. Think.

He'd asked Holmes to read up on the Spaven case, and that meant going through the files. When Great London Road police station had been burnt to the ground, a lot of files had gone up with it, but not the older stuff, because by then the older files had been shipped out to make space. They were stored with all the other ancient cases, all the clanking old skeletons, in a warehouse near Granton Harbour. Rebus had guessed Holmes would sign them out, but maybe not …

It was a ten-minute drive from Fettes to the warehouse. Rebus did it in seven. He allowed himself a grin when he saw Holmes's car in the car park. Rebus walked over to the main door, pulled it open, and was in a vast, dark, echoing space. Regimented rows of green metal shelves ran the length of the warehouse, filled with heavy-duty cardboard boxes, inside which lay the mouldering history of the Lothian and Borders force – and the City of Edinburgh force until its demise – from the 1950s to the 1970s. Documents were still arriving: tea-chests with labels hanging from them sat waiting to be unpacked, and it looked like a changeover was taking place – lidded plastic boxes replacing heavy-duty board. A small elderly man, very trim, with a black moustache and jam-jar glasses, was marching towards Rebus.

'Yes, can I help you?'

The man defined 'clerical'. When he wasn't looking at the floor, he was staring off somewhere past Rebus's right ear. He wore a grey nylon overall over a white shirt with frayed collar and green tweed tie. Pens and pencils protruded from his top pocket.

Rebus showed his warrant card. 'I'm looking for a colleague, DS Holmes, I think he may be looking through some old casenotes.'

The man was studying the warrant card. He walked over to a clipboard and wrote down Rebus's name and rank, plus date and time of arrival.

'Is that necessary?' Rebus asked.

The man looked like he'd never in his life been asked such a thing. 'Paperwork,' he snapped, looking around at the warehouse's contents. 'It's *all* necessary, or I wouldn't be here.'

And he smiled, the overhead lighting glinting from his lenses. 'This way.'

He led Rebus down an alleyway of boxes, then took a right turn and finally, after a moment's hesitation, a left. They came into a clearing, where Brian Holmes sat at what looked like an old school desk, inkwell intact. There was no chair, so he was using an upturned box. His elbows rested on the desk, head in hands. There was a lamp on the desk, bathing the scene in light. The clerk coughed.

'Someone to see you.'

Holmes turned, stood up when he saw who it was. Rebus turned quickly to the clerk.

'Thanks for your help.'

'No trouble. I don't get many visitors.'

The little man shuffled away, footsteps receding into the distance.

'Don't worry,' Holmes said. 'I've laid a trail of breadcrumbs so we can find our way back.' He looked around. 'Isn't this the creepiest place you've ever been?'

'It's straight into the top five. Listen, Brian, there's a problem.' He held up his right hand. 'Fan.' Then his left. 'Shit.' He clapped both hands together. The sound reverberated through the warehouse.

'Tell me.'

'The CC Rider's opening an inquiry into the Spaven case, prior to reopening the case itself. And he's managed to put in charge someone I recently rubbed up the wrong way.'

'Silly you.'

'Silly me. So no doubt they'll be down here some day soon to lift the casenotes. And I don't want them lifting *you*.'

Holmes looked at the bulging files, the faded black ink on each cover. 'The files could get lost, couldn't they?'

'They could. Two problems. One, that would look highly suspicious. Two, I'm assuming Mr Clipboard knows which files you've been consulting.'

'That's true,' Holmes conceded. 'And it went down on his sheet.'

'Along with your name.'

'We could try slipping him some cash.'

'He doesn't look the type. He's not in this for money, is he?'

Holmes looked thoughtful. He also looked terrible: unevenly shaven, his hair uncombed and needing a trim. The bags under his eyes could have carried half a hundredweight of coal.

'Look,' he said at last, 'I'm halfway through ... more than halfway. If

I burn the candle tonight, maybe speed up my reading, I could have it finished by tomorrow.'

Rebus nodded slowly. 'What do you think so far?' He was almost scared to touch the files, to flip through them. It wasn't history, it was archaeology.

'I think your typing hasn't improved. Straight answer: there's something dodgy going on, that much I can read between the lines. I can see exactly where you're covering up, rewriting the true story to fit your version. You weren't quite so subtle in those days. Geddes' version reads better, more confident. He glosses over stuff, he's not afraid to understate. What I'd like to know is, what was the story with him and Spaven in the first place? I know you told me they served together in Burma or somewhere; how did they come to fall out? See, if we knew that, we'd know how valid the chip on Geddes' shoulder was, and maybe how far it would take him.'

Rebus clapped his hands again, this time in muffled applause.

'That's good going.'

'So give me another day, see what else I come up with. John, I *want* to do this for you.'

'And if they catch you?'

'I'll talk my way out, don't worry.'

Rebus's pager sounded. He looked to Holmes.

'Sooner you go,' Holmes said, 'sooner I can get back to it.'

Rebus patted him on the shoulder and headed back along the stacks. Brian Holmes: friend. Difficult to equate with the person who had roughed up Mental Minto. Schizophrenia, the policeman's ally: a dual personality came in handy ...

He asked the clerk if he could use a telephone. There was one on the wall. He called in.

'DI Rebus.'

'Yes, Inspector, apparently you've been trying to reach DCI Templer.'

'Yes.'

'Well, I have a location for her. She's in Ratho, at some restaurant.'

Rebus slammed down the phone, cursing himself for not thinking of it sooner.

The wooden walkway where McLure's body had lain had been blown dry by the wind, leaving nothing to indicate that a death had occurred so recently. The ducks were skimming the water; one of the boats had just left with half a dozen passengers; diners in the restaurant chewed on their food and stared out at the two figures on the canal bank.

'I was in meetings half the day,' Gill said. 'I didn't hear about it until an hour ago. What happened?'

She had her hands deep in coat pockets, the coat a cream Burberry. She looked sad.

'Ask the pathologist. There was a cut on McLure's head, but that doesn't tell us a lot. He could have hit it when he slipped.'

'Or he could have been whacked and pushed in.'

'Or he could have jumped.' Rebus shivered; the death reminded him of the Mitchison options. 'My guess is, all the autopsy will tell us is whether he was alive when he hit the water. Right now I'll tell you he was probably alive, which still doesn't answer the question: accident, suicide, or a whack and a push?' He watched Gill turn away, begin to walk the towpath. He caught up with her. It was starting to rain again, small drops, sparse. He watched them land on her coat, darkening it by degrees.

'Bang goes my big collar,' she said, an edge to her voice. Rebus turned up the collar of her coat, and she caught the joke, smiled.

'There'll be others,' he told her. 'Meantime, a man's dead – don't forget that.' She nodded. 'Listen,' he said, 'the ACC had me on the carpet this afternoon.'

'The Spaven case?'

He nodded. 'Plus he wanted to know what I was doing out here this morning.'

She glanced towards him. 'What did you say?'

'I didn't say anything. But the thing is … McLure ties in to Spaven.'

'What?' He had her full attention now.

'They palled around years back.'

'Jesus, why didn't you tell me?'

Rebus shrugged. 'It didn't seem an issue.'

Gill was thinking hard. 'But if Carswell links McLure to Spaven …?'

'Then my being out here on the very morning Feardie Fergie met the big cheerio is going to look just a tad suspicious.'

'You have to tell him.'

'I don't think so.'

She turned to him, her hands gripping his lapels. 'You're protecting me from the fallout.'

The rain was growing heavier, drops sparkling in her hair. 'Let's just say I'm radiation-proof,' he said, leading her by the hand into the bar.

They ate a snack, neither of them bringing an appetite with them.

Rebus's came with a whisky; Gill's with Highland spring water. They sat facing one another at an alcove table. The place was a third full, nobody near enough to overhear.

'Who else knew?' Rebus said.

'You're the first person I've told.'

'Well, they could find out anyway. Maybe Fergie's nerve went, maybe he owned up. Maybe they just guessed.'

'Plenty of maybes.'

'What else have we got?' He paused, chewing. 'What about the other snitches you inherited?'

'What about them?'

'Snitches hear things, maybe Fergie wasn't the only one who knew about this drugs thing.'

Gill was shaking her head. 'I asked him at the time. He seemed confident it was being kept *very* quiet. You're assuming he was killed. Remember, he has a history of bad nerves, mental problems. Maybe the fear just got too much for him.'

'Do us both a favour, Gill, stick close to the investigation. See what the neighbours say: did he have any visitors this morning? Anyone out of the ordinary or suspicious? See if you can check his phone calls. My bet is it'll go down as an accident, which means no one's going to be working too hard on it. *Push them*, ask favours if you have to. Did he normally go for morning walks?'

She was nodding. 'Anything else?'

'Yes ... who's got the keys to his house?'

Gill made the calls, and they drank coffee until a DC turned up with the keys, fresh from the mortuary. Gill had asked about the Spaven case, Rebus giving only vague answers. Then they'd talked about Johnny Bible, Allan Mitchison ... all shop-talk, steering a wide berth around anything personal. But at one point they'd locked eyes, shared a smile, knowing the questions were there, whether they asked them or not.

'So,' Rebus said, 'what do you do now?'

'About the gen McLure gave me?' she sighed. 'There's nowhere to go with it, it was all so vague – no names or details, no date for the meeting ... it's gone.'

'Well, maybe.' Rebus lifted the keys, shook them. 'Depends whether you want to come snooping or not.'

The pavements in Ratho were narrow. To keep his distance from Gill, Rebus walked on the road. They didn't say anything, didn't need to. This was their second evening together; Rebus felt comfortable sharing everything but close proximity.

'That's his car.'

Gill walked around the Volvo, peered in through the windows. On the dashboard a small red light was blinking: the automatic alarm. 'Leather upholstery. Looks straight out of the showroom.'

'Typical Feardie Fergie car though: nice and safe.'

'I don't know,' Gill mused. 'It's the turbo version.'

Rebus hadn't noticed. He thought of his own aged Saab. 'Wonder what'll happen to it ...'

'Is this his house?'

They walked up to the door, used a mortise and a yale to open it. Rebus turned on the hall lights.

'Do you know if any of our lot has been in here?' Rebus asked.

'As far as I know, we're the first. Why?'

'Just trying out a scenario or two. Say someone came to see him here, and they frightened him. Say they told him to take a walk ...'

'Yes?'

'Well, he still had the presence of mind to double-lock the door. So either he wasn't that scared ...'

'Or whoever was with him double-locked the door, assuming that's what McLure would normally do.'

Rebus nodded. 'One more thing. Alarm system.' He pointed to a box on the wall, its light a steady green. 'It hasn't been switched on. If he was in a flap, he might forget. If he thought he wasn't coming back alive, he wouldn't bother.'

'He might not bother for a short stroll either though.'

Rebus conceded the point. 'Final scenario: whoever double-locked the door forgot or plain didn't know the alarm was there. See, door double-locked but alarm system off – it's not consistent. And someone like Fergie, Volvo driver, my guess is he'd *always* be consistent.'

'Well, let's see if he had anything worth nicking.'

They walked into the living room. It was crammed to bursting with furniture and nick-nacks, some modern, a lot looking like they'd been handed down the generations. But though overfilled, the room was neat, dust-free, with expensive-looking rugs on the floor – far from fire-damaged stock.

'Supposing someone *did* come to see him,' Gill said. 'Maybe we should dust for prints.'

'Definitely maybe. Get forensics on to it first thing.'

'Yes, sir.'

Rebus smiled. 'Sorry, ma'am.'

They kept their hands in their pockets as they walked through the room: the reflex to touch things was always strong.

'No signs of a struggle, and nothing looks like it's been put back in the wrong place.'

'Agreed.'

Past the living room there was another, shorter hallway, leading to a guest bedroom and what had probably once been the lounge: only used when visitors called. Fergus McLure had turned it into an office. There was paperwork everywhere, and on a fold-out dining table sat a new-looking computer.

'I suppose someone's going to have to go through this lot,' Gill said, not relishing the task.

'I hate computers,' Rebus said. He had noticed a fat notepad beside the keyboard. He slipped a hand from his pocket and picked it up by its edges, angling it into the light. There were indents in the paper from the last written sheet. Gill came over to see.

'Don't tell me.'

'Can't make it out, and I don't think the pencil trick would help.'

They looked at one another, spoke their thoughts together.

'Howdenhall.'

'Check the bins next?' Gill said.

'You do it, I'll look upstairs.'

Rebus went back into the front hall, saw more doors, tried them: a small old-fashioned kitchen, family pictures on the walls; a toilet; a box room. He climbed the stairs, his feet sinking into deep-pile carpeting which muffled all sound. It was a quiet house; Rebus got the feeling it had been quiet even when McLure had been there. Another guest bedroom, large bathroom – unmodernised like the kitchen – and main bedroom. Rebus gave his attention to the usual places: beneath the bed, mattress and pillows; bedside cabinets, chest of drawers, wardrobe. Everything was obsessively arranged: cardigans folded just so and layered by colour; slippers and shoes in a row – all the browns together, then the blacks. There was a small bookcase boasting an uninspired collection: histories of carpets and Eastern art; a photographic tour of the vineyards of France.

A life without complications.

Either that or the dirt on Feardie Fergie was elsewhere.

'Found anything?' Gill called up the stairs. Rebus walked back along the corridor.

'No, but you might want to have someone check his business premises.'

'First thing tomorrow.'

Rebus came back down. 'What about you?'

'Nothing. Just what you'd expect to find in bins. Nothing saying, "Dope deal, two-thirty Friday at the carpet auction".'

'Pity,' Rebus said with a smile. He checked his watch. 'Fancy another drink?'

Gill shook her head, stretched. 'I'd better get home. It's been a long day.'

'*Another* long day.'

'Another long day.' She angled her head and looked at him. 'What about you? Are you heading off for another drink?'

'Meaning?'

'Meaning you drink more than you used to.'

'Meaning?'

Her look was intent. 'Meaning I wish you wouldn't.'

'So how much *should* I drink, doctor?'

'Don't take it like that.'

'How do you know how much I drink? Who's been squealing?'

'We went out last night, remember?'

'I only had two or three whiskies.'

'And after I left?'

Rebus swallowed. 'Straight home to bed.'

She smiled sadly. 'You liar. And you were back at it first thing: a patrol car saw you leaving that pub behind Waverley.'

'I'm under surveillance!'

'There are people out there who're worried about you, that's all.'

'I don't believe this.' Rebus threw open the door.

'Where are you going?'

'I need a fucking drink. You can come if you like.'

10

As he drove into Arden Street, he saw a group of people outside the main door to his tenement. They were shuffling their feet and cracking jokes, trying to keep morale up. One or two were eating chips from newspaper – a nice irony, since they had the look of reporters.

'Shit.'

Rebus drove past and kept going, watching in his rearview. There was nowhere to park anyway. He turned right at the junction, then next left, and ended up in a parking space outside Thirlestane Baths. He turned off the ignition and punched the steering-wheel a few times. He could always drive away, maybe head for the M90, race up to Dundee and back, but he didn't feel like it. He took a few deep breaths, feeling the blood pound through him, a rushing noise in his ears.

'Let's do it,' he said, getting out of the car. He walked down Marchmont Crescent to his chippie, then headed home, feeling the fried fat burning his palm through the layers of paper. He took his time walking up Arden Street itself. They weren't expecting him to be on foot, and he was almost on them before someone recognised him.

There was a camera crew, too: Redgauntlet – cameraman, Kayleigh Burgess, and Eamonn Breen. Caught on the hop, Breen flicked a cigarette on to the road and grabbed his microphone. The videocam had a spot attached. Spotlights always made you squint, which in turn made you look guilty, so Rebus kept his eyes nice and wide.

A journalist got in the first question.

'Inspector, any comment on the Spaven inquiry?'

'Is it true the case is being reopened?'

'How did you feel when you heard Lawson Geddes had killed himself?'

At that question, Rebus glanced towards Kayleigh Burgess, who had the grace to look down at the pavement. He was halfway up the path now, only feet from the tenement's main door, but surrounded by reporters. It was like wading through broth. He stopped and turned to face them.

'Ladies and gentlemen of the press, I have a short statement I'd like to make.'

They looked at each other, eyes registering surprise, then held out their tape recorders. A couple of older hacks near the back, who'd been here too often to raise any enthusiasm, were using pen and notepad.

The noise died down. Rebus held his wrapped package aloft.

'On behalf of the chip-eaters of Scotland, I'd like to thank you for providing our nightly wrappings.'

He was inside the door before they could think of anything to say.

In the flat, he left the lights off and walked over to the living-room window, peering down on to the scene outside. A few of the reporters were shaking their heads, calling in on mobile phones to see if they'd be allowed home. One or two were already making for their cars. Eamonn Breen was talking to camera, looking full of himself as usual. One of the younger journalists raised two fingers above Breen's head, turning them into rabbit's ears.

Looking across the road, Rebus saw a man standing against a parked car, arms folded. He was gazing up at Rebus's window, a smile on his face. He unfolded his arms long enough to give Rebus a silent round of applause, then got into his car and started the engine.

Jim Stevens.

Rebus turned back into the room, switched on an Anglepoise lamp, sat down in his chair to eat the chips. But he still didn't have much of an appetite. He was wondering who had leaked the story to the vultures. The CC Rider had only told him this afternoon, and he'd told no one except Brian Holmes and Gill Templer. The answering machine was blinking furiously: four messages. He managed to work the machine without recourse to the manual, and was feeling pleased until he heard the Glaswegian accent.

'Inspector Rebus, it's CI Ancram here.' Brisk and businesslike. 'Just to let you know I'll probably arrive in Edinburgh tomorrow to get the inquiry underway, sooner we start, sooner it'll be over with. Best for all concerned, eh? I did leave a message at Craigmillar for you to phone me, but you don't seem to have been around to act on it.'

'Thank you and good night,' Rebus growled.

Beep. Message two.

'Inspector, it's me again. It would be very useful to know your planned movements for the next week or so, just to maximise my time effectively. If you could type out as full a breakdown as possible, I'd appreciate it.'

'I feel like I'm *having* a fucking breakdown.'

He went back to the window. They were clearing off. The Redgauntlet camera was being loaded into the estate car. Message three. At the sound of the voice, Rebus turned slack-jawed to watch the machine.

'Inspector, the inquiry will be based at Fettes. I'll probably bring one of my own men with me, but otherwise will utilise officers and civilian staff from Fettes. So as from tomorrow morning you can contact me there.'

Rebus walked over to the machine and stared down at it, daring it … daring it …

Beep. Message four.

'Two tomorrow afternoon for our first meeting, Inspector. Let me know if this—'

Rebus snatched up the machine and flung it at the wall. The lid flew open, ejecting the tape.

His doorbell rang.

He checked through the spyhole. Could *not* believe it. Opened the door wide.

Kayleigh Burgess took a step back. 'Christ, you look fierce.'

'I *feel* fierce. What the hell do you want?'

She brought a hand from behind her back, showing a bottle of Macallan. 'Peace offering,' she said.

Rebus looked at the bottle, then at her. 'Is this your idea of entrapment?'

'Absolutely not.'

'Any microphones or cameras about your person?'

She shook her head. Strands of curling brown hair came to rest against her cheeks and the sides of her eyes. Rebus stepped back into the hall.

'Lucky for you I've a drouth on me,' he said.

She walked ahead of him into the living room, giving him the chance to study her body. It was every bit as tidy as Feardie Fergie's house.

'Listen,' he said, 'I'm sorry about your tape machine. Send me the bill, I mean it.'

She shrugged, then saw the answering machine. 'What is it with you and technology?'

'Ten seconds, and already the questions have started. Wait here, I'll get the glasses.' He went into the kitchen and closed the door behind him, then gathered up the press cuttings and newspapers from the table, flinging them into a cupboard. He rinsed two glasses, and took his time drying them, staring at the wall above the sink. What was she after? Information, naturally. Gill's face came into his mind. She'd asked him for a favour, and a man had died. As for Kayleigh Burgess ... maybe *she'd* been responsible for Geddes' suicide. He took the glasses through. She was crouched in front of the hi-fi, studying album spines.

'I've never owned a record player,' she said.

'I hear they're the next big thing.' He opened the Macallan and poured. 'I've no ice, though I could probably chip a block off the inside of the freezer.'

She stood up, took her glass from him. 'Neat's fine.'

She was wearing tight black denims, faded at bum and knees, and a denim jacket with fleece lining. Her eyes, he noticed, were slightly bulbous, her eyebrows arched – natural, he thought, not plucked. Sculpted cheekbones, too.

'Sit down,' he said.

She sat on the sofa, legs slightly apart, elbows on knees, holding the drink up to her face.

'It's not your first today, is it?' she asked him.

He sipped, put the glass on the arm of his chair. 'I can stop any time I want.' He held his arms wide. 'See?'

She smiled, drank, watching him above the rim of the glass. He tried to read the signals: coquette, minx, relaxed, sharp-eyed, calculating, amused ...

'Who tipped you off about the inquiry?' he asked.

'You mean who tipped the media in general, or me personally?'

'Whichever.'

'I don't know who started the story, but one journalist told another and it spread from there. A friend of mine on *Scotland on Sunday* phoned me; she knew we were covering the Spaven case already.'

Rebus was thinking: Jim Stevens, standing on the sideline like the team manager. Stevens, Glasgow-based. Chick Ancram, Glasgow-based. Ancram knowing Rebus and Stevens went way back, spilling the story ...

Bastard. No wonder he hadn't invited Rebus to call him Chick.

'I can almost hear the cogs turning.'

A thin smile. 'Pieces falling into place.' He reached for the bottle – had left it within grabbing distance. Kayleigh Burgess rested against the back of the sofa, sliding her legs under her, looking around.

'Nice room. Big.'

'It needs redecorating.'

She nodded. 'Cornices for definite, maybe around the window. I'd turf that out though.' She was referring to a painting above the fireplace: a fishing-boat in a harbour. 'Where's it supposed to be?'

Rebus shrugged. 'Somewhere that's never existed.' He didn't like the painting either, but couldn't conceive of throwing it out.

'You could strip the door,' she went on, 'it'd come up well from the look of it.' She saw his look. 'I've just bought my own place in Glasgow.'

'Nice for you.'

'The ceilings are too high for my liking, but –' His tone of voice caught her. She stopped.

'Sorry,' Rebus said, 'I'm a bit rusty on chit-chat.'

'But not on irony.'

'I get plenty of practice. How's the programme going?'

'I thought you didn't want to discuss it.'

Rebus shrugged. 'Got to be more interesting than DIY.' He got up to refill her glass.

'It's going OK.' She looked up at him; he kept his eyes on her glass. 'Be better if you agreed to be interviewed.'

'No.' He went back to his chair.

'No,' she echoed. 'Well, with you or without you, the programme will go out. It's already scheduled. Have you read Mr Spaven's book?'

'I'm not a great one for fiction.'

She turned to stare at the piles of books near the hi-fi. They called him a liar.

'I've seldom met a prisoner who didn't profess his or her innocence,' Rebus went on. 'It's a survival mechanism.'

'I don't suppose you've ever come across a miscarriage of justice either?'

'I've seen plenty. But the thing is, usually the "miscarriage" was that the criminal was getting away with it. The whole legal system is a miscarriage of justice.'

'Can I quote you on that?'

'This conversation is strictly *off* the record.'

'You're supposed to make that clear before you say anything.'

He wagged a finger at her. 'Off the record.'

She nodded, raised her glass in a toast. 'Here's to off the record remarks.'

Rebus put his glass to his lips, but didn't drink. The whisky was loosening him up, mixing with the exhaustion and a brain that seemed

119

full to bursting. A dangerous cocktail. He knew he'd have to be more careful, starting straight away.

'Want some music?' he asked.

'Is that a subtle change of subject?'

'Questions, questions.' He went over to the hi-fi, slotted in a tape of *Meddle*.

'Who is it?' she asked.

'Pink Floyd.'

'Oh, I like them. Is it a new album?'

'Not exactly.'

He got her talking about her job, how she got into it, her life all the way back to childhood. Now and again she asked a question about *his* past, but he'd shake his head and lead her back into her own story.

She needs a break, he thought, as in a rest. But she was obsessed with her job, maybe this was as close as she could allow herself to come to a respite: she was with *him*, so it counted as work. It came down to guilt again, guilt and the work ethic. He thought of a story: World War One, Christmastime, the opposing sides emerging from their trenches to shake hands, play a game of football, then back into the trenches, picking up their guns again …

After an hour and four whiskies, she was lying on the sofa with one hand behind her head, the other resting on her stomach. She'd taken her jacket off, and was wearing a white sweatshirt beneath. She'd rolled the sleeves up. The lamplight made golden filaments of the hairs on her arms.

'Better get a taxi …' she said quietly, *Tubular Bells* in the background. 'Who's this again?'

Rebus didn't say anything. There was no need to: she was asleep. He could wake her, help her into a taxi. He could drive her home, Glasgow under an hour away at this time of night. But instead he covered her with his duvet, left the music on so low he could barely hear Viv Stanshall's intros. He sat in his chair by the window, a coat covering him. The gas fire was on, warming the room. He'd wait till she woke up in her own time. Then he'd offer a taxi or his services as driver. Let her choose.

He had a lot of thinking to do, a lot of planning. He had an idea about tomorrow and Ancram and the inquiry. He was turning it, shaping it, adding layers. A lot of thinking to do …

He awoke to streetlamp sodium and the feeling that he hadn't been asleep long, looked at the sofa and saw Kayleigh had gone. He was about to close his eyes again when he noticed her denim jacket still lying on the floor where she'd thrown it.

He got up from the chair, still groggy and suddenly not wanting to be. The hall light was on. The kitchen door was open. The light was on in there too ...

She was standing by the table, paracetamol in one hand, a glass of water in the other. The newspaper clippings were spread in front of her. She started when she saw him, then looked at the table.

'I was looking for coffee, thought it might sober me up. I found these instead.'

'Casework,' Rebus said simply.

'I didn't know you were attached to the Johnny Bible inquiry.'

'I'm not.' He gathered up the sheets and put them back in the cupboard. 'There isn't any coffee, I've run out.'

'Water's fine.' She swallowed the tablets.

'Hangover?'

She gulped water, shook her head. 'I think maybe I can head it off.' She looked at him. 'I wasn't snooping, it's important to me that you believe that.'

Rebus shrugged. 'If it finds its way into the programme, we'll both know.'

'Why the interest in Johnny Bible?'

'No reason.' He saw she couldn't accept that. 'It's hard to explain.'

'Try me.'

'I don't know ... call it the end of innocence.'

He drank a couple of glasses of water, let her wander back into the living room by herself. She came out again with her jacket on, pulling her hair out from behind the collar.

'I'd better go.'

'Do you want me to run you somewhere?' She shook her head. 'What about the bottle?'

'Maybe we can finish it another time.'

'I can't guarantee it'll still be here.'

'I can live with that.' She walked to the front door, opened it, turned back towards him.

'Did you hear about the drowning in Ratho?'

'Yes,' he said, face expressionless.

'Fergus McLure, I interviewed him recently.'

'Really?'

'He was a friend of Spaven.'

'I didn't know that.'

'No? Funny, he told me you pulled him in for questioning during the original case. Anything to say to that, Inspector?' She smiled coldly. 'Thought not.'

He locked the door and heard her walking downstairs, then went back into the living room and stood beside the window, looking down. She turned right, heading for The Meadows and a taxi. There was one light on across the road; no sign of Stevens' car. Rebus fixed his eyes on his own reflection. She knew about the Spaven-McLure connection, knew Rebus had interviewed McLure. It was just the kind of ammo Chick Ancram needed. Rebus's reflection stared back at him, mockingly calm. It took all his willpower to stop him punching out the glass.

11

Rebus was on the run – moving target and all that – morning hangover failing to slow him down. He'd packed first thing, a suitcase only half full, left his pager lying on the mantelpiece. The garage where he usually had his MOT done managed to give the Saab a once-over: tyre pressure, oil level. Fifteen minutes for fifteen quid. Only problem they found, the steering was slack.

'So's my driving,' Rebus told them.

He had calls to make, but avoiding his flat, Fort Apache, or any other cop-shop. He thought of the early-opening pubs, but they were like offices – he was known to work out of them. Too big a chance that Ancram would find him. So he used his local launderette, shaking his head at the offer of a service wash – ten per cent discount this week. A 'promotional offer'. Since when did launderettes need promotional offers?

He used the change machine to turn a five-pound note into coins, got coffee and a chocolate biscuit from another machine, and dragged a chair over to the wall-phone. First call: Brian Holmes at his house, a final red card on the 'investigation'. No answer. He didn't leave a message. Second call: Holmes at work. He disguised his voice and listened to a young DC tell him Brian was a no-show so far.

'Is there any message?'

Rebus put down the receiver without saying anything. Maybe Brian was working from home on the 'investigation', not answering the phone. It was possible. Third call: Gill Templer at her office.

'DCI Templer speaking.'

'It's John.' Rebus looked around the launderette. Two customers with their faces in magazines. Soft motor sound of washers and tumble driers. The smell of fabric conditioner. The manageress was loading powder into a machine. Radio on in the background: 'Double Barrel', Dave & Ansel Collins. Idiot lyric.

'You want an update?'

'Why else would I be phoning?'

'You're a smooth operator, DI Rebus.'

'Tell that to Sade. What have you done about Fergie?'

'The notepad's at Howdenhall, no result yet. A forensic team is going into the house today, checking for prints and anything else. They wondered why they were needed.'

'You didn't tell them?'

'I pulled rank. After all, that's what it's for.'

Rebus smiled. 'What about the computer?'

'I'm going back there this afternoon, look through the disks myself. I'll also question the neighbours about visitors, strange cars, all that.'

'And Fergie's business premises?'

'I'm off to his salesroom in half an hour. How am I doing?'

'So far, I can't complain.'

'Good.'

'I'll phone you later, see how it's going.'

'You sound funny.'

'Funny how?'

'Like you're up to something.'

'I'm not the type. Bye, Gill.'

Next call: Fort Apache, direct line to the Shed. Maclay picked up.

'Hello, Heavy,' Rebus said. 'Any messages for me?'

'Are you kidding? I need asbestos mitts for this phone.'

'DCI Ancram?'

'How did you guess?'

'ESP. I've been trying to reach him.'

'Where are you anyway?'

'Laid low, flu or something.'

'You don't sound too bad.'

'I'm putting on a brave face.'

'Are you at home?'

'At a friend's. She's nursing me.'

'Oh aye? Tell me more.'

'Not just now, Heavy. Look, if Ancram phones again ...'

'Which he will.'

'Tell him I'm trying to reach him.'

'Does your Florence Nightingale have a number?'

But Rebus had hung up. He called his own flat, checking the answerphone was still working after the abuse he'd given it. There were two messages, both from Ancram.

'Give me a break,' Rebus said under his breath. Then he finished his coffee and ate the chocolate biscuit, and sat there staring at the windows of the tumble driers. His head felt like he was inside one, looking out.

He made two more calls – T-Bird Oil and Grampian CID – then decided to take a quick run out to Brian Holmes's, chancing that Nell wouldn't be there. It was a narrow terraced house, a nice size for two people. There was a tiny patch of garden out front, in desperate need of work. Hanging baskets were sited either side of the door, gasping for water. He'd thought Nell a keen gardener.

No one answered the door. He went to the window and looked in. They didn't have net curtains; some younger couples didn't bother these days. The living room was a bomb-site, the floor littered with newspapers and magazines, food wrappings, plates and mugs and empty pint glasses. The wastepaper-bin was spilling beer cans. The TV played to an empty room: daytime soap, a tanned couple face to face. They looked more convincing when you couldn't hear them.

Rebus decided to ask next door. A toddler opened the door to him.

'Hiya, cowboy, is your mum in?'

A young woman was coming from the kitchen, wiping her hands on a dishtowel.

'Sorry to bother you,' Rebus said. 'I was looking for Mr Holmes, he lives next door.'

She looked out of the door. 'His car's gone, he always has the same spot.' She pointed to where Rebus's Saab was parked.

'You haven't seen his wife this morning, have you?'

'Not for ages,' the woman said. 'She used to drop by with sweets for Damon.' She rubbed the kid's hair. He shrugged her off and galloped back into the house.

'Well, thanks anyway,' Rebus said.

'He should be back this evening, he doesn't go out much.'

Rebus nodded. He was still nodding when he got to his car. He sat in the driver's seat, hands rubbing the wheel. She'd walked out on him. How long ago? Why hadn't the stubborn sod said anything? Oh sure, cops were famous for releasing their emotions, talking out their personal crises, Rebus himself a case in point.

He drove to the warehouse: no sign of Holmes, but the clerical clerk said he'd been working right up until closing time last night.

'Did he look like he was finished?'

The clerk shook his head. 'Said he'd see me today.'

Rebus thought about leaving a message, decided he couldn't risk it. He got back into the car and drove.

He drove through Pilton and Muirhouse, didn't want to cut too early on to the busy Queensferry Road. Traffic wasn't bad heading out of town – at least it was moving. He got change ready for the toll at the Forth Bridge.

He was going north. Not just to Dundee this trip. He was going to Aberdeen. He didn't know if he was running away, or heading for a confrontation.

No reason it couldn't be both. Cowards made good heroes sometimes. He stuck a tape into the cassette player. Robert Wyatt, *Rock Bottom*.

'Been there, Bob,' he said. And later: 'Cheer up, it might never happen.'

Saying which he switched tapes. Deep Purple playing 'Into the Fire'. The car accelerated just enough.

Furry Boot Town

12

It was a couple of years since Rebus had been in Aberdeen, and then only for an afternoon. He'd been visiting an aunt. She was dead now; he'd found out only after the funeral. She'd lived near Pittodrie Stadium, her old house surrounded by new developments. The house was probably gone now, flattened. For all the associations with granite, Aberdeen had a feeling of impermanence. These days it owed almost everything it had to oil, and the oil wouldn't be there for ever. Growing up in Fife, Rebus had seen the same thing with coal: no one planned for the day it would run out. When it did, hope ran out with it.

Linwood, Bathgate, the Clyde: nobody ever seemed to learn.

Rebus recalled the early oil years, the sound of Lowlanders scurrying north looking for hard work at high wages: unemployed shipbuilders and steelworkers, school-leavers and students. It was Scotland's Eldorado. You sat in Saturday afternoon pubs in Edinburgh and Glasgow, the racing pages folded open, dream horses circled, and spoke of the great escape you could make. There were jobs going spare, a mini-Dallas was being constructed from the husk of a fishing port. It was unbelievable, incredible. It was magic.

People watching J.R. scheme his way through another episode found it easy to fantasise that the same scenario was being played out on the north-east coast. There was an American invasion, and the Americans – roughnecks, bears, roustabouts – didn't want a quiet, self-contained coastal town; they wanted to raise hell, and started building from the ground up. So the initial stories of Eldorado turned into tales from the darkside: brothels, blood-baths, drunken brawls. Corruption was everywhere, the players spoke millions of dollars, and the locals resented the invasion at the same time as they took the cash and available work. For working-class males based south of Aberdeen, it seemed like the word made flesh, not just a man's world but a hardman's world, where respect was demanded and bought with money. It took only weeks for

129

the switch: fit men came back shaking their heads, muttering about slavery, twelve-hour shifts, and the nightmare North Sea.

And somewhere in the middle, between Hell and Eldorado, sat something approximating the truth, nothing like as interesting as the myths. Economically the north-east had profited from oil, and relatively painlessly at that. Like Edinburgh, commercial development had not been allowed to scar the city centre *too* deeply. But on the outskirts you saw the usual industrial estates, the low-rise factory units, a lot of them with names connecting them to the offshore industry: On-Off; Grampian Oil; PlatTech ...

However, before this there was the glory of the drive itself. Rebus stuck as far as possible to the coastal route, and wondered at the mind-set of a nation who would design a golf course along a clifftop. When he stopped at a petrol station for a break, he bought a map of Aberdeen and checked the location of Grampian Police HQ. It was on Queen Street, in the city centre. He hoped the one-way system wasn't going to be a problem. He'd been to Aberdeen maybe half a dozen times in his life, three of those for childhood holidays. Even though it was a modern city, he still joked about it the way a lot of Lowlanders did: it was full of teuchters, fish-gutters with funny accents. When they asked you where you were from, it sounded like they were saying 'Furry boot ye frae?' Thus, Furry Boot Town, while Aberdonians stuck to 'Granite City'. Rebus knew he was going to have to keep the jokes and jibes in check, at least until he had a feel for the place.

Traffic was bottle-necked heading into the centre, which was fine – it meant he had time to study both map and street names. He found Queen Street and parked, walked into Police HQ and told them who he was.

'I spoke to someone on the phone earlier, a DC Shanks.'

'I'll try CID for you,' the uniform on reception said. She told him to take a seat. He sat down and watched the movement of bodies in and out of the station. He could tell the plainclothes officers from ordinary punters – when you made eye contact, you knew. A couple of the men sported CID moustaches, bushy but neatly trimmed. They were young, trying to look older. Some kids were sitting across from him, looking subdued but with a gleam in their eyes. They were fresh-faced and freckly, with bloodless lips. Two of them were fair-haired, one red-headed.

'Inspector Rebus?'

The man was standing over to his right, could have been there a couple of minutes or more. Rebus stood up and they shook hands.

'I'm DS Lumsden, DC Shanks passed your message on. Something about an oil company?'

'Based up here. One of their employees took a flight out of an Edinburgh tenement.'

'Jumped?'

Rebus shrugged. 'There were others on the scene, one of them's a known villain called Anthony Ellis Kane. I've had word he's working up here.'

Lumsden nodded. 'Yes, I heard Edinburgh CID were asking about that name. Doesn't mean a thing to me, sorry. Normally, we'd assign the Oil Liaison Officer to look after you, but he's on holiday and I'm filling in, which makes me your guide for the duration.' Lumsden smiled. 'Welcome to Silver City.'

Silver for the River Dee which ran through it. Silver for the colour of the buildings in sunlight – grey granite transformed into shimmering light. Silver for the money the oil boom had brought. Lumsden explained as Rebus drove them back down on to Union Street.

'Another myth about Aberdeen,' he said, 'is that the folk are mean. Wait till you see Union Street on a Saturday afternoon. It must be the busiest shopping street in Britain.'

Lumsden wore a blue blazer with shiny brass buttons, grey trousers, black slip-on shoes. His shirt was an elegant blue and white stripe, his tie salmon-pink. The clothes made him look like the secretary of some exclusive golf club, but the face and body told another story. He was six feet two, wiry, with cropped fair hair emphasising a widow's peak. His eyes weren't so much red-rimmed as chlorinated, the irises a piercing blue. No wedding ring. He could have been anywhere between thirty and forty years old. Rebus couldn't quite place the accent.

'English?' he asked.

'From Gillingham originally,' Lumsden acknowledged. 'The family moved around a bit. My dad was in the forces. You did well to spot the accent, most people think I'm a Borderer.'

They were driving to a hotel, Rebus having declared that he'd probably be staying at least the one night, maybe more.

'No problem,' Lumsden had said. 'I know just the place.'

The hotel was on Union Terrace, overlooking the gardens, and Lumsden told him to park outside the entrance. He took a piece of card from his pocket and pressed it to the inside of the windscreen. It stated OFFICIAL GRAMPIAN POLICE BUSINESS. Rebus got his case out of the boot, but Lumsden insisted on carrying it. And Lumsden took care of the details at reception. A porter took the case upstairs, Rebus following.

'Just make sure you like the room,' Lumsden told him. 'And I'll see you in the bar.'

The room was on the first floor. It had the tallest windows Rebus had ever seen, and gave him a view down on to the gardens. The room was baking hot. The porter closed the curtains.

'It's always like this when we get the sun,' he explained. Rebus gave the rest of the room a once-over. It was probably the fanciest hotel room he'd ever been in. The porter was watching him.

'What, no champagne?'

The porter didn't get the joke, so Rebus shook his head and handed him a pound note. The porter explained how the in-house movies worked, told him about room service, the restaurant, and other facilities, then handed Rebus his key. Rebus followed the man back downstairs.

The bar was quiet, the lunchtime crowd having disappeared back to work, leaving their plates, bowls and glasses behind. Lumsden was perched on a stool at the bar, munching peanuts and watching MTV. There was a pint of beer in front of him.

'Forgot to ask your tipple,' he said as Rebus sat down next to him.

'A pint of the same,' Rebus told the barman.

'How's the room?'

'A bit rich for my taste, to be honest.'

'Don't worry, Grampian CID will pick up the tab.' He winked. 'It's a courtesy thing.'

'I must visit more often.'

Lumsden smiled. 'So tell me what you want to do while you're here.'

Rebus glanced at the TV screen, saw the Stones hamming it up in their latest production. Jesus, they looked old. Stonehenge with a blues riff.

'Talk to the oil company, maybe see if I can track down a couple of the deceased's friends. Find out if there's any sign of Tony El.'

'Tony El?'

'Anthony Ellis Kane.' Rebus reached into his pocket for his cigarettes. 'Do you mind?'

Lumsden shook his head twice: once to say he didn't mind, and again to refuse Rebus's offer of one.

'Cheers,' Rebus said, taking a mouthful of beer. He smacked his lips, it was OK. Beer was fine. But the row of optics kept trying to attract his attention. 'So how's the Johnny Bible case going?'

Lumsden scooped more peanuts into his mouth. 'It isn't. Dead slow to stop. Are you attached to the Edinburgh side?'

'Only by association. I've interviewed a few nutters.'

Lumsden nodded. 'Me, too. I'd like to throttle some of them. I had to interview some of our RPOs, too.' He made a face. RPOs: Registered Potential Offenders. These were the 'usual suspects', a list of known perverts, sex attackers, flashers and peepers. In a case like Johnny Bible, they all had to be interviewed, alibis provided and checked.

'I hope you took a bath afterwards.'

'Half a dozen at least.'

'No new leads then?'

'Nothing.'

'You think he's local?'

Lumsden shrugged. 'I don't think anything: you need to keep an open mind. Why the interest?'

'What?'

'The interest in Johnny Bible.'

It was Rebus's turn to shrug. They sat in silence for a moment, until Rebus thought of a question. 'What does an Oil Liaison Officer do?'

'Blunt answer: liaises with the oil industry. It's a major player up here. The thing is, Grampian Police isn't just a dry-land force – our beat includes the offshore installations. If there's a theft on a platform, or a fight, or whatever, anything they bother to report, it's down to us to investigate. You can end up flying three hours out to the middle of hell on a paraffin budgie.'

'Paraffin budgie?'

'Helicopter. Three hours out, chucking your guts up along the way, so you can investigate some minor complaint. Thank Christ we don't usually get involved. It's a real frontier out there, with frontier policing.'

One of the Glasgow uniforms had said the same about Uncle Joe's estate.

'You mean they police themselves?'

'It's a bit naughty, but effective. And if it saves me a six-hour round trip I won't say I'm sorry.'

'What about Aberdeen itself?'

'Reasonably quiet, except at weekends. Union Street on a Saturday night can be like downtown Saigon. There are a lot of frustrated kids around. They've grown up with money and stories of money. Now they want their share, only it's not there any more. Christ, that was quick.'

133

Rebus saw that he'd finished his pint; only the top inch was missing from Lumsden's. 'I like a man who's not afraid to bevvy.'

'I'll get this one,' Rebus said. The barman was standing ready. Lumsden didn't want another, so Rebus ordered an abstemious half. First impressions and all that.

'The room's yours for as long as you need it,' Lumsden said. 'Don't pay cash for that drink, charge it to the room. Meals aren't included, but I can let you have a few addresses. Tell them you're a cop, you'll find the bill pretty reasonable.'

'Tut tut,' Rebus said.

Lumsden smiled again. 'Some fellow officers I wouldn't tell that to, but somehow I think we're on the same wavelength. Am I right?'

'You could be.'

'I'm not often wrong. Who knows, my next posting could be Edinburgh. A friendly face is always an asset.'

'Speaking of which, I don't want my presence here broadcast.'

'Oh?'

'The media are after me. They're making a programme about a case, ancient history, and they want to talk to me.'

'I get the idea.'

'They may try tracking me down, phoning up pretending to be colleagues ...'

'Well, no one knows you're here except me and DC Shanks. I'll try to keep it that way.'

'I'd appreciate it. They may try using the name Ancram. That's the reporter.'

Lumsden winked, finished the bowl of peanuts. 'Your secret's safe with me.'

They finished their drinks and Lumsden said he had to get back to the station. He gave Rebus his telephone numbers – office and home – and took note of Rebus's room number.

'Anything I can do, give me a call,' he said.

'Thanks.'

'You know how to get to T-Bird Oil?'

'I've got a map.'

Lumsden nodded. 'What about tonight? Fancy going for a meal?'

'Great.'

'I'll drop by about seven-thirty.'

They shook hands again. Rebus watched him leave, then headed back to the bar for a whisky. As advised, he charged it to the room, and took it upstairs. With the curtains closed, the room was cooler but still airless. He looked to see if he could open the windows, but couldn't. They had to be twelve feet high. With the curtains closed, he lay on the bed and slipped off his shoes, then replayed his conversation with Lumsden. It was something he did, usually finding things he could have said, better ways of saying them. Suddenly he sat up. Lumsden had mentioned T-Bird Oil, but Rebus couldn't recall telling him the name of the company. Maybe he had ... or maybe he'd mentioned it to DC Shanks over the phone, and Shanks had told Lumsden.

He didn't feel relaxed any more, so prowled the room. In one of the drawers he found material about Aberdeen, tourist stuff, PR stuff. He sat down at the dressing table and started to go through it. The facts came with a zealot's force.

Fifty thousand people in the Grampian region worked in the oil and gas industry, twenty per cent of total employment. Since the early seventies, the area's population had increased by sixty thousand, housing stock had increased by a third, creating major new suburbs around Aberdeen. A thousand acres of industrial land had been developed around the city. Aberdeen Airport had seen a tenfold increase in passenger numbers, and was now the world's busiest heliport. There wasn't a negative comment anywhere in the literature, except for the minor mention of a fishing village called Old Torry, which had been granted its charter three years after Columbus landed in America. When oil came to the north-east, Old Torry was flattened to make way for a Shell supply base. Rebus raised his glass and toasted the memory of the village.

He showered, changed his clothes, and headed back to the bar. A flustered-looking woman in long tartan skirt and white blouse came bustling up to him.

'Are you with the convention?'

He shook his head, and remembered reading about it: pollution in the North Sea or something. Eventually the woman shepherded three corpulent businessmen out of the hotel. Rebus went into the lobby and watched a limo take them away. He checked his watch. Time to go.

Finding Dyce was easy, he just followed signs to the airport. Sure enough, he saw helicopters in the sky. The area around the airport was a mix of farming land, new hotels, and industrial complexes. T-Bird Oil had its headquarters in a modest three-storey hexagon, most of it smoked glass. There was a car park at the front, and landscaped gardens with a path meandering through them to the building itself. In the distance, light aircraft were taking off and landing.

The reception area was spacious and light. Under glass there were models of the North Sea oilfields and of some of T-Bird's production platforms. Bannock was the biggest as well as the oldest. A scale-sized double-decker bus had been placed beside it, dwarfed by the rig. There were huge colour photos and diagrams on the walls, along with a slew of framed awards. The receptionist told him he was expected, and should take the lift to the first floor. The lift was mirrored, and Rebus examined himself. He remembered taking the lift up to Allan Mitchison's flat, Bain shadow-boxing his reflection. Rebus knew if he tried that just now, his reflection would probably win. He crunched down on another mint.

A pretty girl was waiting for him. She asked him to follow her, not exactly an onerous task. They moved through an open plan office, only half the desks in current use. There were TVs switched on to Teletext news, share indices, CNN. They came out of the office into another corridor, much quieter, deep carpeting underfoot. At the second door, which was open, the girl gestured for Rebus to enter.

Stuart Minchell's name was on the door, so Rebus assumed the man rising to his feet to shake hands was Minchell.

'Inspector Rebus? Nice to meet you at last.'

It was true what they said about voices, you could seldom pin the right face and body to them. Minchell spoke with authority, but looked too young – mid-twenties tops, with a sheen to his face, red cheeks, short slicked-back hair. He wore round metal-framed glasses and had thick dark eyebrows, making the face seem mischievous. He still affected wide red braces with his trousers. When he half-turned, Rebus saw his hair at the back had been coaxed into the beginnings of a ponytail.

'Coffee or tea?' the girl was asking.

'No time, Sabrina,' Minchell said. He opened his arms wide to Rebus in apology. 'Change of plan, Inspector. I have to be at the North Sea Conference. I did try reaching you to warn you.'

'That's all right.' Rebus was thinking: shit. If he called Fort Apache, that means they'll know I'm up here.

'I thought we could take my car, talk on the way out there. I should only be half an hour or so. If you've any questions, we can talk afterwards.'

'That'll be fine.'

Minchell was shrugging into his jacket.

'Files,' Sabrina reminded him.

'Check.' He picked up half a dozen, stuffed them into a briefcase.

'Business cards.'

He opened his Filofax, saw he had a supply. 'Check.'

'Cellphone.'

He patted his pocket, nodded. 'Is the car ready?'

Sabrina said she'd check, and went to find her phone.

'We may as well wait downstairs,' Minchell said.

'Check,' said Rebus.

They waited for the lift. When it came, there were already two men inside, which still left room. Minchell hesitated. He looked like he was about to say they'd wait, but Rebus had already stepped into the lift, so he followed, with a slight bow to one of the men, the elder of the two.

Rebus watched in the mirror, saw the elder man staring back at him. He had long yellow-silver hair swept back from his forehead and behind both ears. He rested his hands on a silver-topped cane and wore a baggy linen suit. He looked like a character out of Tennessee Williams, his face chiselled and frowning, gait only slightly stooped despite his years. Rebus looked down and noticed the man was wearing a pair of well-worn trainers. The man brought a notepad out of his pocket, scribbled something on it while still holding his cane, tore the sheet off and handed it to the second man, who read it and nodded.

The lift opened at the ground floor. Minchell physically held Rebus back until the other two had got out. Rebus watched them march to the front door of the building, the man with the note veering off to make a call at reception. There was a red Jaguar parked directly outside. A liveried chauffeur held the back door open for Big Daddy.

Minchell was rubbing his brow with the fingers of one hand.

'Who was that?' Rebus asked.

'That was Major Weir.'

'Wish I'd known, I'd've asked him why I can't get Green Shield stamps with my petrol any more.'

Minchell wasn't in the mood for a joke.

'What was the note all about?' Rebus asked.

'The Major doesn't say much. He communicates better on paper.' Rebus laughed: communication breakdown. 'I'm serious,' Minchell said. 'I don't think I've heard him say more than a couple of dozen words all the time I've worked for him.'

'Something wrong with his voice?'

'No, he sounds fine, a little croaky, but that's to be expected. Thing is, his accent is American.'

'So?'

'So he wishes it was Scottish.'

With the Jag gone, they walked out to the car park. 'He's got this obsession with Scotland,' Minchell went on. 'His parents were Scots migrants, used to tell him stories about the "old country". He got hooked. He only spends maybe a third of the year here – T-Bird Oil stretches around the globe – but you can tell he hates to leave.'

'Anything else I should know?'

'He's a strict teetotaller, one whiff of alcohol from an employee and they're out.'

'Is he married?'

'Widower. His wife's buried on Islay or somewhere like that. This is my car.'

It was a midnight-blue Mazda racing model, low-slung with just enough room for two bucket seats. Minchell's briefcase all but filled the back. He hooked his phone up before turning the ignition.

'He had a son,' Minchell went on, 'but I think he died, too, or was disinherited. The Major won't talk about him. Do you want the good news or the bad?'

'Let's try the bad.'

'Still no sign of Jake Harley, he hasn't returned from his walking holiday. He's due back in a couple of days.'

'I'd like to head up to Sullom Voe anyway,' Rebus said. Especially if Ancram were going to be able to track him to Aberdeen.

'No problem with that. We'll get you up there on a chopper.'

'What's the good news?'

'Good news is, I've arranged for you to take another chopper out to Bannock to talk to Willie Ford. And as it's a day-trip, you won't need any survival training. Believe me, *that's* good news. Part of the training, they belt you into a simulator and tip you into a swimming pool.'

'You've been there?'

'Oh, yes. Anyone making more than ten day-trips a year has to. Scared the hell out of me.'

'But the helicopters are safe enough?'

'Don't worry about that. And you're lucky just now: a nice window.' He saw Rebus's blank look. 'A window in the weather, no major storms brewing. See, oil is an all-year industry, but it's also seasonal. We can't always get to and from the platforms, it depends on the weather. If we want to tow a rig out to sea, we need to plot a window, then hope for the best. The weather out there ...' Minchell shook his head. 'Sometimes it can make you believe in the Almighty.'

'Old Testament variety?' Rebus guessed. Minchell smiled and nodded, then made a call on his phone.

They came out of Dyce and into Bridge of Don, following signs to the Aberdeen Exhibition and Conference Centre. Rebus waited until Minchell had finished his call before asking a question.

'Where was Major Weir headed?'

'Same place we are. He's got to make a speech.'

'I thought you said he doesn't speak.'

'He doesn't. That man with him was his PR guru, Hayden Fletcher. He'll read the speech. The Major will sit beside him and listen.'

'Does that count as eccentric?'

'Not when you're worth a hundred million dollars.'

13

The Conference Centre car park was full of upper-tier management models: Mercs, Beamers, Jags, the occasional Bentley or Roller. A huddle of chauffeurs smoked cigarettes and swapped anecdotes.

'Might have been better PR if you'd all come on bikes,' Rebus said, getting his first view of a demo outside the prism-shaped dome which marked the entrance to the Centre. Someone had unfurled a huge banner from the roof, painted green on white: DON'T KILL OUR OCEANS! Security personnel were up there, trying to haul it in while still retaining their balance and dignity. Someone with a megaphone was leading the chant. There were demonstrators in full combat kit and radiation hoods, and others dressed up as mermaids and mermen, plus an inflatable whale which, gusted by the wind, was in danger of snapping its moorings. Uniformed police patrolled the demo, speaking into their shoulder radios. Rebus guessed there'd be a wagon nearby with the heavier artillery: riot shields, visors, US-style defence batons … It didn't look like that kind of demo, not yet.

'We're going to have to go through them,' Minchell said. 'I *hate* this. We're spending millions on environmental protection. I'm even a member of Greenpeace, Oxfam, you name it. But every bloody year it's the same.' He grabbed his briefcase and cellphone, remote-locked the car and set its alarm, then headed for the doors.

'You're supposed to have a delegate badge to get in,' he explained. 'But just show a warrant card or something. I'm sure it won't be a problem.'

They were close to the main demo now. There was background music through a portable PA, a song about whales, or maybe it was Wales. Rebus recognised the vocal style: The Dancing Pigs. People were shoving flyers at him. He took one of each and thanked them. A young woman was pacing in front of him like a caged leopard. She controlled the megaphone. Her voice was nasal and North American.

'Decisions made now will affect your children's grandchildren! You can't put a price on the future! Put the future first, for everybody's sake!'

She looked at Rebus as he passed her. Her face was blank, no hate, no recrimination, just working. Her bleached hair was rat-tailed, threaded with bright braids, one of which fell down the middle of her forehead.

'Kill the oceans and you kill the planet! Put Mother Earth before profits!'

Rebus was convinced even before he reached the door.

There was a bin inside, where the flyers were being dumped. But Rebus folded his and put them in his pocket. Two guards wanted to see ID, but his warrant card, as predicted, was effective. There were more guards patrolling the concourse – private security, uniformed, wearing shiny caps which meant nothing. They'd probably had a one-day crash course in menacing pleasantry. The concourse itself was full of suits. Messages were being relayed over a PA system. There were static displays, tables piled high with literature, sales pitches for God knows what. Some of the booths looked to be doing good business. Minchell excused himself and said he'd meet Rebus at the main doors in about half an hour. He said he had to do some 'schmoozing'. This seemed to mean shaking hands with people, smiling, giving them a few words and in some cases his business card, then moving on. Rebus quickly lost him.

Rebus didn't see too many pictures of rigs, and those he did see were tension legs and semi-submersibles. The real excitement seemed to be FPSOs – Floating Production, Storage and Offloading Systems – which were like tankers, but did away with the need for a platform altogether. Flowlines connected straight to the FPSO, and it could store 300,000 barrels of oil.

'Impressive, isn't she?' a Scandinavian in a salesman's suit asked Rebus. Rebus nodded.

'No need for a platform.'

'And easier to scrap when the time comes. Cheap *and* environmental.' The man paused. 'Interested in leasing one?'

'Where would I park it?' He walked off before the salesman could translate.

Maybe it was his tracker's nose, but he found the bar with no difficulty and settled at the far end with a whisky and a bowl of nibbles. Lunch had been a petrol station sandwich, so he tucked in. A man came and stood next to him, wiped his face with a huge white handkerchief and asked for a soda water with lots of ice.

'Why do I still come to these things?' the man growled. His accent was pitched somewhere in mid-Atlantic. He was tall and thin, his reddish hair thinning. The flesh around his neck was slack, putting him in his early fifties, though he could have passed for five years younger. Rebus didn't have an answer for him, so said nothing. The drink arrived, and he downed it in one, then ordered another. 'Want one?' he asked.

'No, thanks.'

The man noticed that Rebus's photocard was missing. 'Are you a delegate?'

Rebus shook his head. 'Observer.'

'The newspaper?'

Rebus shook his head again.

'Thought not. Oil's only news when something goes wrong. It's bigger than the nuclear industry, but gets half the coverage.'

'That's good, isn't it, if the news they're printing is all bad?'

The man thought about this, then laughed, showing perfect teeth. 'You've got me there.' He wiped his face again. 'So what exactly are you observing?'

'I'm off duty right now.'

'Lucky you.'

'So what do you do?'

'I work my guts out. But I have to tell you, my company's just about given up trying to sell to the oil industry. They'd rather buy Yank or Scandinavian. Well, fuck them. No wonder Scotland's down the pan … and we want independence.' The man shook his head, then leaned forwards over the bar. Rebus did likewise: co-conspirator. 'Mostly what I do is, I attend boring conventions like this. And I go home at night and wonder what it's all about. You sure about that drink?'

'Go on then.'

So Rebus let the man buy him a drink. The way he had said 'fuck them' made Rebus think he didn't swear that often. It was just something he did to break the ice, to show he was speaking man to man; off the record, as it were. Rebus offered a cigarette, but his friend shook his head.

'Gave them up years ago. Don't think I'm not still tempted.' He paused, looked around the bar. 'Know who I'd like to be?' Rebus shrugged. 'Go on, guess.'

'I wouldn't know where to start.'

'Sean Connery.' The man nodded. 'Think about it, with what he earns per film, he could give a pound to every man, woman and child in this country, and *still* have a couple of mill left over. Isn't that incredible?'

'So if you were Sean Connery, you'd give everyone a pound?'

'I'd be the world's sexiest man, what would I need money for?'

It was a good point, so they drank to it. Only thing was, talking about Sean reminded Rebus of Ancram, Sean's lookalike. He checked his watch, saw that he had to leave.

'Can I buy you one before I go?'

The man shook his head, then produced his business card, doing so in a slick movement, like a magician. 'In case you ever need it. My name's Ryan, by the way.' Rebus read the card: Ryan Slocum, Sales Manager, Engineering Division, and a company masthead: Eugene Construction.

'John Rebus,' he said, shaking Slocum's hand.

'John Rebus,' Slocum said, nodding. 'No business card, John?'

'I'm a police officer.'

Slocum's eyes widened. 'Did I say anything incriminating?'

'Wouldn't bother me if you did. I'm based in Edinburgh.'

'A long way from home. Is it Johnny Bible?'

'Why do you say that?'

'He's killed in both cities, hasn't he?'

Rebus nodded. 'No, it's not Johnny Bible. Take care, Ryan.'

'You too. It's a mad bad world out there.'

'Isn't it just?'

Stuart Minchell was waiting for him at the doors. 'Anything else you'd like to see, or shall we head back?'

'Let's go.'

Lumsden called up to his room, and Rebus came downstairs to meet him. Lumsden was well-dressed, but casual – the blazer swapped for a cream jacket, yellow shirt open at the neck.

'So,' Rebus said, 'do I call you Lumsden all night?'

'First name's Ludovic.'

'Ludovic Lumsden?'

'My parents had a sense of humour. Friends call me Ludo.'

The evening was warm and still light. Birds were noisy in the gardens, and fat seagulls were picking their way along the pavements.

'It'll stay light till ten, maybe eleven,' Lumsden explained.

'Those are the fattest seagulls I've ever seen.'

'I hate them. Look at the state of the pavements.'

It was true, the slabs underfoot were speckled with birdshit. 'Where are we going?' Rebus asked.

'Call it a mystery tour. It's all within walking distance. You like mystery tours?'

'I like having a guide.'

Their first stop was an Italian restaurant, where Lumsden was well known. Everyone seemed to want to shake his hand, and the proprietor took him aside for a quiet word, apologising to Rebus beforehand.

'The Italians up here are docile,' Lumsden explained later. 'They never quite managed to run the town.'

'So who does?'

Lumsden considered the question. 'A mixture.'

'Any Americans?'

Lumsden looked at him, nodded. 'They run a lot of the clubs and some of the newer hotels. Service industry stuff. They arrived in the seventies, never moved away. Do you want to go to a club later?'

Rebus shrugged. 'It sounds almost respectable.'

Lumsden laughed. 'Oh, you want *sleaze*? That's supposed to be what Aberdeen's about, right? You've got the wrong idea. The city is strictly corporate. Later on, if you really want, I'll take you down by the docks: strippers and hard drinkers, but a tiny minority.'

'Living down south, you hear stories.'

'Of course you do: high-class brothels, dope and porn, gambling and alcohol. We hear the stories, too. But as for *seeing* the stuff ...' Lumsden shook his head. 'The oil industry's pretty tame really. The roughnecks have all but disappeared. Oil's gone legit.'

Rebus was almost convinced, but Lumsden was trying too hard. He kept talking, and the more he talked the less Rebus believed. The owner came over for another word, drew Lumsden away to a corner of the restaurant. Lumsden kept a hand on the man's back, patting it. He flattened his tie as he sat down again.

'His son's running wild,' Lumsden explained. He shrugged, as if there were nothing more to say, and told Rebus to try the meatballs.

Afterwards, there was a nightclub, where businessmen vied with young turks for the attentions of the daytime shopworkers turned Lycra vixens. The music was loud and so were the clothes. Lumsden nodded his head to the pulse, but didn't look like he was enjoying himself. He looked like a tour guide. Ludo: player of games. Rebus knew he was being sold a line, the same line any tourists to the north would be sold – this was the country of Baxter's soups, men in skirts, and granny's hieland hame; oil was just another industry, the city and its people had risen above it. There was still a sense of Highland perspective.

There was no down side.

'I thought you might find this place interesting,' Lumsden yelled over the music.

'Why?'

'It's where Michelle Strachan met Johnny Bible.'

Rebus tried to swallow, couldn't. He hadn't noticed the name of the club. He looked with new eyes, saw dancers and drinkers, saw proprietorial arms around unwilling necks. Saw hungry eyes and money used for mating. He imagined Johnny Bible standing quietly by the bar, ticking off possibles in his mind, narrowing the options down to one. Then asking Michelle Fifer for a dance …

When Rebus suggested they move on, Lumsden didn't disagree. So far, they'd paid for one round of drinks: the restaurant meal had been 'taken care of', and the bouncer on the door of the club had nodded them through, bypassing the cash desk.

As they left, a man escorted a young woman past them. Rebus half-turned his head.

'Someone you know?' Lumsden asked.

Rebus shrugged. 'Thought I recognised the face.' He'd seen it only that afternoon: dark curly hair, glasses, olive complexion. Hayden Fletcher, Major Weir's 'PR guru'. He was looking like he'd had a good day. Fletcher's companion glanced back at Rebus and smiled.

Outside, there were still slants of purple light in the sky. In a cemetery across the road, starlings were mobbing a tree.

'Where now?' Lumsden said.

Rebus stretched his spine. 'Actually, Ludo, I think I'll just head back to the hotel. Sorry to wimp out like this.'

Lumsden tried not to look relieved. 'So what's your itinerary tomorrow?'

Suddenly Rebus didn't want him to know. 'Another meeting with the deceased's employer.' Lumsden seemed satisfied.

'And then home?'

'In a couple of days.'

Lumsden tried not to let his disappointment show. 'Well,' he said, 'get a good night's sleep. You know your way back?'

Rebus nodded and they shook hands. Lumsden headed off one way, Rebus the other. He kept walking in the direction of the hotel, taking his time, window-shopping, checking behind him. Then he stopped and consulted his map, saw that the harbour area was almost walking distance. But the first taxi that came along, he flagged it down.

'Where to?' the driver asked.

'Somewhere I can get a good drink. Somewhere down by the docks.' He thought: 'Down Where the Drunkards Roll.'

'How rough do you want?'

'As rough as it gets.'

The man nodded, started off. Rebus leaned forward in his seat. 'I thought the city would be livelier.'

'Ach, it's a bit early yet. And mind, the weekends are wild. Pay-packets coming off the rigs.'

'A lot of drinking.'

'A lot of *everything*.'

'I hear all the clubs are owned by Americans.'

'Yanks,' the driver said. 'They're everywhere.'

'Illegal as well as legal?'

The driver stared at him in his rearview. 'What were you after in particular?'

'Maybe something to get me high.'

'You don't look the type.'

'What does the type look like?'

'It doesn't look like a copper.'

Rebus laughed. 'Off-duty and playing away from home.'

'Where's home?'

'Edinburgh.'

The driver nodded thoughtfully. 'If *I* wanted to get high,' he said, 'I'd maybe think about Burke's Club on College Street. This is us.'

He pulled the cab to a stop. The meter read just over two pounds; Rebus handed over five and told him to keep the change. The driver leaned out of his window.

'You weren't a hundred yards from Burke's when I picked you up.'

'I know.' Of course he knew: Burke's was where Johnny Bible had met Michelle.

As the cab drew away, he took stock of his surroundings. Right across the road was the harbour, boats moored there, lights showing where men were still working – maintenance crews probably. This side of the road was a mix of tenements, shops and pubs. A couple of girls were working the street, but traffic was quiet. Rebus was outside a place called the Yardarm. It promised karaoke nights, exotic dancers, a happy hour, guest beers, satellite TV, and 'a warm welcome'.

As Rebus pushed open the door, he felt the warmth straight off. It was broiling inside. It took him a full minute to work his way to the bar, by which time the smoke was stinging even his hardened eyes. Some of the customers looked like fishermen – cherry faces, slick hair and thick jerseys. Others had hands blackened with oil – dockside mechanics. The women had eyes drooping from drunkenness, faces either too heavily made-up or else needing to be. At the bar, he ordered a double whisky. Now that the metric system had taken over, he could never remember whether thirty-five mils was less or more than a quarter gill. Last time he'd seen so many drunks in the same place had been after a Hibs/ Hearts match. He'd been drinking down Easter Road, and Hibs had won. Pandemonium.

It took him five minutes to engage in conversation with his neighbour, who used to work on the rigs. He was short and wiry, already completely bald in his thirties, and wore Buddy Holly glasses with jam-jar lenses. He had worked in the canteen.

'Best of fucking food every day. Three menus, two shifts. Top quality. The new arrivals always stuffed themselves, but they soon learned.'

'Did you work two weeks on, two off?'

'Everybody did. Seven-day weeks at that.' The man's face was pointing down at the bar as he spoke, like his head was too heavy to lift. 'You got hooked on it. The time I spent on land, I couldn't settle, couldn't wait to get back offshore.'

'So what happened?'

'Times got tougher. I was surplus to requirements.'

'I hear the rigs are hoaching with dope. Did you ever see any?'

'Fuck aye, all over the place. Just for relaxation, understand? Nobody was daft enough to go out to work wired up. One false move, a pipe can have your hand off – I know, I've seen it. Or if you lose your balance, I mean, it's a two-hundred fucking foot drop to the water. But there was plenty of dope, plenty of booze. And I'll tell you, there might not have been any women, but we had scud mags and films up to our ears. Never seen the like. All tastes catered for, and some of them were pretty disgusting. That's a man of the world talking, so you know what I mean.'

Rebus thought he did. He bought the wee man a drink. If his companion leaned any lower over the bar, his nose would be in the glass. When someone announced that the karaoke would start in five minutes, Rebus knew it was time to leave. Been there, done that. He used his map to guide him back towards Union Street. The night was growing livelier. Groups of teenagers were roaming, police wagons –

plain blue Transits – checking them out. There was a strong uniformed presence, but nobody seemed intimidated. People were roaring, singing, clapping their hands. Midweek Aberdeen was like Edinburgh on a bad Saturday night. A couple of woolly suits were discussing something with two young men, while girlfriends stood by chewing gum. A wagon was parked next to them, its back doors open.

I'm just a tourist here, Rebus told himself, walking past.

He took a wrong turn somewhere, ended up approaching his hotel from the opposite direction, passing a large statue of William Wallace brandishing a claymore.

'Evening, Mel,' Rebus said.

He climbed the hotel steps, decided on a nightcap, one to take up to his room. The bar was full of conventioneers, some of them still wearing their delegate badges. They sat at tables awash with empty glasses. A lone woman was perched at the bar, smoking a black cigarette, blowing the smoke ceilingwards. She had peroxide hair and wore a lot of gold. Her two-piece suit was crimson, her tights or stockings black. Rebus looked at her and decided they were stockings. Her face was hard, the hair pulled back and held with a large gold clasp. There was powder on her cheeks, and dark gloss lipstick on her lips. Maybe Rebus's age; maybe even a year or two older – the sort of woman men called 'handsome'. She'd had a couple of drinks, which was perhaps why she smiled.

'Are you with the convention?' she asked.

'No.'

'Thank Christ for that. I swear every one of them's tried chatting me up, but all they can talk about is crude.' She paused. 'As in crude oil – dead crude and live crude. Did you know there was a difference?'

Rebus smiled, shook his head and ordered his drink. 'Do you want another, or does that count as a chat-up line?'

'It does and I will.' She saw him looking at her cigarette. 'Sobranie.'

'Does the black paper make them taste any better?'

'The *tobacco* makes them taste better.'

Rebus got out his own pack. 'I'm a wood-shavings man myself.'

'So I see.'

The drinks arrived. Rebus signed the chit to charge them to his room.

'Are you here on business?' Her voice was deep, west coast or thereabouts, working-class educated.

'Sort of. What about you?'

'Business. So what do you do?'

World's worst reply to a chat-up: 'I'm a police officer.'

She raised one eyebrow, interested. 'CID?'

'Yes.'

'Are you working on the Johnny Bible case?'

'No.'

'The way the papers tell it, I thought every policeman in Scotland was.'

'I'm the exception.'

'I remember Bible John,' she said, sucking on the cigarette. 'I was brought up in Glasgow. For weeks my mum wouldn't let me out of the house. It was like being in the clink.'

'He did that to a lot of women.'

'And now it's all happening again.' She paused. 'When I said I remembered Bible John, your line should have been, "You don't look old enough".'

'Which proves I'm not chatting you up.'

She stared at him. 'Pity,' she said, reaching for her drink. Rebus used his own glass as a prop, too, buying time. She'd given him all the information he needed. He had to decide whether to act on it or not. Ask her up to his room? Or plead ... what exactly? Guilt? Fear? Self-loathing?

Fear.

He saw the way the night could go, trying to extract beauty from need, passion from a certain despair.

'I'm flattered,' he said at last.

'Don't be,' she said quickly. His move again, an amateur chess player thrown against a pro.

'So what do *you* do?'

She turned to him. Her eyes said that she knew every tactic in this game. 'I'm in sales. Products for the oil industry.' She angled her head towards the rest of the men in the bar. 'I may have to work with them, but nobody says I have to share my time off with them.'

'You live in Aberdeen?'

She shook her head. 'Let me get you another.'

'I've an early start tomorrow.'

'One more won't hurt.'

'It might,' Rebus said, holding her gaze.

'Well,' she said, 'bang goes the perfect end to a perfectly shitty day.'

'Sorry.'

'Don't worry about it.'

He felt her eyes on him as he walked out of the bar towards

reception. He had to force his feet up the stairs towards his room. Her pull was strong. He realised he didn't even know her name.

He switched on the TV while he got undressed. Some sub-Hollywood garbage: the women looked like skeletons with lipstick; the men acted with their necks – he'd seen barbers with more Method. He thought of the woman again. Was she on the game? Definitely not. But she'd hit on him quick. He'd told her he was flattered; in truth, he was bemused. Rebus had always found relationships with the opposite sex difficult. He'd grown up in a mining village, a bit behind the times when it came to things like promiscuity. You stuck your hand in a girl's blouse and next thing her father was after you with a leather belt.

Then he'd joined the army, where women were by turns fantasy figures and untouchables: slags and madonnas, there seemed no middle ground. Released from the army, he'd joined the police. Married by then, but his job had proved more seductive, more all-consuming than the relationship – than *any* relationship. Since then, his affairs had lasted months, weeks, mere days sometimes. Too late now, he felt, for anything more permanent. Women seemed to like him – that wasn't the problem. The problem lay somewhere inside him, and it hadn't been eased by things like the Johnny Bible case, by women abused and then killed. Rape was all about power; killing, too, in its way. And wasn't power the ultimate male fantasy? And didn't he sometimes dream of it, too?

He'd seen the post mortem photos of Angie Riddell, and the first thought that had come to him, the thought he'd had to push past, was: *good body*. It had bothered him, because in that instant she'd been just another object. Then the pathologist had got to work, and she had stopped being even that.

He was asleep as soon as his head touched the pillow. His prayer, as every night, was that there would be no dreams. He woke up in darkness, his back drenched in sweat, and to a ticking noise. It wasn't a clock, not even his watch. His watch was on the cabinet. This was closer, much more intimate. Was it coming from the wall? The headboard? He switched the light on, but the sound had stopped. Woodworm maybe? He couldn't find any holes in the headboard's wooden surround. He switched the lamp off and closed his eyes. There it was again: more geiger counter than metronome. He tried to ignore it, but it was too close. It was inescapable. It was the pillow, his feather pillow. There was something inside, something alive. Would it want to crawl into his ear? Lay its eggs there? Mutate or pupate or just enjoy a snack of wax and eardrum? Sweat cooled on his back and on the sheet beneath him. There was no air in the room. He was too tired to get up, too nervy to sleep. He did what he had to do – tossed the pillow towards the door.

No more ticking, but still he couldn't sleep. The ringing phone came as a relief. Maybe it was the woman from the bar. He'd tell her, I'm an alcoholic, a fuck-up, I'm no good for any other human being.

'Hello?'

'It's Ludo here, sorry to wake you.'

'I wasn't asleep. What's the problem?'

'A patrol car's coming to pick you up.' Rebus grimaced: had Ancram tracked him down already?

'What for?'

'A suicide in Stonehaven. Thought you might be interested. The name appears to be Anthony Ellis Kane.'

Rebus shot out of bed. 'Tony El? Suicide?'

'Looks like. The car should be there in five minutes.'

'I'll be ready.'

*

Now that John Rebus was in Aberdeen, things were more dangerous.

John Rebus.

The librarian's list had first thrown up the name, along with an address in Arden Street, Edinburgh EH9. With a short-term reader's ticket, Rebus had consulted editions of *The Scotsman* from February 1968 to December 1969. Four others had consulted the same sets of microfilm during the previous six months. Two were known to Bible John as journalists, the third was an author – he'd written a chapter on the case for a book on Scottish murderers. As for the fourth ... the fourth had given his name as Peter Manuel. It would have meant nothing to the librarian writing out another short-term reader's ticket. But the real Peter Manuel had killed up to a dozen people in the 1950s, and been hanged for it at Barlinnie Prison. It became clear to Bible John: the Upstart had been reading up on famous murderers, and in the course of his studies had come across both Manuel and Bible John. Narrowing his search, he'd decided to concentrate his research on Bible John, learning more about the case by reading newspapers from the period. 'Peter Manuel' had requested not only *Scotsman*s from 1968–70, but *Glasgow Herald*s too.

His was to be thorough research. And the address on his reader's ticket was as fictitious as his name: Lanark Terrace, Aberdeen. The real Peter Manuel had carried out his killing spree in Lanarkshire.

But though the address be false, Bible John wondered about Aberdeen. His own investigations had already led him to site the Upstart in the Aberdeen area. This seemed a further connection. And now John Rebus was in Aberdeen, too ... Bible John had been pondering John Rebus, even before he knew who he was. He was at first an enigma, and now a problem. Bible John had scanned some of the Upstart's most recent cuttings into the computer, and browsed through them while he wondered what to do about the policeman. He read another policeman's words: 'This person needs help, and we would ask him to come forward so that we can help him.' Followed by more speculation. They were whistling in the dark.

Except that one of them was in Aberdeen.

And Bible John had given him his business card.

He'd always known that it would be dangerous, tracking down the Upstart, but he could hardly have expected to bump into a policeman along the way. And not just any officer, but someone who'd been looking at the Bible John case. John Rebus, policeman, based in Edinburgh, address in Arden Street, currently in Aberdeen ... He decided to open a new file on his computer, dedicated to Rebus. He had looked through some recent papers, and thought he'd found why Rebus was in Aberdeen: an oil-worker had fallen from a tenement window in Edinburgh, foul play suspected. Reasonable to conclude that Rebus was working that case rather than any other. But there was still the fact that Rebus had been reading up on the Bible John case. Why? What business was it of his?

And a second fact, more problematical still: Rebus now had his business card. It wouldn't mean anything to him, couldn't, not yet. But there might come a time ... the closer he came to the Upstart, the more risks he would face. The card might mean something to the policeman sometime down the road. Could Bible John risk that? He seemed to have two options: quicken his hunt for the Upstart.

Or take the policeman out of the game.

He would think it over. Meantime, he had to concentrate on the Upstart.

His contact at the National Library had informed him that a reader's ticket required proof of identity: driver's licence, something like that. Maybe the Upstart had forged himself a whole new identity as 'Peter Manuel', but Bible John doubted it. More likely he had managed to talk himself past proving his identity. He would be good at talking. He'd be ingratiating, wheedling. He wouldn't look like a monster. His would be a face women – and men – could trust. He was able to walk out of night clubs with women he'd met only an hour or two before. Getting round a security check would have posed him few problems.

He stood up and examined his face in the mirror. The police had issued a series of photofits, computer generated, ageing the original photofit of Bible John. One of them wasn't a bad likeness, but it was one amongst many. Nobody had so much as looked at him twice; none of his colleagues had remarked on any resemblance. Not even the policeman had seen anything. He rubbed his chin. The bristles showed through red where he hadn't shaved. The house was silent. His wife was elsewhere. He'd married her because it had seemed expedient, one more lie to the profile. He unlocked the study door, walked to the front door and made sure it was locked. Then he climbed the stairs to the upstairs hall, and pulled down the sliding ladder which led up into the attic. He liked it up here, a place only he visited. He looked at a trunk, on top of which sat a couple of old boxes – camouflage. They hadn't been moved. He lifted them off now and took a key from his pocket, unlocked the trunk and snapped open the two heavy brass clasps. He listened again, hearing only silence past the dull beat of his own heart, then lifted the lid of the trunk.

Inside, it was filled with treasure: handbags, shoes, scarves, trinkets, watches and purses – nothing with any means of identifying the previous owner. The bags and purses had been emptied, checked thoroughly for telltale initials or even blemishes and distinguishing marks. Any letters, anything with a name or address, had been incinerated. He settled on the floor in front of the open trunk, not touching anything. He didn't need to touch. He was remembering a girl who'd lived on his street when he'd been eight or nine – she'd been a year younger. They'd played a game. They would take it in turns to lie very still on the ground, eyes closed, while the other one tried to remove as much of their clothing as they could without the one being stripped feeling anything.

Bible John had been quick to feel the girl's fingers on him – he'd played by the rules. But when the girl had lain there, and he'd started working at buttons and zips … her eyelids had fluttered, a smile on her lips … and she'd lain there uncomplaining, even though he knew she must be able to feel his clumsy fingers.

She'd been cheating, of course.

Now his grandmother came to him, with her constant warnings:

153

beware women who wear too much perfume; don't play cards with strangers on trains ...

The police hadn't said anything about the Upstart taking souvenirs. No doubt they wanted to keep it quiet; they'd have their reasons. But the Upstart *would* be taking souvenirs. Three so far. And he'd be hoarding them in Aberdeen. He'd slipped just a little, giving Aberdeen as his address on the reader's card ... Bible John stood up suddenly. He saw it now, saw the transaction between the librarian and 'Peter Manuel'. The Upstart claiming that he needed the use of a reference library. The librarian asking for details, for proof of identity ... The Upstart flustered, saying he'd left all that sort of thing at home. Could he go and fetch it? Impossible, he'd come down from Aberdeen for the day. A long way to travel, so the librarian had relented, issued the ticket. But now the Upstart was obliged to give Aberdeen as his address.

He *was* in Aberdeen.

Revived, Bible John locked the trunk, replaced the boxes exactly as they had been, and went back downstairs. It grieved him that with John Rebus so close, he might have to move the trunk ... and himself with it. In his study, he sat at his desk. Have the Upstart based in Aberdeen but mobile. Have him learn from his first mistakes. So now he plans each cull well in advance. Are the victims chosen at random, or is there some pattern there? Easier to choose prey that wasn't random; but then easier, too, for the police to establish a pattern and eventually catch you. But the Upstart was young: maybe that was one lesson he *hadn't* yet learned. His choice of 'Peter Manuel' showed a certain cockiness, teasing anyone who was able to track him that far. He either knew his victims or he didn't. Two routes to follow. Route one: say he *did* know them, say there existed some pattern linking all three to the Upstart.

One profile: the Upstart was a travelling man – lorry driver, company rep, a job like that. Lots of travel throughout Scotland. Travelling men could be lonely men, sometimes they used the services of a prostitute. The Edinburgh victim had been a prostitute. Often they stayed in hotels. The Glasgow victim had worked as a chambermaid. The first victim – the Aberdeen cull – failed to fit that pattern.

Or did she? Was there something the police had missed, something *he* might find? He picked up his telephone, called Directory Enquiries.

'It's a Glasgow number,' he told the voice on the other end.

14

In the middle of the night, Stonehaven was only twenty minutes south of Aberdeen, especially with a maniac at the wheel.

'He'll still be dead when we get there, pal,' Rebus told the driver.

And so he was, dead in a bed & breakfast bathroom, one arm over the side of the bath Marat-style. He'd slashed his wrists by the book – up and down rather than across. The water in the bath looked cold. Rebus didn't get too close – the arm over the side had leaked blood all across the floor.

'The landlady didn't know who was in the bathroom,' Lumsden explained. 'She just knew whoever it was had been in there long enough. She got no answer, so went to fetch one of her "boys" – this place caters to oil-workers. She tells me she thought Mr Kane was an oil-worker. Anyway, one of her lodgers got the door open and they found this.'

'Nobody saw or heard anything?'

'Suicide tends to be a quiet affair. Follow me.'

They went along narrow passages and up two short flights of stairs to Tony El's bedroom. It was fairly tidy. 'The landlady vacuums and dusts twice a week, sheets and towels are changed twice a week too.' There was a bottle of cheap whisky with the top unscrewed, about a fifth of the bottle left. An empty glass stood beside it. 'Look over here.'

Rebus looked. On the dressing table sat a full set of works: syringe, spoon, cotton wool, lighter, and a tiny polythene bag of brown powder.

'I hear heroin's back in a big way,' Lumsden said.

'I didn't see marks on his arms,' Rebus said. Lumsden nodded that they were there, but Rebus went back to the bathroom to make sure. Yes, a couple of pinpricks on the inside left forearm. He went back to the bedroom. Lumsden was seated on the bed, flicking through a magazine.

'He hadn't been using long,' Rebus said. 'His arms are pretty clean. I didn't see the knife.'

'Look at this stuff,' Lumsden said. He wanted to show Rebus the magazine. A woman with a plastic bag over her head was being entered from behind. 'Some people have sick minds.'

Rebus took the magazine from him. It was called *Snuff Babes*. On the front inside page it stated that it was printed 'with pride' in the USA. It wasn't just illegal; it was the hardest core Rebus had ever seen. Pages and pages of mock-up deaths with sex attached.

Lumsden had reached into his pocket, drew out an evidence bag. Inside was a blood-stained knife. But no ordinary knife: a Stanley.

'I'm not so sure this was suicide,' Rebus said quietly.

So then he had to explain his reasons: the visit to Uncle Joe, how Uncle Joe's son came by his nickname, and the fact that Tony El used to be one of Uncle Joe's henchmen.

'The door was locked from the inside,' Lumsden said.

'And it hadn't been forced when I got here.'

'So?'

'So how did the landlady's "boy" get in?' He took Lumsden back to the bathroom and they examined the door: with the turn of a screwdriver, it could be locked and unlocked from the outside.

'You want us to treat this as murder?' Lumsden said. 'You think this guy Stanley walked in here, spiked Mr Kane, dragged him along to the bathroom, and sliced his wrists open? We just passed half a dozen bedroom doors and came up two flights of stairs – don't you think somebody might have noticed?'

'Have you asked them?'

'I'm telling you, John, no one saw anything.'

'And I'm telling you this has Joseph Toal written all over it.'

Lumsden was shaking his head. He'd rolled up the magazine. It was sticking out of his jacket pocket. 'All I see here is a suicide. And from what you've told me, I'm glad to see the back of the fucker, end of story.'

The same patrol car took Rebus back into the city, still keeping the wrong side of the speed limit.

Rebus felt wide awake. He paced his room, smoked three cigarettes. The city outside his cathedral windows was finally asleep. The adult pay-movie channel was still available. The only other thing on offer was beach volleyball from California. For want of any other distraction he got out the flyers from the demo. They made depressing reading. Mackerel and other species of fish were now 'commercially extinct' in the North Sea, while others, including haddock – staple of the fish supper – wouldn't survive the millennium. Meantime, there were 400 oil installations out there which would one day become redundant, and if they were simply dumped along with their heavy metals and chemicals ... bye-bye fishies.

Of course, it might be that the fish were for the crow road anyway: nitrates and phosphates from sewage, plus agricultural fertilisers ... all drained into the seas. Rebus felt worse than ever, tossed the flyers into the bin. One of them didn't make it, and he picked it up. It told him there was going to be a march and rally on Saturday, with a benefit concert headlined by the Dancing Pigs. Rebus binned it and decided to check his answering machine at home. There were two calls from Ancram, agitated verging on furious, and one from Gill, telling him to call her whatever the hour. So he did.

'Hello?' She sounded like someone had gummed up her mouth.

'Sorry it's so late.'

'John.' She paused to check the time. 'It's so late it's practically early.'

'Your message said ...'

'I know.' She sounded like she was struggling to sit up in bed, yawned mightily. 'Howdenhall worked on that message pad, used ESDA on it, electrostatics.'

'And?'

'Came up with a phone number.'

'Whereabouts?'

'Aberdeen code.'

Rebus felt his spine tingle. 'Where in Aberdeen?'

'It's the payphone in some discotheque. Hang on, I've got the name here ... Burke's Club.'

Clickety-click.

'Does it mean anything to you?' she said.

Yes, he thought, it means I'm up here working at least two cases, maybe three.

'You said a payphone?'

'A public phone. I know because I called it. Not far from the bar by the sound of it.'

'Give me the number.' She did. 'Anything else?'

'The only fingerprints found belonged to Fergie himself. Nothing interesting on his home computer, except that he was trying a few tax dodges.'

'Hold the front page. And his business premises?'

'Nothing so far. John, are you OK?'

'Fine, why?'

'You sound … I don't know, sort of distant.'

Rebus allowed himself a smile. 'I'm right here. Get some sleep, Gill.'

'Night, John.'

'Night-night.'

He decided to try phoning Lumsden at the cop-shop. Conscientious: nearly three a.m. and he was there.

'You should be in the land of Nod,' Lumsden told him.

'Something I meant to ask earlier.'

'What?'

'That club we were in, the one where Michelle Strachan met Johnny Bible.'

'Burke's?'

'I just wondered,' Rebus said. 'Is it above board?'

'Moderately.'

'Meaning what?'

'It skates on thin ice sometimes. There's been a bit of drug dealing on the premises. The owners tried to clean it up, I think they've done a pretty good job.'

'Who owns it?'

'A couple of Yanks. John, what's this about?'

Rebus took less than a second constructing his lie. 'The Edinburgh jumper, he had a book of matches in his pocket. They were from Burke's.'

'It's a popular spot.'

Rebus made a sound of agreement. 'These owners, what were their names again?'

'I didn't say.' Cagey now.

'Is it a secret?'

A humourless laugh. 'No.'

'Maybe you don't want me bothering them?'

'Jesus, John …' A theatrical sigh. 'Erik-with-a-k Stemmons, Judd Fuller. I don't see the point in talking to them.'

'Me neither, Ludo. I just wanted their names.' Rebus attempted an American accent. 'Ciao, baby.' He was smiling when he put down the receiver. He looked at his watch. Ten past three. It was a five-minute walk to College Street. But would the place still be open? He got out the phone book, looked up Burke's – the number listed was the same one Gill had given him. He tried it: no answer. He decided to leave it at that … for the moment.

Spinning in a narrowing gyre: Allan Mitchison … Johnny Bible … Uncle Joe … Fergus McLure's drug deal.

Beach Boys: 'God Only Knows'. Segue to Zappa and the Mothers: 'More Trouble Every Day'. Rebus picked his pillow off the floor, listened to it for a full minute, threw it back on to the bed, then lay him down to sleep.

He was awake early and didn't feel like breakfast, so went for a walk instead. It was a glorious morning. The seagulls were busy hoovering up the night before's leftovers, but the streets were otherwise uncrowded. He walked up to the Mercat Cross, then left along King Street. He knew he was heading in the vague direction of his aunt's house, but doubted he could find it on foot. Instead, he came to something looking like an old school building but calling itself RGIT Offshore. He knew RGIT was Robert Gordon's Institute of Technology, and that Allan Mitchison had studied for a time at RGIT-OSC. He knew Johnny Bible's first victim had studied at Robert Gordon's University, but not what she had studied. Had she taken classes here? He stared at the grey granite walls. The first murder was in Aberdeen. Only later did Johnny Bible move to Glasgow and Edinburgh. Meaning what? Did Aberdeen hold some particular significance for the killer? He'd walked the victim from a nightclub to Duthie Park, but that didn't mean he was local: Michelle herself could have shown him the way. Rebus got out his map again, found College Street, then traced a finger from Burke's Club to Duthie Park. A long walk, residential, nobody had seen them the whole length of the route. Had they taken especially quiet back roads? Rebus folded the map and put it away.

He headed past the City Hospital and ended up on the Esplanade: a long expanse of grass links with bowling green, tennis and putting. There were amusements, all closed this early. People were on the Esplanade – jogging, walking their dogs, morning constitutionals. Rebus joined them. Groynes divided the mostly sandy beach into neat compartments. It was as clean a part of the city as he'd seen, excepting the graffiti – an artist called Zero had been hard at work, making this his or her personal gallery.

Zero the Hero: a character from somewhere ... Gong. Jesus, he hadn't thought of them for years. Pot-head pixies with stoned synths. Floating anarchy.

At the end of the Esplanade, next to the harbour, stood a couple of squares of housing, a village within the city. The squares themselves comprised drying greens and garden sheds. Dogs barked a warning as he passed. It reminded him of the east neuk of Fife, fishermen's

159

cottages, brightly painted but unpretentious. A taxi was cruising the harbour. Rebus waved it down. The R&R was over.

There was a demo outside the headquarters of T-Bird Oil. The young woman with the braided hair who'd been so persuasive the previous day was sitting cross-legged on the grass, smoking a roll-up, looking like she was on her break. The young man currently on the megaphone didn't have half her anger or eloquence, but his friends cheered him on. Maybe he was new to the demonstrating game.

Two young woolly suits, no older than the activists, were in consultation with three or four environmentalists in red boiler-suits and gas masks. The policemen were saying that if they took the gas masks off, conversation might be less of a chore. They were also asking that the demonstration move off land owned by T-Bird Oil. Namely, the patch of grass in front of the main entrance. The demonstrators were saying something about the laws of trespass. Legal knowledge came with the territory these days. It was like rules of unarmed combat to a squaddie.

Rebus was offered the same literature as the day before.

'I already took,' he said with a smile. Braid-hair looked up at him and squinted, like she was taking a photograph.

In the reception area, someone was videoing the demo through the windows. Maybe for police intelligence; maybe for T-Bird's own files. Stuart Minchell was waiting for Rebus.

'Isn't it unbelievable?' he said. 'I hear there are groups like that one outside each of the Six Sisters, plus smaller operations like ours.'

'The Six Sisters?'

'The big North Sea players. Exxon, Shell, BP, Mobil ... I forget the other two. So, ready for the trip?'

'I'm not sure. What are my chances of getting a kip?'

'It might be pretty bumpy. Good news is, we've a plane heading up, so you'll be spared a budgie – at least for today. You'll fly in to Scatsta. It used to be an RAF base. Saves the hassle of changing at Sumburgh.'

'And it's near Sullom Voe?'

'Right next door. Someone'll be there to meet you.'

'I appreciate this, Mr Minchell.'

Minchell shrugged. 'Ever been to Shetland?' Rebus shook his head. 'Well, you're probably not going to see much of it, except from the air. Just remember, when that plane takes off, you're not in Scotland any more. You're a "Sooth-Moother" heading for miles and miles of bugger all.'

15

Minchell drove Rebus to Dyce Airport. The plane was a twin-propeller model with seats for fourteen, but today carrying only half a dozen passengers, all men. Four of them wore suits, and were quick to open their briefcases, disgorging sheafs of paper, ring-bound reports, calculators, pens and laptops. One wore a sheepskin jacket and lacked what the others would probably call 'proper grooming'. He kept his hands in his pockets and stared out of the window. Rebus, who didn't mind an aisle seat, decided to sit beside him.

The man tried to stare him elsewhere. His eyes were bloodshot, grey stubble covering cheeks and chin. In reply, Rebus fastened his seat-belt. The man growled, but shifted upright, allowing Rebus half an arm-rest. Then he went back to window-watching. A car was drawing up outside.

The engine started up, propellers turning. There was a stewardess at the back of the cramped compartment. She hadn't closed the door yet. The man in the window-seat turned to the assembly of suits.

'Prepare to shite yourselves.' Then he started laughing. Whisky fumes from the night before wafted over Rebus, making him glad he'd skipped breakfast. Someone else was boarding the plane. Rebus peered down the aisle. It was Major Weir, dressed in a kilt, sporran attached. The suits froze. Sheepskin was still chuckling. The door slammed shut. Seconds later, the plane began to taxi.

Rebus, who hated flying, tried to think himself into a nice Intercity 125, speeding along terra firma, no intention of suddenly pushing skywards.

'Grab that arm-rest any harder,' his neighbour said, 'and you'll uproot the fucking thing.'

The ascent was like an unpaved road. Rebus thought he could feel fillings popping loose and hear the plane's various bolts and soldered joins snapping. But then they were levelling out, and things settled down. Rebus started breathing again, noticed sweat on his palms and brow. He adjusted the air-intake above him.

'Better?' the man said.

'Better,' Rebus agreed. The wheels retracted, covers closing. The sheepskin explained what the sounds were. Rebus nodded his thanks. He could hear the stewardess behind them.

'I'm sorry, Major, if we'd known you were coming we'd have arranged for coffee to be served.'

She got a grunt for her trouble. The suits were staring at their work, but couldn't concentrate. The plane hit some turbulence, and Rebus's hands went to the arm-rests again.

'Fear of flying,' sheepskin said with a wink.

Rebus knew he had to get his mind off the flight. 'Do you work at Sullom Voe?'

'Practically *run* the place.' He nodded towards the suits. 'I don't work for this lot you know. I'm just cadging a lift. I work for the consortium.'

'The Six Sisters?'

'And the rest. Thirty-odd at the last count.'

'You know, I don't know a damned thing about Sullom Voe.'

Sheepskin gave him a sidelong look. 'You a reporter?'

'I'm a CID detective.'

'Just so long as you're not a reporter. I'm the relief Maintenance Manager. We're always getting grief in the press about cracked pipes and spills. I'll tell you, the only leaks around *my* terminal are the ones to the fucking papers!' He stared out of the window again, as if their conversation had reached a natural end. But a full minute later he turned to Rebus.

'There are two pipelines into the terminal – Brent and Ninian – plus we offload from tankers. Four jetties in near-constant use. I was here from the start, 1973. That's only four years after the first exploration ships chugged into Lerwick. By Christ, I'd have loved to've seen the looks on the fishermen's faces. They probably thought it was the start of bugger all. But oil came and oil stayed, we got to fuck with the islands, and they screwed every penny they could out of the consortium. Every last penny.'

As sheepskin talked, his mouth began to relax. Rebus thought he might still be drunk. He spoke quietly, mostly with his face to the window.

'You should have seen the place in the seventies, kiddo. It was like the Klondike – trailer parks, shanty towns, the roads churned to mud. We had power cuts, not enough fresh water, and the locals fucking hated us. I loved it. There was about one pub we could all drink in. The

162

consortium were choppering in supplies like we were at war. Fuck, maybe we were.'

He turned to Rebus.

'And the weather ... the wind'll strip the skin off your face.'

'So I needn't have brought a razor?'

The big man snorted. 'What takes you to Sullom Voe?'

'A suspicious death.'

'On Shetland?'

'In Edinburgh.'

'How suspicious?'

'Maybe not very, but we have to check.'

'I know all about that. It's like at the terminal, we run hundreds of checks every day, whether they're needed or not. The LPG chilldown area, we had a suspected problem there, and I stress *suspected*. I'll tell you, we had more men on stand-by than God knows what. See, it's not that far from the crude oil storage.'

Rebus nodded, not sure what the man was getting at. He seemed to be drifting off again. Time to reel him in.

'The man who died worked for a while at Sullom Voe. Allan Mitchison.'

'Mitchison?'

'He might've been on maintenance. I think that was his speciality.'

Sheepskin shook his head. 'Name doesn't ... no.'

'What about Jake Harley? He works at Sullom Voe.'

'Oh aye, I've come across him. Don't much like him, but I know the face.'

'Why don't you like him?'

'He's one of those Green bastards. You know, *ecology*.' He almost spat the word. 'What the fuck's ecology ever done for us?'

'So you know him.'

'Who?'

'Jake Harley?'

'I said so, didn't I?'

'He's off on some walking holiday.'

'On Shetland?' Rebus nodded. 'Aye, sounds about right. He's always on about archaeology and whatsit, bird-watching. The only birds I'd spend all day watching don't have fucking feathers on them, let me tell you.'

Rebus to himself: *I thought I was bad, but this guy redefines all the terms.*

'So he's off walking and bird-watching: any idea where he'd go?'

'The usual places. There are a few bird-watchers at the terminal. It's like pollution control. We know we're doing all right as long as the birds don't suddenly start turning up their toes. Like with the *Negrita*.' He almost bit off the end of the word, swallowed hard. 'Thing is, the wind's so fierce, and the currents are fierce too. So you get dispersal, like with the *Braer*. Somebody told me Shetland has a complete change of air every quarter hour. Perfect dispersal conditions. And fuck it, they're only birds. What are they good for, when it comes down to it?'

He rested his head against the window.

'When we get to the terminal, I'll get a map for you, mark some of the places he might go ...' Seconds later, his eyes were closed. Rebus got up and went to the back of the cabin, where the toilet was. As he passed Major Weir, who was seated in the very back row, he saw he was deep in the *Financial Times*. The toilet was no smaller than a child's coffin. If Rebus had been any wider, they'd have had to starve him out. He flushed, thinking of his urine splashing into the North Sea – as far as pollution went, a mere drop in the ocean – and tugged open the accordion doors. He slid into the seat across the aisle from the Major. The stewardess had been sitting there, but he could see her up front in the cockpit.

'Any chance of a keek at the racing results?'

Major Weir lifted his eyes from the newsprint, swivelled his head to take in this strange new creature. The whole process couldn't have taken longer than half a minute. He didn't say anything.

'We met yesterday,' Rebus told him. 'My name's Detective Inspector Rebus. I know you don't say much ...' he patted his jacket ... 'I've a notepad in my pocket if you need one.'

'In your spare time, Inspector, are you some sort of comedian?' The voice was a cultured drawl; urbane just about summed it up. But it was also dry, a little rusty.

'Can I ask you something, Major? Why did you name your oilfield after an oatcake?'

Weir's face reddened with sudden rage. 'It's short for Bannockburn!'

Rebus nodded. 'Did we win that one?'

'Don't you know your history, laddie?' Rebus shrugged. 'I swear, sometimes I despair. You're a *Scot*.'

'So?'

'So your past is important! You need to know it so you can learn.'

'Learn what, sir?'

Weir sighed. 'To borrow a phrase from a poet – a Scots poet, he was talking about words – that we Scots are "creatures tamed by cruelty". Do you see?'

'I think I'm having trouble focusing.'

Weir frowned. 'Do you drink?'

'Teetotal is my middle name.' The Major grunted his satisfaction. 'Trouble is,' Rebus went on, 'my first name's Not-at-all.'

He got it eventually and grudged a frowning smile, the first time Rebus had seen the trick.

'The thing is, sir, I'm up here—'

'I know why you're up here, Inspector. When I saw you yesterday, I had Hayden Fletcher find out who you were.'

'Can I ask why?'

'Because you stared back at me in the elevator. I'm not used to that sort of behaviour. It meant you didn't work for me, and since you were with my personnel manager ...'

'You thought I was after a job?'

'I meant to see to it you didn't get one.'

'I'm flattered.'

The Major looked at him again. 'So why is my company flying you to Sullom Voe?'

'I want to talk to a friend of Mitchison's.'

'Allan Mitchison.'

'You knew him?'

'Don't be ridiculous. I had Minchell report to me yesterday evening. I like to know everything that's going on in my company. I have a question for you.'

'Go ahead.'

'Could Mr Mitchison's death have anything to do with T-Bird Oil?'

'At the moment ... I don't think so.'

Major Weir nodded, lifted his newspaper to eye level. The interview was over.

16

'Welcome to the Mainland,' Rebus's guide said, meeting him on the tarmac.

Major Weir had already been installed in a Range Rover and was speeding from the airfield. A row of helicopters stood in repose nearby. The wind was ... well, the wind was *serious*. It was flapping the helicopters' rotor blades, and it was singing in Rebus's ears. The Edinburgh wind was a pro; sometimes you walked out your front door and it was like being punched in the face. But the Shetland wind ... it wanted to pick you up and shake you.

The descent had been rocky, but before that he'd had his first sighting of Shetland proper. 'Miles and miles of bugger all' didn't do it justice. Hardly any trees, plenty of sheep. And spectacular barren coastline with white breakers crashing into it. He wondered if erosion was a problem. The islands weren't exactly large. They'd crossed to the east of Lerwick, then passed some dormitory towns, which, according to Sheepskin's commentary, had been mere hamlets in the 1970s. He'd woken up by then, and had come armed with a few more facts and fancies.

'Know what we did? The oil industry, I mean? We kept Maggie Thatcher in power. Oil revenue paid for all those tax cuts. Oil revenue paid for the Falklands War. Oil was pumping through the veins of her whole fucking reign, and she never thanked us once. Not once, the bitch.' He laughed. 'You can't help liking her.'

'Apparently there are pills you can take.' But Sheepskin wasn't listening.

'You can't separate oil and politics. The sanctions against Iraq, whole point was to stop him flooding the market with cheap oil.' He paused. 'Norway, the bastards.'

Rebus felt he'd missed something. 'Norway?'

'They've got oil, too, only they've banked the money, used it to kickstart other industries. Maggie used it to pay for a war and a bloody election ...'

As they swung out to sea past Lerwick, Sheepskin had pointed out some boats – bloody big boats.

'Klondikers,' he said. 'Factory ships. They're busy processing fish. Probably doing more environmental damage than the whole North Sea oil industry. But the locals just let them get on with it, they don't give a bugger. Fishing's a heritage thing with them ... not like oil. Aah, fuck the lot of them.'

Rebus still hadn't learned the man's name when they parted on the runway. There was someone waiting for Rebus, a slight grinning man with too many teeth in his head. And he said, 'Welcome to the Mainland.' Then explained what he meant in the car, during the short trip to the Sullom Voe terminal. 'That's what Shetlanders call the main island: Mainland, as opposed to mainland with a small m, which means ... well, the mainland.' A snort for a laugh. He had to wipe his nose on the sleeve of his jacket. He drove the way a kid would when seated in its father's car: bent forward, hands overly busy on the steering-wheel.

His name was Walter Rowbotham, and he was a new recruit to the Sullom Voe Public Relations Department.

'I'd be happy to show you around, Inspector,' he said, still grinning, trying too hard to please.

'Maybe if there's time,' Rebus conceded.

'My pleasure entirely. You know, of course, that the terminal cost one thousand three hundred million just to construct. That's pounds, not dollars.'

'Interesting.'

Rowbotham's face practically lit up, encouraged now. 'The first oil flowed into Sullom Voe in 1978. It is a major employer and has helped contribute greatly to Shetland's low unemployment rate, currently around four per cent or half the Scottish average.'

'Tell me something, Mr Rowbotham.'

'Walter, please. Or Walt if you like.'

'Walt.' Rebus smiled. 'Had any more trouble with the LPG chilldown?'

Rowbotham's face turned pickled baby beet. Jesus, Rebus thought, the media were going to love him ...

They ended up driving through half the installation to get to where Rebus wanted to be, so he heard most of the tour narration anyway and learned more than he hoped he'd ever have to know about debutanising, de-ethanising and depropanising, not to mention surge tanks and

167

integrity meters. Wouldn't it be great, he thought, if you could fit integrity meters to human beings?

At the main administration building they'd been told that Jake Harley worked in the process control room, and that his colleagues were waiting there and knew a police officer was coming to talk to them. They passed the incoming crude lines, the pigging station, and the final holding basin, and at one point Walt thought they were lost, but he had a little orientation map with him.

Just as well: Sullom Voe was huge. It had taken seven years to build, breaking all sorts of records in the process (and Walt knew every one of them), and Rebus had to admit that it was an impressive monster. He'd been past Grangemouth and Mossmorran dozens of times, but they just weren't in the picture. And if you looked out past the crude oil tanks and the unloading jetties, you saw water – the Voe itself to the south; then Gluss Isle over to the west, doing a good impression of unspoilt wilderness. It was like a sci-fi city transported to prehistory.

For all of which, the process control room was about as peaceful a place as Rebus had ever been. Two men and a woman sat behind computer consoles in the centre of the room, while the walls were taken up with electronic charts, softly flashing lights indicating the oil and gas flows. The only sounds were those of fingers on keyboards, and the occasional muted conversation. Walt had decided that it was his job to introduce Rebus. The atmosphere had quieted him, as if he'd walked into the middle of a church service. He went to the central console and spoke in an undertone to the trinity seated there.

The elder of the two men stood up and came to shake Rebus's hand.

'Inspector, my name's Milne. How can we help?'

'Mr Milne, I really wanted to speak to Jake Harley. But since he's made himself scarce, I thought maybe you could tell me a little about him. Specifically, about his friendship with Allan Mitchison.'

Milne wore a check shirt, its sleeves rolled up. He scratched at one arm while Rebus spoke. He was in his thirties, with tousled red hair and a face pitted from teenage acne. He nodded, half-turning to his two colleagues, assuming the role of spokesman.

'Well, we all work beside Jake, so we can tell you about him. Personally, I didn't know Allan very well, though Jake introduced us.'

'I don't think I've ever met him,' the woman said.

'I met him once,' the other man added.

'Allan only worked here for two or three months,' Milne went on. 'I know he struck up a friendship with Jake.' He shrugged. 'Really, that's about it.'

'If they were friends, they must have had something in common. Was it bird-watching?'

'I don't think so.'

'Green issues,' the woman said.

'That's true,' Milne said, nodding. 'Of course, in a place like this, we always end up talking about ecology sooner or later – sensitive subject.'

'Is it a big thing with Jake?'

'I wouldn't go that far.' Milne looked to his colleagues for support. They shook their heads. Rebus realised that nobody was talking much above a whisper.

'Jake works right here?' he asked.

'That's right. We alternate shifts.'

'So sometimes you're working together ...'

'And sometimes we're not.'

Rebus nodded. He was learning nothing; wasn't sure he'd ever actually thought he *would* learn anything. So Mitchison had been into ecology – big deal. But it was pleasant here, relaxing. Edinburgh and all his troubles were a long way away, and felt it.

'This looks like a cushy job,' he said. 'Can anyone apply?'

Milne smiled. 'You'll have to hurry, who knows how long the oil will last?'

'A while yet surely?'

Milne shrugged. 'It's down to the economics of retrieval. Companies are beginning to look west – Atlantic oil. And oil from west of Shetland is being landed at Flotta.'

'On Orkney,' the woman explained.

'They won the contract from us,' Milne went on. 'Five or ten years from now, the profit margin may be bigger out there.'

'And they'll mothball the North Sea?'

All three nodded, like a single beast.

'Have you talked to Briony?' the woman asked suddenly.

'Who's Briony?'

'Jake's ... I don't know, she's not his wife, is she?' She looked to Milne.

'Just a girlfriend, I think.'

'Where does she live?' Rebus asked.

'Jake and her share a house,' Milne said. 'In Brae. She works at the swimming pool.'

Rebus turned to Walt. 'How far is it?'

'Six or seven miles.'

'Take me.'

169

They tried the baths first, but she wasn't on shift, so they tracked down her house. Brae looked to be suffering a crisis of identity, like it had suddenly plopped into being and didn't know what to make of itself. The houses were new but anonymous; there was obviously money around, but it couldn't buy everything. It couldn't turn Brae back into the village it had been in the days before Sullom Voe.

They found the house. Rebus told Walt to wait in the car. A woman in her early twenties answered his knock. She was wearing jogging bottoms and a white singlet, her feet bare.

'Briony?' Rebus asked.

'Yes.'

'Sorry, I don't know your last name. Can I come in?'

'No. Who are you?'

'I'm Detective Inspector John Rebus.' Rebus showed his warrant card. 'I'm here about Allan Mitchison.'

'Mitch? What about him?'

There were a lot of answers to that question. Rebus picked one. 'He's dead.' Then he watched the colour drain from her face. She clung on to the door as if for support, but she still wasn't letting him in.

'Would you like to sit down?' Rebus hinted.

'What happened to him?'

'We're not sure, that's why I want to talk to Jake.'

'You're not sure?'

'Could be an accident. I'm trying to fill in some background.'

'Jake isn't here.'

'I know, I've been trying to reach him.'

'Somebody from personnel keeps phoning.'

'On my behalf.'

She nodded slowly. 'Well, he's still not here.' She hadn't taken her hand off the jamb.

'Can I get a message to him?'

'I don't know where he is.' As she spoke, the colour started to return to her cheeks. 'Poor Mitch.'

'You've no idea where Jake is?'

'He sometimes goes off on a walk. He doesn't know himself where he'll end up.'

'He doesn't phone you?'

'He needs his space. So do I, but I find mine when I swim. Jake walks.'

'He's due back tomorrow though, or the day after?'

She shrugged. 'Who knows?'

Rebus reached into a pocket, wrote on a page of his notebook, tore it out. He held it out to her. 'It has a couple of phone numbers. Will you tell him to call me?'

'Sure.'

'Thanks.' She was staring dully at the piece of paper, her eyes just short of tears. 'Briony, is there anything you can tell me about Mitch? Anything that might help?'

She looked up from the card to him.

'No,' she said. Then, slowly, she closed the door on his face. In that final glimpse of her before the door separated them, Rebus had found her eyes, and seen something there. Not just bewilderment or grief.

Something more like fear. And behind it, a degree of calculation.

It struck him that he was hungry, and gasping for coffee. So they ate in the Sullom Voe canteen. It was a clean white space with potted plants and no smoking signs. Walt was rattling on about how Shetland remained more Norse than Scots; nearly all the place names were Norwegian. To Rebus, it was like the edge of the world, and he liked that. He told Walt about the man on the plane, the one in sheepskin.

'Oh, that sounds like Mike Sutcliffe.'

Rebus asked to be taken to him.

Mike Sutcliffe had changed out of his sheepskin and was dressed in crisp work clothes. They finally found him in heated conversation beside the ballast water tanks. Two underlings were listening to him complain that they could be replaced by gibbons and nobody would notice. He pointed up at the tanks, then out towards the jetties. There was a tanker moored at one of them, it couldn't have been any bigger than half a dozen football pitches. Sutcliffe saw Rebus and lost the thread of his argument. He dismissed the workers and began to move away, only he had to get past Rebus first.

Rebus had a smile ready. 'Mr Sutcliffe, did you get me that map?'

'What map?' Sutcliffe kept walking.

'You said you might have an idea where I could find Jake Harley.'

'Did I?'

Rebus was almost having to jog to keep up with him. He wasn't wearing the smile any more. 'Yes,' he said coldly, 'you did.'

Sutcliffe stopped so suddenly, Rebus ended up in front of him. 'Look, Inspector, I'm up to my gonads in thistles right now. I don't have time for this.'

And he walked, his eyes not meeting Rebus's. Rebus marched alongside, keeping silent. He kept it up for a hundred yards, then stopped. Sutcliffe kept going, looking like he might walk right along the jetty and across the water if he had to.

Rebus went back to where Walt was standing. He took his time, thoughtful. The bum's rush and then some. What or who had changed Sutcliffe's mind? Rebus pictured an old white-haired man in kilt and sporran. The picture seemed to fit.

Walt took Rebus back to his office in the main admin building. He showed Rebus where the phone was, and said he'd be back with two coffees. Rebus closed the office door, and sat down behind the desk. He was surrounded by oil platforms, tankers, pipelines, and Sullom Voe itself – huge framed photos on the walls; PR literature stacked high; a scale model of a super tanker on the desk. Rebus got an outside line and telephoned Edinburgh, weighing up diplomacy against bullshit and deciding it might save time to just tell the truth.

Mairie Henderson was at home.

'Mairie, John Rebus.'

'Oh, Christ,' she said.

'You're not working?'

'Haven't you heard of the portable office? Fax-modem and a telephone, that's all you need. Listen, you owe me.'

'How so?' Rebus tried to sound aggrieved.

'All that work I did for you, and no story at the end of it. That's not exactly *quid pro quo*, is it? And journalists have longer memories than elephants.'

'I gave you Sir Iain's resignation.'

'A full ninety minutes before every other hack knew. And it wasn't exactly the crime of the century to begin with. I *know* you held back on me.'

'Mairie, I'm hurt.'

'Good. Now tell me this is purely a social call.'

'Absolutely. So how are you keeping?'

A sigh. 'What do you want?'

Rebus swung ninety degrees in the chair. It was a comfortable chair, good enough to sleep in. 'I need some digging.'

'I am completely and utterly surprised.'

'The name's Weir. He calls himself Major Weir, but the rank may be spurious.'

'T-Bird Oil?'

Mairie was a *very* good journalist. 'That's the one.'

'He just made a speech at that convention.'

'Well, he had someone else read it out.'

A pause. Rebus flinched. 'John, you're in Aberdeen?'

'Sort of,' he confessed.

'Tell me.'

'Later.'

'And if there's a story ...?'

'You're in pole position.'

'With something longer than a ninety-minute lead time?'

'Absolutely.'

Silence on the line: she knew he could be lying. She was a journalist; she knew these things.

'OK, so what do you want to know about Weir?'

'I don't know. Everything. The interesting stuff.'

'Business or personal life?'

'Both, mainly business.'

'Do you have a number in Aberdeen?'

'Mairie, I'm not *in* Aberdeen. Especially if anyone asks. I'll get back to you.'

'I hear they're reopening the Spaven case.'

'An internal inquiry, that's all.'

'Preliminary to a reopening?'

Walt opened the door, brought in two beakers of coffee. Rebus stood up. 'Look, I have to go.'

'Cat got your tongue?'

'Bye, Mairie.'

'I checked,' Walt said, 'your plane leaves in an hour.' Rebus nodded and took the coffee. 'I hope you've enjoyed your visit.'

Christ, Rebus thought, he means it, too.

17

That evening, once he'd recovered from the flight back to Dyce, Rebus ate at the same Indian restaurant Allan Mitchison had frequented: no coincidence. He didn't know why he wanted to see the place for himself; he just did. The meal was decent, a chicken dopiaza neither better nor worse than he could find in Edinburgh. The diners were couples, young and middle-aged, their conversations quiet. It didn't look the sort of restaurant you'd raise hell in after sixteen days offshore. If anything, it was a place for contemplation, always supposing you were dining alone. When Rebus's bill came, he recalled the sums on Mitchison's credit-card statement – they were about double the present figure.

Rebus showed his warrant card and asked to speak to the manager. The man came bounding up to his table, nervous smile in place.

'Is there some problem, sir?'

'No problem,' Rebus said.

The manager lifted the bill from the table and was about to tear it up, but Rebus stopped him.

'I'd prefer to pay,' he said. 'I only want to ask a couple of questions.'

'Of course, sir.' The manager sat down opposite him. 'What can I do to help?'

'A young man called Allan Mitchison used to eat here regularly, about once a fortnight.'

The manager nodded. 'A policeman came in to ask me about him.'

Aberdeen CID: Bain had asked them to check up on Mitchison, their report back an almost total blank.

'Do you remember him? The customer, I mean?'

The manager nodded. 'Very nice man, very quiet. He came maybe ten times.'

'Alone?'

'Sometimes alone, sometimes with a lady.'

'Can you describe her?'

174

The manager shook his head. There was a clatter from the kitchen, distracting him. 'I just remember he was not always alone.'

'Why didn't you tell the other policeman this?'

The man didn't seem to understand the question. He got to his feet, the kitchen decidedly on his mind. 'But I did,' he said, moving away.

Something Aberdeen CID had conveniently left out of their report ...

There was a different bouncer on the door at Burke's Club, and Rebus paid his entrance money the same as everybody else. Inside, it was seventies night, with prizes for the best period costume. Rebus watched the parade of platform shoes, Oxford bags, midis and maxis, kipper ties. Nightmare stuff: it all reminded him of his wedding photos. There was a *Saturday Night Fever* John Travolta, and a girl who was doing a passable imitation of Jodie Foster in *Taxi Driver*.

The music was a mix of kitsch disco and regressive rock: Chic, Donna Summer, Mud, Showaddywaddy, Rubettes, interspersed with Rod Stewart, the Stones, Status Quo, a blast of Hawkwind and bloody 'Hi-Ho Silver Lining'.

Jeff Beck: up against the wall *now*!

The odd song clicked with him, had the power to send him reeling in the years. The DJ somehow still had a copy of Montrose's 'Connection', one of the very best cover versions of a Stones song. Rebus in the army listened to it in his billet late at night, playing on an early Sanyo cassette player, an earpiece plugged in so nobody else could hear. Next morning, he'd be deaf in one ear. He switched the earpiece about each night so he wouldn't suffer long-term damage.

He sat at the bar. That seemed to be where the single men congregated in silent appraisal of the dance floor. The booths and tables were for couples and office parties, squawks of women who genuinely looked to be enjoying themselves. They wore low-cut tops and short tight skirts, and in the shadowy half-light they *all* looked terrific. Rebus decided he was drinking too quickly, poured more water into his whisky and asked the barman for more ice, too. He was seated at the corner of the bar, less than six feet from the payphone. Impossible to use it when the music was pounding, and there hadn't been much of a let-up yet. Which made Rebus think – the only sensible time to use the payphone would be out of hours, when the place was quiet. But at that time there'd be no punters on the premises, just staff ...

Rebus slipped off his stool and circuited the dance floor. The toilets were signposted down a passageway. He went inside and listened to someone in one of the cubicles snorting something. Then he washed his hands and waited. The toilet flushed, the lock clicked, and a young man in a suit came out. Rebus had his warrant card ready.

'You're under arrest,' he said. 'Anything you say—'

'Hey, wait a minute!' The man still had flecks of white powder in his nostrils. He was mid-twenties, lower management struggling to be middle. His jacket wasn't expensive, but at least it was new. Rebus pushed him against the wall, angled the hand-drier and pushed the button so the hot air blew across his face.

'There,' he said, 'blow some of that talc away.'

The man turned his face away from the heat. He was shaking, his whole body limp, beaten before they really got started.

'One question,' Rebus said, 'and then you walk out of here ... how does the song go? As free as a bird. One question.' The man nodded. 'Where did you get it?'

'What?'

Rebus pushed a bit harder. 'The stuff.'

'I only do this on a Friday night!'

'Last time: where did you get it?'

'Just some guy. He's here sometimes.'

'Is he here tonight?'

'I haven't seen him.'

'What does he look like?'

'Nothing special. Mr Average. You said one question.'

Rebus let the man go. 'I lied.'

The man sniffed, straightened his jacket. 'Can I go?'

'You're gone.'

Rebus washed his hands, loosened the knot in his tie so he could undo his top button. The sniffer might go back to his booth. He might decide to leave. He might complain to the management. Maybe they paid their way so busts like this wouldn't happen. He left the toilet and went looking for the office, couldn't find one. Out in the foyer, there was a staircase. The bouncer was parked in front of it. Rebus told the tux he wanted to speak to the manager.

'No can do.'

'It's important.'

The bouncer shook his head slowly. His eyes didn't move from Rebus's face. Rebus knew what he saw: a middle-aged lush, a pathetic figure in a cheap suit. It was time to disabuse him. He opened his warrant card.

'CID,' he told the tux. 'People are selling drugs on these premises

176

and I'm a heartbeat away from calling in the Drugs Squad. *Now* do I get to talk to the boss?'

He got to talk to the boss.

'My name's Erik Stemmons.' The man came around from his desk to shake Rebus's hand. It was a small office, but well furnished. Good sound-proofing too: the bass from the dance floor was as much as you could hear. But there were video screens, half a dozen of them. Three showing the main dance floor, two the bar, and one a general view of the booths.

'You want to put one in the bogs,' Rebus said, 'that's where the action is. You've got two on the bar: staff problems?'

'Not since we put the cameras in.' Stemmons was dressed in jeans and a white T-shirt, the arms of which he'd rolled up to his shoulders. He had long curling locks, maybe permed, but his hair was thinning and there were tell-tale lines down his face. He wasn't much younger than Rebus, and the younger he tried to look the older he seemed.

'Are you with Grampian CID?'

'No.'

'Thought not. We get most of them in here, good customers. Sit down, won't you?'

Rebus sat down. Stemmons got comfortable behind his desk. It was covered with paperwork.

'Frankly I'm surprised by your allegation,' he went on. 'We cooperate fully with the local police, and this club is as clean as any in the city. You know of course that it's impossible to rule narcotics out of the equation.'

'Someone was snooking up in the toilet.'

Stemmons shrugged. 'Exactly. What can we do? Strip search everyone as they enter? Have a sniffer dog roaming the premises?' He laughed a short laugh. 'You see the problem.'

'How long have you lived here, Mr Stemmons?'

'I came over in '78. Saw a good thing and stayed. That's nearly two decades. I'm practically integrated.' Another laugh; another no reaction from Rebus. Stemmons placed his palms on the desktop. 'Wherever Americans go in the world – Vietnam, Germany, Panama – entrepreneurs follow. And so long as the pickings stay good, why should we leave?' He looked down at his hands. 'What do you *really* want?'

'I want to know what you can tell me about Fergus McLure.'

'Fergus McLure?'

'You know, dead person, lived near Edinburgh.'

Stemmons shook his head. 'I'm sorry, that name means nothing to me.'

Oh, Vienna, Rebus nearly sang. 'You don't seem to have a phone in here.'

'Excuse me?'

'A phone.'

'I carry a mobile.'

'The portable office.'

'Open twenty-four hours. Look, if you've a beef, take it up with the local cops. I don't need this grief.'

'You haven't seen grief yet, Mr Stemmons.'

'Hey.' Stemmons pointed a finger. 'If you've got something to say, say it. Otherwise, the door's the thing behind you with the brass handle.'

'And you're the thing in front of me with the brass neck.' Rebus stood up and leaned across the desk. 'Fergus McLure had information on a drug ring. He died suddenly. Your club's phone number was lying on his desk. McLure wasn't exactly the clubbing type.'

'So?'

Rebus could see Stemmons in a court of law, saying the exact same thing. He could see a jury asking itself the question too.

'Look,' Stemmons said, relenting. 'If I was setting up a drug deal, would I give this guy McLure the number of the club's payphone, which *anyone* might pick up, or would I give him my mobile number? You're a detective, what do you think?'

Rebus saw a judge tossing the case out.

'Johnny Bible met his first victim here, didn't he?'

'Jesus, don't drag that up. What are you, a ghoul or something? We had CID hassling us for weeks.'

'You didn't recognise his description?'

'Nobody did, not even the bouncers, and I pay them to remember faces. I told your colleagues, maybe he met her after she left the club. Who's to say?'

Rebus went to the door, paused.

'Where's your partner?'

'Judd? He's not in tonight.'

'Does he have an office?'

'Next door.'

'Can I see it?'

'I don't have a key.'

Rebus opened the door. 'Does he have a mobile phone too?'

He'd caught Stemmons off guard. The American coughed a response.

'Didn't you hear the question?'

'Judd doesn't have a mobile. He hates telephones.'

'So what does he do in an emergency? Send up smoke signals?'

But Rebus knew damned well what Judd Fuller would do.

He'd use a payphone.

He thought he'd earned a last drink before home, but froze halfway to the bar. There was a new couple in one of the booths, and Rebus recognised both of them. The woman was the blonde from his hotel bar. The man sitting beside her, arms draped along the back of the booth, was her junior by about twenty years. He wore an open-necked shirt and a lot of gold chains around his neck. He'd probably seen someone dressed that way in a film once. Or maybe he was going in for the fancy-dress contest: seventies villain. Rebus knew the warty face straight away.

Mad Malky Toal.

Stanley.

Rebus made the connection, made almost too many of them. He felt dizzy, and found himself leaning against the wall-phone. So he picked up the receiver and slammed home a coin. He had the phone number in his notebook. Partick police station. He asked for DI Jack Morton, waited an age. He pushed more money home, only to have someone come on and tell him Morton had left the office.

'This is urgent,' Rebus said. 'My name's DI John Rebus. Do you have his home number?'

'I can get him to call you,' the voice said. 'Would that do, Inspector?'

Would it? Glasgow was Ancram's home turf. If Rebus handed over his number, Ancram could get to hear of it, and would know where he was … Fuck it, he was only here another day. He reeled the number off and put down the receiver, thanking God the DJ had been playing a slow number: Python Lee Jackson, 'In a Broken Dream'.

Rebus had those to spare.

He sat at the bar, his back to Stanley and his woman. But he could see them distorted in the mirror behind the optics. Dark distant figures, coiling and uncoiling. Of course Stanley was in town: hadn't he killed Tony El? But why? And two bigger questions: was he here in Burke's Club by coincidence?

And what was he doing with the blonde from the hotel?

Rebus was starting to get inklings. He kept an ear out for the telephone, prayed for another slow record. Bowie, 'John, I'm Only

179

Dancing'. A guitar like sawing through metal. It didn't matter: the phone didn't ring.

'Here's one we'd all rather forget,' the DJ drawled. 'But I want to see you up dancing to it anyway, otherwise I might just have to play it again.'

Lieutenant Pigeon: 'Mouldy Old Dough'. The telephone rang. Rebus leapt to it.

'Hello?'

'John? Got the hi-fi loud enough?'

'I'm at a disco.'

'At your age? Is this the emergency – you want me to talk you out of there?'

'No, I want you to describe Eve to me.'

'Eve?'

'Uncle Joe Toal's woman.'

'I've only seen her in photos.' Jack Morton thought about it. 'Blonde out of a bottle, face that could bend nails. Twenty or thirty years ago she *might* have looked like Madonna, but I'm probably being generous.'

Eve, Uncle Joe's lady – chatting Rebus up in an Aberdeen hotel. Coincidence? Hardly. Readying to pump him for information? Nap hand. And up here with Stanley, the two of them looking pretty cosy … He remembered her words: '*I'm in sales. Products for the oil industry.*' Yes, Rebus could guess now what kind of products …

'John?'

'Yes, Jack?'

'This phone number, is that an Aberdeen code?'

'Keep it to yourself. No grassing me up to Ancram.'

'Just one question …?'

'What?'

'Can I really hear "Mouldy Old Dough"?'

Rebus closed the conversation, finished his drink and left. There was a car parked on the other side of the road. The driver lowered his window so Rebus could see him. It was DS Ludovic Lumsden.

Rebus smiled, waved, started to cross the road. He was thinking: I don't trust you.

'Hiya, Ludo,' he said. Just a man who'd been out for a drink and a dance. 'What brings you here?'

'You weren't in your room. I guessed you might be here.'

'Some guess.'

'You lied to me, John. You told me about a book of matches from Burke's Club.'

'Right.'

'They don't do books of matches.'

'Oh.'

'Can I give you a lift?'

'The hotel's only two minutes away.'

'John.' Lumsden's eyes were cold. 'Can I give you a lift?'

'Sure, Ludo.' Rebus walked around the car and got into the passenger seat.

They drove down to the harbour, parked on an empty street. Lumsden turned off the ignition and turned in his seat.

'So?'

'So what?'

'So you went to Sullom Voe today and didn't bother to tell me. So why has my patch suddenly become *your* patch? How would you like it if I started creeping around Edinburgh behind your back?'

'Am I a prisoner here? I thought I was one of the good guys.'

'It's not your town.'

'I'm beginning to see that. But maybe it's not *your* town either.'

'What do you mean?'

'I mean who really runs the place, behind the scenes? You've got kids going mad with frustration, you've got a ready audience for dope and anything else that might give their life a kick. In that club tonight, I saw the lunatic I told you about, Stanley.'

'Toal's son?'

'That's him. Tell me, is he up here for the floral displays?'

'Did you ask him?'

Rebus lit a cigarette, wound down the window so he could flick the ash out. 'He didn't see me.'

'You think we should question him about Tony El.' A statement of fact, no answer required. 'What would he tell us – "sure, I did it"? Come on, John.'

A woman was knocking on the window. Lumsden lowered it, and she was into her spiel.

'Two of you, well, I don't normally do threesomes but you look like nice … Oh, hello Mr Lumsden.'

'Evening, Cleo.'

She looked at Rebus, then Lumsden again. 'I see your tastes have changed.'

'Lose yourself, Cleo.' Lumsden wound the window back up. The woman disappeared into the darkness.

181

Rebus turned to face Lumsden. 'Look, I don't know just how bent you are. I don't know whose money will be paying for my stay at the hotel. There's a lot I don't know, but I'm beginning to get the feeling I *know* this city. I know it because it's much the same as Edinburgh. I know you could live here for years without glimpsing what's beneath the surface.'

Lumsden started to laugh. 'You've been here – what? – a day and a half? You're a tourist here, don't presume to *know* the place. I've been here a hell of a lot longer, and even I couldn't claim that.'

'All the same, Ludo ...' Rebus said quietly.

'Is this leading somewhere?'

'I thought you were the one who wanted to talk.'

'And you're the one who's talking.'

Rebus sighed, spoke slowly as to a child. 'Uncle Joe controls Glasgow, including – my guess – a fair bit of the drug trade. Now his son's up here, drinking in Burke's Club. An Edinburgh snitch had some gen on a consignment headed north. He also had the phone number of Burke's. He ended up dead.' Rebus held up a finger. 'That's one strand. Tony El tortured an oil-worker, who consequently died. Tony El scurried back up here but neatly passed away. That's three deaths so far, every one of them suspicious, and nobody's doing much about it.' A second finger. 'Strand two. Are the two connected? I don't know. At the moment, all that connects them is Aberdeen itself. But that's a start. You don't know me, Ludo, a start is all I need.'

'Can I change the subject slightly?'

'Go ahead.'

'Did you get anything on Shetland?'

'Just a bad feeling. A little hobby of mine, I collect them.'

'And tomorrow you're going out to Bannock?'

'You've been busy.'

'A few phone calls, that's all it took. Know something?' Lumsden started the car. 'I'll be glad to see the back of you. My life was simple until you came along.'

'Never a dull moment,' Rebus said, opening the door.

'Where are you going?'

'I'll walk. Nice night for it.'

'Suit yourself.'

'I always do.'

Rebus watched the car move off, turn a corner. He listened to the engine fade, flicked his cigarette on to the tarmac and started to walk. The first place he passed was the Yardarm. It was Exotic Dancer night, with a scarecrow on the door charging admission. Rebus had been there, done that. The heyday of the exotic dancer had been the late seventies, every pub in Edinburgh seemed to have them: men watching from behind pint glasses, the stripper selecting her three records from the jukebox, a collection afterwards if you wanted her to go a bit further.

'Only two quid, pal,' the scarecrow called, but Rebus shook his head and kept walking.

The same nighttime sounds were around him: drunken whoops, whistles, and the birds who didn't know how late it was. A prowl of woolly suits was questioning two teenagers. Rebus passed by, just another tourist. Maybe Lumsden was right, but Rebus didn't think so. Aberdeen felt so much like Edinburgh. Sometimes, you visited a town or city and couldn't get a handle on it, but this wasn't one of those.

On Union Terrace a low stone wall separated him from the gardens, which were in a gully below. He saw his car still parked across the road, directly outside the hotel. He was about to cross when hands grabbed at his arms and hauled him backwards. He felt the small of his back hit the wall, felt himself tipping backwards, up and over.

Falling, rolling ... Skidding down the steep slope into the gardens, not able to stop himself, so going with the roll. He hit bushes, felt them tear at his shirt. His nose gouged the earth, tears springing into his eyes. Then he was on the flat. Clipped grass. Lying winded on his back, adrenalin masking any immediate damage. More sounds: crashing through bushes. They were following him down. He half rose to his knees, but a foot caught him, sent him sprawling on to his front. The foot came down hard on his head, held it there, so he was sucking grass, his nose feeling ready to break. Someone wrenched his hands behind his back and up, the pressure just right: excruciating pain couldn't overcome the knowledge that if he moved, he'd pop an arm out of its socket.

Two men, at least two. One with the foot. One working the arms. The alcoholic streets seemed a long way off, traffic a distant drone. Now something cold against his temple. He knew the feeling – a handgun, colder than dry ice.

A voice hissing, close to his ear. Blood pounding there, so he had to strain to hear it. A hiss close to a whisper, hard to identify.

'There's a message, so I hope you're listening.'

Rebus couldn't speak. His mouth was full of dirt.

He waited for the message, but it didn't come. Then it did.

Pistol-whipped to the side of his head, just above the ear. An explosion of light behind his eyes. Then darkness.

He woke up and it was still night. Sat up and looked around. His eyes hurt when he moved them. He touched his head – no blood. It hadn't been that kind of thwack. Blunt, not sharp. Just the one by the feel of things. After he'd lost consciousness they'd left him. He searched his pockets, found money, car keys, warrant card and all his other cards. But of course it hadn't been a robbery. It had been a message, hadn't they told him so themselves?

He tried standing. His side hurt. He checked, saw that he'd grazed it coming down the slope. A graze on his forehead too, and his nose had bled a little. He checked the ground around him, but they hadn't left anything. It wouldn't have been professional. All the same, he tried as best he could to trace the route they'd come down, just in case something had been left behind.

Nothing. He hauled himself back over the wall. A taxi driver looked at him in disgust and pressed harder on the accelerator. He'd seen a drunk, a tramp, a loser.

Last year's man.

Rebus limped across the road into the hotel. The woman behind the reception desk was reaching for the phone, ready to summon back-up, but then recognised him from earlier.

'Whatever happened to you?'

'Fell down some steps.'

'Do you want a doctor?'

'Just my key, please.'

'We've a first aid kit.'

Rebus nodded. 'Have it sent up to my room.'

He took a bath, a good long soak, then towelled off and examined the damage. His temple was swollen where the butt had connected, and he had a headache worse than half a dozen hangovers. Some thorns had lodged in his side, but he was able to pick them out with his fingernails. He cleaned the graze, no need for plasters. He might ache in the morning, but he'd probably sleep, so long as the ticking noise didn't come back. A double brandy had arrived with the first aid; he sipped it, hand trembling. He lay on his bed and phoned home, checking the machine. Ancram, Ancram, Ancram. It was too late to phone Mairie, but he tried Brian Holmes's number. A lot of rings later, Holmes picked up.

'Aye?'

'Brian, it's me.'

'What can I do you for?'

184

Rebus had his eyes screwed shut; difficult to think past the pain. 'Why didn't you tell me Nell had walked out?'

'How do you know?'

'I came by your house. I know a batch pad when I see one. Do you want to talk about it?'

'No.'

'Is it the same problem as before?'

'She wants me to leave the force.'

'And?'

'And maybe she's right. But I've tried before, and it's hard.'

'I know.'

'Well, there's more than one way of leaving.'

'How do you mean?'

'Nothing.' And he wouldn't say any more about it. He wanted to talk about the Spaven case. The bottom line from his reading of the notes: Ancram would smell collusion, a certain economy with the truth; which wasn't to say there was anything he could do about it.

'I also notice you interviewed one of Spaven's friends at the time, Fergus McLure. He's just died, you know.'

'Dearie me.'

'Drowned in the canal, out Ratho way.'

'What did the post mortem say?'

'He received a nasty bump to the head some time before entering the water. It's being treated as suspicious, so …'

'So?'

'So if I were you, I'd steer clear. Don't want to hand Ancram any more ammo.'

'Speaking of Ancram …'

'He's looking for you.'

'I sort of missed our first interview.'

'Where are you?'

'Laying low.' With his eyes closed and three paracetamol in his stomach.

'I don't think he went for your flu story.'

'That's his problem.'

'Maybe.'

'So you're finished on Spaven?'

'Looks like.'

'What about that prisoner? The one who was the last to speak to Spaven?'

'I'm on it, but I think he's no fixed abode, could take a while.'

'I really appreciate it, Brian. Do you have a story ready if Ancram finds out?'

'No problem. Take care, John.'

'You too, son.' *Son?* Where had *that* come from? Rebus put down the phone, picked up the TV remote. Beach volleyball would just about do him for tonight …

Dead Crude

18

Oil: black gold. The North Sea's exploration and exploitation rights had been divvied up long ago. The oil companies spent a lot of money on that initial exploration. A block might yield no oil or gas at all. Vessels were sent out laden with scientific equipment, their data studied and discussed – all this before a single test well was sunk. The reserves might lie three thousand metres beneath the sea bed – Mother Nature not keen to give up the hidden trove. But the plunderers had ever more technical expertise; water depths of two hundred metres no longer bothered them. In fact, the latest discoveries – Atlantic oil, two hundred kilometres west of Shetland – involved a water depth of between four and six hundred metres.

If the test drilling proved successful, showing reserves worth the game, a production platform would be built, along with all the various modules to accompany it. In some parts of the North Sea the weather was too unpredictable for tanker loading, so pipelines would have to be installed – the Brent and Ninian pipelines took crude directly to Sullom Voe, while other pipelines carried gas to Aberdeenshire. All this, and still the oil proved stubborn. In many fields, you could expect to recover only forty or fifty per cent of the available reserve, but then the reserve might consist of one and a half billion barrels.

Then there was the platform itself, sometimes three hundred metres high, a jacket weighing forty thousand tonnes, covered in eight hundred tonnes of paint, and with additional weight of modules and equipment totalling thirty thousand tonnes. The figures were staggering. Rebus tried to take them in, but gave up after a while and decided just to be awestruck. He'd only ever once seen a rig, when he'd been visiting relatives in Methil. The street of prefab bungalows led down to the construction yard, where a three-dimensional steel grid lay on its side, towering into the sky. From a distance of a mile, it had been spectacular enough. He recalled it now, staring at the glossy photographs in the brochure, a brochure all about Bannock. The platform, he read, carried fifteen hundred kilometres of electrical cable, and could accommodate nearly two hundred workers. Once the jacket had been towed out to the oilfield and anchored there, over a dozen modules were placed atop it, everything from accommodation to oil and gas separation. The whole structure had been designed to withstand winds of one hundred knots, and storms with hundred-foot waves.

Rebus was hoping for calm seas today.

He was sitting in a lounge at Dyce Airport, only a little nervous about the flight he was about to take. The brochure assured him that safety was paramount in 'such a potentially hazardous environment', and showed him photos of fire-fighting teams, a safety and support vessel on constant standby, and fully equipped lifeboats. 'The lessons of Piper Alpha have been learned.' The Piper Alpha platform, north-east of Aberdeen: over a hundred and sixty fatalities on a summer's night in 1988.

Very reassuring.

The flunkey who'd handed him the brochure had said he hoped Rebus had brought something to read.

'Why?'

'Because the flight can take three hours total, and most of the time it's too noisy for chit-chat.'

Three hours. Rebus had gone into the terminal's shop and bought himself a book. He knew the journey comprised two stages – Sumburgh first, and then a Super Puma helicopter out to Bannock. Three hours out, three hours back. He yawned, checked his watch. It wasn't quite eight o'clock yet. He'd skipped breakfast – didn't like the idea of boaking it back up on the flight. His total consumption this morning: four paracetamol, one glass of orange juice. He held his hands out in front of him: tremors he could put down to aftershock.

There were two anecdotes he liked in the brochure: he learned that a 'derrick' was named after a seventeenth-century hangman; and that the first oil had come ashore at Cruden Bay, where Bram Stoker once took his holidays. From one kind of vampirism to another ... only the brochure didn't put it like that.

There was a television on in front of him, playing a safety video. It told you what to do if your helicopter went down into the North Sea. It all looked very slick on the video: nobody panicked. They slid out of their seats, located the inflatable life-rafts and launched them on to the calm waters of an indoor pool.

'Holy God, what happened to you?'

He looked up. Ludovic Lumsden was standing there, newspaper folded in his jacket pocket, a beaker of coffee in his hand.

'Mugged,' Rebus said. 'You wouldn't know anything about it, would you?'

'Mugged?'

'Two men were waiting for me last night outside the hotel. Threw me over the wall into the gardens, then stuck a gun against my head.' Rebus rubbed the lump on his temple. It felt worse than it looked.

Lumsden sat down a couple of seats away, looked aghast. 'Did you get a look at them?'

'No.'

Lumsden put his coffee on the floor. 'Did they take anything?'

'They weren't *after* anything. They just had a message for me.'

'What?'

Rebus tapped his temple. 'A thumping.'

Lumsden frowned. 'That was the message?'

'I think I was supposed to read between the lines. You wouldn't be any good at translating, would you?'

'What do you mean?'

'Nothing.' Rebus stared at him hard. 'What are you doing here?'

Lumsden was staring at the tiled floor, mind elsewhere. 'I'm coming with you.'

'Why?'

'Oil Liaison. You're visiting a rig. I should be there.'

'Keeping an eye on me?'

'It's procedure.' He looked towards the television. 'Don't worry about ditching, I've had the training. What it boils down to is, you've got about five minutes from the time you hit the water.'

'And after five minutes?'

'Hypothermia.' Lumsden lifted his coffee cup, drank from it. 'So pray we don't hit a storm out there.'

After Sumburgh Airport, there was nothing but sea and a sky wider than any Rebus had seen before, thin clouds strung across it. The twin-engined Puma flew low and loud. The interior was cramped, and so were the survival suits they'd been made to put on. Rebus's was a bright orange one-piece with a hood, and he'd been ordered to keep it zipped up to his chin. The pilot wanted him to keep his hood up, too, but Rebus found that sitting down with the hood tight across his head, the legs of the suit threatened to dissect his scrotum. He'd been in choppers before – back in army days – but for short hops only. Designs might have changed over the years, but the Puma didn't sound any quieter than the old buckets the army had used. Everyone, however, wore earprotectors, through which the pilot could talk to them. Two other men, contract engineers, flew with them. From flying height, the North Sea looked tranquil, a gentle rise and fall showing the currents. The water looked black, but that was just cloud cover. The brochure had gone into great detail concerning anti-pollution measures. Rebus tried to read his book, but couldn't. It juddered on his knees, blurring the words, and he couldn't keep his mind on the story anyway. Lumsden was looking out of the window, squinting into the light. Rebus knew Lumsden was keeping an eye on him, and he was doing so because Rebus had touched a nerve last night. Lumsden tapped his shoulder, pointed through the window.

There were three rigs below them, off to the east. A tanker was moving away from one of them. Tall flares sent bright yellow flames licking into the sky. The pilot told them they would pass to the west of the Ninian and Brent fields before reaching Bannock. Later, he came back on the radio.

'This is Bannock coming up now.'

Rebus looked past Lumsden's shoulder, saw the single platform coming into view. The tallest structure on it was the flare, but there were no flames. That was because Bannock was coming to the end of its useful life. Very little gas and oil were left to exploit. Next to the flare was a tower, like a cross between an industrial chimney and a space rocket. It was painted with red and white stripes, like the flare. It was probably the drilling tower. Rebus made out the words T-Bird Oil on the jacket below it, along with the block number – 211/7. Three large cranes stood against one edge of the platform, while a whole corner was given over to a helipad, painted green with a yellow circle surrounding the letter H. Rebus thought: one gust could have us over the side. There was a two hundred foot drop to the waiting sea. Orange lifeboats clung to the underside of the jacket, and in another corner sat layers of white portacabins, like bulk containers. A ship sat alongside the platform – the safety and support vessel.

'Hello,' said the pilot, 'what's this?'

He'd spotted another boat, circling the platform at a distance of maybe half a mile.

'Protesters,' he said. 'Bloody idiots.'

Lumsden looked out of his window, pointing. Rebus saw it: a narrow boat painted orange, its sails down. It looked to be very close to the safety ship.

'They could get themselves killed,' Lumsden said. 'And good riddance.'

'I do like a copper with a balanced view.'

They swept out to sea again and banked sharply, then headed for the heliport. Rebus was deep in prayer as they seemed to weave wildly, only fifty feet or so above the deck. He could see the helipad, then whitecapped water, then the helipad again. And then they were down, landing on what looked like a fishing net, covering the white capital H. The doors opened and Rebus removed his ear-protectors. The last words he heard were, 'Keep your head down when you get out.'

He kept his head down when he got out. Two men in orange overalls, wearing yellow hard hats and ear-protectors, led them off the helipad and handed out hard hats. The engineers were led one way, Rebus and Lumsden another.

'You'll probably want a mug of tea after that,' their guide said. He saw that Rebus was having trouble with the hat. 'You can adjust the strap.' He showed him how. There was a fierce wind blowing, and Rebus said as much. The man laughed.

'This is dead calm,' he yelled into the wind.

Rebus felt like he wanted to hang on to something. It wasn't just the wind, it was the feeling of how fragile this whole enterprise was. He'd expected to see and smell oil, but the most obvious product around here wasn't oil – it was seawater. The North Sea surrounded him, massive compared to this speck of welded metal. It insinuated itself into his lungs; the salt gusts stung his cheeks. It rose in vast waves as if to engulf him. It seemed bigger than the sky above it, a force as threatening as any in nature. The guide was smiling.

'I know just what you're thinking. I thought the same thing myself first time I came out here.'

Rebus nodded. The Nationalists said it was Scotland's oil, the oil companies had the exploitation rights, but the picture out here told a different story: oil belonged to the sea, and the sea wouldn't give it up without a fight.

Their guide led them to the relative safety of the canteen. It was clean and quiet, with brick troughs filled with plants, and long white tables ready for the next shift. A couple of orange overalls sat drinking tea at one table, while at another three men in checked shirts ate chocolate bars and yoghurt.

'This place is mad at mealtimes,' the guide said, grabbing a tray. 'Tea all right for you?'

Lumsden and Rebus agreed that tea was fine. There was a long serving-hatch, and a woman at the far end smiling at them.

'Hello, Thelma,' their guide said. 'Three teas. Lunch smells good.'

'Ratatouille, steak and chips, or chilli.' Thelma poured tea from a huge pot.

'Canteen's open twenty-four hours,' the guide told Rebus. 'Most guys, when they first arrive, they overeat. The puddings are lethal.' He slapped his stomach and laughed. 'Isn't that right, Thelma?' Rebus recalled the man in the Yardarm telling him much the same thing.

Even seated, Rebus's legs felt shaky. He put it down to the flight. Their guide introduced himself as Eric, and said that seeing how they were police officers, they could skip the introductory safety video.

'Though by rights I'm supposed to show you it.'

Lumsden and Rebus shook their heads, and Lumsden asked how close the platform was to decommissioning.

'Last oil's already been pumped out,' Eric said. 'Pump a final load of seawater into the reservoir and most of us will ship out. Maintenance crew only, until they decide what to do with her. They'd better make up their minds soon, manning this even just with maintenance shifts is an expensive business. You still have to get the supplies out here, the shift changeovers, and you still need the safety ship. It all costs money.'

'Which is all right so long as Bannock is producing oil?'

'Exactly,' said Eric. 'But when it's not producing ... well, the accountants start having palpitations. We lost a couple of days' worth last month, some problem with the heat exchangers. They were out here, waving their calculators about ...' Eric laughed.

He was nothing like the roustabout of legend, the myth of the roughneck. He was a skinny five and a half feet and wore steel-rimmed glasses above a sharp nose and pointed chin. Rebus looked at the other men in the canteen and tried to equate them with the picture of the oil 'bear', face blackened with crude, biceps expanding as he fought to contain a gusher. Eric saw him looking.

'The three over there,' meaning the checked shirts, 'work in the Control Room. Nearly everything these days is computerised: logic circuits, computer monitoring ... You should ask for a look round, it's like NASA or something, and it only takes three or four people to work the whole system. We've come a long way from "Texas Tea".'

'We saw some protesters in a boat,' Lumsden said, scooping sugar into his mug.

'They're off their noggins. These are dangerous waters for a craft that size. Plus they circle too close, all it'd take is a gust to blow them into the platform.'

Rebus turned to Lumsden. 'You're the Grampian Police presence here, maybe you should do something.'

Lumsden snorted and turned to Eric. 'They haven't done anything illegal yet, have they?'

'All they're breaking so far are the unwritten maritime rules. When you've finished your tea, you'll want to see Willie Ford, is that right?'

'Right,' Rebus said.

'I told him we'd meet him in the recky room.'

'I'd like to see Allan Mitchison's room, too.'

Eric nodded. 'Willie's room: the cabins here are twin berths.'

'Tell me,' Rebus said, 'the decommissioning – any idea what T-Bird are going to do with the platform?'

'Might still end up sinking it.'

'After the trouble with Brent Spar?'

Eric shrugged. 'The accountants are in favour. They only need two things: the government on their side, and a good public relations campaign. The latter's already well under way.'

'With Hayden Fletcher in charge?' Rebus guessed.

'That's the man.' Eric picked up his hard hat. 'All finished?'

Rebus drained his mug. 'Lead the way.'

Outside, it was now 'blustery' – Eric's description. Rebus held on to a rail as he walked. Some workers were leaning over the side of the platform. Beyond them, Rebus could see a huge spume of water. He went up to the rail. The support ship was sending jets of water in the direction of the protest boat.

'Trying to scare them off,' Eric explained. 'Keep them from getting too close to the legs.'

Christ, thought Rebus, why today? He could just see the protest boat ramming the platform, forcing an evacuation ... The jets continued their work, all four of them. Someone passed him a pair of binoculars and he trained them on the protest vessel. Orange oilskins – half a dozen figures on the deck. Banners tied to the rails. NO DUMPING. SAVE OUR OCEANS.

'That boat doesn't look too healthy to me,' someone said.

Figures were going below, reappearing, waving their arms as they explained something.

'Stupid buggers, they've probably let the engine flood.'

'She can't be left to drift.'

'Could be a Trojan horse, lads.'

They all laughed at that. Eric moved off, Rebus and Lumsden following. They climbed up and down ladders. At certain points, Rebus could see clear through the latticework of steel flooring to the churning sea below. There were cables and pipes everywhere, but nowhere you could trip over them. Eventually, Eric opened a door and led them down a corridor. It was a relief to be out of the wind; Rebus realised they'd been outdoors for all of eight minutes.

They passed rooms with pool tables in them, and table-tennis tables, dart boards, video games. The video games seemed popular. Nobody was playing table-tennis.

'Some platforms have swimming pools,' Eric said, 'but not us.'

'Is it my imagination,' Rebus asked, 'or did I just feel the floor move?'

'Oh aye,' Eric said, 'there's a bit of give, has to be. In a swell, you'd swear she was going to break free.' And he laughed again. They kept walking along the corridor, passing a library – no one in it – and a TV room.

'We've three TV rooms,' Eric explained. 'Satellite telly only, but mostly the lads prefer videos. Willie should be in here.'

They entered a large room with a couple of dozen stiff-backed chairs and a large-screen TV. There were no windows, and the lights had been dimmed. Eight or nine men sat, arms folded, in front of the screen. They were complaining about something. A man was standing at the video recorder, holding a tape in his hand, turning it over. He shrugged.

'Sorry about this,' he said.

'That's Willie,' Eric said.

Willie Ford was in his early forties, well built but slightly hunched, with a regulation number one haircut: down to the wood. His nose covered a quarter of his face, a beard protected most of the rest. With more of a tan, he might have passed for a Muslim fundamentalist. Rebus walked up to him.

'Are you the policeman?' Willie Ford asked. Rebus nodded.

'The natives look restless.'

'It's this video. It was supposed to be *Black Rain*, you know, Michael Douglas. But instead it's some Jap flick with the same name, all about Hiroshima. Close but no cigar.' He turned to the audience. 'Some you win, guys. You'll have to settle for something else.' Then shrugged and moved away, Rebus following. The four of them went back along the corridor and into the library.

'So you're in charge of entertainment, Mr Ford?'

'No, I just like videos. There's a place in Aberdeen does fortnight rentals. I usually bring some out with me.' He was still holding the

196

video. 'I can't believe this. The last foreign language film that lot watched was probably *Emmanuelle*.'

'You get porn films?' Rebus asked, like he was just making conversation.

'Dozens of them.'

'How strong?'

'It varies.' An amused look. 'Inspector, did you fly out here to ask me about dirty videos?'

'No, sir, I came to ask you about Allan Mitchison.'

Ford's face clouded like the sky outside. Lumsden was watching from the window, maybe wondering if they'd have to stay the night ...

'Poor Mitch,' Ford said. 'I still can't believe it.'

'You shared a room?'

'These past six months.'

'Mr Ford, we don't have too much time, so you'll forgive me if I'm blunt.' Rebus paused to let him digest this. His mind was half on Lumsden. 'Mitch was killed by a man called Anthony Kane, a thug for hire. Kane used to work for a Glasgow ganglord, but recently he's apparently been operating freelance out of Aberdeen. The night before last, Mr Kane turned up dead, too. Do you know *why* Kane would kill Mitch?'

Ford looked stunned, blinked a few times and let his jaw drop open. Eric was looking disbelieving, too, while Lumsden affected a look of merely professional interest. Finally Ford was able to speak.

'I've ... I've no idea,' he said. 'Could it be a mistake?'

Rebus shrugged. 'It could be anything. That's why I'm trying to compose a picture of Mitch's life. For that, I need his friends' help. Will you help me?'

Ford nodded. Rebus sat down on a chair. 'Then you can start,' he said, 'by telling me about him, tell me anything and everything you can.'

At some point, Eric and Lumsden wandered off for lunch. Lumsden brought sandwiches back for Rebus and Willie Ford. Ford talked, pausing only to take drinks of water. He told Rebus what Allan Mitchison had told him of his background – the parents who weren't his real parents; the special school with its dorms. That was why Mitch liked the rigs – the sense of fellowship, and the shared accommodation. Rebus began to see why his flat in Edinburgh had remained unloved. Ford knew a lot about Mitch, knew that his hobbies included hill-walking and ecology.

'Is that how he came to be friends with Jake Harley?'

'Is he the one at Sullom Voe?' Rebus nodded. Ford nodded with him. 'Yes, Mitch told me about him. They were both keen on ecology.'

Rebus thought of the demo boat outside … thought of Allan Mitchison working in an industry that was a target for Green protest.

'How involved was he?'

'He was pretty active. I mean, the work schedule here, you can't be active all the time. Sixteen days out of every month, he was offshore. We get TV news, but not much in the way of newspapers – not the kind Mitch liked to read. But that didn't stop him organising that concert. Poor sod was looking forward to it.'

Rebus frowned. 'What concert?'

'In Duthie Park. Tonight, I think, if the weather holds.'

'The protest concert?' Ford nodded. 'Allan Mitchison *organised* it?'

'Well, he did his bit. Contacted a couple of the bands to see if they'd play.'

Rebus's head birled. The Dancing Pigs were playing that gig. Mitchison was a big fan of theirs. Yet he hadn't had a ticket for their Edinburgh gig … No, because he hadn't needed one – *he would be on the guest list*! Which meant what exactly?

Answer: bugger all.

Except that Michelle Strachan had been murdered in Duthie Park …

'Mr Ford, weren't Mitch's employers worried about his … loyalty?'

'You don't *have* to be in favour of raping the world to get a job in this industry. In fact, as industries go it's a lot cleaner than some.'

Rebus mulled this over. 'Mr Ford, can I take a look at your cabin?'

'Sure.'

The cabin was small. You wouldn't want to suffer claustrophobia of a night. There were two narrow single beds. Above Ford's bed were pinned pictures; nothing above the other bed but holes where the drawing-pins had been.

'I packed away all his stuff,' Ford explained. 'Do you know if there's anyone …?'

'There's no one.'

'Oxfam then, maybe.'

'Whatever you like, Mr Ford. Let's call you the unofficial executor.'

That did it. Ford slumped on his bed, head in hands. 'Oh, Jesus,' he said, rocking. 'Jesus, Jesus.'

Tactful, John. The silver-tongued clarion of bad news. With tears in his eyes, Ford excused himself and left the room.

Rebus got to work.

He opened drawers and the small built-in wardrobe, but eventually found what he wanted beneath Mitchison's bed. A bin-bag and a series of carrier bags: the deceased's worldly goods.

They didn't amount to much. Maybe Mitchison's background had something to do with it. If you didn't burden yourself with stuff, you could high-tail it out of anywhere, any time. There were some clothes, some books – sci-fi, political economics, *The Dancing Wu-Li Masters*. The last one sounded to Rebus like a ballroom competition. He found a couple of envelopes of photographs, went through them. The platform. Workmates. The budgie and its crew. Other groups, onshore this time: trees in the background. Only these didn't look like workmates – long hair, tie-dye T-shirts, reggae hats. Friends? Friends of the Earth? The second packet seemed light. Rebus counted the photos: fourteen. Then he pulled out the negatives: a count of twenty-five. Eleven short. He held the negs up to the light, but couldn't make out much. The missing photos seemed more of the same; group portraits, a couple of them with only three or four figures. Rebus put the negs in his pocket, just as Willie Ford came back into the room.

'Sorry about that.'

'My fault, Mr Ford. I spoke without thinking. You know earlier I asked you about porn?'

'Yes.'

'What about drugs?'

'I don't use them.'

'But if you did …'

'It's a closed circle, Inspector. I don't use, and no one's offered me any. As far as I'm concerned, people could be shooting up round the corner and I'd never know, because I'm not in the loop.'

'But there is a loop?'

Ford smiled. 'Maybe. But on R&R time only. I'd *know* if I was working beside someone who was wired. They know better than to do that. Working on a platform, you need all the wits you've got and any you can borrow.'

'Have there been accidents?'

'One or two, but our safety record's good. They weren't drug-related.'

Rebus looked thoughtful. Ford seemed to remember something.

'You should see what's happening outside.'

'What?'

'They're bringing the protesters aboard.'

So they were. Rebus and Ford went out to take a look. Ford donned his hard hat, but Rebus carried his: he couldn't get it to sit right, and the only thing threatening to fall from the skies was rain. Lumsden and Eric were already there, along with a few other men. They watched the bedraggled figures climb the last few steps. Despite their oilskins, they looked soaked – courtesy of the power hoses. Rebus recognised one of them: it was braid-hair again. She looked glum verging on furious. He moved towards her, until she was looking at him.

'We must stop meeting like this,' he said.

But she wasn't paying him any attention. Instead, she yelled 'NOW!' and snaked to her right, bringing her hand out of her pocket. She already had one half of the handcuffs clamped around her wrist, and now attached the other firmly around the top rail. Two of her companions did likewise, and started yelling protests at the tops of their voices. Two others were hauled back before they could complete the process. The cuffs were snapped shut on themselves.

'Who's got the keys?' an oil-worker was yelling.

'We left them on the mainland!'

'Christ.' The oilman turned to a colleague. 'Go fetch the oxy-acetylene.' He turned to braid-hair. 'Don't worry, the sparks may burn, but we'll have you out of there in a jiffy.'

She ignored him, kept on chanting with the others. Rebus smiled: you had to admire it. Trojan horse with knobs on.

The torch arrived. Rebus couldn't believe they were really going to do it. He turned to Lumsden.

'Don't say a word,' the policeman warned. 'Remember what I said about frontier justice. We're well out of it.'

The torch was lit, a little flare of its own. There was a helicopter overhead. Rebus had half a mind – maybe more than half – to throw the torch over the side.

'Christ, it's the telly!'

They all looked up. The helicopter was hovering low, a video camera pointed straight at them.

'Fucking TV news.'

Oh great, Rebus thought. That's just spot on. Really low-key, John. National television news. Maybe he should just send Ancram a postcard …

19

Back in Aberdeen, he thought he could still feel the deck moving beneath him. Lumsden had headed off home, carrying with him a promise from Rebus that he'd be packed and off the following morning.

Rebus hadn't mentioned he might be back.

It was early evening, cool but bright, the streets busy with last shoppers trudging home and Saturday night revellers starting early. He walked down to Burke's Club. A different bouncer again, so no grief there. Rebus paid his money like a good boy, waded through the music until he reached the bar. The place hadn't been open long, only a few punters in, looking like they'd be moving on if things didn't start happening. Rebus bought an overpriced short loaded with ice, gave the place a once-over in the mirror. No sign of Eve and Stanley. No sign of any obvious dealers. But Willie Ford was right about that: what did dealers look like? Leave aside the junkies and they looked much like anyone else. Their trade was in eye contact, in a shared knowledge with the person whose eyes they were meeting. A cross between a transaction and a chat-up.

Rebus imagined Michelle Strachan dancing in here, beginning the last movements of her life. As he sloshed the ice around his glass, he decided to walk a route from the club to Duthie Park. It might not be the route *she* took, and he doubted it would throw up anything like a clue, but he wanted to do it, same as he'd driven down to Leith to pay his respects to Angie Riddell's patch. He started off down South College Street, saw from his map that if he kept to this route he'd be walking a main thoroughfare alongside the Dee. Lots of traffic: he decided Michelle would have cut through Ferryhill, so did likewise. Here the streets were narrower and quieter; big houses, leafy. A comfortable middle-class enclave. A couple of corner shops were still doing business – milk, ice-lollies, evening papers. He could hear children playing in back gardens. Michelle and Johnny Bible had walked down here at two a.m. It would have been deserted. If they'd been making any noise, it would have been noted behind the net curtains. But no one had reported anything. Michelle couldn't have been drunk. Drunk, her student friends said, she got loud. Maybe she was a bit merry; just enough to have lost her survival instinct. And Johnny Bible ... he'd been quiet, sober, his smile failing to betray his thoughts.

Rebus turned on to Polmuir Road. Michelle's digs were halfway down. But Johnny Bible had persuaded her to keep walking down to the park. How had he managed it? Rebus shook his head, trying to clear it of jumble. Maybe her digs were strict, she couldn't invite him in. She liked it there, didn't want to be kicked out for an infraction of the rules. Or maybe Johnny had commented on the nice mild night, how he didn't want it to end, he liked her so much. Couldn't they just walk down to the park and back? Maybe walk through the park, just the two of them. Wouldn't that be perfect?

Did Johnny Bible *know* Duthie Park?

Rebus could hear something approximating music, then silence, then applause. Yes: the protest concert. The Dancing Pigs and friends. Rebus went into the park, passed a children's play area. Michelle and her beau had come this way. Her body had been found near here, not far from the Winter Gardens and the tea-room ... There was a huge open space at the heart of the park, and a stage had been erected. Several hundred kids comprised the audience. Bootleggers had spread out their merchandise on the grass, alongside tarot readers, hairbraiders, and herbalists. Rebus forced a smile: it was the Ingliston concert in miniature. People were passing through the crowd, rattling collecting tins. The banner which had adorned the roof of the Conference Centre – DON'T KILL OUR OCEANS! – was now flapping atop the stage. Even the inflatable whale was there. A girl in her mid-teens approached Rebus.

'Souvenir T-shirts? Programmes?'

Rebus shook his head, then changed his mind. 'Give me a programme.'

'Three pounds.'

It was a stapled Xerox with a colour cover. The paper was recycled, and so was the text. Rebus flicked through it. Right at the back there was a list of Thank Yous. His eye caught a name a third of the way down: Mitch, 'with love and gratitude'. Allan Mitchison had played his part organising the gig, and here was his reward – and memorial.

'I'll see if I can do better,' Rebus said, rolling the programme into his pocket.

He made for the area behind the stage, which had been cordoned off by means of arranging lorries and vans into a semi-circle, inside which the bands and their entourages moved like zoo exhibits. His warrant card got him where he wanted to be, as well as a few dirty looks.

'You in charge?' he asked the overweight man in front of him. The man was in his fifties, Jerry Garcia with red hair and a kilt, sweat showing through a stained white vest. Beads of perspiration dripped from his overhanging brow.

'Nobody's in charge,' he told Rebus.

'But you helped organise—'

'Look, what's your problem, man? The concert's licensed, the last thing we need is grief.'

'I'm not giving any. I just have a question about the organisation.'

'What about it?'

'Allan Mitchison – Mitch.'

'Yes?'

'Did you know him?'

'No.'

'I hear he was responsible for getting the Dancing Pigs to play.'

The man thought about it, nodded. 'Mitch, right. I don't know him, I mean, I've seen him around.'

'Anyone I could ask about him?'

'Why, man, what's he done?'

'He's dead.'

'Bad number.' He shrugged. 'Wish I could help.'

Rebus made his way back to front-of-stage. The sound system was the usual travesty, and the band didn't sound nearly as good as on their studio album. Notch one up for the producer. The music stopped suddenly, the momentary silence sweeter than any tune. The singer stepped up to the mike.

'We've got some friends we'd like to bring on. A few hours back they were fighting the good fight, trying to save our seas. Put your hands together for them.'

Applause, cheering. Rebus watched two figures walk onstage, still dressed in orange oilskins: he recognised their faces from Bannock. He waited, but there was no sign of braid-hair. When they started their speeches, he turned to go. There was one last collecting tin to be avoided, but he thought better of it, folded a fiver in through the slot. And decided to treat himself to dinner in his hotel: putting it on the room, of course.

*

Insistent noise.

Rebus folded it into his dream, then gave up. One eye open: chinks of light through the heavy curtains. What fucking time was it? Bedside lamp: on. He clawed at his watch, blinked. Six a.m. What? Did Lumsden want rid of him *that* badly?

He swung out of bed, walked stiff-legged to the door, working his muscles. He'd washed a great dinner down with a bottle of wine. In itself the wine would have posed no problem, but as a *digestif* he'd put away four malts, in flagrant disregard of the drinker's rule: never mix the grape and the grain.

Thump, thump, thump.

Rebus pulled open the door. Two woolly suits stood there, looking like they'd been up for hours.

'Inspector Rebus?'

'Last time I looked.'

'Will you get dressed, please, sir?'

'You don't like the outfit?' Y-fronts and a T-shirt.

'Just get dressed.'

Rebus looked at them, decided to comply. When he walked back into the room, they followed, looked around the way cops always do.

'What have I done?'

'Tell them at the station.'

Rebus looked at him. 'Tell me you're fucking joking.'

'Language, sir,' the other uniform said.

Rebus sat on the bed, pulled on clean socks. 'I'd still like to know what this is all about. You know, on the q.t., officer to officer.'

'Just a few questions, sir. Quick as you can.'

The second uniform tugged open the curtains, light stabbing Rebus's eyeballs. He seemed impressed by the view.

'We had a brawl in the gardens a few nights ago. Remember, Bill?'

His colleague joined him at the window. 'And someone jumped off the bridge a fortnight back. Whee, smack on to Denburn Road.'

'Woman in the car got an awful fright.'

They smiled at the memory.

Rebus stood up, looked around him, wondering what to take.

'Shouldn't be too long, sir.'

They were smiling at *him* now. Rebus's stomach did a back-flip. He tried not to think about timbale of haggis ... cranachan with a fruit coulis ... wine and whisky ...

'Feeling a bit rough, sir?'

The uniform looked about as solicitous as a razor blade.

20

'My name's Chief Inspector Edward Grogan. We've a few questions for you, Inspector Rebus.'

So everyone keeps telling me, Rebus thought. But he didn't say anything, just sat there with arms folded and a wronged man's smouldering look. Ted Grogan: Rebus had heard of him. Hard bastard. He looked it, too: bull-necked and bald, his physique more Frazier than Ali. Thin eyes and thick lips; a street-taught fighter. Jutting forehead; simian.

'You already know DS Lumsden.' Sitting over by the door, head bowed, legs apart. He looked exhausted, embarrassed. Grogan sat down opposite Rebus at the table. They were in a biscuit-tin, though they probably had another name for it in Furry Boot Town.

'No point beating around the bush,' Grogan said. He looked about as comfortable on the chair as a prize Aberdeen Angus. 'How did you get the bruises?'

'I told Lumsden.'

'Tell me.'

'I was mugged by a couple of message-boys. Their message was a pistol whipping.'

'Any other scars?'

'They pushed me over a wall, I hit a thorn-bush on the way down. My side's scratched.'

'Is that it?'

'That's it. Look, I appreciate your concern, but—'

'But that's not our concern, Inspector. DS Lumsden says he dropped you off down by the docks, night before last.'

'That's right.'

'I believe he offered you a lift to your hotel.'

'Probably.'

'But you didn't want that.'

Rebus looked over at Lumsden. *What the fuck is going on?* But Lumsden's gaze was still concentrated floorwards. 'I felt like a walk.'

'Back to your hotel?'

'Right.'

'And on the way, you were beaten up?'

'With a pistol.'

A smile, mixing sympathy with disbelief. 'In Aberdeen, Inspector?'

'There's more than one Aberdeen. I don't see what this has to do with anything.'

'Bear with me. So you walked home?'

'To the very expensive hotel Grampian Police provided for me.'

'Ah, the hotel. We'd pre-booked for a visiting Chief Constable, only he cancelled at the last minute. We'd have ended up paying anyway. I believe DS Lumsden used his initiative and decided you might as well stay there. Highland courtesy, Inspector.'

Highland fabrication more like.

'If that's your story.'

'It's not *my* story that's important here. On this walk home of yours, did you see anyone, speak to anyone?'

'No.' Rebus paused. 'I saw a crew of your finest in discussion with a couple of teenagers.'

'You spoke to them?'

Rebus shook his head. 'Didn't want to interfere. This isn't my patch.'

'From what DS Lumsden tells me, you've been acting like it was.'

Rebus caught Lumsden's eyes. They stared right through him.

'Did a doctor look at your injuries?'

'I fixed myself up. Hotel reception had a first aid kit.'

'They asked you if you wanted a doctor.' A statement.

'I said it wasn't necessary. Lowland self-reliance.'

A cool smile from Grogan. 'You spent yesterday on an oil rig, I believe.'

'With DS Lumsden at my heels.'

'And last night?'

'I had a drink, went for a walk, ate dinner at the hotel. I put it on the tab, by the way.'

'Where did you drink?'

'Burke's Club, a dope-dealer's paradise on College Street. My bet is, my attackers started life there. What's the going rate up here for hiring hard men? Fifty for a duffing? Seventy-five per broken limb?'

Grogan sniffed, rose to his feet. 'Those prices might be a wee bit on the high side.'

'Look, with respect, I'm about two hours from out of here. If this is some kind of warning, it's too much too late.'

Grogan spoke very quietly. 'It's not a warning, Inspector.'

'What is it then?'

'You say when you left Burke's you went for a walk?'

'Yes.'

'Where?'

'Duthie Park.'

'A fair hike.'

'I'm a big Dancing Pigs fan.'

'Dancing Pigs?'

'A band, sir,' Lumsden said, 'they were playing a concert last night.'

'It talks.'

'No need for that, Inspector.' Grogan was standing behind Rebus. The invisible interrogator: did you turn to face him, or did you stare at the wall? Rebus had played the trick himself many a time. Objective: unnerve the prisoner.

Prisoner – Jesus.

'You'll remember, sir,' Lumsden said, voice almost atonal, 'that's the route Michelle Strachan took.'

'That's true, isn't it, Inspector? I expect you knew that.'

'How do you mean?'

'Well, you've been taking a great interest in the Johnny Bible case, haven't you?'

'I've been involved tangentially, sir.'

'Oh, tangentially?' Grogan came back into view, showing yellow teeth that looked like they'd been filed short. 'Well, that's one way of putting it. DS Lumsden says you seemed very interested in the Aberdeen side of the case, kept asking him questions.'

'With respect, that's DS Lumsden's interpretation.'

'And what's yours?' Leaning over the desk, fists resting on it. Getting in close. Objective: cow the suspect, show him who's boss.

'Mind if I smoke?'

'Answer the question!'

'*Stop treating me like a fucking suspect!*'

Rebus regretted the outburst immediately – sign of weakness, sign he was rattled. In army training, he'd survived days on end of interrogation techniques. Yes, but back then his head had been emptier; there'd been less to feel guilty about.

'But, Inspector,' Grogan sounding hurt by the flare-up, 'that's precisely what you are.'

Rebus grabbed at the edge of the table, feeling its rough metal edge. He tried to stand, but his legs failed him. He probably looked like he was crapping himself, forced his hands to release the table.

'Yesterday evening,' Grogan said coolly, 'a woman's body was found in a crate on the dockside. Pathologist reckons she was killed some time the previous night. Strangled. Raped. One of her shoes is missing.'

Rebus was shaking his head. Sweet Jesus, he was thinking, not another one.

'There's no sign that she fought back, no skin beneath the fingernails, but she could have lashed out with her fists. She had the look of a strong woman, tenacious.'

Involuntarily, Rebus touched the bruise on his temple.

'You were down near the docks, Inspector, and in a foul mood according to DS Lumsden.'

Rebus was on his feet. 'He's trying to stitch me up!' Attack, they said, was the best form of defence. Not necessarily true, but if Lumsden wanted to play dirty, Rebus would give as good as he got.

'Sit down, Inspector.'

'He's trying to protect his fucking clients! How much do you take a week, Lumsden? How much do they slip you?'

'*I said sit down!*'

'Sod you,' said Rebus. It was like a boil had burst; he couldn't halt the outpour. 'You're trying to tell me I'm Johnny Bible! I'm nearer Bible John's age, for Christ's sake.'

'You were at the docks around the time she was murdered. You arrived back at your hotel cut and bruised, your clothes a mess.'

'This is bullshit! I don't have to listen to this!'

'Yes you do.'

'Charge me then.'

'We've a few more questions, Inspector. This can be as painless as you like, or it can be absolute bastarding agony. You choose, but before you do that – *sit down!*'

Rebus stood there. His mouth was open, and he wiped saliva from his chin. He looked over at Lumsden, who was still seated, albeit tensed, ready to jump if words became deeds. Rebus wouldn't give him the satisfaction. He sat down.

Grogan took a deep breath. The air in the room – what was left of it – was beginning to smell bad. It wasn't even half past seven.

'Bovril and oranges at half time?' Rebus asked.

'That might be a long way off.' Grogan walked to the door, opened it and stuck his head out. Then he held the door wide open so someone outside could come in.

Chief Inspector Chick Ancram.

'Saw you on the news, John. Not exactly telegenic, are you?' Ancram slipped off his jacket and placed it carefully over the back of a chair. He looked like he was about to enjoy himself. 'You weren't wearing your hard hat, mightn't have recognised you otherwise.' Grogan walked over to where Lumsden was sitting, like a tag-team wrestler leaving the ring. Ancram started rolling up his sleeves.

'Going to be a hot one, John, eh?'

'A scorcher,' Rebus muttered. Now he knew why CID liked dawn raids: he felt exhausted already. Exhaustion played tricks with your mind; it made you make mistakes. 'Any chance of a coffee?'

Ancram looked to Grogan. 'I don't see why not. How about you, Ted?'

'I could do with a cup myself.' He turned to Lumsden. 'On you go, son.'

'Fucking message-boy,' Rebus couldn't help saying.

Lumsden sprang to his feet, but Grogan had a restraining hand out. 'Easy, son, just go get those coffees, eh?'

'And DS Lumsden?' Ancram called. 'Make sure Inspector Rebus gets decaf, we don't want him getting all jumpy.'

'Any jumpier and I'd be a kangaroo. Lumsden? I like hundred per cent decaf, no pissing or howking into it, OK?'

Lumsden left the room in silence.

'Now then.' Ancram sat down across from Rebus. 'You're a hard man to catch.'

'You've gone to a lot of trouble.'

'I think you're worth it, don't you? Tell me something about Johnny Bible.'

'Like what?'

'Anything. His methods, background, profile.'

'That could take all day.'

'We've got all day.'

'Maybe you have, but my room's got to be vacated by eleven, or else it's another day's rate.'

'Your room's already empty,' Grogan said. 'Your stuff's in my office.'

'Inadmissible as evidence: you should have had a search warrant.'

Ancram shared a laugh with Grogan. Rebus knew why they were

laughing, he'd've been doing it too if he'd been where they were. But he wasn't. He was where a lot of men and women, some of them barely adult, had been before him. Same chair, same sweaty room, same set-up. Hundreds and thousands of them, suspects. In the eyes of the law, innocent until proven guilty. In the eyes of the interrogator, the other way round. Sometimes to prove to yourself that a suspect was innocent you had to break them. Sometimes you had to go that far before you were sure in your mind. Rebus didn't know how many sessions like this he'd sat in on ... hundreds, certainly. He'd broken maybe a dozen suspects only to find they were innocent. He knew where he was, knew why he was there, but that didn't make it any easier.

'I'll tell *you* something about Johnny Bible,' Ancram said. 'His profile can fit several professions, and one of those is serving or retired police officer, someone who knows our methods and is careful not to leave trace evidence.'

'We've a physical description of him. I'm too old.'

Ancram screwed up his face. 'IDs, John, we all know their failings.'

'I'm not Johnny Bible.'

'Doesn't mean you're not a copycat. Mind, we're not saying you are. All we're saying is, there are questions that have to be asked.'

'So ask them.'

'You came to Partick.'

'Correct.'

'Ostensibly to talk to me about Uncle Joe Toal.'

'Uncannily astute.'

'Yet if memory serves, you ended up asking me a lot of questions about Johnny Bible. And you seemed to know a lot about the Bible John case.' Ancram waited to see if Rebus had a smart comeback. None came. 'While in Partick, you spent a lot of time in the room where the original Bible John files were being checked.' Ancram paused again. 'And now a TV reporter tells me you have cuttings and notes about Bible John and Johnny Bible stashed in your kitchen cupboards.'

Bitch!

'Now wait a minute,' Rebus said.

Ancram sat back. 'I'm waiting.'

'Everything you've said is true. I *am* interested in the two cases. Bible John ... that takes a bit of explaining. And Johnny Bible ... well, for one thing, I knew one of the victims.'

Ancram sat forward. 'Which one?'

'Angie Riddell.'

'In Edinburgh?' Ancram and Grogan exchanged a look. Rebus knew what they were thinking: another connection.

'I was part of the team that picked her up once. I saw her again after that.'

'Saw her?'

'Drove down to Leith, passed the time of day.'

Grogan snorted. 'There's a euphemism I've not heard before.'

'We talked, that's all. I bought her a cup of tea and a bridie.'

'And you didn't tell anyone? Do you know how that looks?'

'Another black mark against me. I've got so many, I could play Al Jolson on stage.'

Ancram got up. He wanted to pace the room, but it wasn't big enough. 'This is bad,' he said.

'How can the truth be bad?' But Rebus knew Ancram was right. He didn't want to agree with Ancram about *anything* – that would be to fall into the interrogator's trap: empathy – but he couldn't make himself disagree on this one point. This *was* bad. His life was turning into a Kinks song: 'Dead End Street'.

'You're up to your oxters, pal,' Ancram said.

'Thanks for reminding me.'

Grogan lit a cigarette for himself, offered one to Rebus, who refused the ploy with a smile. He had his own if he wanted one.

He wanted one – but not enough yet. Instead, he scratched at his palms, clawing his nails across them, a wake-up call to his nerve-endings. There was silence in the room for a minute or so. Ancram rested his backside against the table.

'Christ, is he waiting for the coffee beans to grow or what?'

Grogan shrugged. 'Shift changeover, the canteen'll be busy.'

'You just can't get the staff these days,' Rebus said. Head down, Ancram smiled into his chest. Then he gave a sideways look at the seated figure.

Here we go, thought Rebus: the sympathy routine. Maybe Ancram read his mind, changed his own accordingly.

'Let's talk a bit more about Bible John,' he said.

'Fine with me.'

'I've started on the Spaven casenotes.'

'Oh aye?' Had he got to Brian Holmes?

'Fascinating reading.'

'We had a few publishers interested at the time.'

No smile for that one. 'I didn't know,' the inquisitor said quietly, 'that Lawson Geddes worked on Bible John.'

'No?'

'Or that he was kicked off the inquiry. Any idea why that was?'

Rebus didn't say anything. Ancram spotted the flaw in the armour, stood up and leaned over him.

'You didn't know?'

'I knew he'd worked the case.'

'But you didn't know he'd been ordered off it. No, because he didn't tell you. I found that particular nugget in the Bible John files. But no mention of why.'

'Is this going anywhere other than up the garden path?'

'Did he talk to you about Bible John?'

'Maybe once or twice. He talked a lot about his old cases.'

'I'm sure he did, the two of you were close. And from what I hear, Geddes liked to shoot his mouth off.'

Rebus glared at him. 'He was a good copper.'

'Was he?'

'Believe it.'

'But even good coppers make mistakes, John. Even good coppers can cross the line *once* in their lives. Little birdies tell me you've crossed that line more than a few times yourself.'

'Little birdies shouldn't shit in their own nests.'

Ancram shook his head. 'Your past conduct isn't an issue here.' He straightened up and turned away, letting that remark sink in. He still had his back to Rebus when he spoke. 'You know something? This media interest in the Spaven case, it coincided with the first Johnny Bible killing. Know what that might make people think?' Now he turned round, held up a finger. 'A copper obsessed with Bible John, remembering stories his old sparring partner told him about the case.' Second finger. 'The dirt on the Spaven case is about to be uncovered, years after said copper thought it was buried.' Third finger. 'Copper snaps. There's been this time-bomb in his brain, and now it's activated ...'

Rebus got to his feet. 'You know it's not true,' he said quietly.

'Convince me.'

'I'm not sure I need to.'

Ancram looked disappointed in him. 'We'll want to take samples – saliva, blood, prints.'

'What for? Johnny Bible hasn't left any clues.'

'I also want a forensic lab to look at your clothes, and a team to give your flat the once-over. If you haven't done anything, there should be

212

nothing to object to.' He waited for a reply, got none. The door opened. 'About fucking time,' he said.

Lumsden bearing a tray swimming with spilled coffee.

Break-time. Ancram and Grogan went into the corridor for a chat. Lumsden stood by the door, arms folded, thinking he was on guard duty, thinking Rebus wasn't pumped-up enough to rip his head off.

But Rebus just sat there drinking what was left of his coffee. It tasted disgusting, so probably *was* unleaded. He took out his cigarettes, lit one, inhaled like it might be his last. He held the cigarette vertical, wondered how something so small and brittle could have taken such a hold over him. Not so very different from this case ... The cigarette wavered: his hands were shaking.

'This is you,' he told Lumsden. 'You've sold your boss a story. I can live with that, but don't think I'll forget.'

Lumsden stared at him. 'Do I look scared?'

Rebus stared back, smoked his cigarette, said nothing. Ancram and Grogan came back into the room, all businesslike.

'John,' Ancram said, 'CI Grogan and I have decided this would be best dealt with in Edinburgh.'

Meaning they couldn't prove a thing against him. If there was the slightest possibility, then Grogan would want a home collar.

'There are disciplinary matters here,' Ancram went on. 'But they can be dealt with as part of my inquiry into the Spaven case.' He paused. 'Shame about DS Holmes.'

Rebus went for it, had to. 'What about him?'

'When we went to pick up the Spaven casenotes, some clerk told us there'd been a lot of interest in them recently. Holmes had consulted them three days in a row, apparently for hours at a time – when he should have been on regular duties.' Another pause. 'Your name was down, too. Apparently you visited him. Going to tell me what he was up to?'

Silence.

'Removing evidence?'

'Fuck off.'

'That's the way it looks. Stupid move, whatever it was. He's refusing to talk, facing disciplinary action. He could be out on his ear.'

Rebus kept his face a blank; not so easy to blank his heart.

'Come on,' Ancram said, 'let's get you out of here. My driver can take your car, we'll take mine, maybe have a wee chat on the road.'

Rebus stood up, walked over to Grogan, who straightened his

213

shoulders as if expecting physical assault. Lumsden clenched his fists, ready. Rebus stopped with his face inches from Grogan's.

'Are you on the take, sir?' It was fun to watch the balloon fill with blood, highlighting burst veins and ageing lines.

'John ...' Ancram warned.

'It's an honest question,' Rebus went on. 'See, if you're not, you could do a lot worse than put a surveillance on two Glasgow hoods who seem to be holidaying up here – Eve and Stanley Toal, only his real name's Malky. His dad's called Joseph Toal, Uncle Joe, and he runs Glasgow, where CI Ancram works, lives, splashes out money and buys his suits. Eve and Stanley drink at Burke's Club, where coke isn't something in a long glass with ice. DS Lumsden took me there, looked like he'd been before. DS Lumsden reminded me that Johnny Bible had picked out his first victim there. DS Lumsden drove me down to the harbour that night, I didn't *ask* to be taken there.' Rebus looked over at Lumsden. 'He's a canny operator, DS Lumsden. The games he plays, no wonder he's called Ludo.'

'I won't have malicious comments made about my men.'

'Surveillance on Eve and Stanley,' Rebus stressed. 'And if it's blown, you know where to look.' Same place he was looking now.

Lumsden flew at him, hands at his throat. Rebus threw him off.

'You're as dirty as bilge-water, Lumsden, and don't think I don't know it!'

Lumsden swung a punch; it didn't connect. Ancram and Grogan pulled the two of them apart. Grogan pointed to Rebus, but spoke to Ancram.

'Maybe we'd better keep him here after all.'

'I'm taking him back with me.'

'I'm not so sure about that.'

'I said I'm taking him back, Ted.'

'Long time since I had two men fighting over me,' Rebus said with a smile.

The two Aberdeen officers were looking ready to plough a field with him. Ancram slapped a proprietorial hand on to his shoulder.

'Inspector Rebus,' he said, 'I think we'd best be going, don't you?'

'Do me one favour,' Rebus said.

'What?' They were in the back of Ancram's car, heading for Rebus's hotel, where they'd pick up his car.

'A quick detour down to the docks.'

Ancram glanced at him. 'Why?'

'I want to see where she died.'

Ancram looked at him again. 'What for?'

Rebus shrugged. 'To pay my respects,' he said.

Ancram had only a vague idea where the body had been found, but it didn't take long to find the runs of bright police tape which were there to secure the scene. The docks were quiet, no sign of the crate in which the body had been discovered. It would be in a police lab somewhere. Rebus kept the right side of the cordon, looked around him. Huge white gulls strutted at a safe distance. The wind was fresh. He couldn't tell how close this was to the spot where Lumsden had dropped him off.

'What do you know about her?' he asked Ancram, who stood, hands in pockets, studying him.

'Name's Holden, I think. Twenty-seven, twenty-eight.'

'Did he take a souvenir?'

'Just one of her shoes. Listen, Rebus ... all this interest is because you once bought a prostitute a cup of tea?'

'Her name was Angie Riddell.' Rebus paused. 'She had beautiful eyes.' He gazed towards a rusting hulk chained dockside. 'There's a question I've been asking myself. Do we let it happen, or do we make it happen?' He looked at Ancram. 'Any idea?'

Ancram frowned. 'I'm not sure I understand.'

'Me neither,' Rebus admitted. 'Tell your driver to be careful with my car. The steering's a bit loose.'

The Panic of Dreams

21

They were chasing him up and down monkey-puzzle ladders, the tumorous sea raging beneath, buckling weakened metal. Rebus lost his grip, tumbled down steel steps, gashed his side and dabbed a hand there, finding oil instead of blood. They were twenty feet above him and laughing, taking their time: where was there for him to go? Maybe he could fly, flap his arms and leap into space. The only thing to fear was the drop.

Like landing on concrete.

Was that better or worse than landing on spikes? He had decisions to make; his pursuers weren't far behind. They were never far behind, yet he always stayed in front of them, even wounded. I could get out of this, he thought.

I could get out of this!

A voice directly behind him: 'In your dreams.' Then a push out into space.

Rebus started awake so suddenly his head hit the car roof. His body surged with fear and adrenalin.

'Christ,' Ancram said from the driver's seat, regaining control of the steering-wheel, 'what happened?'

'How long was I asleep?'

'I didn't realise you were.'

Rebus looked at his watch: maybe only a couple of minutes. He rubbed his face, told his heart it could stop hammering any time it liked. He could tell Ancram it was a bad dream; he could tell him it was a panic attack. But he didn't want to tell him anything. Until proven otherwise, Ancram was the enemy as surely as any gun-toting thug.

'What were you saying?' he said instead.

'I was outlining the deal.'

'The deal, right.' The Sunday papers had slid from Rebus's lap. He picked them off the floor. Johnny Bible's latest outrage had made only one front page; the others had been printed too early.

'Right now, I've enough against you to have you suspended,' Ancram said. 'Not such an unusual situation for you, Inspector.'

'I've been there before.'

'Even if I overlook the Johnny Bible questions, there's still the matter of your distinct lack of cooperation with my inquiries into the Spaven case.'

'I had flu.'

Ancram ignored this. 'We both know two things. First, a good cop is going to get into trouble from time to time. I've had complaints made against *me* in the past. Second, these TV programmes almost never uncover new evidence. It's all speculation and maybes, whereas a police investigation is meticulous, and the gen we gather is passed to the Crown Office and pored over by what are supposed to be some of the finest criminal lawyers in the country.'

Rebus turned in his seat to study Ancram, wondering where this was leading. In the mirror, he could see his own car being driven with due care and attention by Ancram's lackey. Ancram kept his eyes on the road.

'See, John, what I'm saying is, why run when you've nothing to fear?'

'Who says I've nothing to fear?'

Ancram smiled. The old pals routine was just that – a routine. Rebus trusted Ancram the way he'd trust a paedophile in a play-park. All the same, when Uncle Joe had lied about Tony El, it was Ancram who'd come up with the Aberdeen info ... Whose side was the man on? Was he playing a double game? Or had he just thought Rebus wouldn't get anywhere, info or no info? Was it a way of covering up that he was in Uncle Joe's pocket?

'If I'm hearing you right,' Rebus said, 'you're saying I've nothing to fear from the Spaven case?'

'This could be true.'

'You'd make it true?' Ancram shrugged. 'In return for what?'

'John, you've ruffled more feathers than a puma in a parrot-house, and you've been about as subtle.'

'You want me to be more subtle?'

Ancram's voice tightened. 'I want you to sit on your arse for once.'

'Drop the Mitchison inquiry?' Ancram didn't say anything. Rebus repeated the question.

'You might find it does you the world of good.'

'And you'd have done Uncle Joe Toal another good turn, eh, Ancram?'

'Wake up to reality. This isn't a linoleum floor, big squares of black and white.'

'No, it's grey silk suits and crisp green cash.'

'It's give and take. People like Uncle Joe don't go away: you get rid of him and a young pretender starts making claims.'

'Better the devil you know?'

'Not a bad motto.'

John Martyn: 'I'd Rather Be the Devil'.

'Here's another,' Rebus said, 'don't rock the boat. Sounds like that's what you're telling me.'

'I'm *advising* you for your own good.'

'Don't think I don't appreciate it.'

'Christ, Rebus, I begin to see why you're always out on a limb: you're not easy to like, are you?'

'Mr Personality six years running.'

'I don't think so.'

'I even cried on the catwalk.' A pause. 'Did you ask Jack Morton about me?'

'Jack has a bizarrely high opinion of you, something I put down to sentiment.'

'Big of you.'

'This is getting us nowhere.'

'No, but it's passing the time.' Rebus saw signs for a service area. 'Are we stopping for lunch?'

Ancram shook his head.

'You know, there's one question you haven't asked me.'

Ancram considered not asking, then caved in. 'What?'

'You haven't asked what Stanley and Eve were doing in Aberdeen.'

Ancram signalled to pull into the service area, braking hard. The driver in Rebus's Saab nearly missed the slip-road, tyres squealing on tarmac.

'Trying to lose him?' Rebus enjoyed seeing Ancram rattled.

'Coffee break,' Ancram snarled, opening his door.

Rebus sat with the tabloid on the table in front of him, reading about Johnny Bible. The victim this time was Vanessa Holden, twenty-seven and married – none of the others had been married. She was director of a company which put on 'corporate presentations': Rebus wasn't entirely sure what that meant. The photo in the paper was the usual smile-for-the-camera job, taken by a friend. She had shoulder-length wavy hair, nice teeth, probably hadn't thought about dying much short of her eightieth birthday.

'We've got to catch this monster,' Rebus said, echoing the last sentence of the story. Then he crumpled the paper and reached for his coffee. Glancing down at the table, he caught a sideways glimpse of Vanessa Holden, and got the feeling he'd seen her before somewhere, just a fleeting glance. He covered her hair with his hand. Old photo; maybe she'd changed hairstyle. He tried to see her face with a few more miles on its clock. Ancram wasn't watching, was talking to the lackey, so he didn't see the shock of recognition hit Rebus's face.

'I have to make a phone call,' Rebus said, rising. The public phone was beside the front door; he'd be in view of the table. Ancram nodded. 'What's the problem?' he said.

'Today's Sunday, I should've been at church. The minister will be worried.'

'This bacon's easier to swallow than that.' Ancram stabbed his fork at the offending article. But he let Rebus go.

Rebus made the call, hoped he'd have enough change: Sunday, cheap rate. Someone at Grampian Police HQ picked up.

'DCI Grogan, please,' Rebus said, his eyes on Ancram. The restaurant was busy with Sunday drivers and their families; no chance of Ancram hearing him.

'I'm afraid he's busy at the moment.'

'This is about Johnny Bible's latest victim. I'm in a phone-box and money's tight.'

'Hold on, please.'

Thirty seconds. Ancram watching him, frowning. Then: 'DCI Grogan speaking.'

'It's Rebus.'

Grogan sucked in breath. 'What the hell do you want?'

'I want to do you a favour.'

'Oh aye?'

'It could make your career.'

'Is this your idea of a joke? Because let me tell you—'

'No joke. Did you hear what I said about Eve and Stanley Toal?'

'I heard.'

'Are you going to do anything?'

'Maybe.'

'Make it a definite ... as a favour to me.'

'And then you'll do me this premier-league favour of yours?'

'That's right.'

Grogan coughed, cleared his throat. 'All right,' he said.

'For real?'

'I keep my promises.'

'Then listen. I've just seen a photo of Johnny's latest victim.'

'And?'

'And I've seen her before.'

A moment's silence. 'Where?'

'She was walking into Burke's Club one night as Lumsden and I were leaving.'

'So?'

'So she was on the arm of someone I knew.'

'You know a lot of people, Inspector.'

'Which doesn't mean I'm connected to Johnny Bible. But maybe the man on her arm is.'

'Do you have a name for him?'

'Hayden Fletcher, works for T-Bird Oil. Public relations.'

Grogan was writing it down. 'I'll look into it,' he said.

'Don't forget your promise.'

'Did I make a promise? I don't recall.' The line went dead. Rebus wanted to hammer the receiver, but Ancram was watching, and besides there were children nearby, drooling over a toy display and devising plans of attack on their parents' pockets. So he replaced the receiver just like any other human being and walked back to the table. The driver got up and went outside, didn't once look at Rebus, so Rebus knew he was under orders.

'Everything OK?' Ancram asked.

'Hunky dory.' Rebus sat down opposite Ancram. 'So when does the inquisition begin?'

'As soon as we can find a vacant torture chamber.' They both ended up smiling. 'Look, Rebus, personally I don't give a midge's IQ what happened twenty years ago between your pal Geddes and this Lenny Spaven. I've seen villains stitched up before: you can't nail them for the thing you *know* they did, so you nail them for something else, something they didn't do.' He shrugged. 'It happens.'

'There were rumours it happened to Bible John.'

Ancram shook his head. 'I don't think so. But see, here's the crux of the matter. *If* your chum Geddes became obsessed with Spaven, and stitched him up – with your help, wittingly or unwittingly ... Well, you know what that means?'

Rebus nodded, but couldn't say the words: they'd been choking him for weeks. They'd choked him back then for a few weeks, too.

'It means,' Ancram went on, 'the real killer got away with it. Nobody's ever tried looking for him, he's scot free.' He smiled at this last phrase, then sat back in his chair. 'Now I'm going to tell you something about Uncle Joe.' He had Rebus's attention. 'He's probably involved in drug dealing. Big profits, unlikely he wouldn't want some. But Glasgow was sewn up years ago, and rather than get into a war we think he's been casting his net wider.'

'As far as Aberdeen?'

Ancram nodded. 'We're compiling a file prior to setting up a surveillance op in conjunction with the Squaddies.'

'And every surveillance you've tried in the past has failed.'

'There's a double loop to this one: if someone leaks word to Uncle Joe, *we'll* know where the leak started.'

'So you end up with either Uncle Joe or the grass? It might work … if you don't go around telling everyone about it.'

'I'm trusting you.'

'Why?'

'Because you could fuck things up, pure and simple.'

'You know, I've been here before, people telling me to lay off, leave everything to them.'

'And?'

'And they've usually had something to hide.'

Ancram shook his head. 'Not this time. But I *do* have something to offer. Like I say, *personally* I've no interest in the Spaven case, but professionally I'm duty bound to do my job. Thing is, there are ways and ways of presenting a report. I could minimise your part in the whole thing, I could leave you out altogether. I'm not telling you to drop any investigation; I'm just asking you to freeze it for a week or so.'

'And let the trail grow cold, maybe enough time for a few more suicides and accidental deaths?'

Ancram looked exasperated.

'Just do your job, Chief Inspector,' Rebus said. 'And I'll do mine.' Rebus got to his feet, looked for the paper with the Johnny Bible story, stuffed it in his pocket.

'Here's the deal,' Ancram said, smouldering. 'I'm going to have a man with you at all times, reporting back to me. It's either that or a suspension.'

Rebus jerked his thumb towards the window. 'Him out there?' The driver was enjoying a smoke in the sunshine. Ancram shook his head.

'Someone who knows you better.'

Rebus came up with the answer a second before Ancram spoke.

'Jack Morton.'

He was waiting for Rebus outside the flat. Water was dribbling down the dishels from where neighbours were cleaning their cars. Jack had been sitting in his own car, windows rolled down, his paper open at the crossword. Now he was out of the car and had his arms folded, head inclined to the sun's rays. He was dressed in a short-sleeved shirt and faded jeans, newish white trainers on his feet.

'Sorry to muck up your weekend,' Rebus told him, as he got out of Ancram's car.

'Remember,' Ancram called to Jack, 'don't let him out of your sight. If he goes for a dump, I want you keeking through the key-hole. If he says he's putting the rubbish out, I want you inside one of the bags. Understood?'

'Yes, sir,' Jack said.

The police driver was asking Rebus where he should park the Saab. Rebus pointed to the double yellow line at the bottom of the street. The windscreen still boasted its Grampian Police Business sign. Rebus was in no hurry to tear it off. Ancram got out of his driving seat and opened the rear door. His driver handed Rebus the keys to the Saab and his suitcase out of the boot, and got into his boss's car, adjusting the seat and the rearview. Rebus and Jack watched Ancram being driven away.

'So,' Rebus said, 'I hear you're with the Juice Church these days.'

Jack wrinkled his nose. 'I can take or leave the holy roller stuff, but it's helped me give up the hooch.'

'That's great.'

'How come I never know when you're being serious?'

'Years of practice.'

'Nice holiday?'

'Nice doesn't begin to describe it.'

'I see your face took a dunt.'

Rebus touched his temple. The swelling was going down. 'Some people get temperamental when you beat them to the sunbeds.'

They climbed the stairwell, Jack a couple of steps behind Rebus.

'Are you seriously not going to let me out of your sight?'

'That's what the boss wants.'

'And what he wants he gets?'

'If I know what's good for me. It's taken me a lot of years to come to the conclusion that I *do* want what's good for me.'

'So speaks the philosopher.' Rebus put his key in the lock, pushed the door open. There was some mail on the hall carpet, but not much.

'You realise this is probably against a couple of dozen laws. I mean, you can't just follow me around if I don't want you to.'

'So take it to the Court of Human Rights.' Jack followed Rebus into the living room. The suitcase stayed out in the hall.

'Fancy a drink?' Rebus asked.

'Ha ha.'

Rebus shrugged, found a clean glass and poured himself some of Kayleigh Burgess's whisky. It went down without touching the sides. He exhaled noisily. 'You must miss it though?'

'All the time,' Jack admitted, slumping on to the sofa.

Rebus poured another. 'I know I would.'

'That's half the battle.'

'What?'

'Admitting you'd have a problem without it.'

'I didn't say that.'

Jack shrugged, got to his feet again. 'Mind if I make a phone call?'

'My home is your home.'

Jack walked over to the telephone. 'Looks like you've got some messages. Want to play them?'

'They'll all be from Ancram.'

Jack lifted the receiver, pressed seven digits. 'It's me,' he said at last. 'We're here.' Then he put the telephone down.

Rebus looked at him above the rim of the glass.

'There's a team on its way,' Jack explained. 'To look the place over. Chick said he'd tell you.'

'He told me. No search warrant, I suppose?'

'If you want it, we can get one. But if I were you, I'd just sit back and let it happen – quick and painless. Plus ... if anything ever comes to court, you'll have the prosecution on a technicality.'

Rebus smiled. 'Are you on my side, Jack?' Jack sat down again, but didn't say anything. 'You told Ancram I'd phoned you, didn't you?'

Jack shook his head. 'I kept my trap shut when maybe I shouldn't.' He sat forward. 'Chick knows we go back, you and me, that's why I'm here.'

'I don't get it.'

'It's a loyalty thing, he's testing my loyalty to him, pitting the past – that's you and me – against *my* future.'

'And how loyal are you, Jack?'

'Don't push it.'

Rebus drained his glass. 'This is going to be an interesting few days.

What happens if I get lucky winching? Are you going to want to hide beneath the bed, like a piss-pot or the fucking bogeyman?'

'John, don't get—'

But Rebus was on his feet. 'This is my home, for Christ's sake! The one place I can hide from all the shite flying around out there! Am I supposed to just sit here and take it? You standing guard, forensics sniffing around like mongrels at a lamp-post – am I supposed to sit here and let you get on with it?'

'Yes.'

'Well fuck that, Jack, and fuck you, too.' The doorbell rang. 'You get it,' Rebus said. 'They're your dogs.'

Jack looked hurt as he made for the door. Rebus went into the hall, grabbed his case and took it into his bedroom. He threw it on the bed and opened it. Whoever had packed it had just stuffed everything in, clean and dirty. The whole lot would have to go to the launderette. He lifted out his wash-bag. There was a note folded below it. It told him that 'certain items of clothing' had been held back by Grampian Police for forensic 'exploration'. Rebus looked: his grass-stained trousers and torn shirt from the night he'd been attacked, they were missing. Grogan was having them tested, just in case Rebus *had* killed Vanessa Holden. Fuck him, fuck them all. Fuck the whole fucking lot of them. Rebus threw the open case across the room, just as Jack came to the doorway.

'John, they say they won't be long.'

'Tell them to take as long as they like.'

'And tomorrow morning there'll be blood tests and a saliva sample.'

'I'll have no trouble with the latter. Just stand Ancram in front of me.'

'He didn't ask for this job, you know.'

'Fuck off, Jack.'

'I wish I could.'

Rebus pushed past him into the hall. He glanced into the living room. There were men in there, some of them he knew, all dressed in white boilersuits and polythene gloves. They were lifting the cushions from his sofa, ruffling the pages of his books. They didn't look like they were enjoying it: small consolation. It made sense that Ancram would use local people: easier than hauling a consignment from weegie-land. The one crouching in front of the corner cupboard got up, turned. Their eyes met.

'*Et tu*, Siobhan?'

'Afternoon, sir,' Siobhan Clarke said, ears and cheeks reddening.

It was about all Rebus needed. He grabbed his jacket, headed for the door.

'John?' Jack Morton called after him.

'Catch me if you can,' Rebus said. Halfway down the stairs, Jack did just that.

'Where are we going?'

'We're going to a pub,' Rebus told him. 'We'll take my car. You won't be drinking, so you can drive me home afterwards. That way we stay the right side of the law.' Rebus pulled the door open. 'Now let's see just how strong your Juice Church really is.'

Outside, Rebus almost collided with a tall man with black curly hair, turning grey. He saw the microphone, heard the man rattle off a question. Eamonn Breen. Rebus ducked his head just enough to catch Breen on the bridge of his nose: no power in the 'Glasgow kiss', just enough to let Rebus past.

'Bastard!' Breen spluttered, dropping the mike and cupping both hands over his nose. 'Did you catch that? Did you?'

Rebus glanced back, saw blood dripping between Breen's fingers, saw the cameraman nodding, saw Kayleigh Burgess over to one side, a pen in her mouth, looking at Rebus with half a smile.

'She probably thought you'd prefer to have a friendly face around,' Jack Morton said.

They were standing in the Oxford Bar, and Rebus had just told him about Siobhan.

'Given the circumstances, I know I would.' Jack was halfway down a pint of fresh orange and lemonade. Ice rattled in the glass when he tipped it. Rebus was on his second pint of Belhaven Best, motoring in fifth: nice and smooth. Sunday evening in the Ox, only twenty minutes after opening time, the place was quiet. Three regulars stood beside them at the bar, heads angled up towards the television, some quiz programme. The quizmaster had topiary where his haircut should have been and teeth transplanted from a Steinway. His job was to hold a card up to just below his face, read out the question, stare at the camera, then repeat the question as though nuclear disarmament depended on the answer.

'So, Barry,' he intoned, 'for two hundred points: which character plays the Wall in Shakespeare's *A Midsummer Night's Dream?*'

'Pink Floyd,' said the first regular.

'Snout,' said the second.

'Cheerio, Barry,' said the third, waving his fingers at the television, where Barry was clearly in trouble. A buzzer sounded. The quizmaster opened the question to the other two contestants.

'No?' he said. 'No takers?' He seemed surprised, but had to refer to his card to find the answer. 'Snout,' he said, looking at the hapless trio, then repeating the name just so they'd remember next time. Another card. 'Jasmine, for a hundred and fifty points: in which American state would you find the town of Akron?'

'Ohio,' said the second regular.

'Isn't he a character in *Star Trek*?' asked the first.

'Cheerio, Jasmine,' said the third.

'So,' Jack asked, 'are we talking?'

'It takes more than my home being raided, my clothes confiscated, and a suspicion of multiple murder hanging over my head to put *me* in the huff. Of course we're fucking talking.'

'Well, that's all-fucking-right then.'

Rebus snorted into his drink, then had to wipe foam off his nose. 'I can't tell you how much I enjoyed nutting that wanker.'

'He probably enjoyed the fact that the whole thing was being filmed.'

Rebus shrugged, reached into his pocket for cigarettes and lighter.

'Go on then,' Jack said, 'give me one.'

'You've stopped, remember?'

'Aye, but there's no AA for smokers. Come on.'

But Rebus shook his head. 'I appreciate the gesture, Jack, but you're right.'

'About what?'

'About looking out for your future. You're dead right. So don't cave in, stick to it. No booze, no cigs, and report my doings back to Chick Ancram.'

Jack looked at him. 'You mean that?'

'Every word of it,' Rebus drained his glass. 'Except the bit about Ancram, of course.'

Then he ordered another round.

'The answer's Ohio,' the quizmaster said, no surprise to anyone in the bar.

'I think,' Jack said a little later on, halfway down his second pint of juice, 'we're about to hit our first crisis of faith.'

'You need a piss?' Jack nodded. 'Well forget it,' Rebus said, 'I'm not going in there with you.'

'Give me your word you'll stay put.'

'Where would I go?'

'John ...'

'OK, OK. Would I get you into trouble, Jack?'

'I don't know, would you?'

Rebus winked at him. 'Off you go to the bog and find out.'

Jack stood his ground as long as he could, then turned and fled. Rebus leaned his elbows on the bar, smoking his cigarette. He was wondering what Jack would do if he ran out on him right now: would he report it to Ancram, or would he keep quiet? Would he be doing himself any favours by reporting it? After all, it showed him in a bad light, and he wouldn't want that. So maybe he'd keep quiet. Rebus could go about his business without Ancram knowing.

Except that Ancram had ways of knowing. The man wasn't solely dependent on Jack Morton. It was an interesting point, nevertheless: a point of faith, apt enough on a Sunday night. Maybe Rebus would drag Jack along to see Father Conor Leary later on. Jack used to be a real hun, a blue-nose, maybe still was. A drink with a Catholic priest might send him scurrying into the night. He looked round and saw Jack at the top of the steps, looking relieved – in both senses of the word.

Poor bastard, Rebus thought. Ancram wasn't being fair on him. You could see the strain around Jack's mouth. Rebus felt tired suddenly, remembered he'd been up since six, and had been on the rack ever since. He drained his glass and gestured towards the door. Jack seemed only too glad to be leaving.

When they got outside, Rebus asked him, 'How close were you in there?'

'To what?'

'Ordering a *real* drink.'

'As close as I ever get.'

Rebus leaned on the roof of the car, waiting for Jack to unlock it. 'Sorry I did that to you,' he said quietly.

'What?'

'Brought you here.'

'I should have the willpower to go into a pub without drinking.'

Rebus nodded. 'Thanks,' he said.

And he had a little smile to himself. Jack would be OK. Jack wouldn't shop him. The man had lost too much self-respect already.

'There's a spare room,' Rebus said, getting into the car, 'but no sheets or anything. We'll make up the sofa if that's OK.'

'That'll be fine,' Jack said.

Fine for Jack, yes, but not so fine for Rebus. It meant he'd have to sleep in his bed. No more nights half-dressed on the chair by the window. No more Stones at two a.m. He knew he had to get busy, had to finish this as fast as he could, one way or another.

Beginning tomorrow.

As they left the Ox, Rebus decided on a detour, directed Jack down towards Leith, let him drive them around for a bit, then pointed to a darkened shop doorway.

'That was her pitch,' he said.

'Whose?' Jack stopped the car. The street was lifeless, the working girls busy elsewhere.

'Angie Riddell's. I knew her, Jack. I mean, I'd met her a couple of times. First time, it was business, I was pulling her in. But then I came down here looking for her.' He looked at Jack, expecting a jokey comment, but Jack's face was serious. He was listening. 'We sat and talked. Next thing I knew, she was dead. It's different when you know someone. You remember their eyes. I don't mean the colour or anything, I mean all the things their eyes told you about them.' He sat in silence for a moment. 'Whoever killed her, he couldn't have been looking at her eyes.'

'John, we're not priests, you know. I mean, this is a *job*, right? You have to be able to lay it aside sometimes.'

'Is that what you do, Jack? Home after a shift, and suddenly everything's OK? Doesn't matter what you've seen out there, your home is your castle, eh?'

Jack shrugged, hands rubbing the steering-wheel. 'It's not my life, John.'

'Good for you, pal.' He looked towards the doorway again, expecting to see something of her there, the trace of a shadow, something left behind. But all he saw was darkness.

'Get me home,' he told Jack, closing his eyes with both thumbs.

*

The Fairmount Hotel was situated in Glasgow's west end, just off the main traffic routes. From the outside, it was an unassuming slab of concrete. Inside, it was a middle-management sort of place, its main business taking place during the week. Bible John booked for the Sunday night only.

News of the Upstart's latest victim had broken on Sunday morning, too late for coverage in the quality press. Instead, he caught the hourly news bulletins on the radio in his room, tuning between half a dozen stations, and watched what TV news he could, making notes between times. The Teletext flashes were brief paragraphs. Almost all he knew was that the victim, a married woman in her late twenties, had been found near the harbour in Aberdeen.

Aberdeen again. It was all fitting together. At the same time, if it was the Upstart, he was breaking his pattern – his first married victim, and perhaps his oldest. Which might mean that the pattern had never been there in the first place. It didn't of necessity negate an existing pattern; it just meant that that pattern had yet to be established.

Which was what Bible John was counting on.

Meantime, he opened the UPSTART file on his laptop and read the notes on the third victim. Judith Cairns, known to her friends as Ju-Ju. Twenty-one years old, shared a rented flat in Hillhead, just across Kelvingrove Park – he could almost see Hillhead from his window. Although she was registered unemployed, Judith Cairns had worked the black economy – some bar work at lunchtimes; a chip shop in the evenings; and weekend mornings as a chambermaid at the Fairmount Hotel. Which was, Bible John was guessing, how the Upstart had come to meet her. A travelling man frequented hotels: he should know. He wondered how close he was to the Upstart – not physically, but mentally. He didn't want to feel close in any way to this brash pretender, this usurper. He wanted to feel unique.

He paced his room, wanting to be back in Aberdeen while the latest inquiry unfolded, but he had work here in Glasgow, work he could not accomplish until the middle of the night. He stared out of the window, imagining Judith Cairns crossing Kelvingrove Park: she must have done it dozens of times. And one time she did it with the Upstart. Once was all he needed.

During the course of the afternoon and evening, more news filtered down of the latest victim. She was now being described as a 'successful twenty-seven-year-old company director'. The word *businessman* was like a shriek in Bible John's head. Not a lorry driver or any other profession; a simple businessman. The Upstart. He sat down at his computer and scrolled back to his notes on the first victim, the student at Robert Gordon's University, studying geology. He needed to know more about her, but couldn't think which route to take. And now there was a fourth victim to occupy him. Perhaps study of number four would mean he wouldn't need the first cull to complete his picture. Tonight might point the way.

He went out late for a walk. It was very pleasant, balmy night air, not much traffic about. Glasgow wasn't such a bad place: he'd been to cities in the States that could eat it for brunch. He remembered the city of his youth, stories of razor gangs and bare-knuckle bouts. Glasgow had a violent history, but that didn't tell the full story. It could be a beautiful city, too, a city for photographers and artists. A place for lovers ...

I didn't want to kill them. He would like to be able to tell Glasgow that, but of course it would be a lie. At the time ... at the last moment ... all he'd wanted in the world was their death. He had read interviews with killers, sat through trial testimony a couple of times, too, wanting someone to explain his feelings to him. No one came close. It was impossible either to describe or to understand.

There were many who especially didn't understand his choice of third victim. It felt pre-ordained, he could have told them. It didn't matter about the witness in the taxi. Nothing mattered, it had all been decided by some higher power.

Or some lower one.

Or merely by some collision of chemicals in his brain, by a genetic mismatch.

And afterwards, there'd been his uncle's offer of a job in the States, so he could afford to leave Glasgow. Leave the whole life behind him and create a new one, a new identity ... as if marriage and a career could ever take the place of what he'd left behind ...

He bought the next morning's edition of the *Herald* at a street corner and retired to a bar to devour it. He drank orange juice and sat in a corner. No one paid him any attention. There were more details about the Upstart's latest victim. She worked in corporate presentations, which meant putting together packages for industry: videos, displays, speech-writing, trade stands ... He studied the photo again. She'd worked in Aberdeen, and there was really only one industry in Aberdeen. Oil. He didn't recognise her, felt sure they'd never met. All the same, he wondered why the Upstart had chosen *her*: could he be sending Bible John a message? Impossible: it would mean he knew who Bible John was. Nobody knew. Nobody.

It was midnight when he returned to the hotel. Reception was deserted. He went up to his room, dozed for a couple of hours, and had the alarm wake him at half past two. He took the carpeted stairs down to reception, which was still deserted. Breaking into the office took thirty seconds. He closed the door after him and sat down in darkness at the computer. It was switched on and in screen saver mode. He nudged the mouse to activate the screen, then got to work. He searched back six weeks from the date of Judith Cairns's murder, checking room registrations and payment methods. He was looking for accounts charged to companies based in or near Aberdeen. His feeling was that the Upstart hadn't come to this hotel looking for a victim, but had been here on business, and had found her by chance. He was looking for the elusive pattern to start emerging.

Fifteen minutes later, he had a list of twenty companies, and of the individuals who had paid with a company credit card. For now, that was all he needed, but he was left with a dilemma: delete the files from the computer, or leave them? With the information deleted, he would have every chance of beating the police to the Upstart. Yes, but someone from the hotel staff would notice, and would be curious. They might contact the police. There would probably be back-ups on floppy. He would actually be helping the police, alerting them to his presence ... No, leave well alone. Do no more than is necessary. The maxim had served him well in the past.

Back in his room, he pored over the list in his notebook. It would be easy to check where each company was based, what it did – work for later. He had a meeting in Edinburgh tomorrow, and would use the trip to do something about John Rebus. He checked Teletext one last time before retiring for the night. After turning off the lights, he opened the curtains, then lay down on the bed. There were stars in the sky, a few of them bright enough to be visible through the streetlight. Dead, a lot of them, or so the astronomers said. So many dead things around, what difference would another one make?

None at all. Not one jot.

22

They took Jack's car to Howdenhall, Rebus sitting in the back, calling Jack his 'chauffeur'. It was a gloss–black Peugeot 405, three years old, turbo version; Rebus disregarded the No Smoking sticker and lit up, but kept the window open beside him. Jack didn't say anything, didn't even look in the rearview. Rebus hadn't slept well in the bed; night sweats, the sheets like a straitjacket. Chase dreams waking him every hour or so, sending him shooting out of bed to stand naked and trembling in the middle of the floor.

Jack for his part had complained first thing of a stiff neck. His second complaint: the kitchen, bare fridge and all. He couldn't go out to the shops, not without Rebus, so they'd made straight for the car.

'I'm gutting,' he complained.

'So stop and we'll eat something.'

They stopped at a bakery in Liberton: sausage rolls, beakers of coffee, a couple of macaroon cakes. Sat eating them in the car, parked double yellow by a bus stop. Buses rattled them as they passed, hinting they should shift. There were messages on the backs of some of them: Please Give Way to This Bus.

'I don't mind the buses,' Jack said. 'It's their drivers I object to. Half of them couldn't pass the time of day, never mind a PSV test.'

Rebus's comment: 'It's not buses that have the choke-hold on this place.'

'You're cheery this morning.'

'Jack, just shut your gub and drive.'

They were ready for him at Howdenhall. The team last night at his flat had taken away all his shoes, so the forensic bods could check for footprints and fail to match them against any left at the scene of Johnny Bible's murders. First thing Rebus had to do this morning was remove the shoes he was wearing. They gave him plastic overshoes to wear, and said his own would be returned to him before he left. The overshoes were too big, uncomfortable – his feet slid around inside them, and he had to curl his toes to keep them from slipping off.

They decided against a saliva test – it was the least reliable – but plucked hairs from his head.

'Could you graft them on to my temples when you're finished?'

The woman with the tweezers smiled, went about her business. She explained that she had to get the roots – PCR analysis wouldn't work on shed hair. There was a test available in some places, but …

'But?'

She didn't answer, but Rebus knew what she'd meant: but they were just going through the motions with him. Neither Ancram nor anyone else was expecting the expensive tests to yield any positive result. The only result would be a nettled, unsettled Rebus. That's what the whole thing was about. Forensics knew it; Rebus knew it.

Blood sample – the need for a warrant had been waived – and fingerprints next, plus they wanted some strands and threads from his clothes. I'm going on the computer, Rebus thought. For all that I'm not guilty, I'll still be a suspect in the eyes of history. Anyone digging the files out in twenty years' time will see that a policeman was interviewed, and gave samples … It was a grim feeling. And once they had his DNA on record … well, that was him on the register. The Scottish DNA database was just beginning to be compiled. Rebus started to wish he'd insisted on a warrant.

Throughout each process Jack Morton stood by, averting his face. And afterwards, Rebus got his shoes back. It felt like the forensic science staff were staring at him; maybe they were, maybe they weren't. Pete Hewitt wandered past – he hadn't been present at the fingerprinting – and made a crack about the biter bit. Jack grabbed Rebus's arm, stopped him from swinging. Hewitt shuffled off double quick.

'We're due at Fettes,' Jack reminded Rebus.

'I'm ready.'

Jack looked at him. 'Maybe we'll stop off somewhere first, get another coffee.'

Rebus smiled. 'Afraid I'll take a swing at Ancram?'

'If you do, bear in mind he's a southpaw.'

'Inspector, do you have any objections to this interview being recorded?'

'What happens to the recording?'

'It'll be dated and timed, copies made: one for you. Transcripts ditto.'

'No objections.'

Ancram nodded to Jack Morton, who set the machine running. They were in an office on the third floor of Fettes. It was cramped, and looked like it had hastily been vacated by a disgruntled tenant. There was a wastepaper-bin by the desk, waiting to be emptied. Paper-clips littered the floor. The walls still bore marks where Sellotaped pictures had been yanked down. Ancram sat behind the scratched desk, the Spaven casenotes piled to one side. He was wearing a formal dark-blue pinstripe with pale blue shirt and tie, and looked like he'd been for a haircut first thing. There were two pens in front of him on the desk – a blue fine-nib Bic with yellow casing, and an expensive-looking lacquered rollerball. His buffed and filed nails tapped against a clean pad of A4 paper. A typed list of notes, queries and points to be raised sat to the right of the pad.

'So, doctor,' Rebus said, 'what are my chances?'

Ancram merely smiled. When he spoke, it was for the benefit of the tape machine.

'DCI Charles Ancram, Strathclyde CID. It's –' he consulted a thin wristwatch – 'ten forty-five on Monday the twenty-fourth of June. Preliminary interview with Detective Inspector John Rebus, Lothian and Borders Police. This interview is taking place in office C25, Lothian Police Headquarters, Fettes Avenue, Edinburgh. Also present is—'

'You forgot the postcode,' Rebus said, folding his arms.

'That was the voice of DI Rebus. Also present is DI Jack Morton, Falkirk CID, currently on secondment to Strathclyde Police, Glasgow.'

Ancram glanced at his notes, picked up the Bic and ran through the first couple of lines. Then he picked up a plastic beaker of water and sipped from it, watching Rebus over the rim.

'Any time you're ready,' Rebus told him.

Ancram was ready. Jack sat by the table on which the tape machine sat. Two mikes ran from it to the desk, one pointing towards Ancram, one towards Rebus. From where he was sitting, Rebus couldn't quite see Jack. It was just him and Ancram, the chessboard set for play.

'Inspector,' Ancram said, 'you know why you're here?'

'Yes, sir. I'm here because I've refused to give up an investigation into possible links between Glaswegian gangster Joseph Toal, the Aberdeen drug market, and the murder of an oil-worker in Edinburgh.'

Ancram flicked through the casenotes, looking bored.

'Inspector, you know that interest in the Leonard Spaven case has been revived?'

'I know the TV sharks have been circling. They think they can smell blood.'

'And can they?'

'Just a leaky old ketchup bottle, sir.'

Ancram smiled; it wouldn't come over on the recording.

'CI Ancram smiles,' Rebus said, for the record.

'Inspector,' referring to his notes, 'what started this media interest?'

'Leonard Spaven's suicide, added to his public notoriety.'

'Notoriety?'

Rebus shrugged. 'The media get a vicarious thrill from reformed thugs and murderers, especially when they show some artistic leaning. The media often aspire to art themselves.'

Ancram seemed to expect more. They sat in silence for a moment. Cassette whirr; motor noise. Someone along the corridor sneezed. No sunshine today: iron-clad skies forecasting rain; a bitter wind off the North Sea.

Ancram sat back in his chair. His message to Rebus: I don't need the notes, I *know* this case. 'How did you feel when you heard Lawson Geddes had killed himself?'

'Gutted. He was a good officer, and a good friend to me.'

'You had your differences though?'

Rebus tried to hold the stare; ended up blinking first. Thought: of such accumulated setbacks were battles lost.

'Did we?' Old trick, answer a question with a question. Ancram's look said it was a tired move.

'I've had my men talk to some serving officers from the time.' A glance towards Jack, not even lasting a second. Drawing Jack in. Good tactics, sowing doubt.

'We had minor disagreements, same as everybody else.'

'You still respected him?'

'Present tense.'

Ancram bowed his head, acknowledging this. Fingered his notes, like stroking a woman's arm. Possessive. But doing it for comfort too, for reassurance.

'So, you worked well together?'

'Pretty well. Mind if I smoke?'

'We'll have a break at ...' checking his watch, 'eleven forty-five. Fair enough?'

'I'll try to survive.'

'You're a survivor, Inspector. Your record speaks for itself.'

'So talk to my record.'

A quick smile. 'When did you find out that Lawson Geddes had it in for Leonard Spaven?'

'I don't understand the question.'

'I think you do.'

'Think again.'

'Do you know why Geddes was kicked off the Bible John inquiry?'

'No.' It was the one question that had power, real power: it could *get* to Rebus.

Because he wanted to know the answer.

'You don't? He never told you?'

'Never.'

'But he talked about Bible John?'

'Yes.'

'See, it's all a bit vague ...' Ancram went into a drawer, hefted two more bulging files on to the desk. 'I've got Geddes's personnel file and reports here. Plus some stuff from the Bible John inquiry, bits and pieces he was involved in. Seems he grew obsessed.' Ancram opened one file, turned pages idly, then looked at Rebus. 'Does that sound familiar?'

'You're saying he was obsessed with Lenny Spaven?'

'I know he was.' Ancram let that sink in, nodding his head. 'I know it from interviews with officers from the time, but more importantly I know it because of Bible John.'

The bastard had hooked Rebus. They were only twenty minutes into the interview. Rebus crossed his legs, tried to look unconcerned. His face was so taut, he knew the muscles were probably visible beneath the skin.

'See,' Ancram went on, 'Geddes tried to tie Spaven to the Bible John case. Now, the notes aren't complete. Either they were destroyed or lost, or else Geddes and his superior didn't write down everything. But Geddes was going after Spaven, no doubt about that. Tucked away in one of the files I found some old photographs. Spaven's in them.' Ancram held the photos up. 'They're from the Borneo campaign. Geddes and Spaven were in the Scots Guards together. My feeling is that something happened out there, and from then on Geddes was out for Spaven's blood. How am I doing so far?'

'Filling the time nicely till the ciggie break. Can I see those photos?'

Ancram shrugged, handed them over. Rebus looked. Old black and whites with crimped edges, a couple of them no bigger than two inches by an inch and a half, the rest four by sixes. Rebus picked Spaven out straight away, the raptor grin hauling him into history. There was a minister in the photos, army uniform and dog collar. Other men posing, dressed in baggy shorts and long socks, faces sweat-shiny, eyes almost scared. Some of the faces were blurred; Rebus couldn't make out Lawson Geddes in any of them. The photos were exteriors, bamboo huts in the background, an old jeep nosing into one shot. He turned them over, read an inscription – Borneo, 1965 – and some names.

'Did these come from Lawson Geddes?' Rebus asked, handing them back.

'I've no idea. They were just in with all the other Bible John junk.' Ancram slipped them back into the file, counting them as he did so.

'They're all there,' Rebus said. Jack Morton's chair scraped the floor: he was checking how long till the tape had to be switched.

'So,' Ancram said, 'we've got Geddes and Spaven serving together in the Scots Guards; we've got Geddes chasing Spaven during the Bible John inquiry – and getting booted off the case; then we wind forwards a few years and what do we have? Geddes still chasing Spaven, but this time for the murder of Elizabeth Rhind. And getting booted off the case again.'

'Spaven definitely knew the victim.'

'No argument there, Inspector.' Pause: four beats. '*You* knew one of the Johnny Bible victims – does it mean you killed her?'

'Come up with her necklace in my flat and ask me again.'

'Ah, well this is where it gets interesting, isn't it?'

'Oh good.'

'You know the word serendipity?'

'I pepper my speech with it.'

'Dictionary definition: the ability to make happy chance finds. Useful word.'

'Absolutely.'

'And Lawson Geddes had the gift, didn't he? I mean, you get an anonymous tip-off about a consignment of stolen clock-radios. So you hoof it over to a garage, no search warrant, no nothing, and what do you find? Leonard Spaven, the clock-radios, and a hat and shoulder-bag – both belonging to the murder victim. I'd call that a *very* happy chance find. Except it wasn't chance, was it?'

'We had a warrant.'

'Signed retrospectively by a tame JP.' Ancram smiled again. 'You think you're doing all right, don't you? You think *I'm* doing all the talking, which means you're saying nothing incriminating. Well listen, I'm talking because I want you to know where we stand. Afterwards, you'll have every opportunity for rebuttal.'

'I'll look forward to that.'

Ancram referred to his notes. Rebus's mind was still half on Borneo and those photographs: what the hell could they have to do with Bible John? He wished he'd looked at them a bit harder.

'I've been reading your own version of events, Inspector,' Ancram went on, 'and I begin to see why you had your pal Holmes take a good look at them.' He looked up. 'That *was* the idea, wasn't it?'

Rebus said nothing.

'See, you weren't quite a seasoned officer back then, for all Geddes had taught you. You wrote a good report, but you were too conscious of the lies you were telling and the gaps you were having to create. I'm good at reading between the lines, practical criticism if you like.'

Rebus had a picture in his mind: Lawson Geddes shivering and wild-eyed on his doorstep.

'So here's how I think it went. Geddes was following Spaven – out on a limb by this time; he'd been ordered off the case. He tracked him to the lock-up one day, waited until Spaven was gone and then broke in. Liked the look of what he saw, and decided to plant some evidence.'

'No.'

'So he breaks in again, only this time he has some of the victim's stuff with him. Now, he didn't get it from an evidence locker, because according to the records nobody removed a hat or a bag from the victim's abode. So how did he get it? Two possibilities. One, he waltzed back into her home and took it. Two, he already had it on him, because right from the start he had the idea of fitting up Spaven.'

'No.'

'To the first or to the second?'

'To both.'

'You'll stand by that?'

'Yes.'

Ancram had been leaning further over the desk as he'd made each point. Slowly he sat back again, glanced at his watch.

'Cigarette break?' Rebus asked.

Ancram shook his head. 'No, I think that's enough for today. You made so many cock-ups in the course of that false report, it's going to take me time to list them all. We'll go through them next meeting.'

'I'm excited already.' Rebus got up and reached into a pocket for his cigarettes. Jack had switched off the recorder and ejected the tape. He handed it to Ancram.

'I'll have a copy made immediately and sent to you for verification,' Ancram told Rebus.

'Thanks.' Rebus inhaled, wished he could hold his breath for ever.

Some people, when they exhaled no smoke came out. He wasn't that selfish. 'One question.'

'Yes?'

'What am I supposed to tell my colleagues when I drag Jack here into the office with me?'

'You'll think of something. You're a more practised liar these days.'

'I wasn't fishing for a compliment, but thanks anyway.' He made to leave.

'A little birdie tells me you put the nut on a TV reporter.'

'I tripped, fell into him.'

Ancram almost smiled. 'Tripped?' Waited till Rebus had nodded. 'Well, it's going to look good, isn't it? They got the whole thing on video.'

Rebus shrugged. 'This little birdie of yours ... anyone in particular?'

'Why do you ask?'

'Well, you have your sources, don't you? In the press, I mean. Jim Stevens for one. Nice little friendship the two of you have got.'

'No comment, Inspector.' Rebus laughed, turned away. 'One more thing,' Ancram said.

'What?'

'When Geddes was trying to pin the murder on Spaven, you interviewed some of Spaven's friends and associates, including ...' Ancram made show of looking for the name in his notes. 'Fergus McLure.'

'What of it?'

'Mr McLure's recently deceased. I believe you went to see him the morning he died?'

Who'd been talking?

'So?'

Ancram shrugged, looked satisfied. 'Just another ... coincidence. By the way, DCI Grogan called me this morning.'

'It must be love.'

'Do you know a pub in Aberdeen called the Yardarm?'

'It's down by the docks.'

'Yes, it is. Ever been inside?'

'Maybe.'

'A drinker in there says definitely. You bought him a drink, talked about the rigs.'

The wee man with the heavy cranium. 'So?'

'So it shows you were at the docks the night *before* Vanessa Holden was murdered. Two nights in a row, Inspector. Grogan's beginning to sound *very* edgy. I think he wants you back in his custody.'

'Are you going to hand me over?' Ancram shook his head. 'No, you wouldn't want that, would you?'

Rebus almost blew some smoke in Ancram's face. Almost. Maybe he was more selfish than he thought ...

'That went as well as could be expected,' Jack Morton said. He was in the driver's seat, Rebus electing to sit in the front with him.

'Only because you thought there'd be a bloodbath.'

'I was trying to remember my first aid training.'

Rebus laughed, releasing tension. He had a headache.

'Aspirin in the glove compartment,' Jack told him. Rebus opened it. There was a little plastic bottle of Vittel there, too. He washed down three tablets.

'Were you ever in the Scouts, Jack?'

'I was a sixer in the Cubs, never made the transfer to Scouts. I had other hobbies by then. Are the Scouts still going?'

'Last I heard.'

'Remember Bob-a-Job week? You had to go round the neighbours, washing windows, digging their gardens. Then at the end, you handed all the cash over to Akela.'

'Who promptly stuck half in his pocket.'

Jack looked at him. 'There's a touch of the cynic in you, isn't there?'

'Maybe just a touch.'

'So where to now? Fort Apache?'

'After what I've just been through?'

'The Ox?'

'You're learning.'

Jack opted for tomato juice – watching his weight, he said – while Rebus had a half-pint and, after a moment's thought, a nip. The lunchtime trade wasn't in yet, but the pies and bridies were heating in preparation. Maybe the barmaid had been in the Girl Guides. They took their drinks through to the back room, settled at a corner table.

'It's funny being back in Edinburgh,' Jack said. 'Never used to drink here, did we? What was the name of the local along Great London Road?'

'I don't remember.' It was true; he couldn't even recall the pub's interior, yet must have been in there two or three hundred times. It was just a place for drink and discussion; what life it had the drinkers brought with them.

'Jesus, the money we wasted in there.'

'There speaks the reformed drinker.'

Jack forced a smile, lifted his glass. 'John, tell me though, why do you drink?'

'It kills my dreams.'

'It'll kill *you* in the end, too.'

'Something's got to.'

'Know what someone said to me? They said you were the world's longest surviving suicide victim.'

'Who said that?'

'Never mind.'

Rebus was laughing. 'Maybe I should apply to the *Guinness Book of Records*.'

Jack drained his glass. 'So what's the itinerary?'

'There's someone I'm supposed to call, a journalist.' He looked at his watch. 'I suppose she might be home. I'm going back to the bar to use the phone. Are you coming?'

'No, I'll trust you.'

'You sure?'

'Fairly.'

So Rebus went to call Mairie, but all he got was her answering machine. He left a brief message, and asked the barmaid if there was a photographer's within walking distance. She nodded, gave him directions, then went back to wiping glasses. Rebus summoned Jack, and they drifted out of the pub into a day that was growing warmer. There was still a blanket of cloud overhead, oppressive, almost thundery. But you just knew the sun was pummelling it, like a child with its pillow. Rebus took his jacket off, slung it over his shoulder. The photographer's was one street further along, so they cut through Hill Street.

The shop carried a window display of portraits – wedding couples seeming to radiate light, young children beaming smiles. Frozen moments of happiness – the great deception – to frame and put in pride of place in your cabinet or on top of the television.

'Holiday snaps, is it?' Jack asked.

'Just don't ask how I got them,' Rebus warned. He explained to the assistant that he wanted reprints made of each negative. She jotted down the instructions and told him it would be next day.

'No chance of one-hour?'

'Not with reprints, sorry.'

Rebus took the receipt from her and folded it into his pocket. Outside again, the sun had given up. It was raining. Rebus kept his jacket off, sweating enough as it was.

'Look,' Jack said, 'you don't have to tell me anything you don't want to, but I wouldn't mind knowing a bit about all this.'

'All what?'

'Your trip to Aberdeen, all the little coded messages between Chick and you, just, well, *everything*.'

'Probably best you don't know.'

'Why? Because I'm working for Ancram?'

'Maybe.'

'Come on, John.'

But Rebus wasn't listening. Two shops down from the photographer's was a small DIY store: paint and brushes and wallpaper rolls. It gave Rebus an idea. Back at the car, he gave directions, telling Jack they were on a mystery tour – remembering Lumsden saying the same thing to him his first night in Furry Boot Town. Near St Leonard's Rebus told Jack to make a left.

'Here?'

'Here.'

It was a do-it-yourself superstore. The car park was almost empty, so they parked close to the doors. Then Rebus hopped out and found a trolley with four working wheels.

'You'd think in a place like this they'd have someone who could fix them.'

'What are we doing here?'

'I need a few things.'

'You need provisions, not bags of plaster.'

Rebus turned to him. 'That's just where you're wrong.'

He bought paint, rollers and brushes, turps, a couple of groundsheets, plaster, a hot-air gun, sandpaper (coarse and fine), and varnish, sticking it all on his credit card. Then he treated Jack to lunch at a nearby café, a haunt of his from St Leonard's days.

And afterwards: home. Jack helped him carry everything upstairs.

'Brought any old clothes with you?' Rebus asked.

'I've a boilersuit in the boot.'

'Better bring it up.' Rebus stopped, stared at his open door, dropped the paint and ran into the flat. A quick check told him there was no one there. Jack was examining the jamb.

'Looks like someone took a crowbar to it,' he said. 'What's missing?'

245

'The hi-fi and telly are still there.'

Jack walked in, checked the rooms. 'Looks much the same as when we left it. Want to call it in?'

'Why? We both know this is Ancram trying to rattle me.'

'I don't see that.'

'No? Funny I get a break-in when I'm being interrogated by him.'

'We should call it in, that way the insurance will cover you for a new door-frame.' Jack looked around him. 'Surprised nobody heard it.'

'Deaf neighbours,' Rebus said. 'Edinburgh's famous for them. All right, we'll call it in. You go back to the store and fetch another lock or something.'

'And what will you be doing?'

'Sitting here, minding the fort. I promise.'

The minute Jack was out of the door, Rebus headed for the telephone. He asked to be put through to DCI Ancram. Then he waited, looking around the room. Somebody breaks in, then leaves without taking the hi-fi. It was almost an insult.

'Ancram.'

'It's me.'

'Something on your mind, Inspector?'

'My flat's been broken into.'

'I'm sorry to hear it. What did they take?'

'Nothing. That's where they slipped up. I thought you should tell them.'

Ancram laughed. 'You think I had something to do with it?'

'Yes.'

'Why?'

'I was hoping you'd tell me. The word "harassment" springs to mind.' As soon as he said it, he thought of *The Justice Programme*: how desperate were they? Desperate enough for a spot of housebreaking? He couldn't see it, not Kayleigh Burgess. Eamonn Breen, however, was another matter entirely ...

'Look, this is a pretty serious allegation. I'm not sure I want to listen to it. Why not calm down and think it over?'

Rebus was doing just that. He hung up on Ancram, got his wallet out of his jacket pocket. It was full of scraps of paper, receipts, business cards. He plucked out Kayleigh Burgess's, phoned her office.

'I'm afraid she's not here this afternoon,' a secretary told him. 'Can I take a message?'

'What about Eamonn?' Trying to sound like a friend. 'Is he in by any chance?'

'I'll just check. What's the name?'

'John Rebus.'

'Hold the line.' Rebus held. 'No, sorry, Eamonn's out as well. Shall I tell him you called?'

'No, it's all right, I'll catch up with him later. Thanks anyway.'

Rebus went through the flat again, more carefully this time. His first thought had been a straight break-in; his second some sort of ruse to wind him up. But now he was thinking of other things someone could have been looking for. It wasn't easy to tell: Siobhan and her friends hadn't exactly left the place as they'd found it. But nor had they been particularly thorough. For instance, they hadn't spent time in the kitchen, hadn't opened the cupboard where he kept all his cuttings and newspapers.

But someone had. Rebus knew which cutting he'd last read, and it was no longer on top of the pile. Instead, it had migrated south three or four layers. Maybe Jack ... no, he didn't think Jack had been snooping.

But someone had. Someone most definitely had.

By the time Jack got back, Rebus had changed into jeans and a gaudy T-shirt bearing the legend DANCING PIGS. A couple of woolly suits had been round to inspect the damage and scribble some notes. They gave Rebus a reference number. His insurers would want it.

Rebus had already moved some of the furniture out of the living room into the hall, and placed a ground-sheet over everything else. The other sheet went on the carpet. He lifted the fishing-boat painting off the wall.

'I like that,' Jack said.

'Rhona gave it to me, the first birthday I had after we were married. Bought it at a craft fair, thought it'd remind me of Fife.' He was studying the painting and shaking his head.

'I take it it didn't?'

'I come from west Fife – mining villages, rough – not the East Neuk.' All fishing creels, tourists and retirement homes. 'I don't think she ever understood.' He took the painting through to the hall.

'I can't believe we're doing this,' Jack said.

'And on police time. Which would you rather do, paint the walls, strip the door, or fit the lock?'

'Paint.' With his blue boilersuit on, Jack looked the part. Rebus handed him the roller, then reached under the sheet to put the hi-fi on. Stones, *Exile on Main Street*. Just right. The two of them got to work.

23

They took a break and walked up Marchmont Road, buying groceries. Jack kept his boilersuit on, said he felt like he was undercover. He had a smudge of paint on his face, but didn't bother wiping it off. He was enjoying himself. He'd sung along to the music, even though he didn't always know the words. They bought junk food mostly, carbohydrate, but added four apples and a couple of bananas. Jack asked if Rebus was going to buy any beer. Rebus shook his head, chose Irn-Bru and bricks of orange juice instead.

'What's all this in aid of?' Jack asked as they sauntered home.

'Clearing the mind,' Rebus answered, 'giving me time to think … I don't know. Maybe I'm thinking of selling.'

'Selling the flat?'

Rebus nodded.

'And doing what exactly?'

'Well, I could buy a round-the-world ticket, couldn't I? Take off for six months. Or stick the money in the bank and live off the interest.' He paused. 'Or maybe buy myself a place outside town.'

'Whereabouts?'

'Somewhere by the sea.'

'That'd be nice.'

'Nice?' Rebus shrugged. 'Yes, I suppose so. I just fancy a change.'

'Right next to the beach?'

'Could be a cliff-top, who knows?'

'What's brought this on?'

Rebus thought about it. 'My home doesn't feel like my castle any longer.'

'Yes, but we bought all the painting stuff before the break-in.'

Rebus didn't have an answer to that.

They worked the rest of the afternoon, windows open to let out the paint fumes.

'Am I supposed to sleep in here tonight?' Jack asked.

'The spare room,' Rebus told him.

The phone rang at half past five. Rebus got to it just as the answering machine cut in.

'Hello?'

'John, it's Brian. Siobhan told me you were back.'

'Well, she should know. How are you?'

'Shouldn't I be asking *you* that?'

'I'm fine.'

'Me, too.'

'You're not pick of the week with DCI Ancram.'

Jack Morton started to take an interest in the call.

'Maybe not, but he's not my boss.'

'He has pull, though.'

'So let him pull.'

'Brian, I know what you're up to. I want to talk to you about it. Can we come round there?'

'We?'

'It's a long story.'

'Maybe I could come see you.'

'This place is a building site. We'll be there in about an hour, all right?'

Holmes hesitated, then said that would be fine.

'Brian, this is Jack Morton, an old friend of mine. He's with Falkirk CID, currently seconded to DI John Rebus.'

Jack winked at Brian. He'd washed the paint off his face and hands. 'What he means is, I'm supposed to keep him out of trouble.'

'UN Peacekeeper, eh? Well, come in.'

Brian Holmes had spent the hour tidying the living room. He saw Rebus's appraisal.

'Just don't go into the kitchen – looks like an Apache raiding party's ridden through.'

Rebus smiled and sat on the sofa, Jack next to him. Brian asked if they wanted anything to drink. Rebus shook his head.

'Brian, I've told Jack a wee bit about what's happened. He's a good man, we can speak in front of him. OK?'

Rebus was taking a calculated risk, hoping the afternoon's bonding had worked. If not, at least they'd made progress on the room: three walls with first coats, and half of one side of the door stripped. Plus a new lock on the door.

Brian Holmes nodded and sat down on a chair. There were photos of

249

Nell on top of the gas fire. It looked like they'd been newly framed and placed there: a makeshift shrine.

'Is she at her mum's?' Rebus asked.

Brian nodded. 'But mostly working late shifts at the library.'

'Any chance she's coming back?'

'I don't know.' Brian made to bite a fingernail, discovered there was nothing there to bite.

'I'm not sure this is the answer.'

'What?'

'You can't make yourself resign, so you're going to let Ancram kick you out: not cooperating, acting the mule.'

'I had a good teacher.'

Rebus smiled. It was true, after all. He'd had Lawson Geddes; and Brian had had him.

'This happened to me once before,' Brian went on. 'At school, I had this really good friend, and we were going to go to university together, only he'd decided to go to Stirling, so I said I'd go there, too. But my first choice had been Edinburgh, and to knock Edinburgh's offer on the head I had to fail Higher German.'

'And?'

'And I sat in the exam hall ... knowing if I just sat there and didn't answer any of the questions, that would be it.'

'But you answered them?'

Brian smiled. 'Couldn't help myself. I got a C pass.'

'Same problem now,' Rebus said. 'If you go this way, you'll always regret it, because in your heart you don't *want* to leave. You like what you're doing. And beating yourself up about it ...'

'What about beating other people up?' Brian looked straight at him as he asked the question. Mental Minto, sporting bruises.

'You lost the head once.' Rebus held up a finger for emphasis. 'It was once too often, but you got away with it. I don't think you'll do that to anyone ever again.'

'I hope you're right.' Holmes turned to Jack Morton. 'I had this suspect in the biscuit-tin, I gave him a smack.'

Jack nodded: Rebus had told him all about it. 'I've been there myself, Brian,' Jack said. 'I mean, it's never come to blows, but I've been close. I've skinned my knuckles on a few walls.'

Holmes held up ten fingers: scrapes all across them.

'See,' Rebus said, 'like I say, you're beating *yourself* up. Mental's got a few marks, but they'll fade.' He tapped his head. 'But when the bruises are in here ...'

'I want Nell back.'

'Of course you do.'

'But I want to be a copper.'

'You've got to make both those clear to her.'

'Christ.' Brian rubbed his face. 'I've tried explaining it ...'

'You've always written a good, clear report, Brian.'

'What do you mean?'

'If the words aren't coming out right, try writing them down.'

'Send her a letter?'

'Call it that if you like. Just put down what it is you want to say, maybe try explaining why you feel that way.'

'Have you been reading *Cosmopolitan* or something?'

'Only the problem page.'

They had a laugh at that, though it didn't really merit one. Brian stretched in his chair. 'I need a sleep,' he said.

'Get an early night, write the letter first thing tomorrow.'

'Maybe I will, aye.'

Rebus started to get to his feet. Brian watched him rise.

'Don't you want to hear about Mick Hine?'

'Who he?'

'Ex-con, the last man to speak to Lenny Spaven.'

Rebus sat down again.

'I had a job tracking him down. Turns out he was here in town all the time, sleeping rough.'

'And?'

'And I had a word with him.' Brian paused. 'And I think you should, too. You'll get a very different picture of Lenny Spaven, believe me.'

Rebus believed him, whatever he meant. He didn't want to, but he did.

Jack was utterly opposed to the idea.

'Look, John, my boss is going to want to talk to this guy Hine, right?'

'Right.'

'How's it going to look when he finds out not just that your pal Brian's been there first, but that *you've* followed up?'

'It's going to look bad, but he hasn't told me not to.'

Jack growled his frustration. They'd dropped his car back at the flat, and were now walking down on to Melville Drive. One side of the road was Bruntsfield Links, the other the Meadows, a flat grassy stretch which could be wonderful on a hot summer's afternoon – a place to relax, to play football or cricket – but scary at night. The paths were lamp-lit, but it was like the wattage had been turned down. Some nights, the walk was positively Victorian. But this was summer, the sky still pink. There were squares of light shining from the Royal Infirmary and a couple of the tall university buildings huddled around George Square. Female students crossed the Meadows in packs, a lesson learned from the animal world. Maybe there were no predators out there tonight, but the fear was just as real. The government had pledged to combat 'the fear of crime'. It was reported on the TV news just before the latest Hollywood shoot-'em-up.

Rebus turned to Jack. 'You going to grass me up?'

'I should.'

'Yes, you should. But will you?'

'I don't know, John.'

'Well, don't let our friendship stand in your way.'

'That helps me a lot.'

'Look, Jack, the water I'm in is so deep, I'd probably die of the bends coming back up. So I might just as well stay down here.'

'Ever heard of the Marianas Trench? Ancram probably has one just like it waiting for you.'

'You're slipping.'

'What?'

'He was Chick before, now he's "Ancram". You better watch yourself.'

'You're sober, aren't you?'

'As a judge.'

'Can't be Dutch courage then, which means it's plain insanity.'

'Welcome to my world, Jack.'

They were headed for the back of the Infirmary. There were benches provided just this side of the perimeter wall. Dossers, travellers, down-and-outs ... whatever you wanted to call them ... they used these benches as beds in the summer. There used to be one old guy, Frank, Rebus saw him every summer, and at the end of every summer he disappeared like a migrating bird, only to reappear the next year. But this year ... this year Frank hadn't appeared. The homeless people Rebus saw were a lot younger than Frank, his spiritual children, if not grandchildren; only they were different – tougher and more frightened, wired and tired. Different game, different rules. Edinburgh's 'gentle-men of the road': twenty years ago you could have measured them in mere dozens. But not these days. Not these days ...

They woke up a couple of sleepers, who denied being Mick Hine and said they didn't know who he was, and then hit lucky with the third bench. He was sitting upright, a pile of newspapers beside him. He had a tiny transistor radio, which he held hard to his ear.

'Are you deaf or does it just need new batteries?' Rebus asked.

'Not deaf, not dumb, not blind. He said another copper might want to talk to me. Do you want a seat?'

Rebus sat down on the bench. Jack Morton rested against the wall behind it, like he'd rather be somewhere out of earshot. Rebus drew out a fiver.

'Here, get some batteries.'

Mick Hine took the money. 'So you're Rebus?' He gave Rebus a long look. Hine was early forties, balding, with a slight squint. He wore a decent enough suit, only it had holes in both knees. Beneath the jacket was a baggy red T-shirt. Two supermarket carrier bags sat on the ground beside him, bulging with worldly goods. 'Lenny talked about you. I thought you'd be different.'

'Different?'

'Younger.'

'I was younger when Lenny knew me.'

'Aye, that's true. Only film stars get younger, have you noticed that? The rest of us get wrinkled and grey.' Not that Hine was either. His face was lightly tanned, like polished brass, and what hair he had was jet black and worn long. He had grazes on his cheeks and chin, forehead, knuckles. Either a stumble or a beating.

'Did you fall over, Mick?'

'I get dizzy sometimes.'

'What does the doctor say?'

'Eh?'

No doctor consulted. 'You know there are hostels, you don't need to be out here.'

'Full up. I hate queuing, so I'm always at the back. Your concern has been noted by Michael Edward Hine. Now, do you want to hear the story?'

'In your own time.'

'I knew Lenny in prison, we shared a cell for maybe four months. He was the quiet type, thoughtful. I know he'd been in trouble before, and yet he didn't fit with prison life. He taught me how to do crosswords, sort out all the jumbled letters. He was patient with me.' Hine seemed to be drifting off, but pulled himself back. 'The man he wrote about is the man he was. He told me himself, he'd done wickedness and never been punished for it. But that didn't make it any easier on his soul, being punished for a crime he didn't commit. Time and again he told me, "I didn't do it, Mick, I swear to God and anybody else who's up there." It was an obsession with him. I think if he hadn't had his writing, he might have done away with himself sooner.'

'You don't think he was got at?'

Hine thought it over before shaking his head firmly. 'I believe he took his own life. That last day, it was like he'd come to a decision, made peace with himself. He was calmer, almost serene. But his eyes ... he wouldn't look at me. It was like he couldn't deal with people any more. He talked, but he was conversing with himself. I liked him such a lot. And his writing was beautiful ...'

'The last day?' Rebus prompted. Jack was peering through the railings at the hospital.

'The last day,' Hine repeated. 'That last day was the most spiritual of my life. I really felt touched by ... grace.'

'Lovely girl,' Jack muttered. Hine didn't hear him.

'You know what his last words were?' Hine closed his eyes, remembering. ' "God knows I'm innocent, Mick, but I'm so tired of saying it over and over." '

Rebus was fidgeting. He wanted to be flippant, ironic, his usual self – but now he found he could identify all too easily with Spaven's epitaph; even perhaps – just a little – with the man himself. Had Lawson Geddes really blinded him? Rebus hardly knew Spaven at all, yet had helped put him in jail for murder, breaching rules and regulations in the process, aiding a man who was feverish with hatred, spellbound by revenge.

But revenge for what?

'When I heard he'd cut his throat, it didn't surprise me. He'd been stroking his neck all day.' Hine leaned forward suddenly, his voice rising. 'And to his dying day he insisted *you* set him up! You and your friend!'

Jack turned towards the bench, ready for trouble. But Rebus wasn't worried.

'Look at me and tell me you didn't!' Hine spat. 'He was the best friend I ever had, the kindest, gentlest man. All gone now, all gone ...' Hine held his head in his hands and wept.

Of all the options open to him, Rebus knew which he favoured – flight. And that's exactly the option he took, Jack working hard to keep up with him as he fled across the grass, back towards Melville Drive.

'Wait up!' Jack called. 'Hold on there!' They were halfway across the playing-field, in the twilit centre of a triangle bordered by footpaths. Jack tugged at Rebus's arm, tried to slow him. Rebus turned and threw the arm off, then swung a punch. It caught Jack on the cheek, spinning him. There was shock on his face, but he was ready for the second blow, blocked it with a forearm, then threw a right of his own – no southpaw. He feinted, made Rebus think he was aiming for the head, then landed one hard into yielding gut. Rebus grunted, felt the pain but rode with it, took two steps back before launching himself. The two men hit the ground in a roll, their blows lacking force, wrestling for supremacy. Rebus could hear Jack saying his name, over and over. He pushed him off, and came up into a crouch. A couple of cyclists had stopped on one of the paths and were watching.

'John, what the fuck are you doing?'

Teeth bared, Rebus swung again, even more wildly, giving his friend plenty of time to dodge and launch a punch of his own. Rebus almost defended himself, but thought better of it. Instead, he waited for the impact. Jack hit him low, the sort of blow that could wind a man without doing damage. Rebus doubled over, fell to hands and knees, and spewed on to the ground, spitting out mostly liquid. He went on trying to cough everything out, even when there was nothing left to expel. And then he started crying. Crying for himself and for Lawson Geddes, and maybe even for Lenny Spaven. And most of all for Elsie Rhind and all her sisters, all the victims he couldn't help and would never ever be able to help.

Jack was sitting a yard or so away, forearms resting on his knees. He was breathing hard and sweating, pulling off his jacket. The crying seemed to take for ever, bubbles of snot escaping from Rebus's nose, fine lines of saliva from his mouth. Then he felt the shuddering lessen, stop altogether. He rolled on to his back, his chest rising and falling, an arm across his brow.

'Christ,' he said, 'I needed that.'

'I haven't had a fight like that since I was a teenager,' Jack said. 'Feel better?'

'Much.' Rebus got a handkerchief out, wiped eyes and mouth, then blew his nose. 'Sorry it had to be you.'

'Rather me than some innocent bystander.'

'That's pretty accurate.'

'Is that why you drink? To stop this happening?'

'Christ, Jack, I don't know. I drink because I've always done it. I like it; I like the taste and the sensation, I like standing in pubs.'

'And you like sleep without dreams?'

Rebus nodded. 'That most of all.'

'There are other ways, John.'

'Is this where you try to sell me the Juice Church?'

'You're a big boy, make up your own mind.' Jack got to his feet, pulled Rebus to his.

'I bet we look like a couple of dossers.'

'Well, you do. I don't know about me.'

'Elegant, Jack, you look cool and elegant.'

Jack touched a hand to Rebus's shoulder. 'OK now?'

Rebus nodded. 'It's daft, but I feel better than for ages. Come on, let's go for a walk.'

They turned and headed back towards the Infirmary. Jack didn't ask where they were going. But Rebus had a destination in mind: the university library in George Square. It was just closing as they walked in, the departing students, folders huddled to chests, giving them plenty of room as they walked up to the main desk.

'Can I help you?' a man asked, looking them up and down. But Rebus was walking around the desk to where a young woman was bowed over a pile of books.

'Hello, Nell.'

She looked up, couldn't place him at first. Then the blood left her face.

'What's happened?'

Rebus held up a hand. 'Brian's fine. Jack here and me ... well, we ...'

'Tripped and fell,' Jack said.

'You shouldn't drink in pubs with stairs.' Now she knew Brian was all right, she was regaining her composure fast, and with it her wariness. 'What do you want?'

'A word,' Rebus said. 'Maybe outside?'

'I'll be finished here in five minutes.'

Rebus nodded. 'We'll wait.'

They went outside. Rebus went to light a cigarette but found the packet crushed, its contents useless.

'Christ, just when I could do with one.'

'Now you know how it feels to give up.'

They sat on the steps and stared at George Square Gardens and the buildings surrounding it, a mishmash of old and new.

'You can almost feel all that brain power in the air,' Jack commented.

'Half the force has been to university these days.'

'And I bet they don't go swinging punches at their friends.'

'I've said I'm sorry.'

'Did Sammy ever go to uni?'

'College. I think she did something secretarial. She works for a charity now.'

'Which one?'

'SWEEP.'

'Working with ex-cons?'

'That's it.'

'Did she do it to have a dig at you?'

Rebus had asked himself the same question many times. He shrugged.

'Fathers and daughters, eh?'

The door swung open behind them. It was Nell Stapleton. She was tall, with short dark hair and a defiant face. No earrings or jewellery.

'You can walk me to the bus stop,' she told them.

'Look, Nell,' Rebus started, realising that he should have thought this through, should have rehearsed; 'all I want to say is, I'm sorry about you and Brian.'

'Thanks.' She was walking quickly. Rebus's knee hurt as he kept up.

'I know I'm unlikely material as marriage guidance, but there's something you have to know: Brian's a born copper. He doesn't want to lose you – it's killing him – but leaving the force would be a slow death in itself. He can't *make* himself leave, so instead he's trying to get into trouble, so the high hiedyins will have no alternative but to boot him out. That's no way to sort a problem.'

Nell didn't say anything for a while. They headed for Potterrow, crossed the road at the lights. They were headed for Greyfriars, plenty of bus stops there.

'I know what you're saying,' she said at last. 'You're saying it's a no-win situation.'

'Not at all.'

'Please, just listen to me.' Her eyes were glistening in the sodium light. 'I don't want to spend the rest of my life waiting for the phone call, the one that tells me there's bad news. I don't want to plan weekends off and holidays away only to have them cancelled because some case or court appearance takes precedence. That's asking too much.'

'It's asking a hell of a lot,' Rebus conceded. 'It's a high-wire act without the safety net. But all the same ...'

'What?'

'You can make it work. A lot of people do. Maybe you can't plan things too far in advance, maybe there'll be cancellations and tears. When the chances come, you take them.'

'Have I wandered into a Dr Ruth show by mistake?' Rebus sighed, and she stopped walking, took his hand. 'Look, John, I know why you're doing this. Brian's hurting, and you don't like to see it. I don't like it either.' A distant siren wailed, down towards the High Street, and Nell shivered. Rebus saw it, looked into her eyes, and found himself nodding. He knew she was right; his own wife had said the same things. And the way Jack was standing, the look on his face, he'd been here before, too. Nell started walking again.

'He'll leave the force, Nell. He'll make them dump him. But for the rest of his life ...' He shook his head. 'It won't be the same. *He* won't be the same.'

She nodded. 'I can live with that.'

'You don't know for sure.'

'No, I don't.'

'You'll take that risk, but you won't risk him staying put?' Her face hardened, but Rebus didn't give her time for a comeback. 'Here's your bus. Just think about it, Nell.'

He turned and walked back towards the Meadows.

They'd made up a bed for Jack in the spare room – Sammy's old bedroom, complete with Duran Duran and Michael Jackson posters. They'd washed themselves and shared a pot of tea – no alcohol, no ciggies. Rebus lay in bed and stared at the ceiling, knew sleep wouldn't come for ages, and that when it did his dreams would be fierce. He got up and tiptoed through to the living room, keeping the lights off. The room was cool, they'd kept the windows open late, but the fresh paint and the old scorched paint from the door left a nice smell. Rebus uncovered his chair and dragged it over to the bay window. He sat down and pulled his blanket over him, felt himself relax. There were lights on across the way and he concentrated on them. I'm a peeper, he thought, a voyeur. All cops are. But he knew he was more than that: he liked to get involved in the lives around him. He had a need to *know* which went beyond voyeurism. It was a drug. And the thing was, when he had all this knowledge, he then had to use booze to blank it out. He saw his reflection in the window, two-dimensional, ghostly.

I'm almost not here at all, he thought.

24

Rebus woke up and knew something was wrong. He showered and dressed and still couldn't put a name to it. Then Jack came slouching through to the kitchen and asked if he'd slept well.

And he had. *That* was what was different. He'd slept very well indeed, and he'd been sober.

'Any word from Ancram?' Jack asked, staring into the fridge.

'No.'

'Then you're probably clear for today.'

'He must be in training for the next bout.'

'So do we crack on with the decorating, or actually go to work?'

'Let's do an hour's painting,' Rebus said. So that's what they did, Rebus keeping half an eye on the street outside. No reporters, no *Justice Programme*. Maybe he'd scared them off; maybe they were biding their time. He hadn't heard anything about an assault charge: Breen was probably too happy with the video footage to consider any further action. Plenty of time to file a complaint after the programme went out …

After the painting, they took Jack's car to Fort Apache. Jack's initial response did not disappoint Rebus.

'What a shit-hole.'

Inside, the station was a frenzy of packing and moving. Vans were already taking crates and boxes to the new station. The desk sergeant had become a shirt-sleeved foreman, making sure the cases were labelled and the moving crew knew where they were to go once they reached their destination.

'It'll be a miracle if it goes to plan,' he said. 'And I notice CID aren't giving a hand.'

Jack and Rebus gave him a round of applause: an old joke, but well intentioned. Then they went to the Shed.

Maclay and Bain were in situ.

'The prodigal son!' Bain exclaimed. 'Where the hell have you been?'

'Helping CI Ancram with his inquiries.'

'You should have called in. MacAskill wants a word, toot-sweet.'

'I thought I told you never to call me that.'

Bain smirked. Rebus introduced Jack Morton. There were nods, handshakes, grunts: the usual procedure.

'You better go see the Boss,' Maclay said. 'He's been fretting.'

'I've been missing him, too.'

'Did you bring us back anything from Aberdeen?'

Rebus searched his pockets. 'Must have slipped my mind.'

'Well,' Bain said, 'you were probably busy.'

'Busier than you two, but that wouldn't be hard.'

'Go see the Boss,' Maclay told him.

Bain was wagging a finger. 'And you should be nice to us, otherwise we might not tell you what our snitches came up with.'

'What?' Local snitches: word out for Tony El's accomplice.

'After you've talked to MacAskill.'

So Rebus went to see his boss, leaving Jack Morton outside the door.

'John,' Jim MacAskill said, 'what have you been playing at?'

'Different games, sir.'

'So I hear, and you've not proved proficient at any of them, eh?'

MacAskill's office was emptying, but there was some way to go. His filing cabinet stood with its drawers gutted, the files themselves spread across the floor.

'Nightmare,' he said, noticing Rebus's look. 'How's your own packing coming?'

'I travel light, sir.'

'I forget, you've not been with us long. Sometimes it seems like for ever.'

'I have that effect on people.'

MacAskill smiled. 'Question one in my mind, this reopening of the Spaven case: is it going to go anywhere?'

'Not if I have my way.'

'Well, Chick Ancram's pretty persistent ... and thorough. Don't depend on him overlooking something.'

'Yes, sir.'

'I've had a word with your boss at St Leonard's. He tells me this is par for the course.'

'I don't know, sir, seems like I'm playing under a handicap.'

'Well, anything I can do, John ...'

'Thank you, sir.'

'I know the way Chick will play it: attrition. He'll sweat the arse off you, run you in circles. He makes it easier for you to lie and say you're guilty than to keep telling the truth. Watch out for that.'

'Will do.'

'Meantime, question one: how are you feeling?'

'I'm all right, sir.'

'Well, there's not much happening around here that we can't handle. So any time off you need, take it.'

'I appreciate that.'

'Chick's west coast, John. He shouldn't be over here.' MacAskill shook his head, went to his drawer for a can of Irn-Bru. 'Bugger,' he said.

'Problem, sir?'

'I've gone and bought the diet stuff.' He opened it anyway. Rebus left him to his packing.

Jack was right outside the door.

'Did you catch any of that?'

'I wasn't listening.'

'My boss just told me I can bunk off whenever I like.'

'Which means we can finish doing up the living room.'

Rebus nodded, but he was thinking of finishing something else instead. He went into the Shed and stood in front of Bain's desk.

'Well?'

'Well,' Bain said, sitting back, 'we did what you asked, put word out with our snitches. And they came up with a name.'

'Hank Shankley,' Maclay added.

'He's not got much of a record, but he's game to make a few quid where he can, no scruples attached. And he gets around. Word is, he's had a windfall and after a couple of drinks he was boasting about his "Glasgow connection".'

'Have you talked to him?'

Bain shook his head. 'Bided our time.'

'Waiting for you to turn up,' Maclay added.

'Have you been rehearsing this routine? Where can I find him?'

'He's a keen swimmer.'

'Anywhere in particular?'

'The Commie Pool.'

'Description?'

'Big building at the top of Dalkeith Road.'

'I meant Shankley.'

'You can't miss him,' Maclay said. 'Late thirties, six feet tall and skinny as a pole, short fair hair. Nordic looking.'

'The description we got,' Bain corrected, 'was albino.'

Rebus nodded. 'I owe you for this, gents.'

'You haven't heard who it was spilled the beans.'

'Who?'

Bain grinned. 'Remember Craw Shand?'

'Claimed to be Johnny Bible?' Bain and Maclay nodded. 'Why didn't you tell me he was a snitch of yours?'

Bain shrugged. 'Didn't want it broadcast. But Craw's a big fan of yours. See, he likes it rough now and then ...'

Outside, Jack made for the car, but Rebus had other plans. He went into a shop and came out with six cans of Irn-Bru, *not* diet, then marched back into the station. The desk sergeant was sweating. Rebus handed him the carrier bag.

'You shouldn't have,' the sergeant said.

'They're for Jim MacAskill,' Rebus said. 'I want at least five to reach him.'

Now he was ready to go.

The Commonwealth Pool, which had been built for the Commonwealth Games in 1970, was sited at the top of Dalkeith Road, at the foot of Arthur's Seat, and just over quarter of a mile from St Leonard's police station. In the days when he swam, Rebus used the Commie Pool at lunchtimes. You found yourself a lane – never an empty lane, it was like easing out of a slip-road on to a motorway – and you swam, pacing yourself so you didn't catch up with the person in front, or let the person behind gain on you. It was OK, but a bit too regimented. The other option was to swim breadths in the open pool, but then you were in with the kids and their parents. There was a separate pool for infants, plus three flumes Rebus had never been down, and elsewhere in the building were saunas, gym, and a café.

They found a space in the overflow car park and went in by the main entrance. Rebus showed ID at the kiosk and gave a description of Shankley.

'He's a regular,' the woman told him.

'Is he here just now?'

'I don't know. I've only just come on.' She turned to ask the other woman in the booth, who was counting coins into polythene bank-bags. Jack Morton tapped Rebus's arm and nodded.

Beyond the kiosk there was a wide open space, with windows looking down on to the main pool. And standing there, glugging Coke from the can, stood a very tall, very thin man with damp, bleached hair. He had a rolled-up towel under one arm. When he turned, Rebus saw that his eyebrows and lashes were fair. Shankley saw two men examining him, placed them immediately. When Rebus and Morton started towards him, he ran.

He turned a corner into the open-plan café, but couldn't see an exit from there, so kept running, ended up beside the children's play area. This was a large netted enclosure totalling three storeys, with slides and walkways and other challenges – a toddler assault course. Rebus liked sometimes to sit with a post-swim coffee watching the kids playing, wondering which would make the best soldier.

Shankley was cornered and knew it. He turned to face them: Rebus and Jack were smiling. The impulse to flee was still too strong: Shankley pushed past the attendant, opened the door to the play area, ducked and went in. Two huge padded rollers stood directly in front of him, like a giant mangle. He was thin enough to squeeze between them.

Jack Morton laughed. 'Where's he going to go from there?'

'I don't know.'

'Let's grab a cup of tea and wait for him to get fed up.'

Rebus shook his head. He'd heard a noise from the top storey. 'There's a kid in there.' He turned to the attendant. 'Isn't there?'

She nodded. Rebus turned to Jack. 'Possible hostage. I'm going in. Stay out here, tell me where Shankley is.'

Rebus took off his jacket and went in.

The rollers were the first obstacle. He was too big to squeeze through, but managed to push his way through the gap between them and the side netting. He remembered his SAS training: assault courses you wouldn't believe. Kept going. A pool of coloured plastic balls to wade through, and then a tube curving upwards, leading to the first floor. A slide nearby – he climbed that. Through the netting he could see Jack, pointing up and towards the far corner. Rebus stayed in a crouch, looked around. Punch-bags, a net across a yawning gap, a cylinder to crawl through … more slides and climbing-ropes. There: far corner, wondering what to do next. Hank Shankley. People in the café were watching, no longer interested in swimming. One floor further up was the kid. Rebus had to get there before Shankley; either that or grab Shankley first. Shankley didn't know anyone was in here with him. Jack was shouting up, distracting him.

'Hey, Hank, we can wait here all day! All night too if we have to!

Come on out, we only want a chat! Hank, you look ridiculous in there. Maybe we'll just padlock it shut and keep you for an exhibit.'

'Shut up!' Flecks of foam from Shankley's mouth. Skinny, gaunt ... Rebus knew it was crazy to worry about HIV, but found himself worrying anyway. Edinburgh was still HIV city. He was about fifteen feet from Shankley when he heard a swooshing sound coming towards him fast. He was passing the exit to one of the tubes when a pair of feet hit him, toppling him on to his side. A boy about eight years old stared at him.

'You're too big for in here, mister.'

Rebus got up, saw Shankley coming for them, and started dragging the kid by the scruff of his neck. He backed up to the slide, then dropped the boy down it. He was turning to confront Shankley when another foot hit him – the albino's. He bounced off the mesh wall and tumbled down the padded slide. The boy was making his way to the entrance, where the attendant gestured for him to hurry. Shankley slid down, both fists out, and clubbed Rebus on the neck. He was sprinting for the kid, but the boy was already through the rollers. Rebus dived at Shankley, brought him down into the plastic balls, caught him with a decent punch. Shankley's arms were tired from swimming; he pummelled Rebus's sides, but it was like being hit by a rag doll. Rebus grabbed a ball, stuffed it into Shankley's mouth, where it wedged, the lips taut and bloodless. Then he hit Shankley in the groin, twice, and that just about did it.

Jack came to help him drag the unresisting figure out. 'You all right?' he asked.

'The kid hurt me more than he did.'

The boy's mother was hugging her son, checking he was all right. She gave Rebus a dirty look. The boy was complaining he still had ten minutes left. The attendant came after Rebus.

'Excuse me,' she said, 'could I have our ball back?'

St Leonard's being so close, they took Shankley there, asked for and were given an empty biscuit-tin, only recently vacated by the smell of it.

'Sit there,' Rebus told Shankley. Then he took Jack outside, spoke in an undertone.

'To fill you in, Tony El killed Allan Mitchison – I still don't know why exactly. Tony had local help.' He tilted his head towards the door. 'I want to know what Hank knows.'

Jack nodded. 'Do I stay dumb, or is there a part for me?'

'You're the good guy, Jack.' Rebus patted his shoulder. 'Always have been.'

They went back into the room as a team, like in the old days.

'Well, Mr Shankley,' Rebus opened, 'so far we've got resisting arrest and assaulting a police officer. Plenty of witnesses, too.'

'I haven't done nothing.'

'Double negative.'

'Eh?'

'If you haven't done nothing, you must have done *some*thing.'

Shankley just looked glum. Rebus had him pegged already: Bain's 'no scruples attached' had given him the clue. Shankley lived to no code whatsoever, except perhaps 'Look after number one'. He didn't give a toss for anything or anyone. There was no intelligence other than a root instinct to survive. Rebus knew he could play on that.

'You don't owe Tony El anything, Hank. Who do you think grassed you up?'

'Tony who?'

'Anthony Ellis Kane. Glasgow hardman relocated to Aberdeen. He was down here to do a job. He needed an associate. Somehow he ended up with you.'

'Not your fault,' Jack chipped in, hands in pockets, 'you're an accessory. We're not doing you for murder.'

'Murder?'

'That young guy Tony El was after,' Rebus explained. 'You scouted out somewhere to take him. That was about the sum of your part, wasn't it? The rest was down to Tony.'

Shankley bit his top lip, showing a bottom row of narrow uneven teeth. His eyes were pale blue with dark flecks in them, his pupils contracted to pencil dots.

'Of course,' Rebus said, 'there's another way we can play it. We could say *you* tossed him out that window.'

'I don't know nothing.'

'Don't know *anything*,' Rebus reminded him. Shankley folded his arms, spread his long legs.

'I want a lawyer.'

'Been watching the *Kojak* repeats, Hank?' Jack asked. He looked to Rebus, who nodded: no more Mr Nice Guy.

'I'm bored with this, Hank. Know what? We're going to take you for fingerprinting now. You left prints all over that squat. You even left behind the carry-out. Prints all over it. You remember touching the bottles? The cans? The bag they were in?' Shankley was trying hard to remember. Rebus's voice grew quieter. 'We've got you, Hank. You're fucked. I'll give you ten seconds to start talking, and that's it – promise. Don't think you can talk to us later, we won't be listening. The judge will have his hearing-aid switched off. You'll be on your own. Know why?' He waited till he had Shankley's attention. 'Because Tony El croaked. Someone sliced him open in a bathtub. Could be you next.' Rebus nodded. 'You need friends, Hank.'

'Listen ...' The Tony El story had woken Shankley up. He sat forward in his chair. 'Look, I'm ... I ...'

'Take your time, Hank.'

Jack asked him if he wanted something to drink. Shankley nodded. 'Cola or something.'

'Fetch me one, too, Jack,' Rebus said. Jack went down the hall to the machine. Rebus bided his time, pacing the room, giving Shankley time to decide how much he was going to tell and with how much gloss. Jack came back, tossed one can at Shankley, handed the other to Rebus, who pulled it open and drank. It wasn't a real drink. It was cold and way too sweet, and the only kick it would give him was from caffeine rather than alcohol. He saw Jack watching him, screwed up his face in reply. He wanted a cigarette, too. Jack read the look, shrugged.

'Now then,' Rebus said. 'Do you have a story for us, Hank?'

Shankley burped, nodded. 'It's like you said. He told me he was here to do a job. Said he had Glasgow connections.'

'What did he mean by that?'

Shankley shrugged. 'Never asked.'

'Did he mention Aberdeen at all?'

Shankley shook his head. 'Glasgow was what he said.'

'Continue.'

'He offered me fifty notes to find him a place where he could take someone. I asked him what he was going to do, and he said ask a few questions, maybe give them a doing. That was all. We waited outside this block of flats, quite posh.'

'The Financial District?'

Another shrug. 'Between Lothian Road and Haymarket.' That was it. 'Saw this young guy come out, and we followed him. For a while, we just watched, then Tony said it was time to strike up his acquaintance.'

'And?'

'Well, we got chatting to him, like. I got to enjoying myself, forgot what was happening. Tony looked like he'd forgotten, too. I thought maybe he was going to call it off. Then we went outside for a taxi, and when the young guy couldn't see us, he gave me a look, and I knew it was still on. But I swear, I only thought the kid was for a kicking.'

'Not so.'

'No.' Shankley's voice dropped. 'Tony had a bag with him. When we got to the flat, he brought out tape and stuff. Tied the kid to the chair. He had a plastic sheet, put a bag over the kid's head.' Shankley's voice cracked. He cleared his throat, took another swallow of cola. 'Then he started taking stuff out of the bag, tools, you know, like a joiner would use. Saws and screwdrivers and that.'

Rebus looked to Jack Morton.

'And that's when I realised the plastic sheet was to catch the blood, the kid wasn't just getting a kicking.'

'Tony planned to torture him?'

'I suppose so. I don't know ... maybe I'd've tried to stop him. I've never done anything like that before. I mean, I've doled it out in my time, but never ...'

The next question used to be the one that counted; Rebus wasn't so sure any more. 'Did Allan Mitchison jump, or what?'

Shankley nodded. 'We had our backs turned. Tony was taking the tools out, and I was just staring at them. The kid had a bag over his head, but I think he saw them. He got between us and went out the window. Must've been scared to death.'

Looking at Shankley, and remembering Anthony Kane, Rebus sensed again how bland monstrosity could be. Faces and voices didn't give any clue; no one sported horns and fangs, dripping blood and all slouching malevolence. Evil was almost ... it was almost child-like: naive, simplistic. A game you played and then woke up from, only to find it wasn't pretend. The real-life monsters weren't grotesques: they were quiet men and women, people you passed on the street and didn't notice. Rebus was glad he couldn't read people's minds. It would be pure hell.

'What did you do?' he asked.

'Packed up and shipped out. We went back to my place first, had a couple of drinks. I was shaking. Tony kept saying it was a mess, but he didn't seem worried. We realised we'd left the hooch – couldn't remember if our dabs were on it. I thought they were. That's when Tony took off. He left me my share, I'll give him that.'

'How far do you live from the flat, Hank?'

'About two minutes' walk. I'm not there much; the kids call me names.'

Life can be cruel, Rebus thought. Two minutes: when he'd arrived at the scene, Tony El might have been only two minutes away. But they'd ended up meeting in Stonehaven ...

'Didn't Tony give you any idea *why* he was after Allan Mitchison?' Shankley shook his head. 'And when did he first approach you?'

'Couple of days before.'

Therefore premeditated. Well, of course it was premeditated, but more than that it meant Tony El had been in Edinburgh, preparing the scheme, while Allan Mitchison had still been in Aberdeen. The night of his death had been his first day of leave. So Tony El hadn't followed him south from Aberdeen ... yet he knew what Allan Mitchison looked like, knew where he lived – there was a telephone in the flat, but unlisted.

Allan Mitchison had been set up by someone who'd known him.

It was Jack Morton's turn. 'Hank, think carefully now, didn't Tony say *anything* about the job, about who was paying him?'

Shankley thought, then nodded slowly. He looked pleased with himself: he'd remembered something.

'Mr H.,' he said. 'Tony said something about Mr H. He clammed up afterwards, like he hadn't meant to.' Shankley almost danced in his seat. He wanted Rebus and Morton to like him. Their smiles told him they did. But Rebus was thinking furiously; the only Mr H. he came up with was Jake Harley. It didn't fit.

'Good man,' Jack cajoled. 'Now think again, tell us something else.'

But Rebus had a question. 'Did you see Tony El jacking up?'

'No, but I knew he was doing it. When we were following the kid, first bar we went in, Tony went to the bog. He came out, and I knew he was on something. Living where I do, it gets so you can tell.'

Tony El a shooter. It didn't mean he wasn't killed. All it meant was, maybe he'd made Stanley's job easier. Tony El sky-high easier to murder than Tony El with defences up. Drugs to Aberdeen ... Burke's Club a magnet for them ... Tony El using – and selling? He wished he'd asked Erik Stemmons about Tony El.

'I need the toilet,' Shankley said.

'We'll get a uniform to take you. Stay here.' Rebus and Morton left the room.

'Jack, I want you to trust me.'

'How far?'

'I want you to stay here and take Shankley's statement.'

'While you do what?'

'Take someone to lunch.' Rebus checked his watch. 'I'll be back here by three.'

'Look, John …'

'Call it parole. I go to lunch, I come back. Two hours.' Rebus held up two fingers. 'Two hours, Jack.'

'Which restaurant?'

'What?'

'Tell me where you're going. I'll phone every quarter of an hour, you better be there.' Rebus looked disgusted. 'And I want to know who your guest is.'

'It's a woman.'

'Name?'

Rebus sighed. 'I've heard of driving a hard bargain, but you've got your HGV.'

'Name?' Jack was smiling.

'Gill Templer. Chief Inspector Gill Templer. OK?'

'OK. Now the restaurant.'

'I don't know. I'll tell you when I get there.'

'Phone me. If you don't, Chick gets to know, OK?'

'It's back to "Chick", is it?'

'He gets to know.'

'All right, I'll phone.'

'With the restaurant's number?'

'With the number. Know what, Jack? You've put me right off eating.'

'Order plenty and bring me a doggie bag.'

Rebus went in search of Gill, found her in her office. She told him she'd already eaten.

'So come and watch me.'

'An offer I can't refuse.'

There was an Italian restaurant on Clerk Street. Rebus ordered a pizza: he could take anything he couldn't eat back to Jack. Then he phoned St Leonard's and left the pizzeria's number, told them to pass it on.

'So,' Gill said when he was seated again, 'been busy?'

'Plenty busy. I went to Aberdeen.'

'What for?'

'That phone number on Feardie Fergie's pad. Plus a few other things.'

'What other things?'

'Not necessarily connected.'

'Tell me, did the trip pass without incident?' She picked up a piece of the garlic bread which had just arrived.

'Not exactly.'

'You surprise me.'

'They say it keeps a relationship on its toes.'

Gill took a bite of bread. 'So what did you find out?'

'Burke's Club is dirty. It's also where Johnny Bible's first victim was last seen alive. The place is run by two Yanks; I only spoke with one of them. I think probably his partner's the grubbier of the two.'

'And?'

'And, also in Burke's I saw a couple of members of a Glaswegian crime family. You know Uncle Joe Toal?'

'I've heard of him.'

'I think he's delivering dope to Aberdeen. From there, I'd guess some of it goes to the rigs – a captive market; a lot of boredom on a rig.'

'You'd know, of course?' she joked. Then she saw the look on his face, and her eyes narrowed. 'You went on a rig?'

'Most terrifying experience of my life, but cathartic with it.'

'Cathartic?'

'An old girlfriend used to use words like that; they rub off on you after a while. The club's owner, Erik Stemmons, denied knowing Fergie McLure. I almost believe him.'

'Which puts his partner in the frame?'

'To my mind.'

'And that's as far as it's got – your mind? I mean, there's no evidence?'

'Not a shred.'

His pizza arrived. Chorizo, mushroom and anchovy. Gill had to look away. The pizza was pre-cut into six fat slices. Rebus lifted one on to his plate.

'I don't know how you can face that.'

'Me neither,' said Rebus, sniffing the surface. 'But it'll make a hell of a doggie bag.'

There was a cigarette machine. If he looked over Gill's right shoulder he could see it there on the wall. Five brands, any of which would suffice. There was a book of matches waiting in the ashtray. He'd ordered a glass of house white, Gill spring water. The wine – 'delicately bouqueted' as the menu put it – arrived, and he gave it the nose test before sipping. It was chilled and sour.

'How's the bouquet?' Gill asked.

'Any more delicate and it'd need Prozac.' The drinks card was in front of him, standing erect in its little holder, listing aperitifs and cocktails and digestifs, plus wines, beers, lagers, spirits. It was the most reading Rebus had done in a couple of days. As soon as he'd finished, he read it again. He wanted to shake the author's hand.

One segment of pizza was enough.

'Not hungry?' Gill asked.

'I'm dieting.'

'You?'

'I want to be fit for my walks along the beach.'

She wasn't following him, shook her head clear of seeming non-sequiturs.

'The thing is, Gill,' he said after another sip of wine, 'I think you were on to something big. And I think it can be salvaged. I just want to be sure it's *your* collar.'

She looked at him. 'Why?'

'Because of all the Christmas presents I've never given you. Because you deserve it. Because it'll be your *first*.'

'It doesn't count if you've done all the work.'

'It'll count all right, all I'm doing is reconnaissance.'

'You mean you're not finished?'

Rebus shook his head, asked the waiter to put the rest of the pizza in a box. He lifted the last piece of garlic bread.

'I'm not nearly finished,' he told her. 'But I might need your help.'

'Oh-oh. Here it comes.'

Rebus spoke quickly. 'Chick Ancram's got me set up for a series of grillings. I've already had one, and between ourselves he didn't cook me more than medium rare. But they take up time, and I might want to head north again.'

'John ...'

'All I need you to do ... *might* need you to do, is telephone Ancram some day and tell him I'm working for you on something urgent, so we'll have to reschedule the interview. Just charm the socks off him and give me some time. That's all I need. I'll try to keep you out of it if I can.'

'So, to recap, all you need is for me to lie to a fellow officer who is carrying out an internal investigation? And meantime, lacking any physical or verbal evidence, you'll be solving the drug-running case?'

'Nicely summarised. I can see why you're the CI instead of me.' He shot to his feet, ran to the payphone. He'd heard it ringing before anyone in the restaurant. It was Jack, checking on him. He reminded Rebus about the doggie bag.

'Being brought to the table as I speak.'

When he got to the table, Gill was checking the bill.

'This is on me,' Rebus said.

'At least let me leave the tip. I ate most of the bread. And besides, my water cost more than your wine.'

'You got the better deal. What's it to be, Gill?'

She nodded. 'I'll tell him anything you like.'

25

Jack still had the power to surprise his old friend: wolfed the pizza. His only comment: 'You didn't eat much.'

'Bit bland for me, Jack.'

Rebus was itching now: for a cigarette and Aberdeen both. There was something up there he wanted; he just didn't know quite what it was.

The truth maybe.

He should have been itching for a drink too, but the wine had put him off. It slopped in his stomach, liquid heartburn. He sat at a desk and read through Shankley's statement. The big man was in a cell downstairs. Jack had worked fast; Rebus couldn't see anything missing.

'So,' he said, 'I'm back from parole. How did I do?'

'Let's not make it a regular date, my heart couldn't take it.'

Rebus smiled, picked up a phone. He wanted to check his machine at home, see if Ancram had plans for him. He did: nine tomorrow morning. There was another message. It was from Kayleigh Burgess. She needed to talk with him.

'I'm seeing someone in Morningside at three, so how about four at that big hotel in Bruntsfield? We can have afternoon tea.' She said it was important. Rebus decided to go out there and wait. He'd have preferred to leave Jack behind ...

'Know what, Jack? You're severely cramping my style.'

'How do you mean?'

'With women. There's one I want to see, but I bet you're going to tag along, aren't you?'

Jack shrugged. 'I'll wait outside the door if you like.'

'It'll be a comfort to know you're there.'

'It could be worse,' stuffing his face with the last of the pizza, 'just think, how do Siamese twins arrange their love lives?'

'Some questions are best left unanswered,' Rebus said.

He thought: Good question though.

It was a nice hotel, quietly upmarket. Rebus worked out a possible dialogue in his head. Ancram knew about the clippings in his kitchen, and Kayleigh was the only possible source. He'd been furious at the time, less angry now. It was her job after all: information, and using that information to elicit other information. It still rankled. Then there was the Spaven-McLure connection: Ancram had picked up on it; Kayleigh knew about it. And finally, above all, there was the break-in.

They waited for her in the lounge. Jack flicked through *Scottish Field* and kept reading out descriptions of estates for sale: 'seven thousand acres in Caithness, with hunting lodge, stabling, and working farm'. He looked up at Rebus.

'Some country this, eh? Where else could you lay your hands on seven thousand acres at knockdown prices?'

'There's a theatre group called 7:84 – know what it means?'

'What?'

'Seven per cent of the population controls eighty-four per cent of the wealth.'

'Are we in the seven?'

Rebus snorted. 'Not even close, Jack.'

'I wouldn't mind a taste of the high life, though.'

'At what cost?'

'Eh?'

'What would you be willing to trade?'

'No, I mean like winning the lottery or something.'

'So you wouldn't take back-handers to drop a charge?'

Jack's eyes narrowed. 'What are you getting at?'

'Come on, Jack. I was in Glasgow, remember? I saw good suits and jewellery, I saw something approaching the smug.'

'They just like to dress nice, makes them feel important.'

'Uncle Joe's not doling out freebies?'

'I wouldn't know if he was.' Jack lifted the magazine to shield his face: matter closed. And then Kayleigh Burgess walked in through the door.

She saw Rebus immediately, and a blush started creeping up her neck. By the time she'd walked over to where he was rising from his chair, it had climbed as far as her cheeks.

'Inspector, you got my message.' Rebus nodded, eyes unblinking. 'Well, thanks for coming.' She turned to Jack Morton.

'DI Morton,' Jack said, shaking her hand.

'Do you want some tea?'

Rebus shook his head, gestured towards the free chair. She sat down.

'So?' he said, determined to make nothing easy for her, not ever again.

She sat with her shoulder-bag in her lap, twisting the strap. 'Look,' she said, 'I owe you an apology.' She glanced up at him, then away, took a deep breath. 'I didn't tell CI Ancram about those cuttings. Or about Fergus McLure knowing Spaven, come to that.'

'But you know he knows?'

She nodded. 'Eamonn told him.'

'And who told Eamonn?'

'I did. I didn't know what to make of it ... I wanted to bounce it off someone. We're a team, so I told Eamonn. I made him promise it'd go no further.'

'But it did.'

She nodded. 'He was straight on the phone to Ancram. See, Eamonn ... he's got a thing about police brass. If we're investigating someone at Inspector level, Eamonn always wants to go over their heads, talk to their superiors, see what gets stirred up. Besides, you haven't exactly made a favourable impression with my presenter.'

'It was an accident,' Rebus said. 'I tripped.'

'If that's your story.'

'What does the footage say?'

She thought about it. 'We were shooting from behind Eamonn. Mostly, what we've got is his back.'

'I'm off the hook then?'

'I didn't say that. Just stick to your story.'

Rebus nodded, getting her drift. 'Thanks. But why did Breen go to Ancram? Why not *my* boss?'

'Because Eamonn knew Ancram was to lead the inquiry.'

'And how did he know *that*?'

'The grapevine.'

A grapevine with few grapes attached. He saw Jim Stevens again, staring up at the window of his flat ... Stirring it ...

Rebus sighed. 'One last thing. Do you know anything about a break-in at my flat?'

Her eyebrows rose. 'Should I?'

'Remember the Bible John stuff in the cupboard? Someone took a crowbar to my front door, and all they wanted was to rifle through it.'

She was shaking her head. 'Not us.'

'No?'

'Housebreaking? We're journalists, for Christ's sake.'

Rebus had his hands up in a gesture of appeasement, but he wanted to push it a little further. 'Any chance Breen would go out on a limb?'

Now she laughed. 'Not even for a story the size of Watergate. Eamonn fronts the programme, he doesn't do any digging.'

'You and your researchers do?'

'Yes, and neither of them seems the crowbar type. Does that leave me in the frame?'

As she crossed one leg over the other, Jack studied them. His eyes had been running all over her like a kid's over a Scalextric set.

'Consider the matter closed,' Rebus said.

'But it's true? Your flat was broken into?'

'Matter closed,' he repeated.

She almost pouted. 'How's the inquiry going anyway?' She held up a hand. 'I'm not snooping, call it personal interest.'

'Depends which inquiry you mean,' Rebus said.

'The Spaven case.'

'Oh, that.' Rebus sniffed, considering his response. 'Well, CI Ancram is the trusting sort. He has real faith in his officers. If you plead innocent, he'll take it at face value. It's a comfort to have superiors like that. For instance, he trusts me so much he's got a minder on me like a limpet on a rock.' He nodded towards Jack. 'Inspector Morton here is supposed to not let me out of his sight. He even sleeps at my flat.' He held Kayleigh's gaze. 'How's that sound?'

She could hardly form the words. 'It's scandalous.'

Rebus shrugged, but she was reaching into her bag, bringing out notebook and pen. Jack glowered at Rebus, who winked back. Kayleigh had to flick through a lot of pages to find a fresh sheet.

'When did this start?' she said.

'Let's see …' Rebus pretended to be thinking. 'Sunday afternoon, I think. After I'd been interrogated in Aberdeen and dragged back here.'

She looked up. 'Interrogated?'

'John …' Jack Morton warned.

'Didn't you know?' Rebus's eyes widened. 'I'm a suspect in the Johnny Bible case.'

On the drive back to the flat, Jack was furious.

'What did you think you were up to?'

'Keeping her mind off Spaven.'

'I don't get it.'

'She's trying to make a programme about Spaven, Jack. She's not doing one on policemen being nasty to other policemen, and she's not doing one on Johnny Bible.'

'So?'

'So now her head's swimming with everything I told her – and not a jot of it has to do with Spaven. It'll keep her ... what's the word?'

'Preoccupied?'

'Good enough.' Rebus nodded, looked at his watch. Five-twenty. 'Shit,' he said. 'Those pictures!'

Traffic was at a crawl as they detoured into the centre of town. Rush-hour Edinburgh was a nightmare these days. Red lights and chugging exhausts, frayed nerves and drumming fingers. By the time they reached the shop it had closed for the night. Rebus checked the opening hours: nine tomorrow. He could pick up the photos on his way to Fettes and only be a little late for Ancram. Ancram: the very thought of the man was like voltage passing through him.

'Let's go home,' he told Jack. Then he remembered the traffic. 'No, second thoughts: we'll stop off at the Ox.' Jack smiled. 'Did you think you'd cured me?' Rebus shook his head. 'I sometimes come off for a couple of days at a stretch, it's no big thing.'

'It could be though.'

'Another sermon, Jack?'

Jack shook his head. 'What about the ciggies?'

'I'll buy a packet from the machine.'

He stood at the bar, resting one shoe on the foot-rail, one elbow on the polished wood. In front of him sat four objects: a packet of cigarettes with seal unbroken; a box of Scottish Bluebell matches; a thirty-five millilitre measure of Teacher's whisky; and a pint of Belhaven Best. He was staring at them with the concentration of a psychic willing them to move.

'Three minutes dead,' a regular commented from along the bar, like he'd been timing Rebus's resistance. A profound question was running through Rebus's mind: did he want them, or did *they* want *him*? He wondered how David Hume would have got on with that. He picked the beer up. No wonder you called it 'heavy': that's just what it was. He sniffed it. It didn't smell too enticing; he knew it would taste OK, but other things tasted better. The aroma of the whisky was fine though – smoky, filling nostrils and lungs. It would sear his mouth, burn going down, and melt through him, the effect lasting not long.

And the nicotine? He knew himself that when he took a few days off the ciggies, he could sense how bad they made you smell – your skin, clothes, hair. Disgusting habit really: if you didn't give yourself cancer, chances were you were giving it to some poor bastard whose only misfortune was in getting too close to you. Harry the barman was waiting for Rebus to act. The whole bar was. They knew something was happening; it was written on Rebus's face – there was almost pain there. Jack stood beside him, holding his breath.

'Harry,' Rebus said, 'take those away.' Harry lifted the two drinks, shaking his head.

'I wish we could get a picture of this,' he said.

Rebus slid the cigarettes along the bar towards the smoker. 'Here, take them. And don't leave them lying too close to me, I might change my mind.'

The smoker lifted the packet, amazed. 'Payback for the singles you've nicked off me in the past.'

'With interest,' Rebus said, watching Harry pour the beer down the sink.

'Does it go straight back into the barrel, Harry?'

'So, do you want anything else, or did you just come in for a seat?'

'Coke and crisps.' He turned to Jack. 'I'm allowed crisps, right?'

Jack was resting a hand on his back, patting him softly. And he was smiling.

They stopped in at a shop on the way to the flat, came out again with the makings of a meal.

'Can you remember the last time you cooked?' Jack asked.

'I'm not that cack-handed.' The answer to the question was 'no'.

Jack, it turned out, enjoyed cooking, but he found Rebus's kitchen lacking the finer tools of his craft. No lemon zester, no garlic crusher.

'Give the garlic here,' Rebus offered, 'I'll stamp on it.'

'I used to be lazy,' Jack said. 'When Audrey left, I tried cooking bacon in the toaster. But cooking's a doddle once you get your head round it.'

'What's it going to be anyway?'

'Low-fat spagbog, with salad if you'll get your arse in gear.'

Rebus got his arse in gear, but found he had to nip out to the deli for the makings of the dressing. He didn't bother with a jacket: it was mild out.

'Sure you can trust me?' he said.

Jack tasted the sauce, nodded. So Rebus went out on his own, and thought about not going back. There was a pub on the next corner, its doors open. But of course he was going back: he hadn't eaten yet. The way Jack slept, if Rebus ever wanted to high-tail it that would be the time.

They set the table in the living room – the first time it had been used for a meal since Rebus's wife had left. Could that be true? Rebus paused, a fork and spoon in his hand. Yes, it was true. His flat, his refuge, suddenly seemed emptier than ever.

Maudlin again: another reason he drank.

They shared a bottle of Highland spring water, chinked glasses.

'Shame it's not fresh pasta,' Jack said.

'It's fresh *food*,' Rebus replied, filling his mouth. 'Rare enough in this flat.'

They ate the salad afterwards – French-style, Jack said. Rebus was reaching for seconds when the phone rang. He picked it up.

'John Rebus.'

'Rebus, it's CI Grogan here.'

'CI Grogan,' Rebus looked to Jack, 'what can I do for you, sir?' Jack came to the phone to listen.

'We've run preliminary tests on your shoes and clothing. Thought you'd like to know you're in the clear.'

'Was there ever any doubt?'

'You're a copper, Rebus, you know there are procedures.'

'Of course, sir. I appreciate you phoning.'

'Something else. I had a word with Mr Fletcher.' Hayden Fletcher: PR at T-Bird. 'He admitted knowing the latest victim. Gave us a detailed breakdown of his movements the night she was killed. He even offered blood for DNA analysis if we thought it would help.'

'He sounds cocky.'

'That just about sums him up. I took an instant dislike to the man, something I don't often do.'

'Not even with me?' Rebus smiled at Jack. Jack mouthed the words 'Go easy'.

'Not even with you,' Grogan said.

'So that's two suspects eliminated. Doesn't get you much further, does it?'

'No.' Grogan sighed. Rebus could imagine him wiping tired eyes.

'What about Eve and Stanley, sir? Did you heed my advice?'

'I did. Mindful of your mistrust of DS Lumsden – an excellent officer, by the way – I set two men on it off my own bat, reporting directly to me.'

'Thank you, sir.'

Grogan coughed. 'They were staying in a hotel near the airport.

Five-star, usually an oil company hang-out. Driving a BMW.' The one from Uncle Joe's cul-de-sac no doubt. 'I've a description of the car and licence details.'

'Not needed, sir.'

'Well, my men followed them to a couple of nightclubs.'

'During business hours?'

'Daylight hours, Inspector. They went in carrying nothing, and came out the same way. However, they also paid visits to several banks in the city centre. One of my men got close enough in one bank to see that they were making a cash deposit.'

'In a bank?' Rebus frowned. Was Uncle Joe the type to trust to banks? Would he let strangers get within a mile of his ill-gained assets?

'That's about it, Inspector. They ate a few meals together, went for a drive down to the docks, then left town.'

'They've gone?'

'Left tonight. My men followed them as far as Banchory. I'd say they were headed for Perth.' And after that, Glasgow. 'The hotel confirms they've checked out.'

'Did you ask the hotel if they're regulars?'

'We did and they are. They started using it about six months ago.'

'How many rooms?'

'They always book two.' There was a smile in Grogan's voice. 'But the story is, the maids only ever had to clean one of them. Seems they were sharing one room, and leaving the other untouched.'

Bingo, Rebus thought. Housey-housey and fucking clickety-click.

'Thanks, sir.'

'Does this help you in something?'

'It might help a lot, I'll be in touch. Oh, something I meant to ask ...'

'Yes?'

'Hayden Fletcher: did he say how he came to know the victim?'

'A business acquaintance. She organised the stand for T-Bird Oil at the North Sea Convention.'

'Is that what "corporate presentations" means?'

'Apparently. Ms Holden designed a lot of the stands, then her company did the actual construction and setting-up. Fletcher met her as part of that process.'

'Sir, I appreciate all of this.'

'Inspector ... if you're coming north again any time, call to let me know, understood?'

Rebus understood that it wasn't an invitation to afternoon tea.

'Yes, sir,' he said, 'good night.'

He put the phone down. Aberdeen beckoned, and he was damned if he'd give anyone prior notice. But Aberdeen could wait another day. Vanessa Holden connected to the oil industry ...

'What is it, John?'

Rebus looked up at his friend. 'It's Johnny Bible, Jack. I just got a strange feeling about him.'

'What?'

'That he's an oilman ...'

They tidied everything away and washed up, then made mugs of coffee and decided to go back to the decorating. Jack wanted to know more about Johnny Bible, and about Eve and Stanley, but Rebus didn't know where to start. His head felt clogged. He kept filling it with new information, and nothing drained away. Johnny Bible's first victim had been a geology student at a university with close ties to the oil industry. Now his fourth victim made stands for conventions, and working in Aberdeen, he could guess who her best clients had been. If there was a connection between victims one and four, was there something he was missing, something linking two and three? A prostitute and a barmaid, one in Edinburgh, the other Glasgow ...

When the telephone rang, he put down his sandpaper – the door was looking good – and picked it up. Jack was using a ladder to reach the cornices.

'Hello?'

'John? It's Mairie.'

'I've been trying to reach you.'

'Sorry, another assignment – a *paying* one.'

'Did you find out anything about Major Weir?'

'A fair bit. How was Aberdeen?'

'Bracing.'

'It'll do that to you. These notes ... probably too much to read over the phone.'

'So let's meet.'

'Which pub?'

'Not a pub.'

'There must be something wrong with the line. Did you just say "not a pub"?'

'How about Duddingston Village? That's about halfway. I'll park by the loch.'

'When?'

'Half an hour?'

'Half an hour it is.'

'We'll never get this room finished,' Jack said, stepping down off the ladder. He had traces of white paint in his hair.

'Grey suits you,' Rebus told him.

Jack rubbed at his head. 'Is it another woman?' Rebus nodded. 'How do you manage to keep them apart?'

'The flat has a lot of doors.'

Mairie was waiting when they got there. Jack hadn't been around Arthur's Seat in years, so they took the scenic route; not that there was much to see at night. The huge hump of a hill, looking like nothing so much as – even kids could see it – a crouched elephant, was a great place to blow off the cobwebs – and anything else you might have on you. At night, though, it was poorly lit and a long way from anywhere. Edinburgh had lots of these glorious empty spaces. They were fine and private places right up until the moment you met your first junkie, mugger, rapist or gay-basher.

Duddingston Village was just that – a village in the midst of a city, sheltering beneath Arthur's Seat. Duddingston Loch – more outsize pond than true loch – looked down on to a bird sanctuary and a path known as the Innocent Railway: Rebus wished he knew where it got the name.

Jack stopped the car and flashed his lights. Mairie switched hers off, unlocked her door, and came loping towards them. Rebus leaned into the back to open the door, and she got in. He introduced her to Jack Morton.

'Oh,' she said, 'you worked the Knots and Crosses case with John.' Rebus blinked. 'How do you know that? It was before your time.' She winked at him. 'I've done my research.'

He wondered what else she might know, but hadn't time to speculate. She handed him a brown A4 envelope.

'Thank God for e-mail. I've a contact on the *Washington Post* and he got me most of what's there.'

Rebus switched on the interior light. There was a spot-lamp specially for reading by.

'Usually he wants to meet me in pubs,' Mairie told Jack, 'right seedy ones at that.'

Jack smiled at her, turned in his seat with his arm hanging down over the headrest. Rebus knew Jack liked her. Everyone liked Mairie from the off. He wished he knew her secret.

'Seedy pubs suit his personality,' Jack said.

'Look,' Rebus interrupted, 'will you two bugger off and go look at the ducks or something?'

Jack shrugged, checked it was OK with Mairie, and opened his door. Alone, Rebus settled deeper into his seat and started to read.

Number one: Major Weir was not a Major. It was a nickname, earned in adolescence. Two, his parents had handed on to him their love of all things Scottish – up to and including a craving for national independence. There were a lot of facts about his early years in industry, latterly the oil industry, and reports of Thom Bird's demise – nothing suspicious about it. A journalist in the States had started writing an unauthorised biography of Weir, but had given up – rumour had it he was paid not to finish the book. A couple of stories, unsubstantiated: Weir left his wife amid much acrimony – and later, much alimony. Then something about Weir's son, either deceased or disinherited. Maybe off in some ashram or feeding the African hungry, maybe working in a burger parlour or Wall Street futures. Rebus turned to the next sheet, only to find there wasn't one. The story had finished mid-sentence. He got out of the car, walked to where Mairie and Jack were in huddled conversation.

'It's not all here,' he said, waving what sheets he had.

'Oh, yes.' Mairie reached into her jacket, brought out a single folded sheet and handed it over. Rebus stared at her, demanding an explanation. She shrugged. 'Call me a tease.'

Jack started laughing.

Rebus stood in the glare of the headlights and read. His eyes widened and his mouth fell open. He read it again, then for a third time, and had to run a hand through his hair to make sure the top of his head hadn't just blown off.

'Everything all right?' Mairie asked him.

He stared at her for a moment, not really seeing anything, then pulled her to him and planted a kiss on her cheek.

'Mairie, you're perfect.'

She turned to Jack Morton.

'I second that,' he said.

*

Sitting in his car, Bible John had watched Rebus and friend drive out of Arden Street. His business had kept him an extra day in Edinburgh. Frustrating, but at least he'd been able to take another look at the policeman. It was hard to tell from a distance, but Rebus seemed to sport bruises on his face, and his clothes were dishevelled. Bible John couldn't help but feel a little disappointed: he'd been hoping for a more worthy adversary. The man looked dead done in.

Not that he thought them adversaries, not really. Rebus's flat had not thrown up much, but it *had* revealed that Rebus's interest in Bible John was connected to the Upstart. Which went some way towards explaining it. He hadn't stayed as long in the flat as he would have liked. Being unable to pick the lock, he'd been forced to break the door. He couldn't know how long it would take for neighbours to spot something. So he had been swift, but then there'd been so little in the flat worth his attention. It told him something about the policeman. He felt now that he *knew* Rebus, at least to a degree – he felt the loneliness of his life, the gaps where sentiment and warmth and love should have been. There was music, and there were books, but neither in great quantity nor of great quality. The clothes were utilitarian, one jacket much like another. No shoes. He found that bizarre in the extreme. Did the man possess only one pair?

And the kitchen: lacking in utensils and produce. And the bathroom: needing redecorating.

But back in the kitchen, a small surprise. Newspapers and cuttings hastily hidden, easily found. Bible John, Johnny Bible. And evidence that Rebus had gone to some trouble: the original papers must have been bought from a dealer. An investigation within the official investigation, that was what it looked like. Which made Rebus more interesting in Bible John's eyes.

Paperwork in the bedroom: boxes of old correspondence, bank statements, very few photographs – but enough to show that Rebus had once been married, and had a daughter. Nothing recent though: no photos of the daughter grown-up, no recent photos at all.

But the one thing he'd come here for … his business card … no sign of it at all. Which meant either that Rebus had thrown it away, or that he carried it with him still, in a jacket pocket or wallet.

In the living room, he noted Rebus's telephone number, then closed his eyes, making sure he had committed the flat's layout to memory. Yes, easy. He could come back here at dead of night and walk through the place without disturbing anything or anyone. He could take John Rebus any time he wanted to. Any time at all.

He wondered about Rebus's friend though. The policeman didn't seem the gregarious type. They'd been painting the living room together. He couldn't know if it was connected to the break-in; probably not. A man Rebus's age, maybe a little younger, quite a tough-looking individual. Another policeman? Perhaps. The man's face had lacked

Rebus's intensity. There was something in Rebus – he had noticed it during their first meeting, and it had been reinforced this evening – a singleness of purpose, a sense of determination. Physically, Rebus's friend seemed the superior, but that wouldn't make Rebus a pushover. Physical strength could take a person only so far.

After that, it was down to attitude.

26

They were waiting outside the photo shop when it opened next morning. Jack looked at his watch for only the fifteenth time.

'He'll kill us,' he said for the ninth or tenth. 'No, I mean it, really he will.'

'Relax.'

Jack looked about as relaxed as a headless chicken. When the manager started unlocking the shop, they sprinted from the car. Rebus had the stub ready in his hand.

'Give me a minute,' the manager said.

'We're late for something.'

Coat still on, the manager browsed through a box of photograph packets. Rebus imagined family days out, holidays abroad, red-eyed birthdays and blurred wedding receptions. There was something faintly desperate and yet touching about collections of photographs. He'd looked through a lot of photo albums in his time – usually seeking clues to a murder, a victim's acquaintances.

'You'll have to wait anyway while I unlock the till.' The manager handed over the packet. Jack glanced at the price, slapped down more than enough to cover it, and dragged Rebus out of the shop.

He drove to Fettes like there was a murder scene waiting there. Traffic honked and squealed as he did his stunt-driver routine. They were still twenty minutes late for the meeting. But Rebus didn't mind. He had his reprints, the missing photos from Allan Mitchison's cabin. They were similar to the other pictures: group shots, but with fewer figures. And in all of them, braid-hair, standing right next to Mitchison. In one, she had an arm around him; in another, they were kissing, grinning as their lips met.

Rebus wasn't surprised, not now.

'I hope they were bloody well worth it,' Jack said.

'Every penny, Jack.'

'That's not what I meant.'

Chick Ancram sat with hands clasped, his face the colour of rhubarb crumble. The files were in front of him, as though they hadn't been moved since the previous meeting. His voice had a slight vibrato. He was in control, but only just.

'I had a phone call,' he said, 'from someone called Kayleigh Burgess.'

'Oh yes?'

'She wanted to ask me a few questions.' He paused. 'About you. About the role DI Morton is currently playing in your life.'

'It's gossip, sir. Jack and myself are just good friends.'

Ancram slapped both hands down on the desk. 'I thought we had a deal.'

'Can't say I remember.'

'Well, let's hope your long-term memory's better.' He opened a file. 'Because now the fun really begins.' He nodded for a sheepish Jack to switch on the tape recorder, then started off by giving date and time, officers present ... Rebus felt as if he'd explode. He really thought if he sat there a second longer, his eyeballs would fly from their sockets like those jokeshop glasses with spring-loaded eyes. He'd felt like this before, just before a panic attack. But he wasn't panicking now; he was just *charged*. He stood up. Ancram broke off what he'd been saying.

'Something the matter, Inspector?'

'Look,' Rebus rubbed at his forehead, 'I can't think straight ... not about Spaven. Not today.'

'That's for me to decide, not you. If you're feeling ill, we can call for a doctor, but otherwise ...'

'I'm not ill. I just ...'

'Then sit down.' Rebus sat down, and Ancram went back to his notes. 'Now, Inspector, on the night referred to, your report states that you were at Inspector Geddes' house, and there was a telephone call?'

'Yes.'

'You didn't actually hear the conversation?'

'No.' Braid-hair and Mitchison ... Mitch the organiser, protester. Mitch the oil-worker. Killed by Tony El, henchman to Uncle Joe. Eve and Stanley, working Aberdeen, sharing a room ...

'But DI Geddes told you it was to do with Mr Spaven? A tip-off?'

'Yes.' Burke's Club, police hang-out, maybe an oil-workers' hang-out too. Hayden Fletcher drinking there. Ludovic Lumsden drinking there. Michelle Strachan meets Johnny Bible there ...

'And Geddes didn't say who the call was from?'

'Yes.' Ancram looked up, and Rebus knew he'd given the wrong answer. 'I mean, no.'

'No?'

'No.'

Ancram stared at him, sniffed, concentrated on his notes again. There were pages and pages of them, specially prepared for this session: questions to be asked, 'facts' double-checked, the whole case stripped down and rebuilt.

'Anonymous tip-offs are pretty rare in my experience,' Ancram said.

'Yes.'

'And they're almost always made to a police station's general desk. Would you agree?'

'Yes, sir.' Was Aberdeen the key then, or did the answers lie further north? What did Jake Harley have to do with it? And Mike Sutcliffe – Mr Sheepskin – hadn't Major Weir warned him off? What was it Sutcliffe had said? He'd said something on the plane, then stopped suddenly ... Something about a boat ...

And did any of it connect to Johnny Bible? *Was* Johnny Bible an oilman?

'So it would be rational to deduce that DI Geddes knew the caller, wouldn't it?'

'Or they knew him.'

Ancram shrugged this aside. 'And this tip-off just happened to concern Mr Spaven. Didn't that strike you at the time as a bit of a coincidence, Inspector? Seeing as Geddes had been warned off Spaven already? I mean, it must have been clear to you that your boss was *obsessed* with Spaven?'

Rebus got up again and started pacing the small room as best he could.

'Sit down!'

'With respect, sir, I can't. If I sit there any longer, I'm going to stick my fist in your face.'

Jack Morton covered his eyes with one hand.

'What did you say?'

'Wind the tape back and take a listen. And that's why I'm up and walking: crisis management if you like.'

'Inspector, I'd caution you—'

Rebus laughed. 'Would you? That's big of you, sir.' Ancram was rising to his feet. Rebus turned away and walked to the far wall, turned round again and stopped.

'Look,' he said, 'a simple question: do you want to see Uncle Joe fucked?'

'We're not here to—'

'We're here to put on a show – you know that as well as I do. The brass are sweaty about the media; they want the force to look good if that programme ever gets made. This way, everyone sits back and says there was an inquiry. TV seems to be about the only thing brass are afraid of. Villains don't scare them, but ten minutes of negative coverage, dearie me, no. Can't have that. All for a programme which will be stared at by a few million, half of them with the sound down, the other half not taking it in, then forgotten about the very next day. So,' he took a deep breath, 'simple yes or no.' Ancram didn't say anything, so Rebus repeated the question.

Ancram signalled for Jack to turn off the machine. Then he sat back down.

'Yes,' he said quietly.

'I can see that it happens.' Rebus kept his voice level. 'But I don't want *you* getting sole credit. If it's anyone's, the collar belongs to CI Templer.' Rebus went back to his chair, propped himself on the edge of it. 'Now *I* have a couple of questions.'

'Was there a phone call?' Ancram asked, surprising Rebus. They stared at one another. 'Tape's off, this is between the three of us. Was there ever a phone call?'

'I answer yours and you answer mine?' Ancram nodded. 'Of course there was a phone call.'

Ancram almost smiled. 'You liar. He came to your house, didn't he? What did he tell you? Did he say you wouldn't need a search warrant? You must've known he was lying.'

'He was a good cop.'

'Every time you come out with that line, it sounds thinner. What's the matter: stopped finding it convincing?'

'He was.'

'But he had a problem, a little personal demon called Lenny Spaven. You were his friend, Rebus, you should have stopped him.'

'Stopped him?'

Ancram nodded, eyes gleaming like moons. 'You should have helped him.'

'I tried,' Rebus said, his voice a whisper. It was another lie: Lawson by that time had been a junkie with a craving, and only one thing would help – the taste itself.

Ancram sat back, trying not to look satisfied. He thought Rebus was cracking. The inner doubts had been sown – not for the first time. Ancram could now water them with sympathy.

'You know,' he said, 'I'm not blaming you. I think I know what you were going through. But there was a cover-up. There was that one central lie: the tip-off.' He lifted his notes an inch off the desk. 'It's written all over these, and it throws everything else into the pot, because if Geddes had been following Spaven, what was to stop him planting a little evidence along the way?'

'It wasn't his style.'

'Not even when pushed to the limit? Had you seen him there before?'

Rebus couldn't think of a thing to say. Ancram had been leaning forward in his seat again, palms against the desk. He sat back. 'What did you want to ask?'

When Rebus was a child, they'd lived in a semi-detached with a close separating it from the next house along. The close had led to both back gardens. Rebus played football there with his dad. Sometimes he placed a foot against either wall and pushed his way up towards the roof of the close. And sometimes he'd just stand in the middle and throw a small hard rubber ball as hard as he could against the stone floor. The ball would bounce like anything, zipping back and forth, floor to roof to wall to floor to roof …

His head felt like that now.

'What?' he said.

'You said you had a couple of questions.'

Slowly, Rebus's head came back to the here and now. He rubbed his eyes. 'Yes,' he said. 'First off, Eve and Stanley.'

'What about them?'

'Are they close?'

'You mean how do they get on? All right.'

'Just all right?'

'No flare-ups to report.'

'I was thinking more of jealousy.'

Ancram cottoned on. 'Uncle Joe and Stanley?'

Rebus nodded. 'Is she clever enough to play one off against the other?' He'd met her, thought he already knew the answer. Ancram just shrugged. The conversation had obviously taken an unexpected turn.

'Only,' Rebus said, 'in Aberdeen they were sharing a hotel room.'

Ancram narrowed his eyes. 'You're sure of this?' Rebus nodded. 'They must be mad. Uncle Joe'll kill them both.'

'Maybe they don't think he can.'

'How do you mean?'

'Maybe they think they're stronger than him. Maybe they reckon in a war the muscle-men would change sides. Stanley's the one people are scared of these days, you said as much yourself. Especially with Tony El gone.'

'Tony was history anyway.'

'I'm not so sure.'

'Explain.'

Rebus shook his head. 'I need to talk to a couple of people first. Have you heard of Eve and Stanley working together in the past?'

'No.'

'So this Aberdeen jaunt ...?'

'I'd say it's a newish excursion.'

'Hotel records say the past six months.'

'So the question is, what's Uncle Joe setting up?'

Rebus smiled. 'I think you know the answer to that: drugs. He's lost the market in Glasgow, it's already been divvied up. So he can fight for a piece, or he can play away from home. Burke's will take the stuff and sell it on, especially with someone from CID in their pocket. Aberdeen's still a nice market, not the hotbed of fifteen or twenty years ago, but a market nonetheless.'

'So tell me, what are you going to do that the rest of us can't?'

Rebus shook his head. 'I still don't know if you're on the level; I mean, you might be see-sawing.'

This time Ancram really did smile. 'I could say the same about you and the Spaven case.'

'Probably.'

'I won't be satisfied until I know. I think maybe that makes us similar.'

'Look, Ancram, we walked into that lock-up and the bag was *there*. Does it matter how *we* came to be there?'

'It could have been planted.'

'Not with my knowledge.'

'Geddes never confided? I thought the two of you were close?'

Rebus was on his feet. 'I may not be around for a day or two. All right?'

'No, it's not all right. I'll expect you here tomorrow, same time.'

'For Christ's sake ...'

'Or we can turn the machine back on right now and you can tell me what you know. That way, you'll have all the time in the world. And I think you'll find it easier to live with yourself, too.'

'Living with myself has never been the problem. Breathing the same air as people like you – *that's* my problem.'

'I've already told you, Strathclyde Police and the Squaddies are planning an operation …'

'One that'll get nowhere, because for all we know half the Glasgow force is in Uncle Joe's pocket.'

'I'm not the one who goes visiting him at home, with a word put in by a certain Morris Cafferty.'

There was a sudden tightening around Rebus's chest. Coronary, he thought. But it was only Jack Morton, arms holding him, stopping him moving in on Ancram.

'Tomorrow morning, gentlemen,' Ancram said, like they'd had a useful session.

'Yes, sir,' Jack said, hustling Rebus out of the room.

Rebus told his friend to get them on to the M8.

'No way, José.'

'Then park near Waverley, we'll take the train.'

Jack didn't like the way Rebus looked: like his wiring was shorting out. You could almost see the sparks behind his eyes.

'What are you going to do in Glasgow? Walk up to Uncle Joe and say, "Oh, by the way, your woman's shagging your son"? Even you can't be *that* stupid.'

'Of course I'm not that stupid.'

'Glasgow, John,' Jack pleaded. 'It's not our territory. I'll be back in Falkirk in a few weeks, and you …'

Rebus smiled. 'Where'll I be, Jack?'

'God and the Devil know.'

Rebus was still smiling; thought to himself: I'd rather be the devil.

'You've always got to be the hero, haven't you?' Jack asked.

'Time loves a hero, Jack,' Rebus told him.

On the M8, halfway between Edinburgh and Glasgow, slowed by syrupy traffic, Jack tried again.

'This is crazy. I mean *really* crazy.'

'Trust me, Jack.'

'Trust you? The guy who tried to lay me out two nights back? With friends like you …'

'… you'll never be short of enemies.'

'There's still time.'

'Not really, you just think there is.'

'You're talking out your arse.'

'Maybe you're just not listening.' Rebus felt calmer now they were on the road. To Jack, he looked like someone had pulled the plug on him: no more sparks. He almost preferred the model with the faulty wiring. The lack of emotion in his friend's voice was chilling, even in the overheated car. Jack slid his window down a little further. The speedometer was steady on forty, and that was them in the outside lane. Traffic to their left was *really* crawling. If he could find a space, he'd move to the inside – anything to delay their arrival.

He'd oftentimes admired John Rebus – and heard him praised by other officers – for his tenacity, the way he worried at a case terrier-style, more often than not tearing it open, spilling out secret motives and hidden bodies. But that same tenacity could also be a weakness, blinding him to danger, making him impatient and reckless. Jack knew why they were headed for Glasgow, thought he knew pretty well what Rebus would want to do there. And, as ordered by Ancram, Jack would be close by when the crap came tumbling down.

It was a long time since Rebus and Jack had worked together. They'd been an effective team, but Jack had been glad enough of the posting out of Edinburgh. Too claustrophobic – the town and his partner both. Rebus had seemed even then to spend more time living in his own head than in the company of others. Even the pub he chose to haunt was one with fewer than usual distractions: TV, one fruit machine, one cigarette machine. And when group activities were arranged – fishing trips, golf competitions, bus runs – Rebus never signed up. He was an irregular regular, a loner even in company, his brain and heart only fully engaged when he was working a case. Jack knew the score only too well. Work had a way of wrapping itself around you, so you were cut off from the rest of the world. People you met socially tended to treat you with suspicion or outright hostility – so you ended up mixing only with other cops, which bored your wife or girlfriend. *They* began to feel isolated too. It was a bastard.

There were plenty of people on the force who coped, of course. They had understanding partners; or they could shut work out whenever they went home; or it was just a job to them, a way of keeping up with the mortgage. Jack would guess CID was split fifty-fifty between those for whom it was a vocation, and those who could fit into any other type of office life, anywhere, any time.

He didn't know what else John Rebus could do. If they kicked him off the force ... he'd probably drink his pension dry, become just another old ex-cop hanging on to a fund of stories, telling them too often to the same people, trading one form of isolation for another.

It was important that John should stay on the force. It was therefore important to keep him off Shit Street. Jack wondered why nothing in life was ever easy. When he'd been told by Chick Ancram that he'd be 'keeping an eye' on Rebus, he'd been pleased. He'd seen them going out together, reminiscing about cases and characters, haunts and high points. He should have known better. *He* might have changed – become a 'yes man', a pencil-pusher, a careerist – but John was the same as always ... only worse. Time had seasoned his cynicism. He wasn't a terrier now: he was a fighting dog with locking jaws. You just knew that no matter how bloody he got, how much pain there was behind the eyes, the grip was there to the death ...

'Traffic's beginning to shift,' Rebus said.

It was true; whatever the problem had been, it was clearing. The speedo was up to fifty-five. They'd be in Glasgow in no time at all. Jack glanced over at Rebus, who winked without moving his eyes from the road ahead. Jack had a sudden image of himself propping up a bar, dipping into his pension for another drink. Fuck that. For his friend's sake, he'd go the ninety minutes, but no more: no extra time, no penalties. Definitely no penalties.

They made for Partick police station, since their faces were known there. Govan had been another possibility, but Govan was Ancram's HQ and not a place they could do business on the q.t. The Johnny Bible investigation had picked up some momentum from the most recent murder, but all the Glasgow squad were really doing was reading through and filing material sent from Aberdeen. It made Rebus shiver to think he'd walked past Vanessa Holden in Burke's Club. For all that Lumsden had been trying to stitch him up, Aberdeen CID had one thing right: quite a string of coincidences tied Rebus to the Johnny Bible inquiry. So much so that Rebus was beginning to doubt coincidence had much to do with it. Somehow, he couldn't yet say how exactly, Johnny was connected to one of Rebus's other investigations. At present it was no more than a hunch, nothing he could do anything about. But it was there, niggling him. It made him wonder if he knew more about Johnny Bible than he thought ...

Partick, new and bright and comfortable – basically your state of the art cop-shop – was still enemy territory. Rebus couldn't know how many friendly ears Uncle Joe might have on-site, but he thought he might know a quiet spot, a place they could make their own. As they wandered through the building, a few officers nodded or greeted Jack by name.

'Base camp,' Rebus said at last, turning into the deserted office which was temporary home to Bible John. Here he was, spread out across tables and the floor, pinned and taped to the walls. It was like standing in the middle of an exhibition. The last photofit of Bible John, the one compiled by his third victim's sister, was repeated around the room, along with her description of him. It was as if by repetition, by piling image upon image, they could will him into physical being, turn wood pulp and ink into flesh and blood.

'I hate this room,' Jack said as Rebus closed the door.

'So does everyone else by the look of things. Long tea-breaks and other business to attend to.'

'Half the force weren't alive when Bible John was on the go. He's lost any sort of meaning.'

'They'll be telling their grandkids about Johnny Bible though.'

'True enough.' Jack paused. 'Are you going to do it?'

Rebus saw that his hand was lying on the receiver. He picked it up, punched in the numbers. 'Did you doubt me?' he asked.

'Not for a minute.'

The voice that answered was gruff, unwelcoming. Not Uncle Joe, not Stanley. One of the body-builders. Rebus gave as good as he got.

'Malky there?'

Hesitation: only his close friends called him Malky. 'Who wants to know?'

'Tell him it's Johnny.' Rebus paused. 'From Aberdeen.'

'Haud on.' Clatter as the receiver was dropped on to a hard surface. Rebus listened closely, heard television voices, game-show applause. Watching: Uncle Joe maybe, or Eve. Stanley wouldn't like game-shows; he'd never get a question right.

'Phone!' the body-builder called.

A long wait. Then a distant voice: 'Who is it?'

'Johnny.'

'Johnny? Johnny who?' The voice closer.

'From Aberdeen.'

The receiver was picked up. 'Hello?'

Rebus took a deep breath. 'For your own sake you better sound natural. I know about you and Eve, know what you've been up to in Aberdeen. So if you want to keep it quiet, sound natural. Don't want Muscle Man to get even the slightest suspicion.'

A rustling sound, Stanley turning away for privacy, tucking the phone into his chin.

'So what's the story?'

'You've got a nice scam going, and I don't want to fuck it up unless I

295

have to, so don't do anything that would make me do that. Understood?'

'No bother.' The voice was not used to attempting levity when its brain demanded bloody restitution.

'You're doing all right, Stanley. Eve'll be proud of you. Now we need to talk, not just you and me, the three of us.'

'My dad?'

'Eve.'

'Oh, right.' Calming again. 'Eh ... no problem with that.'

'Tonight?'

'Eh ... OK.'

'Partick police station.'

'Wait a minute ...'

'That's the deal. Just to talk. You're not walking into anything. If you're worried, keep your gob shut until you hear the deal. If you don't like it, you can walk. You won't have said anything, so there's nothing to fear. No charges, no tricks. It's not you I'm interested in. Are we still on?'

'I'm not sure. Can I call you back?'

'I need a yes or no right now. If it's no, you might as well pass me across to your dad.'

Condemned men laughed with more humour. 'Look, for myself, there's no problem. But there are other parties involved.'

'Just tell Eve what I've told you. If she won't come, that doesn't mean you shouldn't. I'll get some visitors' passes for you. False names.' Rebus looked down at a book open in front of him, found two straight off. 'William Pritchard and Madeleine Smith. Can you remember that?'

'I think so.'

'Repeat them.'

'William ... something.'

'Pritchard.'

'And Maggie Smith.'

'Close enough. I know you can't just sneak off, so we'll leave the time open. Get here when you can. And if you start thinking of bottling it, just remember all those bank accounts and how lonely they'll be without you.'

Rebus put down the phone. His hand was hardly trembling.

27

They notified the front desk and got visitors' passes made up, and after that there was nothing to do but wait. Jack said the room felt cold and musty at the same time; he had to get out. He suggested the canteen or a corridor or anywhere, but Rebus shook his head.

'You go. I think I'll stay here, see if I can decide what to say to Bonnie and Clyde. Bring me back a coffee and maybe a filled roll.' Jack nodded. 'Oh, and a bottle of whisky.' Jack looked at him. Rebus smiled.

He tried to remember his last drink. He recalled standing in the Ox with two glasses and a packet of cigs. But before that ... Wine with Gill?

Jack had said the room was cold; it felt stifling to Rebus. He took off his jacket, loosened his tie and undid the top button of his shirt. Then he wandered around the office, peering into desk drawers and grey cardboard boxes.

He saw: interview transcripts, their covers faded and curling at the edges; hand-written reports; typed reports; evidence summaries; maps, mostly hand-drawn; duty logs; ream after ream of witness statements – descriptions of the man seen in the Barrowland Ballroom. Then there were the photographs, matt black and whites, ten by eight and smaller. The Ballroom itself, interior and exterior. It looked more modern than the word 'ballroom' conjured up, reminded Rebus a bit of his old school – flat building panels with the occasional window. Three spots sat atop a concrete canopy, pointing up towards the windows and the sky. And on the canopy itself – a useful shelter from the rain while you were waiting either to be admitted or, afterwards, for your lift – the words 'Barrowland Ballroom' and 'Dancing'. Most of the exterior pictures had been taken on a wet afternoon, women caught on the periphery with plastic rain-mates, men in bunnets and long coats. More photographs: police frogmen searching the river; the loci, CID in their trademark pork-pie hats and raincoats – a back lane, the back court of a tenement, another back court. Typical locations for a cuddle and a feel-up, maybe going a wee bit further. Too far for the victims. There was a photo of

Superintendent Joe Beattie, holding out an artist's impression of Bible John. Looking between the portrait and Beattie, the men's expressions seemed similar. Several members of the public had commented on it. Mackeith Street and Earl Street – victims two and three were killed on the streets where they lived. He'd taken them so close to their homes: why? So they'd relax their defences? Or had he been vacillating, putting off the attacks? Nervous to ask for a kiss and a cuddle, or just plain scared and with his conscience battling his deep desire? The files were full of such aimless speculation, and more structured theories from professional psychologists and psychiatrists. In the end they'd been as helpful as Croiset the psychic detective.

Rebus thought of meeting Aldous Zane in this very room. Zane had been in the papers again – he'd inspected the latest locus, given the same rambling spiel, and been flown home. Rebus wondered what Jim Stevens was up to now. He remembered Zane's handshake, the way it had tingled. And Zane's impressions of Bible John – though Stevens had been present, the paper hadn't bothered printing them. A trunk in the attic of a modern house. Well, Rebus could have come up with better than that himself, if some paper had put him up in a posh hotel.

Lumsden had put him up in a posh hotel, probably thinking CID would never know. Lumsden had tried to get pally with him, telling him they were alike, showing Rebus that he had stature in the city – free meals and drinks, free entrance to Burke's Club. He'd been testing Rebus, seeing how open he'd be to a bung. But at whose behest? The club's owners? Or Uncle Joe himself …?

More photos. There seemed no end to them. It was the onlookers who interested Rebus, the people who didn't know they'd been snapped for posterity. A woman in high heels, good legs – all you could see of her were heels and legs, the rest hidden behind a WPC taking part in a reconstruction. Woolly suits searching the back courts off Mackeith Street, looking for the victim's handbag. The courts looked like bomb-sites – drying-poles poking up out of stunted grass and rubble. Roadside motor cars: Zephyrs, Hillman Imps, Zodiacs. A world ago. A bundle of posters sat in one box, the rubber band long ago perished. Photofits of Bible John along with varying descriptions: 'Speaks with a polite Glasgow accent and has an erect posture'. Very helpful. The phone number of the inquiry HQ. They'd received thousands of phone calls, boxes of them. Brief details of every one, with more detailed back-up notes if the call seemed worth checking.

Rebus's eyes moved over the remaining boxes. He chose one at random – a big flat cardboard box, inside which were newspapers from the time, intact and unread for quarter of a century. He examined front pages, then turned to the back to look at the sports. A few of the crosswords had been half-done, probably by a bored detective. Slips of paper stapled to each banner-head gave page numbers with Bible John coverage. But Rebus wasn't going to find anything there. He looked at the other stories instead and smiled at some of the adverts. Some seemed artless by today's standards; others hadn't aged at all. In the personal ads, people were selling lawnmowers, washing machines, and record players at knock-down prices. In a couple of papers, Rebus found the same ad, framed like a public notice: 'Find a New Life and a Good Job in America – Booklet Tells You How'. You had to send off a couple of stamps to an address in Manchester. Rebus sat back, wondering if Bible John had got that far.

In October '69, Paddy Meehan had been sentenced at the High Court in Edinburgh and had shouted out, 'You've made a terrible mistake – I'm innocent!' That made Rebus think of Lenny Spaven; he shook the thought away and turned to a new paper. November 8: gales forced the evacuation of the Staflo oil rig; November 12: a report that the owners of the *Torrey Canyon* had paid out £3 million in compensation after losing 5,000 tons of Kuwaiti crude into the English Channel. Elsewhere, Dunfermline had decided to allow *The Killing of Sister George* to be shown in the town, and a brand new Rover three-and-a-half litre would cost you £1,700. Rebus turned to late December. The SNP chairman was predicting that Scotland stood 'on the threshold of a decade of destiny'. Nice one, sir. December 31: Hogmanay. The *Herald* wished its readers a happy and prosperous 1970, and led with the story of a shootout in Govanhill: one constable dead, three wounded. He put the paper down, the gust blowing some photos off the desk. He picked them up: the three victims, so full of life. Victims one and three shared some facial similarities. All three looked hopeful, like the future just might bring them everything they were dreaming of. It was good to have hope, and never to give up. But Rebus doubted many people managed that. They might smile for the camera, but if caught unawares they'd more likely look bedraggled and exhausted, like the bystanders in the photos.

How many victims were there? Not just Bible John or Johnny Bible, but all the killers, the punished and the never found. The World's End murders, Cromwell Street, Nilsen, the Yorkshire Ripper ... And Elsie Rhind ... If Spaven hadn't killed her, then the murderer must have been hooting with laughter all through the trial. And he was still out there, maybe with other scalps added to his tally, other unsolveds. Elsie

Rhind lay in her grave unavenged, a forgotten victim. Spaven had committed suicide because he couldn't bear the weight of his innocence. And Lawson Geddes ... had he killed himself over grief for his wife, or because of Spaven? Had cold realisation finally crept over him?

The bastards were all gone; only John Rebus was left. They wanted to shift their burdens on to him. But he was refusing, and he'd go on refusing, denying. He didn't know what else he could do. Except drink. He wanted a drink, wanted one desperately. But he wasn't going to have one, not yet. Maybe later, maybe sometime. People died and you couldn't bring them back. Some of them died violently, cruelly young, without knowing why they'd been chosen. Rebus felt surrounded by loss. All the ghosts ... yelling at him ... begging him ... shrieking ...

'John?'

He looked up from the desk. Jack was standing there with a mug in one hand and a roll in the other. Rebus blinked, his vision was going: it was like he was looking at Jack through a heat haze.

'Christ, man, are you all right?'

His nose and lips were wet. He wiped at them. The photos on the desk were wet too. He knew he'd been crying and pulled out a handkerchief. Jack put the mug and roll down and rested an arm along his shoulders, squeezing gently.

'Don't know what's up with me,' Rebus said, blowing his nose.

'Yes you do,' Jack said quietly.

'Yes, I do,' Rebus acknowledged. He gathered up the photographs and newspapers and stuffed them all back into their boxes. 'Stop looking at me like that.'

'Like what?'

'I wasn't talking to you.'

Jack lifted his backside on to a desk. 'Not many defences left, have you?'

'Doesn't look like it.'

'Time to get your act together.'

'Ach, Stanley and Eve won't be here for a while yet.'

'You know that's not—'

'I know, I know. And you're right: time to get my act together. Where do I start? No, don't tell me – the Juice Church?'

Jack just shrugged. 'Your decision.'

Rebus picked up the roll and bit into it. A mistake: the block in his throat made it hard to swallow. He gulped at the coffee, managed to finish the roll – bland ham and wet tomato. Then remembered he had to make another call: a Shetland number.

'I'll be back in a minute,' he told Jack.

In the toilets he washed his face. Tiny red veins had burst in the whites of his eyes; he looked like he'd been on a bender.

'Stone cold sober,' he told himself, heading back to the telephone. Briony, Jake Harley's girlfriend, picked up.

'Is Jake there?' Rebus asked.

'No, sorry.'

'Briony, we met the other day, DI Rebus.'

'Oh, yes.'

'Has he been in touch?'

A long pause. 'Sorry, I missed that. The line's not great.'

It sounded just fine to Rebus. 'I said, has he been in touch?'

'No.'

'No?'

'That's what I said.' Edgy now.

'OK, OK. Aren't you a bit worried?'

'What about?'

'Jake.'

'Why should I be?'

'Well, he's been off on his own longer than intended. Maybe something's happened.'

'He's all right.'

'How do you know?'

'I just do!' Almost shouting now.

'Calm down. Look, why don't I get—'

'Just leave us alone!' The phone died on him.

Us. Leave *us* alone. Rebus stared at the receiver.

'I could hear her from over here,' Jack said. 'Sounds like she's cracking up.'

'I think she is.'

'Boyfriend trouble?'

'Boyfriend *in* trouble.' He put the receiver down. There was an incoming call.

'DI Rebus.'

It was the front desk, telling him the first of his visitors had arrived.

Eve looked much as she had that night in the bar of Rebus's hotel – dressed for business in a two-piece suit, conservative blue rather than vamp red, and with the gold jewellery on wrists, fingers and neck, and the same gold clasp pulling back her peroxide hair. She had a handbag with her, and tucked it under her arm as she clipped on her visitor's pass.

'Who's Madeleine Smith?' she asked as they climbed the stairs.

'I got her name out of a book, I think she was a murderess.'

She gave Rebus a look which managed to be hard and amused at the same time.

'This way,' Rebus said. He led her to the Bible John room, where Jack was waiting. 'Jack Morton,' Rebus said, 'Eve ... I don't know your last name. It's not Toal, is it?'

'Cudden,' she said coldly.

'Sit down, Ms Cudden.'

She sat down, reached into her bag for the black cigarettes. 'Do you mind?'

'Actually, there's no smoking allowed,' Jack said, sounding apologetic. 'And neither Inspector Rebus nor myself are smokers.'

She looked at Rebus. 'Since when?'

Rebus shrugged. 'Where's Stanley?'

'He'll be here. We thought it wise to leave separately.'

'Uncle Joe won't suspect?'

'Well, that's *our* problem, not yours. As far as Joe knows, Malky's going out on the ran-dan, and I'm visiting a friend. She's a good friend, she'll not let on.'

Her tone told Rebus she'd used the friend before – other times, other assignations.

'Well,' he said, 'I'm glad you arrived first. I wanted to have a private word.' He rested against a desk, folded his arms to stop his hands shaking. 'That night in the hotel, you were setting me up, yes?'

'Tell me what you know.'

'About you and Stanley?'

'Malky.' Her face creased. 'I hate that nickname.'

'OK then, *Malky*. What do I know? I know just about everything. The two of you head north every now and then on business for Uncle Joe. I'd guess you're go-betweens. He needs people he can trust.' He gave a twist to the last word. 'People who won't share their hotel bedroom, leaving the other one vacant. People who won't rip him off.'

'Are we ripping him off?' Disregarding Jack, she'd lit up. There were no ashtrays in sight, so Rebus placed a wastepaper-bin beside her, inhaling the smoke as he did so. Wonderful smoke. Almost a contact high.

'Yes,' he said, retreating to the desk. They'd placed Eve's chair in the middle of the floor, Rebus to one side of her, Jack the other. She looked comfortable enough with the arrangement. 'I don't see Uncle Joe as a bank account kind of villain. I mean, he probably wouldn't trust the banks in Glasgow, never mind Aberdeen. Yet there you are, you and Malky, dumping wads of cash into several accounts. I have dates, times, bank details.' An exaggeration, but he reckoned he could wing it. 'I've got statements from hotel employees, including maids who never need to clean Malky's room. Funny, he doesn't strike me as the tidy sort.'

Eve exhaled smoke down her nostrils, managed a smile. 'All right,' she said.

'Now,' Rebus went on, wanting to rid her of the confident smile, 'what would Uncle Joe say to all this? I mean, Malky's blood, but you're not, Eve. I'd say you were expendable.' Pause. 'And I'd say you know it, have done for a while.'

'Meaning?'

'Meaning I don't see you and Malky as an item, not long-term. He's too thick for you, and he'll never be rich enough to make up for that. I can see what he sees in *you*: you're an accomplished seducer.'

'Not that accomplished.' Her eyes found his.

'Pretty good though. Good enough to hook Malky. Good enough to talk him into skimming from the Aberdeen money. Let me guess: your story was that the two of you would bugger off together when there was enough set by?'

'My language may not have matched yours.' Her eyes were calculating slits, but the smile had gone. She knew Rebus was going to deal; she wouldn't be here otherwise. She was wondering what she could get away with.

'But you wouldn't, right? Just between us, you were planning to clear off by yourself.'

'Was I?'

'I'm banking on it.' He stood up, walked towards her. 'I don't want you, Eve. Good fucking luck to you, I say. Take the money and run.' He lowered his voice. 'But I want Malky. I want him for Tony El. And I want the answers to some questions. When he gets here, you're going to talk to him. You're going to persuade him to cooperate. Then we'll talk, and it'll go down on tape.' Her eyes widened. 'The story is, it's my insurance in case you decide to stick around.'

'But in reality?'

'It'll take Malky down, and Uncle Joe with him.'

'And I walk away?'

'Promise.'

'How do I know I can trust you?'

'I'm a gentleman, remember? You said as much in the bar.'

She smiled again, her eyes not moving from his. She looked like a cat: same morals, same instinct. Then she nodded her head.

Malcolm Toal arrived at the station fifteen minutes later, and Rebus left him with Eve in an interview room. The station was evening quiet, not yet late enough for pub rowdies, knife fights, blow-ups before bed. Jack asked Rebus how he wanted to play it.

'Just sit there and look like everything I say is the word of God, that'll be good enough for me.'

'And if Stanley makes a move?'

'We can handle him.' He'd already told Eve to find out if Malky was carrying. If he was, Rebus wanted the weaponry on the table by the time he returned. He went into the toilets again, just to steady his breathing and look at himself in the mirror. He tried to relax his jaw muscles. In the past, he'd have been reaching for the quarter-bottle of whisky in his pocket. But tonight there was no quarter-bottle, no Dutch courage. Which meant for once he'd be relying on the real thing.

Back in the interview room, Malky looked at him with eyes like lasers, proof that Eve had said her piece. Two Stanley knives lay on the table. Rebus nodded, satisfied. Jack was busy setting up the recorder and breaking the seals on a couple of tapes.

'Has Ms Cudden explained the situation, Mr Toal?' Malky nodded. 'I'm not interested in the pair of you, but I *am* interested in everything else. You slipped up, but you can still get out of this, same as you've been planning all along.' Rebus tried not to look at Eve, who was looking anywhere but at lovelorn Stanley. Christ, she was a tough one. Rebus really had taken a liking to her; he almost liked her better now than he had that night in the bar. Jack nodded that the recorder was running.

'OK, now we're recording I'd like to make it clear that this is for my own personal insurance, and won't be used against the pair of you at any time, so long as you clear off afterwards. I'd like you to introduce yourselves.' They did, Jack checking the levels and adjusting them.

'I'm Detective Inspector John Rebus,' Rebus said, 'and with me is Detective Inspector Jack Morton.' He paused, pulled out the third chair at the table and sat down, Eve to his right, Toal to his left. 'Let's start with that night in the hotel bar, Ms Cudden. I'm not a great believer in coincidence.'

Eve blinked. She'd expected the questions to relate to Malky alone. Now she saw that Rebus really *was* going to have some insurance.

'It wasn't coincidence,' she said, fumbling for another Sobranie. The packet slipped, and Toal picked it up, taking out a cigarette, lighting it for her, then handing it over. She could hardly bear to take it – or else wanted Rebus to think that. But Rebus was looking at Toal, surprised by the gesture. There was unexpected affection in 'Mad Malky', a real joy at being close to his lover, even in the present situation. He seemed very different from the scowling complainer Rebus had met at the Ponderosa: younger now, face shining, eyes wide. Hard to believe he could kill in cold blood – but not impossible. He was dressed in the same awful non-style of their previous meeting – the trousers from a shell-suit with an orange leather jacket and a blue patterned shirt, set off with scuffed black slip-on shoes. His mouth moved like he was chewing gum, even though he wasn't. He sat low in the chair, legs open, hands resting between his thighs, high up near the crotch.

'It was planned,' Eve went on. 'Well, sort of. I thought there was a good chance you'd hit the bar before you went to bed.'

'How come?'

'The word is, you like to drink.'

'Says who?'

She shrugged.

'How did you know which hotel I'd be in?'

'I was told.'

'Who by?'

'The Yanks.'

'Tell me their names.' By the book, John.

'Judd Fuller, Erik Stemmons.'

'They both told you?'

'Stemmons specifically.' She smiled. 'Coward that he is.'

'Go on.'

'I think he thought handing you to us was a better option than putting Fuller on to you.'

'Because Fuller would have been harder on me?'

She shook her head. 'He was thinking of himself. If *we* went after you, the two of them were in the clear. Judd's difficult to control sometimes.' Toal snorted at that. 'Erik would rather he didn't get worked up.'

Probably Stemmons had reined in Fuller, so all Fuller's men had done was pistol-whip Rebus rather than put him out of the game. One yellow card: he couldn't see Fuller giving a second. Rebus wanted to ask her more. He wanted to know how far she'd have gone to find out what he knew ... But somehow he thought that line of questioning might blow *all* Malky's fuses.

'Who told the Yanks where I was staying?'

He already knew the answer – Ludovic Lumsden – but wanted it on tape if possible. But Eve shrugged, and Toal shook his head.

'Tell me what you were doing in Aberdeen.'

Eve busied herself with her cigarette, so Toal cleared his throat.

'Working for my dad.'

'Doing what specifically?'

'Selling an' that.'

'Selling?'

'Dope – speed, skag, anything and everything.'

'You sound very relaxed, Mr Toal.'

'Mibbe resigned would be nearer the mark.' Toal sat up in his chair. 'Eve says we can trust you. I wouldn't know about that, but I know what my dad'll do when he finds out we've been skimming.'

'So I'm the lesser of two evils?'

'You said it, not me.'

'All right, let's get back to Aberdeen. You were supplying drugs?'

'Aye.'

'Who to?'

'Burke's Club.'

'The individuals' names?'

'Erik Stemmons and Judd Fuller. Specifically Judd, though Erik knows the score, too.' He smiled at Eve. 'Score,' he repeated. She nodded, letting him know she got the joke.

'Why specifically Judd Fuller?'

'Erik runs the club, does the business side of things. Doesnae' like getting his hands dirty, you know, pretends everything's above board.'

Rebus remembered Stemmons' office – paperwork everywhere. Mr Businessman.

'Can you give me a description of Fuller?'

'You've met him: he gave you that beating.' Toal grinned. The man with the pistol: had he sounded American? Had Rebus been listening that hard?

'I didn't see him though.'

'Well, he's six feet, black hair, it always looks wet. Brylcreem or something. Back-combs it, long, like that *Saturday Night Fever* guy.'

'Travolta?'

'Aye, in that other film. You know.' Toal made like he was spraying the room with bullets.

306

'*Pulp Fiction*?'

Toal clicked his fingers.

'Except Judd's face is thinner,' Eve added. 'In fact, he's thinner all round. He does like wearing dark suits though. And there's a scar on the back of one of his hands, looks like it was sewn together too tight.'

Rebus nodded. 'Does Fuller deal only drugs?'

Toal shook his head. 'Naw, he's got fingers in every pie: prozzies, porn, casinos, a bit of reset, fake designer stuff – watches and shirts an' that.'

'All-round entrepreneur,' Eve added, flicking ash into the waste-bin. She was being careful to say nothing that would incriminate her.

'And Judd and Erik aren't the only ones. There are some Yanks in Aberdeen worse than they are: Eddie Segal, Moose Maloney ...' Toal saw the look on Eve's face and ground to a halt.

'Malcolm,' she said sweetly, 'we do want to get out of this alive, don't we?'

Toal's face reddened. 'Forget I said that,' he told Rebus. Rebus nodded, but the machine wouldn't forget.

'So,' Rebus said, 'why did you kill Tony El?'

'Me?' Toal said, going into his act. Rebus sighed and looked at the tips of his shoes.

'I think,' Eve prodded, 'that means the Inspector wants *everything*. We don't talk to him, he has a word with your dad.'

Toal stared at her, but she held it; he broke off first. His hands went back to his crotch. 'Yeah,' he said, 'well, I was under orders.'

'Who from?'

'Dad, of course. See, Tony was still working for us. He was day-to-day running of the Aberdeen end. All that stuff about him leaving, that was just a story. But after you came and spoke to Dad ... he went through the fucking roof, because Tony had been doing outside hits, endangering the operation. And now you were on to him, so ...'

'So Tony had to go?' Rebus was remembering that Tony El had bragged to Hank Shankley about his 'Glasgow connections' – he hadn't been lying.

'That's right.'

'And I don't suppose you were too upset to see the back of him?' Eve smiled. 'Not particularly upset, no.'

'Because to save his own neck, Tony might have grassed the two of you?'

'He didn't know we were skimming, but he found out about the hotel arrangements.'

'Biggest mistake he ever made,' Toal said, grinning again. He was getting cockier by the minute, enjoying telling the story, basking in the knowledge that everything was going to be fine. As he grew cockier, so Eve seemed to regard him with less and less good grace. She'd be relieved to be free of him, Rebus could see that. The poor little bastard.

'You had CID fooled, they thought it was suicide.'

'Well, when you've a cop or two in your pocket ...'

Rebus looked at Toal. 'Say that again.'

'A cop or two on the payroll.'

'Names?'

'Lumsden,' Toal said. 'Jenkins.'

'Jenkins?'

'He's something to do with the oil industry,' Eve explained.

'Oil Liaison Officer?'

She nodded.

Who'd been on holiday when Rebus had arrived, Lumsden standing in . for him. With those two on your side, you'd have no trouble supplying the production platforms with whatever they needed – a real captive market. And when the workers came ashore, you had further delights for them: clubs, prozzies, booze and gambling. The legit and the illicit working side by side, each feeding the other. No wonder Lumsden had tagged along on the trip out to Bannock; he was protecting his investment.

'What do you know about Fergus McLure?'

Toal looked to Eve, ready to talk but seeking permission. She nodded, keeping her own mouth shut.

'He had a little accident, got too close to Judd.'

'Fuller killed him?'

'Hands on, that's what Judd said.' There was a hint of hero worship in Toal's voice. 'Told McLure they had to talk somewhere private, said walls had ears. Moseyed down to the canal with him, a dunt to the head with his gun, and into the water.' Toal shrugged. 'He was back in Aberdeen in time for a late breakfast.' He smiled at Eve. 'Late.' Presumably another joke, but she was beyond smiling back. She just wanted out of there.

Rebus had other questions, but he was beginning to tire. He decided to leave it at that. He got up and nodded for Jack to switch off the machine, then told Eve she could go.

'What about me?' Toal asked.

'You don't leave together,' Rebus reminded him. Toal seemed to accept this. Rebus saw Eve along the corridor and down the stairs.

Neither of them said a word, not even goodbye. But he watched her leave before asking the desk officer for a couple of uniforms, a.s.a.p. at the interview room.

When he got back, Jack had just finished rewinding the tapes, and Toal was on his feet, doing some stretching exercises. There was a knock, and the two uniforms came in. Toal stood up straight, sensing something was wrong.

'Malcolm Toal,' Rebus said, 'I am charging you with the murder of Anthony Ellis Kane on the night of—'

With a roar, Mad Malky flew at Rebus, hands scrabbling at his neck.

The woolly suits eventually got him into a cell, and Rebus sat on a chair in the interview room, watching his hands shaking.

'You OK?' Jack asked.

'Know what, Jack? You're like a broken record.'

'Know what, John? You're always needing it asked.'

Rebus smiled and rubbed his neck. 'I'm fine.'

As Toal had run at him, Rebus had kneed the young man in the groin with enough force to lift him off his feet. After that, the uniforms had found him just about manageable, especially with a Vulcan death grip to his carotid.

'What do you want to do?' Jack asked.

'One copy of the tape goes to CID here. It'll give them enough to go on until we get back.'

'From Aberdeen?' Jack guessed.

'And points north.' Rebus pointed to the machine. 'Stick the copy back in and turn it on.' Jack did so. 'Gill, here's a little present for you. I hope you'll know what to do with it.' He nodded, and Jack stopped recording and ejected the tape.

'We'll drop it off at St Leonard's.'

'So we *are* going back to Edinburgh?' Jack was thinking of tomorrow's meeting with Ancram.

'Only long enough for a change of clothes and a doctor's line.'

Outside in the car park, a solitary figure was waiting: Eve.

'Going my way?' she asked.

'How did you know?'

She smiled her most feline smile. 'Because you're like me – you've got unfinished business in Aberdeen. I'm only going to be there as long as it takes to visit a few banks and close a few accounts, but there are those two hotel rooms …'

A good point: they'd need a base, preferably one Lumsden didn't know about.

'He's in a cell?' she asked.

'Yes.'

'How many men did you need?'

'Just the two.'

'I'm surprised.'

'We all surprise ourselves some time,' Rebus said, opening the back door of Jack's car for her.

Rebus wasn't surprised to find Gill Templer's office locked up for the night. He looked around the night shift and saw Siobhan Clarke trying to make herself inconspicuous, dreading their first meeting since she'd been part of the search team at his flat. He walked up to her, the yellow padded envelope in his hand.

'It's OK,' he said, 'I know why you were there. I think I should thank you.'

'I just thought ...'

He nodded. The relief on her face made him wonder what she'd been going through.

'Working on anything?' he asked, figuring she was owed a minute's conversation. Jack and Eve were downstairs in the car, getting to know one another.

'I've been on Johnny Bible background: deadly dull.' She perked up. 'One thing though. I was going through the old newspapers in the National.'

'Yes?' Rebus had been there, too: he wondered if that were her story.

'One of the librarians told me someone was looking at recent newspapers and asking about people calling up ones from 1968 to '70. I thought the combination was a bit odd. The recent papers were all from just before the first Johnny Bible murder.'

'And the others were the years Bible John was operating?'

'Yes.'

'A journalist?'

'That's what the librarian says. Only, the card he handed over was a fake. He contacted the librarian by telephone.'

'Did the librarian have anything?'

'A few names. I took them down, on the off chance. A couple of them *are* journalists. One is you. The others, God knows.'

Yes, Rebus had spent a long day poring over the old stories, arranging for photocopies to be made of the relevant pages ... building his collection.

'And the mysterious journalist?'

'No idea. I got a physical description, but it doesn't help much. Early fifties, tall, fair-haired ...'

'Doesn't rule too many people out, does it? Why the interest in recent papers? No, wait ... Looking for cock-ups.'

Siobhan nodded. 'That's what I thought. And at the same time asking about people who'd shown an interest in the original Bible John case. It might sound crazy, but maybe Bible John's out there looking for his offspring. Thing is, whoever he was ... he's got your name now, *and* your address.'

'Nice to have a fan.' Rebus thought for a moment. 'Those other names ... can I see?'

She found the relevant page in her notebook. One name leapt out: Peter Manuel.

'Something?' she asked.

Rebus pointed. 'Not his real name. Manuel was a killer back in the fifties.'

'Then who ...?'

Reading up on Bible John, using a killer's name as an alias. 'Johnny Bible,' Rebus said quietly.

'I'd better have another word with that librarian.'

'First thing in the morning,' Rebus advised. 'Speaking of which ...' He handed her the envelope. 'Can you see to it that Gill Templer gets this?'

'Sure.' She shook it. The cassette rattled. 'Anything I should know about?'

'Definitely not.'

She smiled. 'Now you've whetted my curiosity.'

'Then unwhet it.' He turned to leave. He didn't want her to see how shaken he was. Someone else was hunting Johnny Bible, someone who now had Rebus's name and address. Siobhan's words: *Bible John ... looking for his offspring.* Description: tall, fair-haired, early fifties. The age was right for Bible John. Whoever it was knew Rebus's address ... and his flat had been broken into, nothing stolen, but his newspapers and cuttings disturbed.

Bible John ... looking for his offspring.

'How's the inquiry?' Siobhan called.

'Which one?'

'Spaven.'

'A doddle.' He stopped, turned back to her. 'By the way, if you're really bored ...?'

'Yes?'

'Johnny Bible: there could just be an oil connection. The last victim worked for oil companies and drank with oilmen. First victim studied at RGIT, geology, I think. Find out if there's any connection to oil, see if there's something we can link to victims two and three.'

'You think he lives in Aberdeen?'

'Right now, I think I'd lay money on it.'

Then he was gone. One more stop to make before the long haul north.

*

Bible John was driving through the streets of Aberdeen.

The town was quiet. He liked it that way. The trip to Glasgow had been useful, but the fourth victim had proved more useful still.

From the hotel computer, he had his list of twenty companies. Twenty guests of the Fairmount Hotel who had paid by corporate credit card in the weeks before Judith Cairns's murder. Twenty companies based in the north-east. Twenty individuals he needed to check, any one of whom could be the Upstart.

He'd played with the connection between the victims, and numbers one and four had given him his answer: oil. Oil was at the heart of it. Victim one had studied geology at Robert Gordon's, and in the north-east the study of geology was in so many ways connected to the subject of oil exploration. Victim four's company numbered oil companies and their ancillaries among its best clients. He was looking for someone connected to the oil industry, someone so very like himself. The realisation had shaken him. On the one hand, it made it even more imperative he track down the Upstart; on the other, it made the game that much more dangerous. It wasn't physical danger – he had long since conquered that particular fear. It was the danger of losing his hard-fought-for identity as Ryan Slocum. He almost felt he *was* Ryan Slocum. But Ryan Slocum was just a dead man, a newspaper obituary he'd come across. So he'd applied for a duplicate birth certificate, pleading the original's loss in a house fire. This had been in pre-computer days, easy to get away with.

So his own past ceased to exist ... for a time, at least. The trunk in the attic told a different story, of course. It gave the lie to his change of identity: you couldn't change the man you were. His trunk full of souvenirs, most of them American ... He had made arrangements for the trunk to be moved soon, when his wife was out of the house. A moving company would send a Transit. The trunk would be taken to a self-storage warehouse. It made sense as a precaution, but he still regretted it; it was like saying the Upstart had won.

No matter what the outcome.

Twenty companies to check. So far he had dismissed four possible suspects as being too old. A further seven companies were not involved in the oil industry in any way that he could see – they went to the bottom of the list. Leaving nine names. It was a slow business. He'd used guile during telephone calls to the companies' offices, but guile would only go so far. He'd also had recourse to the telephone book, finding addresses for the names, watching their homes, waiting for a glimpse of a face. Would he know the Upstart when he saw him? He felt he would; at least, he'd recognise the type. But then Joe Beattie had said the same about Bible John – that he'd recognise him in a crowded room. As if a man's heart showed in the creases and contours of his face, a sort of phrenology of sin.

He parked the car outside another house, called his office to check for messages. In his line of work, they expected him to be out of the office for long periods of the day, if not for days and weeks at a time. It was the perfect career, really. No messages, nothing for him to think about but the Upstart … and himself.

In the early days, he had lacked patience. This was no longer the case. This slow stalking of the Upstart would only make the final confrontation sweeter. But this thought was tempered with another: that the police could be closing in, too. After all, the information was there for them to find: it was just a matter of making the connections. So far only the Edinburgh prostitute failed to fit the pattern, but if he could connect three out of four, he'd be satisfied. He could bet, too, that once he knew the Upstart's identity he could place him in Edinburgh at the time she was killed: hotel records maybe; or a receipt for petrol from an Edinburgh filling station … Four victims. One more already than the Bible John of the sixties. It was galling, he had to say it. It rankled.

And someone would pay for it. Very soon.

North of Hell

'Scotland will be reborn the day
the last minister is strangled with
the last copy of the *Sunday Post.*'

Tom Nairn

28

It was after midnight when they reached the hotel. It was situated near the airport, one of the shiny new constructions Rebus had passed on his way to T-Bird Oil. There was too much glare in the lobby, too many mirrors reflecting full-length portraits of three weary figures with meagre luggage. Maybe they would have provoked suspicion, but Eve was a regular and had a business account, so that was that.

'It all goes through the taxi firm,' she explained, 'so this is my treat. Just sign out of the rooms when you're finished, they'll send the bill to Joe's Cabs.'

'Your usual rooms, Ms Cudden,' the clerk said, handing over the keys, 'plus one a few doors further along.'

Jack had been looking through the hotel directory. 'Sauna, health club, weight gym. We should fit right in, John.'

'It's all oil execs,' Eve said, leading them to the lifts. 'They like that kind of thing. Keeps them fit enough to handle the hokey-cokey. And I don't mean the dance.'

'Do you sell everything direct to Fuller and Stemmons?' Rebus asked.

Eve stifled a yawn. 'You mean, do I deal myself?'

'Yes.'

'Would I be that stupid?'

'What about the punters – any names?'

She shook her head, smiled tiredly. 'You never stop, do you?'

'It takes my mind off things.' Specifically: Bible John, Johnny Bible ... out there somewhere, and maybe not so very far away ...

She handed their room keys to Rebus and Jack. 'Sleep well, boys. I'll probably be long gone when you wake up ... and I won't be coming back.'

Rebus nodded. 'How much will you be taking with you?'

'About thirty-eight thou.'

'A decent skim.'

317

'Decent profits all round.'

'How soon till Uncle Joe finds out about Stanley?'

'Well, Malcolm won't be in a hurry to tell him, and Joe's used to him disappearing for a day or two on the trot … With any luck, I won't even be in the country when the bomb goes off.'

'You look the lucky type to me.'

They left the lift at the third floor and checked the numbers on their keys. Rebus ended up next door to Eve: Stanley's old room. Jack was two doors further down.

Stanley's old room was a good size and boasted what Rebus guessed were the usual corporate embellishments: mini-bar, trouser press, a little saucer of chocolates on the pillow, a bathrobe laid out on the turned-down bed. There was a notice clipped to the robe. It asked him not to take it home with him. If he wanted to, he could purchase one from the health club. 'Thank you for being a considerate guest.'

The considerate guest made himself a cup of Café Hag. There was a price list on top of the mini-bar, detailing the delights within. He stuck it in a drawer. The wardrobe boasted a mini-safe, so he took the mini-bar key and locked it inside. Another barrier for him to get past, another chance to change his mind if he *really* wanted that drink.

Meantime, the coffee tasted fine. He had a shower, wrapped himself in the bathrobe, then sat on his bed and stared at the connecting door. Of course, there would have to be a connecting door: couldn't have Stanley hopping around the corridor at all hours. There was a simple lock his side, as there would be on the other. He wondered what he would find if he unlocked the door: would Eve's be standing open? If he knocked, would she let him in? What about if *she* knocked? He turned his eyes from the door, and they settled on the mini-bar. He felt peckish – there would be nuts and crisps inside. Maybe he could …? No, no, no. He turned his attention back to the connecting door, listened hard, couldn't hear any movement from Eve's room. Maybe she was already asleep – early start and all that. He found he wasn't feeling tired any more. Now he was here, he wanted to get to work. He pulled open his curtains. It had started to rain, the tarmac glistening and black like the back of a huge fat beetle. Rebus pulled a chair over to the window. Wind was driving the rain, making shifting patterns in the sodium light. As he stared, the rain began to resemble smoke, billowing out of the darkness. The car park below was half full, the cars huddled like cattle while their owners stayed snug and dry.

Johnny Bible was out there, probably in Aberdeen, probably connected to the oil industry. He thought about the people he'd met these past days, everyone from Major Weir to Walt the tour guide. It was ironic that the person whose case had brought him here – Allan Mitchison – was not only connected to oil but was also the only candidate he could rule out, being long dead by the time Vanessa Holden met her killer. Rebus felt guilty about Mitchison. His case was becoming swamped by the serial killings. It was a job, something Rebus had to do. But it wasn't wedged in his throat the way the Johnny Bible case was, something he had either to cough up or choke on.

But he wasn't the only one with an interest in Johnny. Someone had broken into his flat. Someone had been checking library records. Someone using a false identity. Someone with something to hide. Not a reporter, not another policeman. Could Bible John really be out there still? Dormant somewhere until brought to life by Johnny Bible? Enraged by the act of imitation, by its temerity and the cold fact that it brought the original case back up into the light? Not only enraged, but feeling endangered, too – externally and internally: fear of being recognised and caught; fear of not being the bogeyman any longer.

A new bogeyman for the nineties, someone to be scared of again. One mythology erased and replaced by another.

Yes, Rebus could feel it. He could sense Bible John's hostility to the young pretender. No flattery in imitation, none at all …

And he knows where I live, Rebus thought. He's been there, touched my obsession, and wondered how far I'm willing to take it. But why? Why would he place himself in danger like that, breaking into a flat in the middle of the day? Looking for what exactly? Looking for something in particular? But *what*? Rebus turned the question over in his mind, wondered if a drink would help, got as far as the safe before turning back, standing there in the middle of the room, his whole body crackling with need.

The hotel felt asleep; easy to imagine the whole country asleep and dreaming blameless dreams. Stemmons and Fuller, Uncle Joe, Major Weir, Johnny Bible … everyone was innocent in sleep. Rebus walked over to the connecting door and unlocked it. Eve's door was slightly ajar. Silently, he pushed it wide open. Her room was in darkness, curtains closed. Light from his own room lay like an arrow along the floor, pointing towards the king-size bed. She lay on her side, one arm on top of the covers. Her eyes were closed. He took one step into her room, not merely a voyeur now but an intruder. Then he just stood there, watching her. Maybe he'd have stayed that way for long minutes.

'Wondered how long it would take you,' she said.

Rebus walked across to her bed. She reached both arms up to him.

She was naked beneath the covers, warm and sweet-smelling. He sat down on the bed, took her hands in his.

'Eve,' he said quietly, 'I need one favour from you before you go.'

She sat up. 'Not counting this?'

'Not counting this.'

'What?'

'I want you to phone Judd Fuller. Tell him you need to see him.'

'You should stay away from him.'

'I know.'

She sighed. 'But you can't?' He nodded, and she touched his cheek with the back of her hand. 'OK, but now I want a favour in return.'

'What?'

'Take the rest of the night off,' she said, pulling him towards her.

He woke up alone in her bed, and it was morning. He checked to see if she'd left a note or anything, but of course she hadn't: she wasn't the type.

He walked through the open doorway and locked his door after him, then switched off the lights in his room. There was a knock at his door: Jack. Rebus pulled on pants and trousers and was halfway to the door when he remembered something. He walked back to the bed and removed the chocolates from the pillow, then pulled the covers down, messing them up. He surveyed the scene, punched a head-shaped dent in one pillow, then answered the door.

And it wasn't Jack at all. It was one of the hotel staff, carrying a tray.

'Morning, sir.' Rebus stood aside to let him in. 'Sorry if I woke you. Miss Cudden specified the time.'

'That's OK.' Rebus watched the young man slide the tray on to the table by the window.

'Would you like me to open it?' Meaning the half bottle of champagne resting in an ice-bucket. There was a jug of fresh orange juice, a crystal glass, and a folded copy of the morning's *Press & Journal*. In a slim porcelain vase stood a single red carnation.

'No.' Rebus lifted the bucket. 'This, you can take away. The rest is fine.'

'Yes, sir. If you'll just sign ...?'

Rebus took the proffered pen, and added a hefty tip to the bill. Fuck it, Uncle Joe was paying. The young man broke into a big grin, making Rebus wish he was this generous every morning.

'Thank *you*, sir.'

When he'd gone, Rebus poured a glass of juice. The fresh-squeezed stuff, cost a fortune in the supermarket. Outside, the roads were still damp, and there was plenty of cloud overhead, but the sky looked like it might break into a grin of its own before the morning was out. A light aircraft took off from Dyce, probably Shetland-bound. Rebus looked at his watch, then called Jack's room. Jack answered with a noise somewhere between an inquiry and an oath.

'Your morning alarm call,' Rebus trilled.

'Fuck off.'

'Come by for orange juice and coffee.'

'Give me five minutes.'

Rebus said that was the least he could do. Next he tried phoning Siobhan at home – got her machine. Tried her at St Leonard's, but she wasn't there. He knew she wouldn't be slow in going about the work he'd given her, but he wanted to stick close to her, needed to know when she got a result. He put down the phone and looked at the tray again, then smiled.

Eve had left him a message after all.

The dining room was quiet, most tables taken by single men, some of them already at work on portable phones and laptops. Rebus and Jack got stuck in – juice and cornflakes, then the Full Highland Breakfast with a big pot of tea.

Jack tapped his watch. 'Quarter of an hour from now, Ancram's going to hit the roof.'

'Might knock some sense into him.' Rebus scraped a pat of butter on to his toast. Five-star hotel, but the toast was still cold.

'So what's our plan of attack?'

'I'm looking for a girl, she's in photos with Allan Mitchison, an environmental protester.'

'Where do we start?'

'You sure you want in on this?' Rebus looked around the dining room. 'You could spend the day here, try the health club, watch a film … It's all on Uncle Joe.'

'John, I'm sticking by you.' Jack paused. 'As a friend, not Ancram's dog's-body.'

'In that case, our first port of call's the Exhibition Centre. Now eat up, it's going to be a long day, believe me.'

'One question.'

'What?'

'How come *you* got the orange juice this morning?'

The Exhibition Centre was almost deserted. The various stalls and stands – many of them, as Rebus now knew, designed by Johnny Bible's fourth victim – had been dismantled and taken away, the floors hoovered and polished. There were no demonstrators outside, no inflatable whale. They asked to speak to someone in charge, and were eventually taken to an office where a brisk, bespectacled woman introduced herself as 'the Deputy' and asked them how she could help.

'The North Sea Conference,' Rebus explained, 'you had a bit of trouble with protesters.'

She smiled, her mind on other things. 'Bit late to do anything about that, isn't it?' She moved some papers around her desk, looking for something.

'I'm interested in one particular protester. What was the name of the group?'

'It wasn't that organised, Inspector. They came from all over: Friends of the Earth, Greenpeace, Save the Whale, God alone knows.'

'Did they cause any trouble?'

'Nothing we couldn't handle.' Another frozen smile. But she was looking harassed: she really had misplaced something. Rebus got to his feet.

'Well, sorry to trouble you.'

'No trouble. Sorry I can't help.'

'Don't worry about it.'

Rebus turned to go. Jack bent down and retrieved a sheet of paper from the floor, handed it to her.

'Thanks,' she said. Then she followed them out of her office. 'Look, a local pressure group was responsible for the march on the Saturday.'

'What march?'

'It ended at Duthie Park, there was some music afterwards.'

Rebus nodded: Dancing Pigs. The day he'd visited Bannock.

'I can give you their phone number,' she said. The smile was human now.

Rebus telephoned the group's headquarters.

'I'm looking for a friend of Allan Mitchison's. I don't know her name, but she's got short fair hair, with some of it braided, you know, with beads and stuff. One braid hangs down past her forehead to her nose. Sort of an American accent, I think.'

'And who might you be?' The voice was cultured; for some reason, Rebus visualised the speaker sporting a beard, but it wasn't the kilted Jerry Garcia, different accent.

'My name's Detective Inspector John Rebus. You know Allan Mitchison is dead?'

A pause, then an exhalation: cigarette smoke. 'I heard. Bloody shame.'

'Did you know him well?' Rebus was trying to recall the faces in the photographs.

'He was the shy type. Only met him a couple of times. Big fan of Dancing Pigs, that's why he tried so bloody hard to get them to top the bill. I was amazed when it worked. He bombarded them with letters, you know. Maybe a hundred or more, probably wore down their resistance.'

'And his girlfriend's name?'

'Not given out to strangers, I'm afraid. I mean, I've only your word for it you're a police officer.'

'I could come over—'

'I don't think so.'

'Look, I'd really like to talk to you ...'

But the telephone was dead.

'Want to take a run down there?' Jack suggested.

Rebus shook his head. 'He won't tell us anything he doesn't want to. Besides, I've got the feeling by the time we got there he'd have gone out for the day. Can't afford to waste time.'

Rebus tapped his pen against his teeth. They were back in his bedroom. The telephone had a speaker, and he'd kept it on so Jack could hear. Jack was helping himself to last night's chocolates.

'Local cops,' Rebus said, picking up the receiver. 'That gig was probably licensed, maybe Queen Street will have records of other organisers.'

'Worth a go,' Jack agreed, plugging in the kettle.

So Rebus spent twenty minutes knowing how a pinball feels, as he was shunted from one office to another. He was pretending to be a Trading Standards Officer, interested in bootleggers, following up on an operation at an earlier Dancing Pigs concert. Jack nodded his approval: not a bad story.

'Yes, John Baxter here, City of Edinburgh Trading Standards. I was just explaining to your colleague ...' And off he went again. When he was passed on to yet another voice, and recognised it as belonging to the first person he'd spoken to, he slammed down the phone.

'They couldn't organise the proverbial piss-up.'

Jack handed him a cup of tea. 'End of the road?'

'No chance.' Rebus consulted his notebook, picked up the phone again and was put through to Stuart Minchell at T-Bird Oil.

'Inspector, what a pleasant surprise.'

'Sorry to keep pestering you, Mr Minchell.'

'How's your investigation?'

'To be honest, I could use a bit of help.'

'Fire away.'

'It's about Bannock. The day I went out there, some protesters were brought aboard.'

'Yes, I heard. Handcuffed themselves to the rails.' Minchell sounded amused. Rebus remembered the platform, the strong gusts, the way his hard-hat wouldn't stay on, and the helicopter overhead, filming everything ...

'I was wondering what happened to the protesters. I mean, were they placed under arrest?' He knew they weren't: a couple of them had been at the concert.

'Best person to ask would be Hayden Fletcher.'

'Do you think you could ask for me, sir? On the quiet, as it were.'

'I suppose so. Give me your number in Edinburgh.'

'That's all right, I'll call you back ... say, twenty minutes?' Rebus glanced towards the window: he could almost see the T-Bird headquarters from here.

'Depends if I can find anyone.'

'I'll try again in twenty minutes. Oh, and Mr Minchell?'

'Yes?'

'If you should need to speak to Bannock, could you put a question from me to Willie Ford?'

'What's the question?'

'I want to know if he knew Allan Mitchison had a girlfriend, blonde with braided hair.'

'Braided hair.' Minchell was writing it down. 'Can do.'

'If so, I'd like her name, and an address if possible.' Rebus thought of something else. 'When the protesters came to your headquarters, you had them videoed, didn't you?'

'I don't remember.'

'Could you find out? It would be security, wouldn't it?'

'Do I still have twenty minutes for all this?'

Rebus smiled. 'No, sir. Let's make it half an hour.'

Rebus put down the phone and drained his tea.

'How about another phone call now?' Jack asked.

'Who to?'

'Chick Ancram.'

'Jack, look at me.' Rebus pointed to his face. 'Could a man this ill possibly pick up the telephone?'

'You'll swing.'

'Like a pendulum do.'

Rebus gave Stuart Minchell forty minutes.

'You know, Inspector, you make working for the Major seem like a picnic by comparison.'

'Glad to be of service, sir. What have you got?'

'Just about everything.' A rustle of paper. 'No, the protesters weren't arrested.'

'Isn't that a bit generous, under the circumstances?'

'It would only have generated more bad publicity.'

'Something you don't need right now?'

'The company did get names out of the protesters, but they were false. At least, I'm assuming Yuri Gagarin and Judy Garland are aliases.'

'Sound reasoning.' Judy Garland: Braid-Hair. Interesting choice.

'So they were detained, given something hot to drink, and flown back to the mainland.'

'Very decent of T-Bird.'

'Yes, isn't it?'

'And the video recording?'

'That was, as you guessed, our security staff. Precautionary, I'm told. If there's trouble, we have physical evidence.'

'They don't use the film to identify the protesters?'

'We're not the CIA, Inspector. We're an oil company.'

'Sorry, sir, go on.'

'Willie Ford says he knew Mitch *had* been seeing someone in Aberdeen – past tense. But they never discussed her. Mitch was – quote – "a dark horse on the question of his love life" – unquote.'

Dead ends everywhere.

'Is that everything?'

'That's it.'

'Well, thank you, sir, I really appreciate this.'

'My pleasure, Inspector. But next time you want a favour, try not to make it on a day when I'm due to sack a dozen of our workforce.'

'Hard times, Mr Minchell?'

'A book by Dickens, Inspector Rebus. Goodbye.'

Jack was laughing. 'Good line,' he said approvingly.

'So it should be,' Rebus said, 'he was less than a mile away.' He walked over to the window, watched another plane taking off in the near-distance, the roar of its jets fading as it headed north.

'Had enough for one morning?'

Rebus didn't say anything. He'd been expecting Eve to call. There was that favour. He wondered if she'd do it. She owed him, but crossing Judd Fuller didn't sound like the wisest move on the dance floor. She'd been dancing her own little steps for years: why trip up now?

Jack repeated his question.

'One option left,' Rebus said, turning to face him.

'What's that?'

'Flight.'

At Dyce Airport, Rebus showed his warrant card and asked if there were any flights out to Sullom Voe.

'Not for a while,' he was told. 'Maybe in four or five hours.'

'We're not fussy who we fly with.'

Shrugs, shakes of the head.

'It's important.'

'You could always hitch a ride to Sumburgh.'

'That's miles from Sullom Voe.'

'Only trying to be helpful. You could rent a car.'

Rebus thought about it, then had a better idea. 'How soon could we be out of here?'

'To Sumburgh? Half an hour, forty minutes. There's a helicopter stopping there on its way out to Ninian.'

'Fine.'

'Let me talk to them.' She picked up her telephone.

'We'll be back in five minutes.'

Jack followed Rebus over to the public telephones, where Rebus made a call to St Leonard's. He was put through to Gill Templer.

'I'm halfway through listening to the tape,' she said.

'Better than *Saturday Night Theatre*, isn't it?'

'I'm going through to Glasgow later on. I want to talk to him myself.'

'Good idea, I've left a copy of the tape with Partick CID. Have you seen Siobhan this morning?'

'I don't think so. Which shift is she working? If you like, I can try to find her.'

'Don't bother, Gill, long distance doesn't come cheap.'

'Oh hell, where are you now?'

'Ill in bed, if Ancram comes asking.'

'And looking for that favour?'

'A phone number, actually. Lerwick police station. I'm assuming such a thing exists.'

'It does,' she said. 'Under the auspices of Northern Division. There was a conference in Inverness last year, they were complaining about keeping tabs on Orkney and Shetland.'

'Gill ...'

'I've been looking it up while I talk.' She reeled the number off; it went into his notebook.

'Thanks, Gill. Bye.'

'John!'

But he'd cut her off. 'How are you for change, Jack?' Jack showed him some coins. Rebus took most of them, then called Lerwick and asked if they could lend a car for half a day. He explained it was a murder inquiry, Lothian and Borders. Nothing to get het up about, they'd only be interviewing a friend of the victim.

'Well now, a car ...' the voice drawled, like Rebus had asked for a spaceship. 'When would you be arriving?'

'We're on a chopper out of here in about half an hour.'

'Two of you?'

'Two of us,' Rebus said, 'which rules out a motorbike.'

His reward: a deep gurgling laugh. 'Not necessarily.'

'Can you do it?'

'Well, I can do *some*thing. Only problem might be if the cars are out elsewhere. Some of our calls are to the back of beyond.'

'If there's no one to meet us at Sumburgh, I'll phone again.'

'You do that now. Cheerio.'

Back at the desk, they found they were on the flight in thirty-five minutes.

'I've never been on a helicopter,' Jack said.

'An experience you'll never forget.'

Jack frowned. 'Can you try that again with a bit more enthusiasm?'

29

There were half a dozen planes on the ground at Sumburgh Airport, and the same number of helicopters, most of them connected as if by umbilical cord to neighbouring fuel tankers. Rebus walked into the Wilsness Terminal, unzipping his survival suit as he went, then saw that Jack was still outside, taking in the coastal scenery and bleak inland plain. There was a fierce wind rising, and Jack had his chin tucked into his suit. Post-flight, he looked pale and slightly queasy. Rebus for one had spent the entire time trying not to remember his outsized breakfast. Jack eventually saw him signalling, and came in from the cold.

'Doesn't the sea look blue?'

'Same colour you'd turn after two more minutes out there.'

'And the sky ... incredible.'

'Don't go New Age on me, Jack. Let's get these suits off. I think our escort with the Escort has just arrived.'

Only it was an Astra, snug with three of them inside, especially when the uniformed driver was built like a rock formation. His head – minus the diced cap – brushed the roof of the car. The voice was the same as on the telephone. He'd shaken Rebus's hand as though greeting some foreign emissary.

'Have you been to Shetland before?'

Jack shook his head; Rebus admitted he'd been once, but added no further details.

'And where would you like me to take you?'

'Back to your base,' Rebus said from the cramped back seat. 'We'll drop you off and turn the car in when we're finished.'

The woolly suit – whose name was Alexander Forres – boomed his disappointment. 'But I've been two decades on the force.'

'Yes?'

'This would be my first murder inquiry!'

'Look, Sergeant Forres, we're only here to talk to a friend of the victim. It's background – routine and boring as hell.'

'Ach, all the same … I was quite looking forward to it.'

They were heading up the A970 to Lerwick, twenty-odd miles north of Sumburgh. The wind buffeted them, Forres' huge hands tight on the steering-wheel, like an ogre choking an infant. Rebus decided to change the subject.

'Nice road.'

'Paid for with oil money,' Forres said.

'How do you like being ruled from Inverness?'

'Who says we are? You think they come checking up on us every week of the year?'

'I'd guess not.'

'You'd guess right, Inspector. It's like Lothian and Borders – how often does someone from Fettes bother travelling down to Hawick?' Forres looked at Rebus in the rearview. 'Don't go thinking we're all idiots up here, with just enough sense to set light to the boat come Up-Helly-Aa.'

'Up-Helly what?'

Jack turned towards him. 'You know, John, where they burn a longboat.'

'Last Tuesday in January,' Forres said.

'Odd form of central heating,' Rebus muttered.

'He's a born cynic,' Jack told the sergeant.

'Well, it'd be sad for him if he died one.' Forres' eyes were still on the rearview.

On the outskirts of Lerwick, they passed ugly pre-fabricated buildings which Rebus guessed were connected to the oil industry. The police station itself was in the New Town. They dropped Forres off, and he went in to fetch them a map of Mainland.

'Not that you could get very lost,' he'd told them. 'There are only the three big roads to worry about.'

Rebus looked at the map and saw what he meant. Mainland comprised a shape in the vague form of a cross, the A970 its spine, the 971 and 968 its arms. Brae was as far north again as they'd just come. Rebus was going to be driving, Jack navigating – Jack's decision; he said it would give him a chance to sight-see.

The drive was by turns awe-inspiring and bleak: coastal vistas giving way to interior moorland, scattered settlements, a lot of sheep – many of them on the road – and few trees. Jack was right though, the sky *was* amazing. Forres had told them this season was 'simmer dim' – a time of year without true darkness. But in winter, daylight became a precious commodity. You had to respect people who chose to live miles from everything you took for granted. Easy enough to be a hunter-gatherer in a city, but out here ... It wasn't the sort of scenery to inspire conversation. They found their dialogues crumbling into grunts and nods. As close as they were in the speeding car, they were in isolation each from the other. No, Rebus was damned sure he couldn't survive out here.

They took a left fork towards Brae, and found themselves suddenly on the island's west coast. It was still hard to know what to make of the place – Forres was the only born and bred Shetlander they'd met. What architecture they'd seen in Lerwick had been a mix of Scottish and Scandinavian styles, a sort of Ikea baronial. Out in the country, the crofts were the same as any in the Western Isles, but the names of the settlements showed Scandinavian influence. As they drove through Burravoe and into Brae, Rebus realised he felt just about as foreign as he ever had in his life.

'Where to now?' Jack asked.

'Give me a minute. When I was here before, we came into town the other way ...' Rebus got a fix on where they were, and eventually led them to the house Jake Harley shared with Briony. Neighbours looked out at the police car like they'd never seen one before; maybe they hadn't. Rebus tried Briony's door – no answer. He knocked harder, the sound echoing emptily. A look in through the living-room window: untidy, but not a mess. A woman's untidiness, not quite professional enough. Rebus went back to the car.

'She works at the swimming pool, let's give it a shot.'

The pool, with its blue metal roof, was hard to miss. Briony was pacing the edge of the pool, watching children at play. She wore the same uniform of singlet and jogging bottoms as when they'd last met, but now had tennis shoes on her feet. Her ankles were bare: lifesavers didn't bother with socks. She had a referee's tin whistle strung around her neck, but the kids were behaving themselves. Briony saw Rebus and recognised him. She put the whistle in her mouth and gave three short blasts: a recognised signal – another staff member took her place poolside. She walked up to Rebus and Jack. The temperature was getting on for tropical, with humidity to match.

'I told you,' she said, 'Jake's still not shown up.'

'I know, and you said you weren't worried about him.'

She shrugged. She had short dark hair which fell straight most of the way before ending in kiss-curls. The style took half a dozen years off her, turning her into a teenager, but her face was older – slightly hardened, whether by climate or circumstance Rebus couldn't say. Her eyes were small, as were nose and mouth. He tried not to think of a hamster, but then she twitched her nose and the picture was complete.

'He's a free agent,' she said.

'But you were worried last week.'

'Was I?'

'When you closed the door on me. I've seen the look enough times to know.'

She folded her arms. 'So?'

'So one of two things, Briony. Either Jake's in hiding because he's in fear of his life.'

'Or?'

'Or he's already dead. Either way, you can help.'

She swallowed. 'Mitch ...'

'Did Jake tell you why Mitch was killed?'

She shook her head. Rebus tried not to smile: so Jake had been in touch since they'd last spoken.

'He's alive, isn't he?'

She bit her lip, then nodded.

'I'd like to talk to him. I think I can get him out of this mess.'

She tried to gauge the truth of this, but Rebus's face was a mask. 'Is he in trouble?' she asked.

'Yes, but not with us.'

She looked back at the pool, saw everything was under control. 'I'll take you,' she said.

They drove back through the moorland and down past Lerwick, heading for a place called Sandwick on the eastern side of Mainland, just ten miles north of where their helicopter had originally landed.

Briony didn't want to talk during the drive, and Rebus guessed she didn't know much anyway. Sandwick turned out to be a spread of land taking in older settlements and oil-era housing. She directed them to Leebotten, a nestling of sea-front cottages.

'Is this where he is?' Rebus asked as they got out of the car. She shook her head and pointed out to sea. There was an island out there, no sign of habitation. Cliffs and rocky approaches. Rebus looked to Briony.

'Mousa,' she said.

'How do we get there?'

'Boat, always supposing somebody's willing to take us.' She knocked on a cottage door. It was opened by a middle-aged woman.

331

'Briony,' the woman said simply, more statement of fact than greeting.

'Hello, Mrs Munroe. Is Scott in?'

'He is.' The door opened a little wider. 'Come in, won't you?'

They entered one decent-sized room which seemed kitchen and living room both. A large wooden table took up most of the space. By the fireplace were two armchairs. A man was rising from one of them, unhooking wire reading-glasses from his ears. He folded them and put them in his waistcoat pocket. The book he'd been reading lay open on the floor: it was a family-sized Bible, black leather cover and brass clasps.

'Well now, Briony,' the man said. He was middle-aged or a little after, but his weatherbeaten face was that of an old man. His hair was silver, cut short with the careful simplicity of a home barber. His wife had gone to the sink to fill the kettle.

'No thanks, Mrs Munroe,' Briony said, before turning back to the man. 'Have you seen Jake lately, Scott?'

'I was over there a couple of days back, he seemed fine.'

'Could you take us across?'

Scott Munroe looked to Rebus, who stuck out a hand.

'Detective Inspector Rebus, Mr Munroe. This is DI Morton.'

Munroe shook both hands, putting no power into it: what had he to prove?

'Well, the wind's dropped a bit,' Munroe said, rubbing the grey stubble on his chin. 'So I suppose that's all right.' He turned to his wife. 'Meg, what about some bread and ham for the lad?'

Mrs Munroe nodded and silently set about her work, while her husband readied himself. He found oilskins for all of them and waterproof boots for himself, by which time a parcel of sandwiches and flask of tea sat waiting. Rebus stared at the flask, knowing Jack was doing the same, both gasping for a drink.

But there was no time for that. They were off.

It was a small boat, freshly painted and with an outboard motor. Rebus had had visions of them rowing across.

'There's a jetty,' Briony said when they were underway, rising and falling against the choppy water. 'A ferry usually takes visitors across. We'll have a bit of a hike, not much.'

'It's a bleak spot to choose,' Rebus yelled above the wind.

'Not that bleak,' she said with the ghost of a smile.

'What's that?' Jack said, pointing.

It stood on the edge of the island, next to where sloping strata of rock eased down into the dark water. Sheep grazed on the grass around the structure. To Rebus, it looked like some gigantic sandcastle or upturned flower-pot. As they got closer he saw it had to be over forty feet high, maybe fifty feet in diameter at its base, and was constructed from large flat stones, thousands of them.

'Mousa Broch,' Briony said.

'What is it?'

'Like a fort. They lived there, it was easy to defend.'

'Who lived there?'

She shrugged. 'Settlers. Maybe a hundred years BC.' There was a low-walled area behind the broch. 'That was the Haa; it's just a shell now.'

'And where's Jake?'

She turned to him. 'Inside the broch, of course.'

They landed, Munroe saying he'd circle the island and be back for them in an hour. Briony carried the bag of provisions, and struck out towards the broch, watched by the slow-chewing sheep and a few strutting birds.

'You live in a country all your life,' Jack was saying, the hood of his oilskin up to protect him from the wind, 'and you never even *know* stuff like this is out there.'

Rebus nodded. It *was* an extraordinary place. The feel of his feet on the grass wasn't like walking across lawn or field; it was like he was the first person ever to walk there. They followed Briony through a passageway and into the heart of the broch itself, sheltered from the wind but with no roof to protect them from threatening rain. Munroe's 'one hour' was a warning: any later and they'd be in for a rough if not dangerous crossing.

The blue nylon one-man tent looked incongruous pitched in the broch's central court. A man had risen out of it to hug Briony. Rebus bided his time. Briony handed over the bag of tea and sandwiches.

'God,' Jake Harley said, 'I've got too much food here as it is.'

He didn't look surprised to see Rebus. 'I thought she'd crack under pressure,' he said.

'No pressure necessary, Mr Harley. She's worried about you, that's all. I was worried too for a while there – thought you might have had an accident.'

Harley managed a smile. 'By which you don't really mean "accident"?' Rebus nodded. He was staring at Harley, trying to see him as 'Mr H.', the person who had ordered Allan Mitchison's execution. But that seemed way off the mark.

'I don't blame you for going into hiding,' Rebus said. 'Probably the safest thing you could have done.'

'Poor Mitch.' Harley looked down at the ground. He was tall, well built, with short, thinning black hair and metal-rimmed glasses. His face had retained a touch of the schoolboy, but he was badly needing a shave and to wash his hair. The tent's flaps were open, showing ground-mat, sleeping bag, a radio and some books. Leaning against the interior wall of the broch was a red rucksack, and nearby a camping-stove and carrier bag filled with rubbish.

'Can we talk about it?' Rebus asked.

Jake Harley nodded. He saw that Jack Morton was more interested in the broch itself than in their conversation. 'Isn't it incredible?'

'Bloody right,' Jack said. 'Did it ever have a roof?'

Harley shrugged. 'They built lean-tos in here, so maybe they didn't need a roof up there. The walls are hollow, double-thick. One of the galleries still leads to the top.' He looked around. 'There's a lot we don't know.' Then he looked at Rebus. 'It's been here two thousand years. It'll be here long after the oil's gone.'

'I don't doubt that.'

'Some people can't see it. Money's made them short-sighted.'

'You think this is all about money, Jake?'

'Not all of it, no. Come on, I'll show you the Haa.'

So they walked back out into the wind, crossing the grazing land and coming to the low wall around what had been a good-sized stone-built house, only the shell of which remained. They circuited the boundary, Briony walking with them, Jack further back, reluctant to leave the broch.

'Mousa Broch has always been lucky for the hunted. There's a story in the *Orkneyinga Saga*, an eloping couple took shelter here ...' He smiled at Briony.

'You found out Mitch was dead?' Rebus asked.

'Yes.'

'How?'

'I phoned Jo.'

'Jo?'

'Joanna Bruce. Mitch and her had been seeing one another.' So at last Braid-Hair had a name.

'How did she know?'

'It was in the Edinburgh paper. Jo's a media checker – she reads all the papers first thing every morning to see if there's anything the various pressure groups should know.'

'You didn't tell Briony?'

Jake took his girlfriend's hand and kissed it. 'You'd only have worried,' he told her.

'Two questions, Mr Harley: why do you think Mitch was killed, and who was responsible?'

Harley shrugged. 'As to who did it ... I'd never be able to prove anything. But I know why he was killed – it was my fault.'

'Your fault?'

'I told him what I suspected about the *Negrita*.'

The ship Sheepskin had mentioned on the flight to Sullom Voe; afterwards clamming up.

'What happened?'

'It was a few months back. You know Sullom Voe has some of the strictest procedures going? I mean, time was tankers would swill out their dirty bilges as they approached the coast – it saved pumping them ashore at the terminal ... saved time, which meant *money*. We used to lose black guillemots, great northern divers, shags, eider ducks, even the otters. That doesn't happen now – they tightened up. But mistakes still happen. That's all the *Negrita* was, a mistake.'

'An oil spill?'

Harley nodded. 'Not a big one, not by the standards we've managed to set with *Braer* and *Sea Empress*. The first mate, who should have been in charge, was in the sick bay – bad hangover apparently. A crew member who hadn't done the job before hit the wrong sequence of levers. The thing was, the crew member didn't have any English. That's not unusual these days: the officers might be British, but the hired help is the cheapest the company can get, which usually means Portuguese, Filipino, a hundred other nationalities. My guess is, the poor sod just didn't understand the instructions.'

'It was hushed up?'

Harley shrugged. 'Never really news in the first place, not a big enough spill.'

Rebus frowned. 'So what's the problem?'

'Like I say, I told Mitch the story ...'

'How did you know?'

'The crew landed at the terminal. They were in the canteen. I got talking to one of them, he looked awful – I can speak a bit of Spanish. He told me he did it.'

Rebus nodded. 'And Mitch?'

'Well, Mitch found out something that *had* been covered up. Namely the tanker's real owners. It's not easy with these boats – they're registered here, there and everywhere, leaving a real paper trail in their wake. Not always easy to get details from some of the registration ports. And sometimes the name on the papers doesn't mean much – companies own other companies, more countries are involved ...'

'A real maze.'

'Purposely so: a lot of the tankers out there are in shocking condition. But maritime law is international – even if we wanted to stop them landing, we couldn't, not without the say-so of all the other signatories.'

'Mitch found out that T-Bird Oil owned the tanker?'

'How did you know?'

'An educated guess.'

'Well, that's what he told me.'

'And you think someone at T-Bird had him killed? But why? Like you say, it wasn't a newsworthy spill.'

'It would be with T-Bird in the frame. They're going all out to persuade the government to let them dump their platforms at sea. They're talking up the environment and their record in that area. We're Mr Clean, so let us do what we want.' Harley showed bright white teeth as he spoke, the words almost a sneer. 'So tell me, Inspector, am I being paranoid? Just because Mitch gets thrown out of a window doesn't mean he was assassinated, right?'

'Oh, he was assassinated all right. But I'm not sure the *Negrita* had much to do with it.' Harley stopped walking and looked at him. 'I think you'd be quite safe going back home, Jake,' Rebus said. 'In fact, I'm sure of it. But first, there's something I need.'

'What?'

'An address for Joanna Bruce.'

30

The trip back was a real follicle transplant – hairier even than the trip out. They'd taken Jake and Briony back to Brae, then dropped the car off at Lerwick and begged a lift to Sumburgh. Forres was still in the huff, but relented eventually and checked the flights back, one of which gave them enough time for a Cup-a-Soup at the station.

At Dyce, they climbed back into Jack's car and sat there for a couple of minutes, adjusting to being back on the ground. Then they headed south on the A92, using the directions Jake Harley had given them. It was the same road Rebus had been taken on the night Tony El had been killed. They had Stanley for that – no matter what. Rebus wondered what else the young psychopath might spill, especially now he'd lost Eve. He'd know she'd flown; he'd know she wouldn't have left the loot behind. Maybe Gill would have twisted more stories out of him.

It could be the making of her.

They saw signposts to Cove Bay, followed Harley's instructions and came to a lay-by, behind which were parked a dozen vans, caravans, buses and campers. Bumping over ineffectual earth mounds, they came into a clearing in front of a forest. Dogs were barking, kids out playing with a punctured football. Clothes-lines hung between branches, and someone had lit a bonfire. A few adults had parked themselves around the fire, passing joints, one woman strumming a guitar. Rebus had been to travellers' camps before. They came in two designs. There was the old-style gypsy camp, with smart caravans and builders' lorries, the inhabitants – Romanies – olive-skinned and lapsing into a tongue Rebus couldn't understand. Then there were the 'New Age travellers': usually with buses which had passed their last MOT on a wing and a prayer. They were young and savvy, cut dead wood for fuel, and worked the social security system, despite government attempts to render it unworkable. They gave their kids names the kids would kill them for when they grew up.

Nobody paid Rebus and Jack any heed as they walked towards the camp-fire. Rebus kept his hands in his pockets, and tried not to make fists of them.

'Looking for Jo,' he said. He recognised the guitar chords: 'Time of the Preacher'. He tried again. 'Joanna Bruce.'

'Bummer,' someone said.

'That could be arranged,' Jack cautioned.

The joint went from hand to hand. 'Decade from now,' someone else said, 'this won't be illegal. It might even be on prescription.'

Smoke billowed from grinning mouths.

'Joanna,' Rebus reminded them.

'Warrant?' the guitarist asked.

'You know better than that,' Rebus told her. 'I only need a warrant if I want to bust this place. Want me to fetch one?'

'Macho Man!' someone sang.

'What do you want?'

There was a small white caravan hooked up to an antiquated Land Rover. She'd opened the caravan door – just the top half – and was leaning out.

'Can you smell the bacon, Jo?' the guitarist asked.

'Need to talk to you, Joanna,' Rebus said, walking towards the caravan, 'about Mitch.'

'What about him?'

'Why he died.'

Joanna Bruce looked at her fellow travellers, saw that Rebus had their attention, and unlocked the bottom half of her door. 'Better come in,' she said.

The caravan was cramped and unheated. There was no TV, but untidy stacks of magazines and newspapers, some of them with articles clipped out, and on the small folding table – benches either side, the whole thing convertible into a bed – a laptop computer. Standing, Rebus's head touched the caravan roof. Joanna shut down the computer, then gestured for Rebus and Jack to take the bench seats, while she balanced atop a pile of magazines.

'So,' she said, folding her arms, 'what's the story?'

'My question exactly,' Rebus replied. He nodded towards the wall behind her, where some photos had been pinned for decoration. 'Snap.' She looked round at the pictures. 'I've just had another lot of those developed,' Rebus explained: they were the originals missing from Mitch's envelope. She sat there with a face like stone, giving nothing away. There was kohl around her eyes and her hair was white fire in the glow from the gas lighting. For a full half-minute, the soft roar of igniting gas was the only sound in the caravan. Rebus was giving her time to change her mind, but she was using that time to erect further barricades, her eyes closing to slits, mouth pressed shut.

'Joanna Bruce,' Rebus mused. 'Interesting choice of name.' She half-opened her mouth, closed it again.

'Is Joanna your real first name, or did you change that too?'

'What do you mean?'

Rebus looked at Jack, who was sitting back, trying to look the part of the relaxed visitor, telling her it wasn't two against one, that she'd no need to be afraid. When Rebus spoke, he spoke to Jack's face.

'Your real surname's Weir.'

'How ... who told you that?' Trying to laugh it off.

'Nobody needed to. Major Weir had a daughter; they fell out; he disowned her.' And changed her sex to a son, maybe to muddy the water. Mairie's source had said as much.

'He didn't disown her! *She* disowned *him*!'

Rebus turned to her. Her face and body were animated now, clay come to life. Her fists gouged at her knees.

'Two things put me on track,' he said quietly. 'One, that surname: Bruce, as in Robert the ... as any student of Scottish history would know. Major Weir is daft on Scots history, he even named his oilfield after Bannockburn, which as we know was won by Robert the Bruce. Bruce and Bannock. I'm guessing you picked the name because you thought it would rile him?'

'It riles him all right.' Half a smile.

'The second thing was Mitch himself, once I knew you two were friends. Jake Harley tells me Mitch had gleaned some gen on *Negrita*, top-secret stuff. Well, Mitch might have been resourceful in some areas, but I couldn't see how he'd manage to work his way back through a paper trail. He travelled light, no sign of any notes or anything like that, either in his flat or in his cabin. I'm assuming he got the gen from you?' She nodded. 'And you'd have to seriously have it in for T-Bird Oil to bother with that sort of labyrinth in the first place. But we already know you've got something against T-Bird – the demo outside their HQ; chaining yourself to Bannock in full view of the TV cameras. I thought maybe it was something personal ...'

'It is.'

'Major Weir's your father?'

Her face turned sour and strangely childlike. 'Only in the biological sense. Even then, if you could get a gene transplant I'd be at the front of the queue.' Her voice sounded more American than ever. 'Did he kill Mitch?'

'Do *you* think he did?'

'I'd like to think so.' She stared at Rebus. 'I mean, I'd like to think he'd sink that low.'

'But?'

'But nothing. Maybe he did, maybe he didn't.'

'You reckon he had the motive?'

'Sure.' Not aware she was doing it, she picked at a nail and then bit it, before starting on another. 'I mean, *Negrita* and the way T-Bird's culpability was hushed up ... and now the dumping. He had plenty of economic reasons.'

'Was Mitch threatening to go to the media with the story?'

She removed a sliver of nail from her tongue. 'No, I think he was trying blackmail first. Keep quiet about everything, so long as T-Bird went for ecological scrapping of Bannock.'

'Everything?'

'What?'

'You said "everything", like there was more.'

She shook her head. 'No.' But she wasn't looking at him.

'Joanna, let me ask you something: why didn't *you* go to the media, or try blackmail on your father? Why did it have to be Mitch?'

She shrugged. 'He had the *chutzpah*.'

'Did he?'

Another shrug. 'What else?'

'See, the way it looks to me ... you don't mind tormenting your father – as publicly as possible. You're at the front of every demo, you make sure your picture's on TV ... but if you actually came forward and let the world know who you *are*, that would be even more effective. Why the secrecy?'

Her face turned childlike again, her mouth busy with fingers, knees together. The single braid fell between her eyes, like she wanted to hide from the world but be caught at the same time – a child's game.

'Why the secrecy?' Rebus repeated. 'Seems to me it's precisely because this is so personal between you and your father, like some sort of private game. You like the idea of torturing him, letting him wonder when you'll go public with any of this.' He paused. 'Seems to me maybe you were using Mitch.'

'No!'

'Using him to get at your father.'

'No!'

'Which means he had something you found useful. What could that be?'

She got up. 'Get out!'

'Something that drew the two of you together.'

She clamped her hands over her ears, shaking her head.

'Something from your past ... your childhoods. Something like blood between you. How far back does it go, Jo? Between you and your father – how far into the past does it stretch?'

She swung around and slapped his face. Hard. Rebus rode it, but it still stung.

'So much for non-violent protest,' he said, rubbing the spot.

She slumped down on the magazines again, ran a hand over her head. It came to rest on one of her braids, which she twirled nervously. 'You're right,' she said, so quietly Rebus almost didn't hear.

'Mitch?'

'Mitch,' she said, remembering him at last. Allowing herself that pain. Behind her, lighting flickered over the photographs. 'He was so uptight when we met. Nobody could believe it when we started seeing one another – chalk and cheese they said. They were wrong. It took a while, but one night he opened up to me.' She looked up. 'You know his background?'

'Orphaned,' Rebus said.

She nodded. 'Then institutionalised.' She paused. 'Then abused. He said there were times he'd thought of coming forward, telling people, but after all this time ... he wondered what good it would do.' She shook her head, tears forming. 'He was the most unselfish person I've ever met. But inside, it was like he was eaten away, and Jesus, I know *that* feeling.'

Rebus got it. 'Your father?'

She sniffed. 'They call him "an institution" in the oil world. Me, I was institutionalised ...' A deep breath, nothing theatrical about it: a necessity. 'And then abused.'

'Christ,' Jack said quietly. Rebus's heart was racing; he had to fight to keep his voice level.

'For how long, Jo?'

She looked up angrily. 'You think I'd let the prick get away with it *twice*? I ran as soon as I could. Kept running for years, then thought: fuck it, *I'm* not to blame. I'm not the one who should be doing this.'

Rebus nodded understanding. 'So you saw a bond between Mitch and you?'

'That's right.'

'And you told him your own story?'

'Quid pro quo.'

'Including your father's identity?' She started to nod, but stopped, swallowed instead. 'That's what he was blackmailing your father with – the incest story?'

'I don't know. Mitch was dead before I could find out.'

'But that was his intention?'

She shrugged. 'I guess.'

'Jo, I think we'll need a statement from you. Not now, later. All right?'

'I'll think about it.' She paused. 'We can't prove anything, can we?'

'Not yet.' Maybe not ever, he was thinking. He slid out of the seat, Jack following.

Outside, there were more songs around the camp-fire. Candles danced inside Chinese lanterns strung from the trees. Faces had turned shiny orange, like pumpkins. Joanna Bruce watched from her doorway, leaning against the bottom half of the door as before. Rebus turned to say goodbye.

'Will you be camped here a while?'

She shrugged. 'The way we live, who knows?'

'You like what you're doing?'

She gave the question serious thought. 'It's a life.'

Rebus smiled, moved away.

'Inspector!' she called. He turned back to her. Kohl was dribbling down her cheeks. 'If everything's so wonderful, how come everything's so fucked up?'

Rebus didn't have an answer to that. 'Don't let the sun catch you crying,' he told her instead.

On the drive back, he tried answering her question for himself, found he couldn't. Maybe it all had to do with balance, cause and effect. Where there was light, there must needs be dark. It sounded like the start of a sermon, and he hated sermons. He tried out his own personal mantra instead: Miles Davis, 'So What?' Only, it didn't sound so clever now.

It didn't sound clever at all.

Jack was frowning. 'Why didn't she come forward with any of this?' he asked.

'Because as far as she's concerned, it's got nothing to do with us. It didn't even have anything to do with Mitch, he just blundered in.'

'Sounded more like he was invited.'

'An invitation he should have refused.'

'You think Major Weir did it?'

'I'm not sure. I'm not even sure it matters. He's not going anywhere.'

'How do you mean?'

'He's in this little private hell she's constructed for the two of them. As long as he knows she's out there, demonstrating against everything he holds dear ... that's his punishment and her revenge. No getting away from it for either of them.'

'Fathers and daughters, eh?'

'Fathers and daughters,' Rebus agreed. And past misdemeanours. And the way they refused to go away ...

They were beat when they got back to the hotel.

'Round of golf?' Jack suggested.

Rebus laughed. 'I could just about manage coffee and a round of sarnies.'

'Sounds good to me. My room in ten minutes.'

Their rooms had been made up, fresh chocolates on the pillows, clean bathrobes laid out. Rebus changed quickly, then phoned reception to ask if there were any messages. He hadn't checked before – hadn't wanted Jack to know he was expecting one.

'Yes, sir,' the receptionist trilled. 'I've a phone message for you here.' Rebus's heart rose: she hadn't just upped and run. 'Shall I read it to you?'

'Please.'

'It says, "Burke's, half an hour after closing. Tried another time, another place, but he wasn't having any." There's no name.'

'That's fine, thanks.'

'You're welcome, sir.'

Of course he was welcome: business account. The whole world sucked up to you if you were corporate. He got the outside line, tried Siobhan at home, got her machine again. Tried St Leonard's, was told she wasn't there. Tried her at home again, deciding this time to leave his telephone number on her machine. Halfway through, she picked up.

'What's the use of an answering machine when you're home?' he asked.

'Call filtering,' she said. 'I get to check if you're a heavy breather or not before I talk to you.'

'My breathing's under control, so talk to me.'

'First victim,' she said. 'I spoke to someone at Robert Gordon's. Deceased was studying geology, and it included time spent offshore.

People who study geology up there almost always get a job in the oil industry, the whole course is geared towards it. Because she spent time offshore, deceased did a survival module.'

Rebus was thinking: chopper simulator, ducked in a swimming pool.

'So,' Siobhan went on, 'she spent time at OSC.'

'The Offshore Survival Centre.'

'Which deals with nothing but oil people. I got them to fax me staff and student rolls. So much for the first victim.' She paused. 'Victim two seemed completely different: older, different set of friends, different city. But she was a prostitute, and we know that a lot of businessmen use that sort of service when they're away from home.'

'I wouldn't know.'

'Victim four worked closely with the oil industry, which left Judith Cairns, the Glasgow victim. Variously employed, including part-time cleaning at a city-centre hotel.'

'Businessmen again.'

'So tomorrow they begin faxing me names. They weren't keen, client confidentiality and all that.'

'But you can be persuasive.'

'Yes.'

'So what are we hoping for? A guest at the Fairmount who's got a connection with Robert Gordon's?'

'It'll be in my prayers.'

'How soon tomorrow will you know?'

'That's down to the hotel. I may have to drive over there and gee them up.'

'I'll phone you.'

'If you get the machine, leave a number where I can reach you.'

'Will do. Cheers, Siobhan.' He put the telephone down, went along to Jack's room. Jack was wearing his robe.

'I might have to splash out on one of these,' he said. 'Sarnies are on their way up, ditto a big pot of coffee. I'm just going to take a shower.'

'Fine. Listen, Siobhan might be on to something.' He filled Jack in.

'Sounds promising. Then again ...' Jack shrugged.

'Christ, and I thought I was cynical.'

Jack winked, went into the bathroom. Rebus waited till he could hear the shower running, and Jack humming what sounded like 'Puppy Love'. Jack's clothes were on a chair. Rebus fished in the jacket pockets, came up with car keys, pocketed them for himself.

He wondered what time Burke's closed on a Thursday night. He

344

wondered what he was going to say to Judd Fuller. He wondered how badly Fuller would take it, whatever it was.

The shower stopped. 'Puppy Love' segued into 'What Made Milwaukee Famous'. Rebus liked a man with catholic tastes. Jack emerged, wrapped in his robe and doing prizefighter impressions.

'Back to Edinburgh tomorrow?'

'First thing,' Rebus agreed.

'To face the music.'

Rebus didn't say he might well be facing the music long before that. But when the sandwiches arrived, he found he'd lost his appetite. Thirsty though: four cups of coffee. He needed to stay awake. Long night coming, no moon in the sky.

Darkness on the short drive in, thin rain falling. Rebus felt jolted by coffee, loose wires sparking where his nerves should be. One-fifteen in the morning: he'd rung Burke's, the bar-side payphone, asked a punter what time the place shut.

'Party's nearly finished, ya radge!' Phone slammed home. Background music: 'Albatross', so it was moon-dance time. Two or three slows, your last chance to grab a breakfast partner. Desperate times on the dance floor; as desperate in your forties as in your teens.

Albatross.

Rebus tried the radio – vacuous pop, pounding disco, telephone chat. Then jazz. Jazz was OK. Jazz was fine, even on Radio Two. He parked near Burke's, watched a dumb-show as two bouncers took on three farm-boys whose girlfriends were trying to pull them away.

'Listen to the ladies,' Rebus muttered. 'You've proved yourselves for tonight.'

The fight dissolved into pointed fingers and swearing, the bouncers, arms not touching their sides, waddling back inside. A final kick at the doors, saliva hitting the porthole-styled windows, then hauled away and up the road. Opening curtain on another north-east weekend. Rebus got out and locked the car, breathed the city air. Shouts and sirens up on Union Street. He crossed the road and headed for Burke's.

The doors were locked. He kicked at them, but nobody answered: probably thinking the farm-boys were back. Rebus kept kicking. Someone poked a head round the interior doors, saw he didn't look like a punter, shouted something back into the club. Now a bouncer came out, jangling a chain of keys. He looked like he wanted to go to bed, day's work done. The door rattled, and he opened it an inch.

'What?' he growled.

'I've an appointment with Mr Fuller.'

The bouncer stared at him, pulled the door wide. The lights were on in the main bar, staff emptying ashtrays and wiping down tables, collecting an enormous number of glasses. With the lights up, the interior looked as bleak as any moorland vista. Two men who looked like DJs – ponytails, black sleeveless T-shirts – sat smoking at the bar, sinking bottles of beer. Rebus turned to the bouncer.

'Mr Stemmons around?'

'I thought your appointment was with Mr Fuller.'

Rebus nodded. 'Just wondered if Mr Stemmons was available.' Talk to him first – the sane member of the cast; businessman, therefore a listener.

'He might be upstairs.' They went back into the foyer, climbed to where Stemmons and Fuller had their offices. The bouncer opened a door. 'In you go.'

In Rebus went, ducking too late. The hand hit his neck like a side of beef, flooring him. Fingers sought his throat, probing for the carotid artery, applying pressure. No brain damage, Rebus thought, as the edges of his vision darkened. Please, God, let there be no damage ...

31

He woke up drowning.

Sucking foam and water in through his nose, his mouth. Fizzing taste – not water, beer. He shook his head wildly, opened his eyes. Lager trickled down his throat. He tried coughing it out. Someone was standing behind him, holding the now-empty bottle, chuckling. Rebus tried turning and found his arms were on fire. Literally. He could smell whisky, see a shattered bottle on the floor. His arms had been doused in the stuff and set alight. He cried out, wriggled. A bar towel flapped at the flames and they died. The smouldering towel fell with a slap on to the floor. Laughter echoing around the walls.

The place reeked of alcohol. It was a cellar. Bare lightbulbs and aluminium kegs, boxes of bottles and glasses. Half a dozen brick pillars supporting the ceiling. They hadn't tied Rebus to one of these. Instead, he hung suspended from a hook, the rope fraying his wrists, arms readying to pop from sockets. Rebus shifted more weight on to his feet. The figure from behind tossed the beer-bottle into a crate and came round to stand in front of him. Slick black hair with a kiss-curl at the front, and a large hooked nose in the centre of a face lush with corruption. A diamond glinted in one of the teeth. Dark suit, white T-shirt. Rebus took a wild guess – Judd Fuller – but reckoned the time for introductions was past.

'Sorry I don't have Tony El's ingenuity with power tools,' Fuller said. 'But I do what I can.'

'From where I'm standing, you're doing fine.'

'Thanks.'

Rebus looked around. They were alone in the cellar, and nobody'd thought to tie his legs together. He could kick Fuller in the balls and ...

The punch came low, hitting him just above the groin. It would have doubled him up, if his arms had been free. As it was, he instinctively raised his knees, lifting his feet off the floor. His shoulder-joints told him this was not the brightest move.

Fuller was walking away, flexing the fingers of his right hand. 'So, cop,' he said, his back to Rebus, 'how do you like it so far?'

'I'm ready for a break if you are.'

'Only break you're going to get is your goddamn neck.' Fuller turned to him, grinned, then picked up another beer-bottle, smacked it open against a wall and gulped half the contents.

The smell of the alcohol was overpowering, and the few mouthfuls Rebus had swallowed seemed already to be having an effect. His eyes stung; so did his hands where the flames had licked them. His wrists were already blistering.

'We have a nice club here,' Fuller was saying. 'Everybody has fun. You can ask around, it's a popular spot. What gives you the right to spoil the party?'

'I don't know.'

'You made Erik upset the night you talked to him.'

'Does he know about this?'

'He'll *never* get to know about this. Erik's happier not knowing. He has an ulcer, you know. He *worries*.'

'Can't think why that is.' Rebus stared at Fuller. If you caught his face in the right kind of shadow, he resembled a young Leonard Cohen, the Travolta comparison *way* off.

'You're a nuisance, that's all you are, an itch that needs to be scratched.'

'You don't get it, Judd. You're not in America. You can't just hide a body here and hope nobody stumbles across it.'

'Why not?' Fuller opened his arms wide. 'Boats head out of Aberdeen all the time. Weight you down and tip you into the North Sea. Know how hungry the fish are out there?'

'I know it's *over*fished – do you want some trawler netting me?'

'Option two,' Fuller said, raising two fingers, 'the mountains. Let the fucking sheep find you, nibble you clean to the bone. Plenty of options, don't think we haven't used them before.' He paused. 'Why did you come here tonight? What did you *ever* hope you were going to do?'

'I don't know.'

'When Eve phoned … she couldn't hide it, it was in her voice – I knew she was shitting me, setting me up. But I have to admit, I was expecting something a little more challenging.'

'Sorry to disappoint you.'

'I'm glad it's you, though, I've been wanting to see you again.'

'Well, here I am.'

'What did Eve tell you?'

'Eve? She didn't tell me anything.'

A roundhouse kick took time: Rebus did what he could, turned sideways on to it, caught it in the ribs. Fuller followed up with a punch to the face, his hand moving so slowly Rebus could see the scar on its back – a long ugly welt. A tooth split in half, one of his root-canal jobs. Rebus spat the tooth and some blood at Fuller, who backed off a little, impressed at the damage.

Rebus knew he was dealing with someone who at best could be termed unpredictable, at worst psychotic. Without Stemmons to keep him in check, Judd Fuller looked capable of anything.

'All I did,' Rebus lisped, 'was do a deal with her. She set up the meeting with you, and I let her go.'

'She must have told you *some*thing.'

'She's a hard nut to crack. I got even less from Stanley.' Rebus tried to sound defeated: not difficult. He wanted Fuller to go for the whole story.

'Stanley and her have gone off together?' Fuller chuckled again. 'Uncle Joe's going to shit monkeys.'

'Putting it mildly.'

'So tell me, cop, how much do you know? Make it good, maybe we can work something out.'

'I'm open to offers.'

Fuller shook his head. 'I don't think so. Ludo already sniffed you out about that.'

'He didn't exactly have the cards you've got.'

'Well, that's true.' Fuller took a swipe at Rebus's face with the jagged neck of his bottle. Instead of connecting, Rebus felt air brush his cheek. 'Next time,' Fuller said, 'I might get careless. You could lose your looks.'

As if the condemned man cared for beauty. But Rebus was shaking.

'Do I look like martyr material? All I was doing was my job. It's what they pay me for, I'm not married to it!'

'But you're persistent.'

'Blame fucking Lumsden, he got right up my back!' A memory came to him unbeckoned: closing time at the Ox, nights when they'd stumbled out into the cold, joking about getting locked in the cellar and drinking the place dry. Now all Rebus wanted was out.

'How much do you know?' The jagged glass was an inch from his nose. Fuller stretched his arm until the bottle was beneath Rebus's nostrils. Lager fumes, the cold touch of glass, pressing upwards.

349

'Remember the old joke?' Fuller asked. 'Ask yourself how you'd smell without a nose.'

Rebus sniffed. 'I know the lot,' he spat.

'And how much is that?'

'The dope comes up from Glasgow, straight to here. You sell it, and ship it out to the rigs. Eve and Stanley collected the cash, Tony El was Uncle Joe's man on the spot.'

'Proof?'

'Almost non-existent, especially with Tony El dead and Eve and Stanley on the run. But—' Rebus swallowed.

'But what?'

Rebus kept his mouth shut. Fuller flicked the bottle up and pulled it away. Rebus's nose dribbled fresh blood.

'Maybe I'll just bleed you dry! "But what?"'

'But it doesn't matter,' Rebus said, trying to wipe his nose on his shirt. His eyes were watering. He blinked, tears streaking both cheeks.

'Why not?' Fuller interested.

'Because people are blabbing.'

'Who?'

'You know I can't—'

The bottle flew to his right eye. Rebus screwed his eyes shut. 'All right, all right!' The bottle stayed where it was, so close he had to focus past it. He took a deep breath. Time to stir the shit. His big plan. 'How many cops on your payroll?'

Fuller frowned. 'Lumsden?'

'He's been talking ... and someone's been talking to him.'

Rebus could almost hear the cogs creaking inside Fuller's head, but even he had to work it out eventually.

'Mr H?' Fuller's eyes widened. 'Mr H. talked to Lumsden, I heard about that. But it was supposed to be about the woman who got herself killed ...' Fuller busied himself thinking.

Mr H. – the man who'd paid Tony El. And now Rebus knew who Mr H. was – Hayden Fletcher, interviewed by Lumsden about Vanessa Holden. Fletcher had paid Tony El to take care of Allan Mitchison – the two men had probably met right here. Maybe Fuller himself had introduced them.

'It's not just you. They've been grassing up Eddie Segal, Moose Maloney ...' Rebus pulling out the names Stanley had mentioned.

'Fletcher and Lumsden?' Fuller said to himself. He shook his head, but Rebus could see he was halfway convinced. He stared at Rebus, who tried to look as beaten as a man could be – no great acting required.

'There's a Scottish Crime Squad operation coming,' Rebus said. 'Lumsden and Fletcher are in their pockets.'

'They're dead men,' Fuller said at last.

'Why stop when you're having fun?'

A cold, wicked smile. Fletcher and Lumsden were for the future: but Rebus was right here.

'We'll go for a little ride,' Fuller said. 'Don't worry, you did all right. I'll make it quick. One bullet to the back of the head. You won't go out screaming.' He let the bottle drop to the floor and crunched glass on his way to the stairs. Rebus looked around fast, no way of knowing how long he had. The hook looked pretty solid – it had held his weight so far, no problem. If he could stand on a box, get some height, then he could unhook the ropes. There was the empties' crate, not three feet away. Rebus stretched, his arms in agony, felt with his shoe, just touched the rim of the crate and started to drag it. Fuller had climbed up through a trapdoor, but left it open. Rebus could hear a voice echoing in the bar. Maybe Fuller wanted a bouncer, someone to witness the policeman's demise. The crate caught in a dip in the floor, wouldn't budge. Rebus tried to lift it with the toe of his shoe, couldn't. He was soaked: blood, booze and sweat. The box gave, and he hauled it beneath him, climbed on to it and pushed with his knees. He freed the rope from the hook and brought his arms down slowly, trying to enjoy the pain, feeling blood tingle its way back along them. His fingers stayed numb and cold. He chewed at the knots in the rope, couldn't budge them. There was plenty of broken glass around, but sawing through would take too long. He bent down, picked up a broken bottle, then saw something even better.

A cheap pink plastic lighter. Fuller had probably used it to ignite the whisky on Rebus's arms, dropped it afterwards. Rebus picked it up, looked around. There was a lot of booze down here. No way out except the ladder. He found a rag, opened a bottle of whisky and stuffed it into the neck. Not quite a petrol bomb, but a weapon at any rate. One option: ignite it and toss it into the club, get the fire alarm going and wait for the cavalry. Supposing they came. Supposing that would stop Judd Fuller ...

Option two: think again.

He looked around. CO_2 cylinders; plastic crates; runs of rubber tubing. Hanging on the wall: a small fire extinguisher. He grabbed the fire extinguisher, primed it, got it under one arm so he could carry the whisky bottle up the steps.

The club looked dead, dimly lit. Someone had left a glitterball turning, throwing glass jewels across walls and ceiling. He was halfway across the dance floor when the door flew open, Fuller standing there, lit from behind by the foyer. He had a set of car keys between his teeth, dropped them as his mouth opened. He was reaching into his jacket pocket when Rebus got the rag lit, tossed the bottle two-handed. It turned in the air, shattered in front of Fuller. A pool of blue flame spread across the floor. Rebus was still coming, fire extinguisher ready. The gun was in Fuller's hand as the spray caught him full in the face. Rebus followed it up with a head-butt to the bridge of Fuller's nose and a knee hard into the groin. Not exactly textbook stuff, but powerfully effective. The American sank to his knees. Rebus kicked him in the face and ran, pulled open the door to the outside world and almost fell into Jack Morton.

'Christ Almighty, man, what have they done to you?'

'He's got a gun, Jack, let's get the fuck out of here.'

They sprinted for the car. Jack got the keys from Rebus's pocket. Into the car and accelerating away, Rebus feeling a bewildering mix of emotions, chief among them elation.

'You smell like a brewery,' Jack said.

'Jesus, Jack, how did you get here?'

'Took a taxi.'

'No, I mean …'

'You can thank Shetland.' Jack sniffed. 'That wind up there, I've got a cold coming. Went to get the hankie out of my trouser pocket … no car keys. No car in the car park, and no John Rebus tucked up in bed.'

'And?'

'And reception repeated the message they gave you, so I phoned for a taxi. What the hell happened?'

'I took a beating.'

'I'd say that was an understatement. Who's got the gun?'

'Judd Fuller, the American.'

'We'll stop at the nearest phone, get an armed response unit over there.'

'No.'

Jack turned. 'No?' Rebus was shaking his head. 'Why not?'

'I was taking a calculated risk, Jack.'

'Time to buy a new calculator.'

'I think it worked. Now all we need to do is give it a bit of time.'

Jack thought about it. 'You want them turning on each other?' He nodded. 'Never were one to play by the book, were you? The note was from Eve?' Rebus nodded. 'And you thought you'd leave me out. Know

352

something? When I saw the keys were gone, I was so angry, I almost said "Stuff it, let him do what he wants, it's his neck".'

'It almost was.'

'You're a stupid bastard.'

'Years of dedicated practice, Jack. Can you stop and untie me?'

'I like you better tied up. Casualty or a doctor call-out?'

'I'll be fine.' The nosebleed had already stopped; there was no pain from the dead tooth.

'So what *did* you do there?'

'I fed Fuller a line, and I found out Hayden Fletcher hired Allan Mitchison's killer.'

'And you're telling me there wasn't an easier way?' Jack shook his head slowly. 'If I live to be a hundred, I swear I'll never understand you.'

'I'll take that as a compliment,' Rebus said, leaning his head back against the seat.

Back at the hotel, they decided it was time to leave Aberdeen. Rebus had a bath first, and Jack checked his injuries.

'Strictly an amateur sadist, our Mr Fuller.'

'He did apologise at the start.' Rebus checked his gap-toothed smile in the mirror.

Every bit of his body ached, but he'd live, and he didn't need a doctor to agree with him. They loaded the car, signed out without fuss, and got back on the road.

'What an end to our holidays,' Jack commented. But his audience of one was already asleep.

*

When he had narrowed the list to four individuals, four companies, it was time to use the 'key' – Vanessa Holden herself.

More of the suspects had turned out to be too old, or not right in some other way: one, first name Alex, had turned out to be a woman.

Bible John made the call from his own office, door closed. He had his notepad in front of him. Four companies, four individuals.

Eskflo	James Mackinley
LancerTech	Martin Davidson
Gribbin's	Steven Jackobs
Yetland	Oliver Howison

The call was to Vanessa Holden's company. A receptionist answered.

'Hello,' he told her, 'Queen Street CID here, Detective Sergeant Collier. General question: I was wondering if you'd ever undertaken any work for Eskflo Fabrication?'

'Eskflo?' The receptionist sounded dubious. 'Let me put you through to Mr Westerman.'

Bible John wrote the name on his notepad, circled it. When Westerman answered, he repeated his question.

'Is this to do with Vanessa?' the man asked.

'No, sir, though I was sorry to hear about Ms Holden. You have my deepest sympathies – same goes for everyone here.' He looked around the walls of his office. 'And I'm sorry to have to call at such a distressing time.'

'Thank you, Detective Sergeant. It's been a great shock.'

'Of course, and rest assured, we're following up several lines of inquiry concerning Ms Holden. But my present request concerns a suspected fraud.'

'Fraud?'

'Nothing to do with yourselves, Mr Westerman, but we're investigating several companies.'

'Including Eskflo?'

'Indeed.' Bible John paused. 'You'll appreciate that I'm telling you this in the strictest confidence?'

'Oh, of course.'

'Now, the companies I'm concerned with are ...' He made show of shuffling some papers, eyes on the notepad. 'Here we are: Eskflo, LancerTech, Gribbin's, and Yetland.'

'Yetland,' said Westerman, 'we did some work for them recently. No, wait ... We pitched for a contract, didn't get it.'

'And the others?'

'Look, can I get back to you? I'm going to have to go to the files. I seem to be having trouble concentrating.'

'I understand, sir. I'm due out on a call ... how about if I phone again in an hour?'

'Perhaps if I call you when I'm ready?'

'I'll phone again in an hour, Mr Westerman. I do appreciate this.'

He put the phone down, bit a fingernail. Would Westerman try phoning Queen Street CID, asking for a DS Collier? He'd give him forty minutes.

But in the end, he gave him thirty-five.

'Mr Westerman? That call didn't take as long as I thought. I wonder if you've come up with anything for me?'

'Yes, I think I've got what you need.'

Bible John concentrated on the tone of voice, listening for any doubt or suspicion, any inkling Westerman might have that he was not talking to a policeman. He found none.

'As I said,' Westerman continued, 'we pitched for a Yetland contract but didn't get it. That was in March this year. Lancer ... we did a panel display for them in February. They had a stand at the Safety at Sea conference.'

Bible John consulted his list. 'Do you happen to know who your contact was?'

'I'm sorry, Vanessa handled it. She was very good with clients.'

'The name Martin Davidson doesn't ring any bells?'

'I'm afraid not.'

'Not to worry, sir. And the other two companies ...?'

'Well, we've worked for Eskflo in the past, but not for a couple of years. And Gribbin's ... well, to be honest, I've never heard of them.'

Bible John ringed Martin Davidson's name. Put a question mark beside James Mackinley: a lag-time of a couple of years? Doubtful, but possible. Decided that Yetland was a distant third, but just to be sure ...

'Would Yetland have dealt with yourself or Ms Holden?'

'Vanessa was on holiday around then. It was just after Safety at Sea, she was exhausted.'

Bible John scored both Yetland and Gribbin's off his list.

'Mr Westerman, you've been a big help. I appreciate it.'

'Glad to help. Just one thing, Detective Sergeant?'

'Yes, sir?'

'If you ever find the bastard who killed Vanessa, give him one from me.'

Two M. Davidsons in the phone book, one James Mackinley and two J. Mackinleys. Addresses noted.

Then another phone call, this time to Lancer Technical Support.

'Hello, it's the Chamber of Commerce here, just a general question. We're compiling a database on local companies connected to the oil business. That would include LancerTech, wouldn't it?'

'Oh, yes,' the receptionist said. 'Definitely.' She sounded a bit frazzled. Background noise: staff talking, a photocopier, another phone ringing.

'Can you give me a thumbnail sketch?'

'Well ... we, erm, we design safety aspects into oil platforms, support vessels ...' She sounded like she was reading from a crib-sheet. 'That sort of thing.' Her voice trailed off.

'I'm just writing that down,' Bible John told her. 'If you work in safety design, can I take it you have links to RGIT?'

'Oh yes, close links. We cooperate on half a dozen projects. A couple of our staff are partly based there.'

Bible John underlined the name Martin Davidson. Twice.

'Thank you,' he said. 'Goodbye.'

Two M. Davidsons in the phone book. One might be a woman. He could telephone, but that would be to give the Upstart advance warning ... What would he do with him? What did he want to do with him? He had begun his task in anger, but was now composed ... and more than a little curious. He could call the police, an anonymous tip-off, that's what they were waiting for. But he knew now that he wasn't going to do that. At one point, he'd assumed he could simply dispatch the wretch and resume his life as before, but that just wasn't possible. The Upstart had changed everything. His fingers went to his tie, checked the knot. He ripped the sheet from his notepad and tore it into tiny pieces, letting them flutter into the waste-bin.

He wondered if he should have stayed in the States. No, there would always have been the craving for home. He remembered one of the early theories about him – that he had been a member of the 'Exclusive Brethren'. And in a sense, he had been and still was. And intended to remain a member.

Good understanding giveth favour, but the way of transgressors is hard.

Hard it was, hard would always be. He wondered if he had 'good understanding' of the Upstart? He doubted it, and wasn't sure he wanted to understand.

The truth was, now he was here, he didn't know what he wanted. But he knew what he needed.

32

They crash-landed in Arden Street at breakfast time, neither of them feeling much like breakfast. Rebus had taken over the driving at Dundee, so Jack could crawl into the back seat for an hour. It was like driving back after one of his all-nighters, the roads quiet, rabbits and pheasant in the fields. The cleanest time of day, before everyone got busy messing it up again.

There was mail behind the door of the flat, and so many messages on his machine the red indicator was almost solid.

'Don't you dare leave,' Jack said, before shuffling into the guest room, leaving the door open. Rebus made a mug of coffee, then slumped into his chair by the window. The blisters on his wrists looked like nettle-rash. His nostrils were crusted with blood.

'Well,' he said to the waking world, 'that went as well as could be expected.' He closed his eyes for five minutes. The coffee was cold when he opened them again.

His phone was ringing. He got to it before the machine.

'Hello?'

'CID awakes. It's like a Ray Harryhausen film.' Pete Hewitt from Howdenhall. 'Look, I shouldn't be doing this, but strictly off the record ...'

'What?'

'All those forensic checks we ran on you – nothing. I expect they'll get round to telling you officially, but I thought I'd put your mind at rest.'

'If only you could, Pete.'

'Hard night?'

'Another one for the record books. Thanks, Pete.'

'Bye, Inspector.'

Rebus didn't put down the receiver; called Siobhan instead. Got her answering machine. Told her he was at home. Another home number, this time answered.

'What?' The voice groggy.

'Morning, Gill.'

'John?'

'Alive and kicking. How did it go?'

'I talked with Malcolm Toal, I think he's good as gold – that is, when he's not hitting his head against the cell wall – but ...'

'But?'

'But I've passed everything on to the Squaddies. They're the experts, after all.' Silence. 'John? Look, I'm sorry if you think I bottled out ...'

'You can't see me smiling. You played it just right, Gill. You'll get your share of the glory, but let them do the dirty work. You've learned.'

'Maybe I had a good teacher.'

He laughed quietly. 'No, I don't think so.'

'John ... thanks ... for everything.'

'Want to know a secret?'

'What?'

'I'm on the wagon.'

'Good for you. I'm really impressed. What happened?'

Jack slouched into the room, yawning and scratching his head.

'I had a good teacher,' Rebus said, replacing the receiver.

'I heard the phone,' Jack said. 'Any coffee on the go?'

'In the kettle.'

'Want one?'

'Go on then.' Rebus went into the hall and picked up his mail. One envelope was fatter than the others. London postmark. He tore it open as he walked through to the kitchen. There was another envelope inside, fat, with his name and address printed on it. There was also a single sheet of notepaper. Rebus sat down at the table to read it.

It was from Lawson Geddes' daughter.

My father left the enclosed envelope with instructions that it should be sent on to you. I'm just back from Lanzarote, having had to arrange not only the funeral but the sale of my parents' house and the sorting out and removal of all their things. As you may remember, Dad was a bit of a magpie. Apologies for the slight delay in sending this on, which I trust you will understand. Hoping all is well with you and your family.

She'd signed it Aileen Jarrold (*née* Geddes).

'What is it?' Jack asked as Rebus tore open the second envelope. He read the first couple of lines, then looked up at Jack.

'It's a very long suicide note,' he said. 'From Lawson Geddes.'

Jack sat down and they read it together.

John, I'm sitting here writing this in the full and certain knowledge that I'm about to top myself: we always called it the coward's way out, remember? I'm not so sure about that now, but I get the feeling I'm maybe being more selfish than cowardly exactly, selfish because I know the telly are looking at Spaven again – they've even sent a team to the island. This isn't about Spaven, it's about Etta. I miss her, and I want to be with her, even if all the afterlife consists of is my bones lying next to hers somewhere.

As Rebus read, the years melted away again. He could hear Lawson's voice, and see him swaggering into the station, or marching into a pub like he was the landlord, a word for everybody whether he knew them or not ... Jack got up for a minute and returned with two mugs of coffee. They read on.

With Spaven dead and me out of the way, there'll only be you left for the telly people to hassle. I don't like to think of that – I know you'd nothing to do with any of it. So here's this letter, after all these years, and maybe it'll explain things. Show it to whoever you need to. They say dying men tell no lies, and maybe they'll accept that the following is the truth as I know it.

I knew Lenny Spaven back in the Scots Guards. He was always getting into trouble, finding himself consigned to jankers or even on occasion the glass-house. He was a skiver, too, and that's how he came to be involved with the minister. Spaven used to attend the Sunday church service (I say 'church' – in Borneo it was a tent, back home it was a Nissen hut). But I suppose a lot of places can be churches in the sight of God. Maybe I'll ask him when I see him. It's ninety-odd degrees outside, and I'm drinking firewater – the old usquebaugh. *It tastes better than ever.*

Rebus caught the sudden tang of whisky at the back of his mouth: memory playing tricks. Lawson used to drink Cutty Sark.

Spaven helped the minister out, laying hymnaries on the chairs, then counting them back in at the end. You know yourself there are some buggers in the army would steal a hymnary as soon as anything else. There weren't many regular attenders. If things got hairy, a few more souls would turn up, praying it wouldn't be them being nailed into a box at the end of play. Well, like I say, Spaven had it cushy. I didn't have much to do with him, or with any of the church types.

The thing is, John, there was a murder – a prostitute near our camp. A native girl from the kampong. *The villagers blamed it on us, and even the Gurkhas knew it was probably a British soldier. There was an investigation – civil and military. Funny really, I mean, there we were going hell for leather killing people – it was what we got paid for – and there they were looking into a single murder. Anyway, they never found anyone for it. Thing is though, that prozzy was strangled, and one of her sandals was never recovered.*

Rebus turned a page.

Well, all that was behind me. I was a bobby, back in Scotland and happy with my lot. Then I got roped into the Bible John case. You've got to remember, we didn't know him as 'Bible John' until very late on. It was after the third victim that we got the description of him quoting from the Bible. That's when the papers came up with the name. Well, when I thought about someone quoting from the Bible, a strangler and rapist, I remembered Borneo. I went to my boss and told him all about it. He said it was a long shot of Olympic standards, but that I could chase it up in my own time if I liked. You know me, John, never one to resist a challenge. Besides, I had a shortcut planned – Lenny Spaven. I knew he was back in Scotland, and he'd have info on all the church-goers. So I got in touch with him, but he'd gone from bad to rotten, didn't want anything to do with it. I'm the persistent type, and he complained about me to my boss. That got me a warning to ease off, but I wasn't about to ease off. I knew what I wanted: I reckoned Lenny might have photos from his days in Borneo, maybe with him and the rest of the flock. I wanted to show them to the woman who'd shared the taxi with Bible John. I wanted to see if she recognised anyone. But bloody Spaven kept standing in my way. Eventually, I did manage to get some photos – going the long way round, talking to the army first, then tracking down the minister from the time. It took weeks.

Rebus looked at Jack. 'The photos Ancram showed us.' Jack nodded.

We showed the photos to the eye-witness. Mind, they were eight or nine years out of date, and not very good to start with, water damaged some of them. She said she couldn't be sure, she thought one of them 'was like him' – her words. But as my boss said, there were hundreds of men out there in the big wide world who bore a physical resemblance to the killer: we'd interviewed most of them. That wasn't good enough for me. I got the man's name, he was called Ray Sloane – an unusual enough name, and it wasn't hard to track him down. Only he'd cleared out. He'd been living in a bedsit in Ayr, working as a toolmaker. But he'd recently given notice and moved on, nobody knew where. I was convinced in my mind that he could be the man we were looking for, but I couldn't convince my boss to go all-out on finding him.

See, John, that delay while I was dealing with the army, it was all down to Spaven. If he'd helped, I'd have been on to Sloane before he'd had a chance to pack up and ship out. I know it, I can feel it. I might have had him. Instead of which, I had nothing but my anger and frustration, both of which I vented too publicly. The boss kicked me off the inquiry, and that was that.

'Your coffee's getting cold,' Jack said. Rebus took a gulp, turned another page.

Or at least it was until Spaven came back into my life, moving to Edinburgh much the same time I did. It was like he was haunting me, and I couldn't forgive him for what he'd done. If anything, as time passed I grew to despise him even more. That's why I wanted him for the Elsie Rhind killing. I admit it, to you and to anyone else reading this, I wanted him so badly it was like a hard ball in my stomach, something only surgery would remove. When I was told to ease off on him, I didn't. When I was told to steer clear, I steered closer. I followed him — on my own time — I tracked him every day and every night. I went without sleep for the best part of three days. But it was worth it when I saw him make for that lock-up, somewhere we didn't know about. I was elated, ecstatic. I didn't know what we'd find inside, but I had the feeling we'd find something. That's why I came rushing over to your house, why I dragged you back there with me. You asked me about a search warrant, and I told you not to be so stupid. I put a lot of pressure on you, using our long friendship as blackmail — I was feverish, I'd have done anything, and that surely included breaking rules I now saw as being there to punish the police and protect the villains. So in we went, and found the heaps of boxes, all that knock-off from the factory job in Queensferry. Plus the bag. Elsie Rhind's, as it turned out. I nearly dropped to my knees to thank God for finding it.

I know what a lot of people thought — yourself included. They thought I'd planted it there. Well, I swear on my deathbed (except I'm writing this at the table) that I did not. I found it fair and square, even though I made us break the rules to accomplish it. But you see, that one crucial piece of evidence would have been ruled inadmissible because of the way we'd come to find it, which is why I persuaded you — against your better judgement — to stick to the story I invented. Am I sorry I did it? Yes and no. It can't be very comfortable for you just now, John, and it can't have been a nice thing to have lived with all these years. But we got the murderer, and in my mind — and I've spent God knows how long thinking about it, reliving it, running through the way I played it — that's what really counts.

John, I hope all this fuss dies down. Spaven's not worth it. Nobody's giving much thought to Elsie Rhind, are they? The victim can never win. Chalk this one up to Elsie Rhind. Just because a villain can write doesn't make him less of a villain. I read that the commandants at the concentration camps used to put their feet up at night and read the classics while listening to a bit of Beethoven. Monsters can do that. I know this now. I know because of Lenny Spaven.

Your friend, Lawson.

Jack patted Rebus's back. 'He's just cleared you, John. Wave this in Ancram's face and that's the end of that.'

Rebus nodded, wishing he could feel relief, or any other sensible emotion.

'What's wrong?' Jack asked.

Rebus tapped the paper. 'This is,' he said. 'I mean, most of it is probably right, but it's still a lie.'

'What?'

Rebus looked at him. 'The stuff we found in the lock-up ... I saw it in Elsie Rhind's house the first time we went round there. Lawson must have lifted it later.'

Jack looked uncomprehending. 'Are you sure?'

Rebus flew to his feet. 'No, I'm not sure, and that's the real bastard of it! I'll never be sure.'

'I mean, it was twenty years ago, your mind plays tricks.'

'I know. Even at the time, I wasn't a hundred per cent sure I'd seen them before – maybe I saw a different bag, different hat. I went round to her place, took another look. This was when we had Spaven in custody. I looked for the hat and the bag I'd seen there ... and they were gone. Ah, shit, maybe I didn't see them at all, only thought I did. It doesn't change the fact that I *think* I saw them. I *think* Lenny Spaven was set up, and I've always thought it ... and I've never done a thing about it.' He sat down again. 'Never even told anyone till now.' He tried to pick up his mug but his hand was shaking. 'DTs,' he said, forcing a smile.

Jack was thoughtful. 'Does it matter?' he said at last.

'You mean whether I'm right or not? Jesus, Jack, I don't know.' Rebus rubbed his eyes. 'It was all so long ago. Does it matter if the killer got away? Even if I'd come forward at the time, it would have maybe cleared Spaven but it wouldn't have got us the real killer, would it?' He let out a breath. 'I've been spinning it in my head all these years, the grooves are worn almost to nothing.'

'Time to buy a new record?'

Rebus smiled for real this time. 'Maybe you're right.'

'One thing I don't understand ... why didn't Spaven himself explain

362

any of this? I mean, he never touches on it in his book. He could have just said why Geddes had it in for him.'

Rebus shrugged. 'Look at Weir and his daughter.'

'You mean it was personal?'

'I don't know, Jack.'

Jack picked up the letter, turning its pages. 'Interesting about the Borneo pics though. Ancram thought they were relevant because they showed Spaven. Now we find it was this guy Sloane that Geddes was after.' Jack checked his watch. 'We should nip over to Fettes, show this to Ancram.'

Rebus nodded. 'Let's do it. But first, I want a photocopy of Lawson's letter. Like you say, Jack, I might not believe it, but it's here in black and white.' He looked up at his friend. 'Which should be good enough for *The Justice Programme*.'

Ancram looked like he should have been fitted with a pressure valve. He was so angry he'd almost swung all the way round to calm. His voice was the first wisp of smoke from a sleeping volcano.

'What is it?'

Rebus was trying to hand him a sheet of paper, folded in half. They were in Ancram's office. Ancram was seated, Rebus and Jack standing.

'Look and see,' Rebus said.

Ancram stared at him, then unfolded the headed note.

'It's a doctor's line,' Rebus explained. 'Forty-eight-hour stomach bug. Dr Curt was very clear that I should isolate myself. He said it could be catching.'

When he spoke, Ancram's voice was little more than whisper. 'Since when do pathologists hand out sick notes?'

'You haven't seen the queues at my health centre.'

Ancram crunched the note into a ball.

'It's dated and everything,' Rebus said. Of course it was: Dr Curt had been their last call before heading north with Eve.

'Shut up, sit down, and listen to me while I tell you why you're on an official reprimand. And don't think a reprimand's going to be the end of the affair.'

'Maybe you should read this first, sir,' Jack said, handing over Geddes' letter.

'What is it?'

'Not so much the end of the affair, sir,' Rebus told him, 'more like the heart of the matter. While you're digesting it, maybe I could have a browse through the files.'

'Why?'

'Those Borneo pics, I'd like another look.'

After the first few sentences of Lawson Geddes' confession, Ancram was hooked. Rebus could have walked out unnoticed with the files under his arm. But instead he slipped the photos out of their packet and went through them, checking the back of each for identifying names.

In one photo, third from the left was marked as Pvt. Sloane, R. Rebus stared at the face. Slightly blurred, with some water damage and fading. A fresh-faced young man, not long out of teens, his smile slightly crooked, maybe the fault of his teeth.

Bible John had one tooth which overlapped another, according to the eye-witness.

Rebus shook his head. That really was stretching the evidence, and Lawson Geddes had done enough of that in his time for both of them. Without knowing exactly why, and checking first that Ancram was still immersed in the letter, Rebus slid the photo into his pocket.

'Well,' Ancram said at last, 'this will obviously have to be discussed.'

'Obviously, sir. No interview today then?'

'Just a couple of questions. Number one, what the devil happened to your nose and tooth?'

'I got too close to a fist. Anything else, sir?'

'Yes, what the hell have you been doing with Jack?'

Rebus turned, saw what Ancram meant: Jack fast asleep on a chair by the wall.

'So,' Jack said, 'this is the big challenge.'

They'd come to the Oxford Bar, just for somewhere to be. Rebus ordered two orange juices, then turned to Jack. 'You want some breakfast?' Jack nodded. 'And four packets of crisps, any flavour,' Rebus told the barmaid.

They raised their glasses, said 'Cheers', and drank.

'Fancy a smoke?' Jack asked.

'I'd kill for one,' Rebus said, laughing.

'So,' Jack said, 'what's been achieved?'

'Depends on your point of view,' Rebus said. He'd been asking himself the same question. Maybe the Squaddies would nab all the drug players: Uncle Joe, Fuller, Stemmons. Maybe before that happened, Fuller would have done something with Ludovic Lumsden and Hayden Fletcher. Maybe. Hayden Fletcher was a regular at Burke's. He met Tony El there, maybe even scored nose-talc from him. Maybe Fletcher was the type who liked to hang out with gangsters – some people were like that. Seeing the Major was worried, and learning that Allan Mitchison was the problem ... it would have been easy to talk it over with Tony El, and for Tony to see the chance of some easy cash ... Maybe Major Weir himself ordered Mitch's death. Well, his was the one certain punishment, his daughter would make sure of that. And had Tony El ever actually intended to kill Mitch? Rebus couldn't even be sure of that. Maybe he'd have torn the bag from Mitch's head at the last minute. Then maybe he'd have warned him to forget all about T-Bird Oil.

It seemed part of some larger pattern, accidents forming themselves into a dance of association. Fathers and daughters, fathers and sons, infidelities, the illusions we sometimes call memory. Past errors harped on, or made good by spurious confession. Bodies littered down the years, mostly forgotten except by the perpetrators. History turning sour, or fading away like old photographs. Endings ... no rhyme or reason to them. They just happened. You died, or disappeared, or were forgotten. You became nothing more than a name on the back of an old photo, and sometimes not even that.

Jethro Tull: 'Living in the Past'. Rebus had been a slave to that rhythm for far too long. It was the work that did it. As a detective, he lived in people's pasts: crimes committed before he arrived on the scene; witnesses' memories ransacked. He had become a historian, and the role had bled into his personal life. Ghosts, bad dreams, echoes.

But maybe now he had a chance. Look at Jack: he'd reinvented himself. Good news week.

The phone rang, was answered by the barmaid, who nodded towards Rebus. He took the receiver.

'Hello?'

'I tried your first home, decided to try your second home.'

Siobhan. Rebus straightened up.

'What did you get?'

'A name: Martin Davidson. Stayed at the Fairmount three weeks before the Judith Cairns murder. The room was charged to his employer, a firm called LancerTech, as in technical support. Based in Altens, just outside Aberdeen. They design the safety elements into platform equipment, that sort of thing.'

'You've talked to them?'

'Soon as I got his name. Don't worry, I didn't mention him. I just asked a couple of general questions. Receptionist said I was the second person in two days to ask her the same thing.'

'Who was the other person?'

'Chamber of Commerce, she said.' They were quiet for a moment.

'And Davidson fits with Robert Gordon's?'

'He hosted some seminars earlier this year. His name was down on the staff roll.'

A solid connection. Rebus could feel it like a punch. His knuckles were white on the receiver.

'There's more,' Siobhan said. 'You know how businesses sometimes stay faithful to one hotel chain? Well, the Fairmount has a sister establishment here. Martin Davidson of LancerTech was in town the night Angie Riddell was killed.'

Rebus saw her picture again: Angie. Hoped she was getting ready to rest.

'Siobhan, you're a genius. Have you told anyone else?'

'You're the first. After all, you gave me the tip.'

'I gave you a hunch, that's all. It might not have paid off. This is down to you. Now take it to Gill Templer – she's your boss – tell her what you've just told me, let her pass it on to the Johnny Bible team. Stick to procedure.'

'It's him, isn't it?'

'Pass the news along, and make sure you get the credit. Then we'll wait and see. All right?'

'Yes, sir.'

He put down the receiver, told Jack what she'd just told him. Then they just stood there, drinking their drinks, staring at the mirror behind the bar. Calmly at first, then with more agitation. Rebus was the first to say what they both knew.

'We need to be there, Jack. *I* need to be there.'

Jack looked at him, nodded. 'Your turn to drive or mine?'

33

British Telecom had listings for two Martin Davidsons in Aberdeen. But Friday afternoon, he was most likely still at work.

'Doesn't mean we'll find him at Altens,' Jack said.

'Let's go there anyway.' Practically Rebus's only thought the whole drive: he *needed* to see Martin Davidson, not necessarily speak to him, just clap eyes on him. Eye contact: Rebus wanted *that* memory.

'He could be working at OSC, or anywhere else for that matter,' Jack went on. 'He might not even be in Aberdeen.'

'Let's go there anyway,' Rebus repeated.

Altens Industrial Estate was south of the city, signposted off the A92. They found a map at the entrance to the estate, and used it to wind their way in towards LTS – Lancer Technical Support. There was what looked like a jam at one point, cars blocking the road, nobody going anywhere. Rebus got out to take a look, and almost wished he hadn't. They were police cars, unmarked but with tell-tale static coming from their radios. Siobhan had passed on the info, and someone had been fast to act.

A man was bearing down on Rebus. 'What the hell are you doing here?'

Rebus shrugged, hands in pockets. 'Informal observer?'

DCI Grogan narrowed his eyes. But his mind was elsewhere; he'd no time or inclination for argument.

'Is he inside?' Rebus asked, nodding towards the LTS building, a typical industrial unit of windowless white corrugation.

Grogan shook his head. 'We came steaming down here, now it seems he hasn't come in today.'

Rebus frowned. 'Day off?'

'Not officially. The switchboard tried his home, no answer.'

'Is that where you're headed?'

Grogan nodded.

Rebus didn't ask if they could tag along; Grogan would only say no.

But once the convoy was moving, no one would notice an extra car at the tail.

He got back into the Peugeot and told Jack about it, while Jack reversed and found a parking spot out of the way. They watched the police cars execute three-point turns and head back out of the estate, then eased their way in behind the last of them.

They headed north over the Dee and along Anderson Drive, passing more buildings belonging to Robert Gordon's University, and several oil company HQs. At last they headed off Anderson Drive, past Summerhill Academy, and into a tight maze of suburban streets with green-field sites beyond.

A couple of the cars left the convoy, probably to circle around and come at Davidson's house from the other direction, blocking him in. Brake lights came on, the cars stopping in the middle of the road. Doors opened, officers appearing. Quick confabs, Grogan issuing orders, pointing to left and right. Most eyes were on a single house, its curtains closed.

'Reckon he's flown?' Jack asked.

'Let's find out.' Rebus undid his seat-belt and opened the door.

Grogan was sending men to the neighbouring houses, some to ask questions, some to nip out the back door and work their way round the back of the suspect's house.

'Hope this isn't a wild goose chase,' Grogan muttered. He saw Rebus, but still barely registered his presence.

'Men in position, sir.'

People had come out of their houses, wondering what was going on. Rebus could hear the distant chimes of an ice-cream van.

'Armed Response Unit standing by, sir.'

'I don't think we'll need them.'

'Right you are, sir.'

Grogan sniffed, ran a finger under his nose, then selected two men to go with him to the suspect's door. He pressed the bell, and there was a collective holding of breath while they waited. Grogan rang again.

'What can they see round the back?'

One of Grogan's men radioed to ask. 'Curtains are closed upstairs and down, no sign of life.'

Just like at the front.

'Buzz a JP, say we need a warrant.'

'Right, sir.'

'And meantime, take a sledgehammer to that bloody door.'

The officer nodded, gave a signal, and a car boot was opened. Inside was like the back of a builder's van. Out came the sledgehammer. Three blows and the door was open. Ten seconds later there were cries for an ambulance. Ten seconds after that, someone suggested a hearse instead.

Jack was a good copper: the boot of *his* car held scene of crime equipment, including overshoes and gloves, and the all-over plastic boilersuits which made you look like a walking condom. Officers were being kept out of the house so as not to contaminate the scene. They stood crammed in the doorway, trying to see what they could. When Rebus and Jack stepped forward, no one recognised them, so took them for forensics. The crowd parted for a moment, and both men were inside.

The rules on contamination didn't seem to extend to senior officers and their flunkeys: Grogan stood in the living room, hands in pockets, examining the scene. The body of a young man lay on the black leather sofa. His fair hair was matted over a deep cut. More blood had dried on his face and neck. There were signs of a struggle: the glass and chrome coffee table overturned, magazines crumpled underfoot. A black leather jacket had been thrown over the man's chest, a gentle act after the bloodshed. Stepping closer, Rebus saw marks on the neck, visible below the blood-lines. On the floor in front of the body sat a large green holdall, the sort you took to the gym or for a weekend trip. Rebus peered inside, saw a backpack, a single shoe, Angie Riddell's necklace ... and a length of plastic-covered clothes-line.

'I think we can rule out suicide,' Grogan muttered.

'Knocked unconscious, then strangled,' Rebus guessed.

'You reckon it's him?'

'That bag isn't just sitting there for fun. Whoever did this, they knew who he was, and wanted us to know, too.'

'An accomplice?' Grogan asked. 'A mate, someone he blabbed to?'

Rebus shrugged again. He was intent on the corpse's face, felt cheated by it: the closed eyes, the repose. *I've come all this way, thanks to you, you bastard* ... He stepped closer, lifted the jacket a couple of inches and peered beneath. A black slip-on shoe had been stuffed into Martin Davidson's left armpit.

'Oh, Christ,' Rebus said, turning to Grogan and Jack. 'Bible John did this.' He saw disbelief mingled with horror in their faces. Rebus lifted the jacket a little higher so they could see the shoe. 'He's been here all the time,' he said. 'He never went away ...'

The Scene of Crime team did their business, photographing and videoing, bagging and taping potential evidence. The pathologist examined the body, then said it could be removed and taken to the mortuary. There were reporters outside, kept at a distance by police cordons. Once the SOC team had finished upstairs, Grogan took Rebus and Jack up for a look. He didn't seem to mind them being there, probably wouldn't have minded if he'd had Jack the Ripper himself for an audience: Grogan was the man who'd be on TV tonight, the man who tracked down Johnny Bible. Only he hadn't, of course – someone had beaten them to it.

'Tell me again,' Grogan said, as they climbed the stairs.

'Bible John took souvenirs – shoes, clothes, handbags. But he also placed a sanitary towel in the left armpit. Downstairs ... that was him letting us know who did this.'

Grogan shook his head. He would take some convincing. Meantime, he had things to show them. The main bedroom was just that, but beneath the bed were boxes of magazines and videos – hard core S&M, similar to the stuff in Tony El's bedroom, text in English and several other languages. Rebus wondered if one of the American gangs had brought it to Aberdeen.

There was a small guest bedroom with a padlock on it. Crowbarred open, it gave the lie to one area of speculation. A couple of the CID men had been wondering if Johnny Bible were tricking them – killing an innocent man and setting him up to look like the killer. The guest bedroom said Martin Davidson was Johnny Bible. It had been turned into a shrine to Bible John and other killers: dozens of scrapbooks, cuttings and photos pinned to the cork boards which lined the walls, videos of documentaries about serial killers, paperback books, heavily annotated, and at the centre of it all a blow-up of one of the Bible John flyers: the face almost smiling, a kindly face, and above it the same basic question: Have You Seen This Man?

Rebus almost answered yes; there was something about the shape of the face, he'd seen it before somewhere ... somewhere recently. He took the Borneo photo from his pocket, looked at Ray Sloane, then back at the poster. They were very alike, but that wasn't the similarity that was niggling Rebus. There was something else, *someone* else ...

Then Jack asked him something from the doorway, and Rebus lost it.

They followed everyone back to Queen Street. Rebus and Jack had, by association, become part of the team. There was quiet jubilation, tempered with the knowledge that another murderer was in their midst.

But as at least one officer put it, 'If he did for that bastard, good luck to him.'

Which, Rebus guessed, would be the reaction Bible John would be hoping for. He'd be hoping they wouldn't try too hard to find him. *If* he'd come out of retirement, then it had been to one end only – the killing of his impersonator. Johnny Bible had taken the glory, the achievement away from his predecessor; now there'd come the revenge.

Rebus sat in the CID office, staring into space, thinking. When someone handed him a cup, he raised it to his lips. But then Jack's hand stopped him.

'It's whisky,' he warned. Rebus looked down, saw sweet liquid the colour of honey, gazed at it for a moment, then put the cup down on the desk. There was laughter in the office, cheering and singing, like a football crowd after a result: same songs, same chants.

'John,' Jack said, 'remember Lawson.' It sounded like a warning.

'What about him?'

'He became obsessed.'

Rebus shook his head. 'This is different. I *know* it was Bible John.'

'What if it was?'

Rebus shook his head slowly. 'Come on, Jack, after everything I told you? After Spaven and everything else? You know better than to ask that.'

Grogan was waving Rebus over to a telephone. Smiling, with whisky breath, he handed Rebus the receiver.

'Someone wants a word.'

'Hello?'

'What in God's name are *you* doing there?'

'Oh, hello, Gill. Congratulations, looks like everything's coming right for once.'

She melted a little. 'Siobhan's doing, not mine. I only passed the info along.'

'Make sure that goes on record.'

'I will.'

'I'll talk to you later.'

'John ... when are you coming back?' Not what she'd wanted to ask.

'Tonight, maybe tomorrow.'

'OK.' She paused. 'See you then.'

'Fancy doing something on Sunday?'

She sounded surprised by the question. 'What sort of thing?'

'I don't know. A drive, a walk, somewhere down the coast?'

'Yes, OK.'

'I'll call you. Bye, Gill.'

'Bye.'

Grogan was refilling a cup. There were at least a couple of crates of whisky, and three of bottled beer.

'Where do you get this stuff?' Rebus asked.

Grogan smiled. 'Oh, you know.'

'Pubs? Clubs? Places you're owed a favour?'

Grogan just winked. More officers were arriving all the time – uniforms, civilian staff, even people who looked to be off-duty: all had heard, and all wanted to be part of it. The top brass looked stiff but smiling, declining refills.

'Maybe Ludovic Lumsden gets it for you?'

Grogan's face creased. 'I know you think he shafted you, but Ludo's a good copper.'

'Where is he?'

Grogan looked around. 'No idea.'

In fact, no one knew where Lumsden was; he hadn't been seen all day. Someone had called him at home, but only got an answering machine. His bleeper was turned on, but he wasn't responding. A patrol car, detouring past his house, reported no sign of him, though his car was outside. Rebus got an idea, and went downstairs to the comms room. There were people at work here – taking incoming calls, keeping communications open with patrol cars and beat officers. But they had a bottle of whisky of their own, and plastic cups to go round. Rebus asked if he could see the day's sheets.

He only had to look back an hour. A call from a Mrs Fletcher, reporting her husband missing. He'd gone to work that morning as usual, but hadn't arrived, and hadn't come home since. The sheet listed details of his car and a brief description. Patrols had been requested to keep a look-out. In another twelve hours or so, they'd start to deal with it more seriously.

Christian name of missing spouse: Hayden.

Rebus recalled Judd Fuller talking about dumping bodies at sea, or inland, places they'd never be found because no one ever went there. He wondered if that would be the fate of Lumsden and Fletcher ... No, he couldn't do it. He wrote a message on the back of one of the sheets and handed it to the duty officer, who read it silently before reaching for the mike.

'Any patrol in the vicinity of the city centre, to College Street, Burke's Club. Apprehend Judd Fuller, co-owner, and bring to Queen Street for questioning.' The comms officer turned to Rebus, who nodded. 'And check the cellar,' he continued, 'persons possibly being held there against their will.'

'Please repeat,' one patrol car said. The message was repeated. Rebus went back upstairs.

In spite of the party, some work was still being done. Rebus saw Jack manoeuvring one of the secretaries into a corner, chatting her up twenty to the dozen. Near them, a couple of desk-bound officers were making phone calls. Rebus picked up a spare receiver, called Gill.

'It's me.'

'What's happened?'

'Nothing. Listen, you passed all the stuff about Toal and Aberdeen on to the Scottish Crime Squad?'

'Yes.'

'Who's your contact there?'

'Why?'

'Because whoever it is, I've a message for them. I think Judd Fuller has picked up DS Ludovic Lumsden and a man called Hayden Fletcher, and intends to make sure they're not seen again.'

'What?'

'A patrol car's gone out to the club, God knows what they'll find, but the Squaddies should keep an eye on it. If they're found, they'll be brought back to Queen Street. The Squaddies might want someone on the scene.'

'I'll get on it. Thanks, John.'

'Any time.'

I'm getting soft in my old age, he thought. Or maybe I've just relocated my conscience.

He went walkabout, asked a few drinkers the same question, and eventually had the Oil Liaison officer, DI Jenkins, pointed out to him. Rebus just wanted to look at him. His name was mentioned in Stanley's confession, along with Lumsden. The Squaddies would be wanting a word with him. He was smiling, looking unconcerned, tanned and rested after his holiday. It gave Rebus a warm glow to realise the man would soon be sweating under an internal inquiry.

Maybe he wasn't getting so soft after all.

He walked over to the working officers, looked down over their shoulders. They were doing the preliminary work on the murder of Martin Davidson, collating information from neighbours and employer, trying to track down a next of kin, and all the time keeping the media at bay.

One of them slammed his phone down and suddenly had a big grin on his face. He reached for his mug of whisky and drained it.

'Something?' Rebus asked.

A balled-up piece of paper hit the officer on the head. Laughing, he threw it back.

'Neighbour came off the night shift,' he said, 'found a car blocking his drive. Had to park on the street. Says he hadn't seen the car before, and took a good look so he'd know it again. Woke up around lunchtime, and it was gone. Metallic blue BMW, 5 Series. He even got part of the licence plate.'

'Hell's bells.'

The officer was reaching for his phone. 'Shouldn't take too long.'

'It better not,' Rebus replied, 'or DCI Grogan may not be sober enough to take it in.'

34

Grogan caught Rebus in the hallway, slapped an arm around him. He was missing his tie, and the top two buttons of his shirt were open, showing tufts of wiry grey hair. He'd danced a jig with a couple of WPCs and was sweating profusely. The shift had changed; or rather, a new shift had come on, while the old shift stayed put, not wanting to break the spell. There was occasional talk of pubs and restaurants, nightclubs and bowling alleys, but nobody seemed to leave, and there was communal applause when an Indian restaurant nearby delivered boxes and bags full of food – courtesy of the brass, who by then actually *had* left the scene. Rebus had helped himself to pakora, keema nan, and chicken tikka, while one CID officer tried to explain to another why his saying 'Bhajis, we don' need no steenking bhajis' was a joke.

Judging by Grogan's breath, he hadn't taken a meal break. 'My wee Lowland laddie,' he said. 'How are you doing? Enjoying our Highland hospitality?'

'It's a great party.'

'So why the face like a thistle?'

Rebus shrugged. 'It's been a long day.' And a long night before it, he could have added.

Grogan patted his back. 'You're welcome back here any time, any time at all.' Grogan made towards the toilets, paused and turned. 'Any sign of Ludo?'

'He's in the City Hospital, next bed along from a man called Hayden Fletcher.'

'What?'

'There's a Crime Squad officer on the ward, too, waiting for them to wake up and give their statements. *That's* how clean Lumsden is. About time you woke up to the fact.'

Rebus went downstairs to the interview rooms, opened the door of the one *he'd* been interviewed in. There were two more Squaddies inside. And smoking a cigarette at the table, Judd Fuller. Rebus had come down earlier, just for a look, and to explain to the officers what had happened, referring them back to Gill's tapes and notes.

'Evening, Judd,' Rebus said now.

'Do I know you?'

Rebus walked up to him. 'You stupid bastard, you let me get away but you still went on using the cellar.' He shook his head. 'Erik will be disappointed.'

'Screw Erik.'

Rebus nodded. 'Every man for himself now, eh?'

'Let's get it over with.'

'What?'

'Why you're here.' Fuller looked up at him. 'You want a free hit at me, this is the only chance you're ever going to get. So make it good.'

'I don't need to hit you, Judd.' Rebus grinned, showing the stunted tooth.

'Then you're yellow.'

Rebus shook his head slowly. 'I used to be, but not any more.'

He turned his back and walked.

Back in CID, the party was in full swing. A cassette player had been wired up, accordion reels at distorted volume. Only two couples were dancing, and then not very well: there was barely room between the desks for professional ceilidh enthusiasts. Three or four bodies lay slumped at their desks, heads on arms. Someone else lay prone on the floor. Rebus counted nine empty whisky bottles, and someone had been sent out for more cases of beer. Jack was still talking with the secretary, his cheeks red from the heat in the room. The place was beginning to smell like a changing room at full-time.

Rebus walked around the room. The walls were still covered with material pertaining to Johnny Bible's local victims: maps, diagrams, duty rosters, photographs. He studied the photos, as if memorising the smiling faces. He saw that the fax machine had just finished spewing something out. Car ownership details, metallic blue BMWs. Four in Aberdeen, but only one with the same sequence of letters the witness recalled. Registered to a company called Eugene Construction with a Peterhead address.

Eugene Construction? *Eugene Construction?*

Rebus emptied his pockets on to a desktop, finding petrol receipts, notebook, scraps of paper with telephone numbers, Rennies, a book of matches ... there: business card. Given to him by the man he'd met at the convention. Rebus studied the card. Ryan Slocum, Sales Manager, Engineering Division. The parent company: Eugene Construction, with a Peterhead address. Trembling, Rebus lifted the Borneo photo and looked at it, remembering the man he'd met that day in the bar.

'*No wonder Scotland's down the pan. And we want independence.*'

He'd handed over his business card, then Rebus had announced that he was a policeman.

'*Did I say anything incriminating ...? Is it Johnny Bible?*'

The face, the eyes, the height ... close to the man in the photograph. Close. Ray Sloane ... Ryan Slocum. Someone had broken into Rebus's flat, looking for something, taking nothing. Looking for something that might incriminate them? He looked again at the business card, then reached for a phone, eventually tracked Siobhan down at home.

'Siobhan, the guy you talked to at the National Library ...?'

'Yes?'

'He gave you a description of the so-called journalist?'

'Yes.'

'Give it to me again.'

'Hang on.' She went to fetch her notebook. 'What's this about anyway?'

'I'll tell you later. Read it out.'

' "Tall, fair-haired, early fifties, longish face, no distinguishing features." '

'Anything about the accent?'

'Nothing down here.' She paused. 'Oh, yes, he *did* say something. He said it was twangy.'

'Like American?'

'But Scottish.'

'It's him.'

'Who?'

'Bible John, just like you said.'

'*What?*'

'Stalking his offspring ...' Rebus rubbed his forehead, pinched the bridge of his nose. He had his eyes screwed shut. Was it or wasn't it? *Was* he obsessed? How different was Johnny Bible's shrine from the scene in his own kitchen, the table covered in cuttings?

'I don't know,' he said. But he did know. He did. 'Talk to you later,' he told Siobhan.

'Wait!'

But that was the one thing he couldn't do. He needed to know. He needed to know right now. He looked round the room, saw dissolution and reverie, nobody who could drive, no back-up.

Except Jack.

Who had one arm around the secretary now, and was whispering in her ear. She was smiling, holding her cup with a steady hand. Maybe she was drinking the same thing Jack was: cola. Would Jack give him the keys? Not without an explanation, and Rebus wanted to do this alone, needed to. His motive: confrontation, and maybe exorcism. Besides, Bible John had cheated him out of Johnny Bible.

Rebus called downstairs. 'Any cars going begging?'

'Not if you've been drinking.'

'Try me with a breath test.'

'There's an Escort parked outside.'

Rebus searched desk drawers, found a phone book. Peterhead ... Slocum R. No listing. He could try BT, but an unlisted check would take time. Another option: get on the road. It was what he wanted anyway.

The city streets were wild: another Friday night, young souls at play. Rebus was singing 'All Right Now'. Segue into: 'Been Down So Long'. Thirty miles north to Peterhead, deep-water port. Tankers and platforms went there for servicing. Rebus wound the motor up, not much traffic heading out of the city. Sky glowing dull pink. Simmer dim, as the Shetlanders called it. Rebus tried not to think about what he was doing. Breaking rules he'd advised others not to break. No back-up. No real authority up here, a long way from home.

He had the address for Eugene Construction, got it from Ryan Slocum's business card. *I stood next to Bible John in a bar. He bought me a drink.* Rebus shook his head. Probably a lot of other people could say the same, if only they knew; Rebus wasn't so special. The company's phone number was on the card, but all he'd got was an answering machine. It didn't mean no one was there: security wouldn't necessarily answer the phones. The card also had a pager number for Slocum, but Rebus wasn't about to use that.

The company was housed behind a tall mesh fence. It took twenty minutes of driving around and asking questions before he found it. It wasn't dockside, which was where he'd expected it to be. There was a country business park on the edge of town, and Eugene Construction bordered that. Rebus drove up to the gates. They were locked. He sounded his horn. There was a gatehouse, its lights on, but nobody in. Past the gates were barriers, painted red and white. His headlamps picked them out, and then behind them, coming forwards, a sauntering figure in guard's uniform. Rebus left the car running, walked up to the gate.

'What is it?' the guard asked.

He pressed his warrant card to the mesh. 'Police. I need a home address for one of your employees.'

'Can't it wait till morning?'

Gritted teeth. 'Afraid not.'

The guard – sixties, retirement age, low-slung paunch – rasped at his chin. 'I don't know,' he said.

'Look, who do you contact in an emergency?'

'My office.'

'And they contact someone from the company?'

'I suppose so. Haven't had to test it. Some kids tried to scale the fence a few months back, but they –'

'Could you phone in?'

'– heard me coming and ran away sharpish. What?'

'Could you phone in?'

'I suppose so, if it's an emergency.' The guard walked towards his hut.

'And could you let me in while you're at it? I'll need to use your phone afterwards.'

The guard scratched his head, muttered something, but shook a chain of keys from his pocket and walked up to the gate.

'Thanks,' Rebus told him.

The hut was sparsely furnished. Kettle, mug, coffee and a little jar of milk sat on a rusted tray. There was a one-bar electric heater, two chairs, and a paperback novel on the desk: a western. Rebus took the telephone and explained the situation to the guard's supervisor, who asked to speak to the guard again.

'Yes, sir,' the guard said, 'ID and everything.' Staring at Rebus like he might be leader of a heist gang. He put Rebus back on, and the supervisor handed him the name and phone number he needed. Rebus made the call, waited.

'Hello?'

'Is that Mr Sturges?'

'Speaking.'

'Sir, I'm sorry to disturb you at this hour. My name's Detective Inspector John Rebus. I'm calling from your company's gatehouse.'

'Not a break-in or something?' The man sighed. A break-in meant he'd have to get dressed and go down there.

'No, sir, I just need some information on one of your employees.'

'Can't it wait till morning?'

'Afraid not.'

'Who is it anyway?'

'Ryan Slocum.'

'Ryan? What's wrong?'

'A serious illness, sir.' Rebus had used the lie before. 'An elderly relative. They need Mr Slocum's permission to operate.'

'Good God.'

'That's why it's urgent.'

'Yes, I see, I see.' It always worked: grandmas in peril. 'Well, it's not every employee whose address I know off the top of my head.'

'But you know Mr Slocum's?'

'Been to dinner there a few times.'

'He's married?' Enter a spouse into the equation. Rebus hadn't imagined Bible John married.

'Wife's name's Una, lovely couple.'

'And the address, sir?'

'Well, it's the phone number you'll be wanting?'

'Both actually. That way, if no one's home, we can send someone round to wait.'

Rebus copied the details into his notebook, thanked the man and put down the phone.

'Any idea how to get to Springview?' he asked the guard.

35

Springview was a modern development on the coast road south of town. Rebus parked outside Three Rankeillor Close, shut off the engine, and took a good long look at the house. There was a landscaped garden to the front – clipped lawn, rockery, shrubs and flower beds. No fence or hedge separated the garden from the pavement in front. The other properties were the same.

The house itself was a newish two-storey with gabled roof. To the right of the house was an integral garage. There was an alarm box above one of the bedroom windows. A light was on behind the living-room curtains. The car parked on the gravel driveway was a white Peugeot 106.

'Now or never, John,' Rebus told himself, taking a deep breath as he got out of the car. He walked up to the front door and rang the bell, then stepped back off the doorstep. If Ryan Slocum himself answered, Rebus wanted a bit of distance. He remembered his army training – unarmed combat – and an old maxim: shoot first, ask questions later. Something he should have remembered when he'd gone to Burke's Club.

A woman's voice came through the door. 'Yes? What is it?'

Rebus realised he was being watched through a spy-hole. He stepped back up on to the doorstep, so she could get a close look. 'Mrs Slocum?' Holding his warrant card up in front of him. 'CID, madam.'

The door was flung open. A small, slender woman stood there, black cusps beneath her eyes, her hair short and dark and untidy.

'Oh my God,' she said, 'what's happened?' Her accent was American.

'Nothing, madam.' Relief washed over her face. 'Why should there be?'

'Ryan,' she said, sniffing back tears. 'I don't know where he is.' She sought a handkerchief, realised the box was back in the living room, and told Rebus he'd better come in. He followed her into the large, well-furnished room, and while she was pulling out paper hankies took the opportunity to open the curtains a little. If a blue BMW turned up, he wanted to know about it.

'Working late maybe?' he said, already knowing the answer.

'I tried his office.'

'Yes, but he's a sales manager, could he be entertaining a client?'

'He always phones, he's very dutiful that way.'

Dutiful: odd choice of word. The room looked the sort that got cleaned before it was ever dirty; Una Slocum looked like the cleaner. Her hands twitched with the bundle of tissues, her whole face drawn with tension.

'Try to calm down, Mrs Slocum. Is there anything you could take?' He'd bet she had a doctor's prescription somewhere in the house.

'In the bathroom, but I don't want any. They make me dopey.'

Towards the far end of the room, a large mahogany dining table and six straight-backed chairs sat in front of a trio of wall units. China dolls behind glass, bathed by recessed lighting. Some silverware. No family photographs ...

'Maybe a friend who could ...?'

Una Slocum sat down, got up again, remembering she had a guest. 'Some tea, Mr ...?'

'Rebus, Inspector Rebus. Tea would be great.'

Give her something to do, keep her mind busy. The kitchen was only slightly smaller than the living room. Rebus peered out into the back garden. It looked enclosed, no easy way for Ryan Slocum to sneak up on the house. Rebus's ears were primed for car noises ...

'He's gone,' she said, stopping suddenly in the middle of the floor with the kettle in one hand, teapot in the other.

'What makes you say that, Mrs Slocum?'

'A suitcase, some clothes ... they're gone.'

'Business, maybe? Something at the last minute?'

She shook her head. 'He'd have left a note or something, a message on the machine.'

'You've checked?'

She nodded. 'I was in Aberdeen all day, shopping, walking around. When I got back, the house felt different somehow, emptier. I think I knew right off.'

'Has he said anything about leaving?'

'No.' The ghost of a smile. 'But a wife gets to know, Inspector. Another woman.'

'A woman?'

Una Slocum nodded. 'Isn't it always? He's been so ... I don't know, just *different* lately. Short-tempered, distracted … spending time away from home when I knew he'd no business meetings.' She was still nodding, confirming it to herself. 'He's gone.'

'And you've no idea where he could be?'

She shook her head. 'Wherever *she* is, that's all.'

Rebus walked back through to the living room, checked the window: no BMW. A hand touched his arm, and he spun. It was Una Slocum. 'Jesus,' he said. 'I nearly died.'

'Ryan always complains I never make any noise. It's the carpet.'

Half-inch Wilton, yards of it.

'Have you any children, Mrs Slocum?'

She shook her head. 'I think Ryan would have liked a son. Maybe that was the problem …'

'How long have you been married?'

'A long time, fifteen years, nearer sixteen.'

'Where did you meet?'

She smiled, drifting back. 'Galveston, Texas. Ryan was an engineer, I was a secretary in the same company. He'd emigrated from Scotland some time before. I could tell he missed home, I always knew we'd end up coming back.'

'How long have you been here?'

'Four and a half years.' And no killings during that time, so maybe Bible John *had* come out of retirement for this one job … 'Of course,' Una Slocum said, 'we go back now and then to see my folks. They're in Miami. And Ryan goes over three or four times a year on business.'

Business. Rebus added a rider to his previous thought: *or maybe not*.

'Is he a churchgoer, Mrs Slocum?'

She stared at him. 'He was when we met. It tailed off, but he's been attending again.'

Rebus nodded. 'Any chance I could look around? He may have left a clue where he was headed.'

'Well … I suppose that would be all right.' The kettle came to the boil and clicked off. 'I'll make the tea.' She turned to go, paused, turned back. 'Inspector, what are you doing here?'

Rebus smiled. 'A routine inquiry, Mrs Slocum, to do with your husband's work.'

She nodded as though this explained everything, then walked silently back to the kitchen.

'Ryan's study's to the left,' she called. So Rebus started there.

It was a small room, made smaller by the furniture and bookshelves. There were dozens of books about the Second World War, a whole wall covered with them. Papers were laid out neatly on the desk – stuff from Slocum's work. In the drawers were more work files, plus others for tax, house and life insurance, pension. A life put into compartments. There was a small radio, and Rebus turned it on. Radio Three. He turned it off again, just as Una Slocum put her head round the door.

'Tea's in the living room.'

'Thank you.'

'Oh, another thing, he's taken his computer.'

'Computer?'

'You know, a laptop. He used it a lot. He kept this door locked while he worked, but I could hear the clatter of keys.'

There was a key on the inside of the door. When she'd gone, Rebus closed the door and locked himself in, then turned and tried to imagine this as the den of a murderer. He couldn't. It was a workspace, nothing more. No trophies, and no place to hide them. No bag filled with souvenirs, like Johnny Bible had collected. And no shrine, no scrapbooks of horror. No indication at all that this person lived a double life ...

Rebus unlocked the door, went through to the living room, checked the window again.

'Find anything?' Una Slocum was pouring tea into fine china cups. A Battenberg cake had been sliced on a matching plate.

'No,' Rebus admitted. He took a cup and a slice of cake from her. 'Thank you.' Then retreated to the window again.

'When your husband's a salesman,' she went on, 'you get used to seeing him irregularly, to having to attend boring parties and gatherings, to being hostess at dinner parties where the guests are not ones you'd have chosen for yourself.'

'Can't be easy,' Rebus agreed.

'But I never complained. Maybe Ryan would have paid me more attention if I had.' She looked at him. 'You're sure he's not in trouble?'

Rebus put on his most sincere face. 'I'm positive, Mrs Slocum.'

'I suffer from nerves, you know. I've tried everything – pills, potions, hypnosis ... But if something's in you, there's not much they can do, is there? I mean, if it's there from the time you're born, a little ticking time bomb ...' She looked around. 'Maybe it's this house, so new and all, nothing for me to do.'

Aldous Zane had predicted a house like this, a modern house ...

'Mrs Slocum,' Rebus said, eyes on the window, 'this might sound like a daft request, and I've no way to explain it, but do you think I could take a look at your attic?'

A chain on the first-floor landing. You tugged at it and the trapdoor opened, the wooden steps sliding down to meet you.

'Clever,' Rebus said. He began to climb, Una Slocum staying on the landing.

'The light switch is just to your right when you get up,' she called.

Rebus poked his head into space, half-expecting a shovel to come crashing down on it, and fumbled for the switch. A single bare bulb illuminated the floored attic.

'We talked about converting it,' Una Slocum called. 'But why bother? The house is too big for us as it is.'

The attic was a few degrees cooler than the rest of the house, testament to modern insulation. Rebus looked around, not sure what he might find. What had Zane said? Flags: the Stars and Stripes and a swastika. Slocum had lived in the US, and seemed fascinated by the Third Reich. But Zane had also seen a trunk in the attic of a large, modern house. Well, Rebus couldn't see anything like that. Packing cases, boxes of Christmas decorations, a couple of broken chairs, a spare door, a couple of hollow-sounding suitcases ...

'I haven't been up here since last Christmas,' Una Slocum said. Rebus helped her up the last couple of steps.

'It's big,' Rebus said. 'I can see why you thought of converting it.'

'Planning permission would have been the problem. All the houses here are supposed to stay the same. You spend a fortune on a place, then you aren't allowed to do anything with it.' She lifted a folded piece of red cloth from one of the suitcases, brushed dust from it. It looked like a tablecloth, maybe a curtain. But when she shook it, it unfurled into a large flag, black on a white circle with red border. A swastika. She saw the shock on Rebus's face.

'He used to collect this sort of stuff.' She looked around, her face creasing into a frown. 'That's odd.'

Rebus swallowed. 'What?'

'The trunk's gone.' She pointed to a space on the floor. 'Ryan must have moved it.' She looked around, but it obviously wasn't anywhere in the attic.

'Trunk?'

'A big old thing, he's had it for ever. Why would he move it? Come to that, *how* would he move it?'

'What do you mean?'

'It was heavy. He kept it locked, said it was full of old stuff, mementoes of his life before we met. He promised he'd show me some day ... Do you think he took it with him?'

385

Rebus swallowed again. 'A possibility,' he said, making for the stairs. Johnny Bible had a holdall, but Bible John needed a whole trunk. Rebus began to feel queasy.

'There's more tea in the pot,' Mrs Slocum said as they went back down to the living room.

'Thanks, but I really must be going.' He saw her try to hide a look of disappointment. It was a cruel life when the only company you had was a policeman chasing your husband.

'I'm sorry,' he said, 'about Ryan.' Then he glanced out of the window one last time.

And there was a blue BMW parked by the kerb.

Rebus's heart kicked at his chest. He couldn't see anyone in the car, no one moving towards the house ...

Then the doorbell rang.

'Ryan?' Mrs Slocum was making for the door. Rebus caught her and pulled her back. She squealed.

He put a finger to his lips, motioned for her to stay where she was. His gorge was rising, as if he might bring up the curry from earlier. His whole body felt electric. The bell went again. Rebus took a deep breath, ran to the door and hauled it open.

A young man stood there, denim jacket and jeans, spiky gelled hair, acne. He was holding out a set of car keys.

'Where did you get it?' Rebus roared. The youth took a step back, stumbled off the step. 'Where did you get the car?' Rebus was out of the door now and looming over him.

'Work,' the youth said. 'P-part of the s-service.'

'What is?'

'Returning your c-car. From the airport.' Rebus stared at him, demanding more. 'We do valet cleaning, all that. And if you drop your car off and want it taking back to your house, we do that, too. Sinclair Car Rentals ... you can check!'

Rebus held out a hand, pulled the youth to his feet.

'I was only going to ask if you wanted it put away,' the youth said, ashen-faced.

'Leave it where it is.' Rebus tried to control his trembling. Another car had drawn up, a horn sounded.

'My lift,' the youth explained, the terror still not completely gone from his face.

'Where was Mr Slocum headed?'

'Who?'

'The car's owner.'

The youth shrugged. 'How should I know?' He put the keys in Rebus's hand, headed back down the drive. 'We're not the gestapo,' his parting shot.

Rebus handed the keys to Mrs Slocum, who was staring at him like she had questions, like she wanted to start again from the beginning. Rebus shook his head, marched off. She looked at the keys in her hand.

'What am I going to do with two cars?'

But Rebus was gone.

He told his story to Grogan.

The Chief Inspector was almost sober – and very ready to go home. He'd already been talked to by the Crime Squad. They'd said they'd have more questions for him tomorrow, all to do with Ludovic Lumsden. Grogan listened with growing impatience, then asked what evidence there was. Rebus shrugged. They could place Slocum's car near the scene of the murder, and at a curious hour of the morning. But they couldn't do more than that. Maybe forensics would throw up some connection, but they both guessed Bible John was too smart to allow that to happen. Then there was the story outlined in Lawson Geddes' letter – a dead man's tale – and the photo from Borneo. But that meant nothing without a confession from Ryan Slocum that he'd once been Ray Sloane, had lived in Glasgow in the late sixties and had been – and still was – Bible John.

But Ryan Slocum had disappeared.

They contacted Dyce Airport, but there was no record of his having taken a plane out of there, and no taxi or car rental company would admit seeing him. Had he already left the country? What had he done with the trunk? Was he lying low in some hotel nearby, waiting for the fuss to die?

Grogan said they'd make enquiries, put out an alert to ports and airports. He didn't see what else they could do. They'd send someone out to talk with Mrs Slocum, maybe go through the house with a fine-toothed comb ... Tomorrow maybe, or the day after. Grogan didn't sound too enthusiastic. He'd found his serial killer for today, and had little inclination to go chasing ghosts.

Rebus found Jack in the canteen, drinking tea and eating chips and beans.

'Where did you get to?'

Rebus sat down beside him. 'Thought maybe I was cramping your style.'

Jack shook his head. 'Tell you what though, I nearly asked her back to that hotel.'

'Why didn't you?'

Jack shrugged. 'She told me she could never trust a man who didn't drink. Do you feel like heading back?'

'Why not?'

'John, where *did* you get to?'

'I'll tell you on the way back. It might help keep you awake ...'

36

Next morning, after a few hours' sleep on the chair, Rebus telephoned Brian Holmes. He wanted to know how he was doing, and whether Ancram's threats had evaporated in the light of Lawson Geddes' letter. The call was answered quickly.

'Hello?' A woman's voice: Nell's. Softly, Rebus put the receiver down. So she was back. Did that mean she'd come to terms with Brian's work? Or had he promised to give it up? Rebus was sure to find out later.

Jack wandered through. He reckoned his job of 'minder' was finished, but had stayed the night anyway – too tired to contemplate the miles home to Falkirk.

'Thank God it's the weekend,' he said, rubbing both hands through his hair. 'Any plans?'

'I thought I might nip down to Fettes, see what the score is with Ancram.'

'Good idea, I'll come with you.'

'You don't need to.'

'But I want to.'

They took Rebus's car for a change. But when they got to Fettes, Ancram's office was bare, no sign of it ever having been occupied. Rebus telephoned Govan, and was put through.

'Is that it finished?' he asked.

'I'll write up my report,' Ancram said. 'No doubt your boss will want to discuss it with you.'

'What about Brian Holmes?'

'It'll all be in the report.'

Rebus waited. 'All of it?'

'Tell me something, Rebus, are you clever or just spawny?'

'Is there a difference?'

'You've really mucked things up. If we'd gone ahead against Uncle Joe, we could have had the mole.'

'You'll have Uncle Joe instead.' Ancram grunted a response. 'You *know* who the mole is?'

'I have a hunch. Lennox, you met him that day in The Lobby.' DS Andy Lennox: freckles and ginger curls. 'Thing is, I've no hard evidence.'

Same old problem. In law, *knowing* was not enough. Scots law was stricter still: there must needs be corroboration.

'Maybe next time, eh?' Rebus offered, putting down the phone.

They drove back to the flat so Jack could pick up his car, but then he had to climb the stairs with Rebus, having forgotten some of his kit.

'Are you ever going to leave me alone?' Rebus asked.

Jack laughed. 'Starting any minute.'

'Well, while you're here you can help me shift the stuff back into the living room.'

It didn't take long. The last thing Rebus did was hook the fishing-boat back on the wall.

'So what now?' Jack asked.

'I suppose I could see about getting this tooth fixed. And I said I'd meet up with Gill.'

'Business or pleasure?'

'Strictly off-duty.'

'A fiver says you end up talking shop.'

Rebus smiled. 'Five says you're on. What about you?'

'Ach, I thought while I'm in town I might check out the local AA, see if there's a meeting. It's been too long.' Rebus nodded. 'Want to tag along?'

Rebus looked up, nodded. 'Why not?' he said.

'The other thing we could do is keep on with the decorating.'

Rebus wrinkled his nose. 'The mood's passed.'

'You're not going to sell?' Rebus shook his head. 'No cottage by the sea?'

'I think I'll settle for where I am, Jack. It seems to suit me.'

'And where's that exactly?'

Rebus considered his answer. 'Somewhere north of hell.'

He got back from his Sunday walk with Gill Templer and stuck a fiver in an envelope, addressed it to Jack Morton. Gill and he had talked about the Toals and the Americans, about how they'd go down on the strength of the tape. Rebus's word might not be enough to convict Hayden Fletcher of conspiracy to murder, but he'd have a damned good go. Fletcher was being brought south for questioning. Rebus had a busy week ahead. His telephone rang as he was tidying the living room.

'John?' the voice said. 'It's Brian.'

'Everything all right?'

'Fine.' But Brian's voice was hollow. 'I just thought I'd ... the thing is ... I'm putting in my papers.' A pause. 'Isn't that what they say?'

'Jesus, Brian ...'

'Thing is, I've tried to learn from you, but I'm not sure you were the right choice. A bit too intense maybe, eh? See, whatever it is you've got, John, I just don't have it.' A longer pause. 'And I'm not sure I even want it, to be honest.'

'You don't have to be like me to be a good copper, Brian. Some would say you should strive to be what I'm not.'

'Well ... I've tried both sides of the fence, hell, I've even tried sitting *on* the fence. No good, any of it.'

'I'm sorry, Brian.'

'Catch you later, eh?'

'Sure thing, son. Take care.'

He sat down in his chair, stared out of the window. A bright summer's afternoon, a good time to go for a walk through the Meadows. Only Rebus had just come back from a walk. Did he really want another? His phone rang again and he let the machine take it. He waited for a message, but all he could hear was static crackle, background hiss. There was someone there; they hadn't broken the connection. But they weren't about to leave a message. Rebus placed a hand on the receiver, paused, then lifted it.

'Hello?'

He heard the other receiver being dropped into its cradle, then the hum of the open line. He stood for a moment, then replaced the receiver and walked into the kitchen, pulled open the cupboard and lifted out the newspapers and cuttings. Dumped the whole lot of them into the bin. Grabbed his jacket and took that walk.

Afterword

The genesis of this book was a story I heard very early in 1995, and I worked on the book all through that year, finishing a satisfactory draft just before Christmas. Then on Sunday January 29 1996, just as my editor was settling down to read the manuscript, the *Sunday Times* ran a story headlined 'Bible John "living quietly in Glasgow"', based on information contained in a book to be published by Mainstream in April. The book was *Power in the Blood* by Donald Simpson. Simpson claimed that he had met a man and befriended him, and that eventually this man had confessed to being Bible John. Simpson also claimed that the man had tried to kill him at one point, and that there was evidence the killer had struck outside Glasgow. Indeed, there remain many unsolved west-coast murders, plus two unsolveds from Dundee in 1979 and 1980 – both victims were found stripped and strangled.

It may be coincidence, of course, but the same day's *Scotland on Sunday* broke the story that Strathclyde Police had new evidence in the ongoing Bible John investigation. Recent developments in DNA analysis had given them a genetic fingerprint from a trace of semen left on the third victim's tights, and police had been asking as many of the original suspects as they could find to come forward to have a blood sample taken and analysed. One such suspect, John Irvine McInnes, had committed suicide in 1980, so a member of his family had given a blood sample instead. This seems to have proved a close enough match to warrant exhuming McInnes' body so as to carry out further tests. In early February, the body was exhumed (along with that of McInnes' mother, whose coffin had been placed atop her son's). For those interested in the case, the long wait began.

As I write (June 1996), the wait is still going on. But the feeling now is that police and their scientists will fail – indeed, already have failed – to find incontrovertible proof. For some, the seed has been sown anyway – John Irvine McInnes will remain the chief suspect in their minds – and it is true that his personal history, compared alongside the psychological profile of Bible John compiled at the time, makes for fascinating reading.

But there is real doubt, too – some of it also based on offender profiling. Would a serial killer simply cease to kill, then wait eleven years to commit suicide? One newspaper posits that Bible John 'got a fright' because of the investigation, and this stopped him killing again, but according to at least one expert in the field, this simply fails to fit the recognised pattern. Then there's the eye-witness, in whom chief investigator Joe Beattie had so much faith. Irvine McInnes took part in an identity parade a matter of days after the third murder. Helen Puttock's sister failed to pick him out. She had shared a taxi with the killer, had watched her sister dance with him, had spent hours in and out of his company. In 1996, faced with photos of John Irvine McInnes, she says the same thing – the man who killed her sister did not have McInnes' prominent ears.

There are other questions – would the killer have given his real first name? Would the stories he told the two sisters during the taxi ride be true or false? Would he have gone ahead and killed his third victim, knowing he was leaving a witness behind? There are many out there, including police officers and numbering people like myself, who would refuse to be convinced even by a DNA match. For us, he's still out there, and – as the Robert Black and Frederick West cases have shown – by no means alone.

Acknowledgements

Thanks to: Chris Thomson, for permission to quote from one of his songs; Dr Jonathan Wills for his views on Shetland life and the oil industry; Don and Susan Nichol, for serendipitous help with the research; the Energy Division of the Scottish Office Industry Department; Keith Webster, Senior Public Affairs Officer, Conoco UK; Richard Grant, Senior Public Affairs Officer, BP Exploration; Andy Mitchell, Public Affairs Advisor, Amerada Hess; Mobil North Sea; Bill Kirton, for his offshore safety expertise; Andrew O'Hagan, author of *The Missing*; Jerry Sykes, who found the book for me; Mike Ripley, for the video material; the inebriated oil-worker Lindsey Davis and I met on a train south of Aberdeen; Colin Baxter, Trading Standards Officer *extraordinaire*; my researchers Linda and Iain; staff of the Caledonian Thistle Hotel, Aberdeen; Grampian Regional Council; Ronnie Mackintosh; Ian Docherty; Patrick Stoddart; and Eva Schegulla for the e-mail. Grateful thanks as ever to the staffs of the National Library of Scotland (especially the South Reading Room) and Edinburgh Central Library. I'd also like to thank the many friends and authors who got in touch when the Bible John case hit the headlines again early in 1996, either to commiserate or to offer suggestions for tweaks to the plot. My editor, Caroline Oakley, had faith throughout, and referred me to the James Ellroy quote at the start of my own book ... Finally, a special thank you to Lorna Hepburn, who told me a story in the first place ...

Any 'implags' will be from the following: *Fool's Gold* by Christopher Harvie; *A Place in the Sun* by Jonathan Wills; *Innocent Passage: The Wreck of the Tanker Braer* by Jonathan Wills and Karen Warner; *Blood on the Thistle* by Douglas Skelton; *Bible John: Search for a Sadist* by Patrick Stoddart; *The Missing* by Andrew O'Hagan.

Major Weir's quote – 'creatures tamed by cruelty' – is actually the title of Ron Butlin's first poetry collection.